W9-BNW-887

FATAL JUDGMENT

Books by Irene Hannon

Heroes of Quantico Series

Against All Odds

An Eye for an Eye

In Harm's Way

Guardians of Justice Series

Fatal Judgment

GUARDIANS *of* JUSTICE #1

FATAL JUDGMENT

A NOVEL

IRENE HANNON

a division of Baker Publishing Group
Grand Rapids, Michigan

Published by Revell
a division of Baker Publishing Group
P.O. Box 6287, Grand Rapids, MI 49516-6287

Printed in the United States of America

ISBN 978-1-61129-227-5

Published in association with MacGregor Literary.

To Sister Marie Blanche Marschner,
who taught me freshman English.

Thank you for inspiring me, encouraging me—
and teaching me how to diagram a sentence!
Your enthusiasm, appreciation, and respect for language
opened my eyes to the power, the passion,
and the possibilities of words.

1

At the vibrating summons from his BlackBerry, Deputy U.S. Marshal Jake Taylor clenched his hands on the steering wheel and stifled a groan. Except for the two hours of semi-restful downtime he'd enjoyed during the flight back to St. Louis from Denver, he'd been operating for almost twenty-four adrenaline-packed hours on high-alert status. His plan had been to head straight for his rented condo, ignore the boxes waiting to be unpacked, and crash.

But a quick glance at caller ID told him that plan was probably toast.

Taking a deep breath, he pressed the talk button and greeted his boss. "Hi, Matt. What's up?"

"Sorry to call so late. Did I wake you?"

"No. The flight was delayed. I'm on my way home from the airport."

"You might want to pull over."

Not good.

A drive-through coffee shop came into view, and Jake swung into the parking lot, grateful for the providential timing and the establishment's late hours. Since the LED dial on his dashboard clock was inching toward midnight and he suspected sleep wouldn't be on his agenda in the foreseeable future, a hefty dose of caffeine was in order.

"I'm stopping for some coffee as we speak." He pulled behind the car already at the order window.

"Good idea. Everything go okay?"

"Yeah. We had it covered. He didn't even get off a shot." Arresting a person on the U.S. marshals' most-wanted list was always dicey. And as Jake had expected, Ray Carlson—whose string of warrants included murder, arson, narcotics trafficking, and firearms and explosives violations—had merited the deployment of a full contingent of deputy marshals from the service's elite Special Operations Group.

"Good. That's the way we like arrests to go down. Listen, I hate to pull you into another tough situation before you catch your breath, but Todd just left for Beauregard for some sniper training."

Meaning Matt thought this job warranted SOG attention. Todd was the only other St. Louis–based member of the select tactical group headquartered in Louisiana.

"What's the problem?" Jake extracted a small notebook from his pocket and balanced it on the steering wheel, keeping an eye on the car ahead of him.

"There was an attempted murder earlier tonight at the home of a federal judge. The judge's sister was shot. She's alive, but it's not looking good. Until we have a handle on what happened, I want a protective detail on the judge 24/7. I'd like you to head it up."

Not for the first time, he wished he'd had more time to prep before his transfer to St. Louis. Jake knew few of the judges here that the Marshals Service was charged with protecting. But no sooner had he arrived in town two weeks ago than he'd been called away to work the Carlson arrest. And during his prior six-month deployment to Iraq, he'd been focused on improving that country's judicial and witness security—and staying alive. Future assignments back home hadn't been on his radar screen.

"Who's the judge?" Pen poised, Jake figured he could get the basics from Matt now and fill in the rest later.

"Elizabeth Michaels."

He stopped breathing.

Liz Michaels? Doug's wife?

No. It couldn't be the same person.

Could it?

Even as that question echoed in his mind, he had a sinking feeling he knew the answer.

"Jake? You there?"

"Yeah." He took a breath. Kept his inflection neutral. "I haven't done my homework on the Eighth District judges in this area yet, but the name is familiar. I knew an attorney years ago from Jefferson City named Liz Michaels."

The car in front of Jake pulled away from the drive-through window, and he eased forward to place his order.

"Same person. She was in private practice there for quite a while, then served as a state circuit court judge for three years. She was appointed to the federal bench four months ago."

A muscle in Jake's jaw clenched as he pressed the mute button on his phone and addressed the barista. "Large Americano. And throw in an extra shot of espresso."

The silence lengthened as he dug for his wallet, and when Matt spoke again he could tell from his boss's tone that the man was frowning.

"Is there a problem?"

Yeah. A big one.

He'd rather go back to Iraq than head Liz Michaels's protective detail.

But there was only one response a professional could give.

"No. No problem."

"Good. I'll get you some relief as soon as this thing is sorted out. But I'd like you to stick close for the first twenty-four hours. I'll send Spence over to assist."

"Okay. Where is she?"

"St. John's. It was the closest Level I trauma center. Two police officers are with her in the ER. They'll stay there until you arrive. What's your ETA?"

Jake exited the drive-through and headed toward westbound I-64.

"Ten, fifteen minutes tops."

"I'll be in touch."

The line went dead.

After slipping the BlackBerry back onto his belt, Jake reached for his cup and took a swig of the potent coffee. Then another.

It was going to be a long, unpleasant night.

Fourteen minutes later, the buzz from the espresso beginning to dent his fatigue, Jake found a parking spot near the ER and walked past the media vans. He drew no more than a few disinterested glances from the news crews milling about in the chill of the October night. Dressed in jeans, a wrinkled cotton shirt, and a scuffed leather jacket, with twenty-four hours' worth of stubble roughening his jaw, he assumed the reporters didn't consider him anyone worth noticing.

They might have revised their opinion if they'd seen the SOG-issued .45 caliber Springfield tucked in the holster on his belt.

Unlike the media, however, the police officers at the door gave him their full attention as he approached.

Hand hovering near his holster, the older of the two officers stepped forward. "May I help you, sir?"

"Deputy Marshal Jake Taylor." He'd already withdrawn his credentials from his pocket, and he flipped them open.

The officer examined them, then nodded. "We were told you were on the way. Your brother is waiting to brief you. I'll take you back." He led the way inside, motioning for another officer to take his place at the door.

So Cole was on this case. Meaning the crime had happened in the jurisdiction of the St. Louis County PD. That was one piece of good news, at least. His brother was an excellent detective. But he'd have preferred a different venue for their first get-together since his homecoming. One that included a loaded pizza and a few laughs.

A midnight rendezvous in an emergency room didn't even come close.

As Jake followed the officer down a brightly lit corridor, blinking against the glare while his eyes transitioned from real-world darkness to a world that never slept, the acid from the coffee gurgled in his stomach, sending a vague wave of nausea through him.

He hated hospitals. Had for four years. If he could have avoided this one, he would have.

For a lot of reasons.

He caught sight of one of them as he passed a doorway flanked by two more officers. While his glimpse through the half-ajar door was fleeting, and though he hadn't seen her in five years, Jake had no problem recognizing the sole occupant of the room.

One quick, assessing sweep was all he needed to conclude that Liz Michaels hadn't changed much. She had the same long, honey-blonde hair parted to one side. The same lithe figure, bordering on too thin. The same preference for classic, elegant attire. Except tonight the silky, cream-colored open-necked blouse tucked into her dark brown slacks had maroon stains at the cuffs and splotches of the same color on the front.

Blood.

Her posture also suggested uncharacteristic defeat. He remembered her as the chin-up, look-the-world-in-the-eye-with-confidence type. Tonight, no hint of that self-assurance was evident. She sat head bowed, eyes closed, her fingers laced as she rested her elbows on the arms of the plastic chair. There wasn't a trace of color in her cheeks.

He almost felt sorry for her.

"Detective . . . Marshal Taylor is here."

Realizing he'd slowed while passing the room where Liz sat, he picked up his pace to join his brother a few yards away.

Cole raised his disposable coffee cup in salute and gave him a wry smile as the escorting officer returned to his post. "Welcome to St. Louis."

Sarcasm twisted Jake's lips. "Thanks a lot. I'd rather be home in bed."

"Join the club." Cole gave him a sweeping appraisal. "But I must admit you look like you need the sleep more than I do. A lot more, in fact. Must be your advanced age."

"I'm only three years older than you."

"Yeah. But thirty-eight is a lot closer to forty than thirty-five." Cole grinned. "How come you didn't let me know you were back?"

"I just got in an hour ago."

Cole grimaced. "Ouch. I take it you didn't get any shut-eye on the flight home."

"Nope." As they both knew, dozing off on a plane was against the rules for armed marshals.

"When's the last time you slept?"

"I can't remember." Jake surveyed his brother. Cole's dark hair was a bit disheveled, and the white shirt beneath his sport coat had lost most of its starch. "You look like you've put in a long day too."

"That's why we get paid the big bucks, right?" Cole smirked and hefted his cup again. "You want some coffee?"

"I had an Americano with three shots of espresso on the way here, thanks."

"Smart choice. You're going to need it." He drained the dark dregs and made a face. "And I thought the coffee at the office was bad." Tossing the cup in a nearby trash can, he gestured toward a darkened room. "We don't have much yet, but I can brief you on the basics in there."

Without waiting for a reply, he entered, flipped on the light, and shut the door behind Jake. Settling into one of the two hard plastic chairs, he withdrew a small notebook from his pocket. "Make yourself comfortable."

Jake cast a skeptical eye at the rigid chair. "Right."

"I hear you." Cole shifted in his seat. "They ought to make the people who design these things sit in them for an hour every day."

Blowing out a resigned breath, Jake sat. "Okay. What do you have?"

"According to Judge Michaels, she arrived home from the courthouse about 7:30, as usual. She checked on her sister, who had been lying down. The sister got up, and the judge ran across the street to get a FedEx package that had been dropped off at her neighbor's house. She was gone about ten minutes. Her neighbor carried it back for her, and after he left she found her sister slumped on the couch in front of the television in the family room. She'd been shot in the head from behind at close range."

Jake's lips compressed into a grim line. Not a pretty image. No wonder Liz looked shell-shocked.

"Any suspects?"

"The sister's husband. Judge Michaels says he was abusive, and that she'd been after her sister for years to leave him. She finally did. Yesterday. After he beat her up again. We alerted her local PD in Springfield, and they've been to the house. No one's there. We issued a BOLO alert about an hour ago."

Jake frowned. An abusive husband who was angry enough to kill his wife might also be inclined to seek revenge on the woman who'd offered her shelter.

Cole read his mind. "We had the same thought." He tucked his notebook back in his pocket. "And trust me, we're more than happy to turn the good judge over to you guys."

"Thanks a lot." Any lingering hope of getting some shut-eye tonight evaporated. "How's the sister?"

"Critical. Not likely to make it. She's in surgery now. We kept the judge here instead of moving her to the surgical waiting room because it was easier to secure." He rose. "I need to ask her a few more questions. Might as well introduce you."

"We've met." Jake stood too. "She's Doug Stafford's wife."

"Whoa!" Cole's eyebrows rose. "The connection didn't register."

"No reason it would. Michaels isn't an uncommon name. And I doubt I've mentioned her to you more than a couple of times."

"Well, at least you're acquainted. That might make things easier."

Jake let that remark pass. He'd never shared his opinion of Doug's wife with Cole.

But as he followed his brother down the hall, *easy* wasn't the word that came to mind about this assignment.

Not even close.

This can't be happening.

Elbows resting on the arms of the uncomfortable plastic chair, Liz leaned forward and massaged her temples. She felt like she was in an episode of *The Twilight Zone*. Five hours ago, she and her sister had been getting ready to share a spaghetti dinner.

Now Stephanie was fighting for her life.

From a gunshot wound.

It was surreal.

But she was alive, thank God. Although she wouldn't be if she hadn't sensed a presence behind her and shifted at the last instant. At least that was the speculation of the doctor who'd spoken with her hours ago, then left her alone to wait. And worry. And lament the day Stephanie had ever said "I do" to Alan Long.

She hoped that once the police found him, he rotted in prison for the rest of his miserable life.

As a surge of anger ripped through her, she rose suddenly—startling the officer stationed at the door.

"Everything okay, Judge?" He gave her a worried scan and

wrapped one hand around the edge of the half-closed door, blocking her exit.

Her anger spiked up a notch. What kind of stupid question was that? The only way to make everything okay was to rewind the clock. Start the day over. Edit out the bad stuff.

But none of those things were going to happen. And that wasn't this young cop's fault.

"Would you like a soft drink or some coffee, ma'am?"

Shoulders slumping, she sank back into her chair. "Coffee would be good."

And see if you can round up a miracle while you're at it.

Two minutes later, when the door swung open again, she expected a coffee delivery. Instead, the detective stepped through. She searched her memory for his name. Gave up. If he'd told it to her, it hadn't registered. Besides, she wasn't in the mood to talk to him again. She'd already told him everything she knew.

"I have a few more questions, Judge. And I wanted to let you know the U.S. Marshals would be taking over your security."

Liz knew such protection was protocol for federal judges. She'd just never expected to need it. And she wasn't sure she did now. Obviously, Alan had . . .

Her train of thought derailed as a tall, dark-haired man stepped into the room behind the detective.

Jake Taylor.

Her husband's best friend from college.

Shock rippled through her.

Though their paths had only crossed twice—once when he'd been the best man at her wedding, the second time at Doug's funeral five years ago—there was no mistaking those intense brown eyes nor his formidable presence.

She also recognized his dispassionate gaze. It was the same cool, aloof manner he'd displayed toward her at the service for Doug, and it hadn't warmed one degree over the years.

She'd never understood what she'd done to incur his antipathy—and had long since given up trying to figure it out. The more important question was, what was he doing in St. Louis?

"I understand you know my brother, Jake," the detective said.

The tall, dark-haired detective and Jake were brothers. She studied them, seeing the obvious resemblance now that they stood side by side. They had the same perennial-tan coloring, same strong chin, same athletic build—though the detective was about an inch shorter than Jake's six-one, six-two height.

"Yes. Hello, Jake."

"Liz."

The officer returned with her cup of coffee, edging around the other two men in a room that had suddenly grown crowded. "I hope black is okay."

"Fine. Thank you."

As she reached for it, she saw Jake's focus shift to the stains on her long-sleeved blouse.

She'd been trying to ignore them all evening. And she did her best to do so now as she took the coffee. But she couldn't control the tremors in her fingers, and the steaming liquid sloshed dangerously close to the edge. She wrapped both hands around the flimsy cup.

As the younger cop exited, the detective spoke again. "Jake will be handling security for you."

She carefully balanced the cup on her leg. "Why? My sister's husband got what he came after." Bitterness etched her words.

The men exchanged a glance, and the detective moved the other chair in the room closer to her. "You want to grab a seat? There are more chairs in the hall." He raised an eyebrow in Jake's direction.

"I'll stand."

Propping his shoulder against the wall, Jake folded his arms across his chest and looked down at her.

"We'd feel more comfortable if you had security until we apprehend your sister's husband," the detective told her as he sat.

Liz processed his comment. "You think he might come after me?"

"It's possible. You harbored his wife. He clearly has an anger problem. If he's the perpetrator, he's already killed once—or tried to. I doubt he'd hesitate a second time."

She reasoned through that, trying to nudge her numb brain into analytical mode. "If he wanted me dead too, why wouldn't he have taken care of both of us at once?"

The detective shrugged. "He could've been watching for you to return and seen your neighbor coming with you. Or he might have been spooked by something. We won't know that until we find him."

Jake had remained silent during the exchange, and she tipped her head back to look up at him. He towered over her in the small space, hovering like a keen-eyed hawk waiting to swoop down on his quarry. For the first time, she noticed the shadows of fatigue beneath his lower lashes, his rumpled clothes and the stubble on his chin. The scruffy look didn't fit. Meaning he must have had a very long day.

But his eyes remained alert. Focused. Razor sharp. Just the way she remembered.

"Are there any security cameras at your house?" he asked.

"No."

"What about cameras at the neighbors' houses, Cole?"

Cole. Liz tucked the name away as she took a careful sip of the too-hot coffee.

"We already checked. Nothing. Judge Michaels, is there anyone else you know of who might have had a reason to want your sister dead?"

"No. Stephanie is one of the kindest, sweetest people I've ever known." She blinked to clear away the sudden blur of moisture. "The only one who ever mistreated her was Alan. I tried over and over to convince her to leave him. But she always said he was a good person at heart, and that he couldn't help these rages that came over him from time to time."

She rummaged in the pocket of her slacks for a tissue. "The only reason she finally left him was because she just found out she was pregnant, and she was afraid for the b-baby." Her voice caught, and a tear slipped down her cheek. She swiped at it, balling the tissue into her fist.

"Let's assume for a minute your sister wasn't the specific target." Cole leaned closer to her, his posture intent. "Is there anything in the house important enough to kill for?"

"You think robbery might have been the motive?" She squinted at him, taken aback by that notion.

"We need to explore every option."

She chewed at her lower lip and considered the question, then shook her head. "No. I did bring home some case notes for an upcoming trial, but there was nothing sensitive or incriminating in them. And I don't have many personal items of great value."

"We'd like you to look around and see if anything is missing once the evidence technicians are finished. Sometime tomorrow."

She felt the blood drain from her face. "I'm not sure I can . . ." Her voice choked, and she swallowed. "Going back there will be very difficult."

"I understand that. But if your sister's husband has an alibi, we need to consider other motives." Cole rose. "If you have any other thoughts about what happened tonight, let Jake know and he'll pass them on."

"Okay."

Standing, he directed his parting comment to his brother. "I'll be in touch."

She watched as he exited and pulled the door half closed behind him.

Several beats of silence passed. Her husband's best friend remained standing, eyes veiled.

"I'm sorry about your sister."

"Thanks." She felt like a bug under a microscope, and gestured to the chair Cole had vacated. "You might want to sit. It's going to be a long night."

After a brief hesitation, he pushed off from the wall, eased the chair away from her, and dropped into it.

The silence lengthened again. Liz wasn't up to small talk, but the quiet in the room felt uncomfortable. "I thought you were based in Washington."

"I was. But they needed more help here, and I volunteered to transfer. Family ties and all that. I only arrived two weeks ago."

Just her luck.

"Was Jennifer able to get a . . . teaching job here?" It took her a moment to summon up the profession of the woman she'd never met. She'd always regretted not being able to go with Doug to the wedding in Virginia six years ago, after new evidence in a case she was handling came to light days before the trial was scheduled to begin. That hellish week of twenty-hour days could still make her shudder.

A muscle twitched in his cheek. "Jen died four years ago."

Another wave of shock rippled through her. "I didn't . . . I had no idea. I'm sorry."

"So am I." The words came out gravelly, and he cleared his throat.

"Was it an illness?"

"No. Head injuries from a skiing accident." He shifted in his seat. "Have you had any updates on your sister?"

She got the hint. Subject closed.

"No. They took her to surgery hours ago. I was about to ask one of the officers if he would . . ."

The words died in her throat when a fortyish man dressed in scrubs pushed open the door and stepped inside. Jake rose at once and moved in front of her.

"It's okay," she spoke up. "This is Dr. Lawrence. The surgeon."

His posture relaxed a fraction.

"I'll wait outside." He started to exit.

"You don't have to leave." She swallowed, trying to control the tremor in her voice. Whatever the doctor had to say, she didn't want to face it alone. Despite Jake's reserve, his solid presence felt somehow reassuring.

He hesitated, one hand on the door, then stepped back into the room and gestured to the empty chair. "Take my seat, Doctor. I suspect you've had a long night."

"Thanks. I have." The man pulled the chair closer to her and sat, his eyes weary.

At his grim expression, Liz's heart stuttered and she tried to brace herself. Though he hadn't uttered a word, she already knew the bottom line.

The news was bad.

2

As the surgeon settled into his seat, Jake noticed two things.

The shakes had spread from Liz's hands to her whole body.

And her grip on the disposable coffee cup was about to send a geyser of hot liquid spurting into the air—and onto her lap.

Closing the distance between them, he reached for the cup. "I'll hold this for a few minutes."

Instead of relinquishing her grip, she lifted her chin, giving him an up-close view of green eyes flecked with gold—and dulled by shock.

She'd had about all she could take, he realized. And while he might not like her personally, he was responsible for her well-being. That included protecting her from self-inflicted burns.

He peeled the fingers of one of her hands away from the cup and gave it a slight tug, gentling his voice. "Let it go, Liz. I'll give it back after you talk to the doctor."

She blinked and looked down. So did he. His much-larger hand partly covered hers, and he couldn't help noticing that beside his fingers, hers seemed slender. And fragile. And very feminine.

A weird catch in his respiration startled him, and the instant she released her grip he retreated to the farthest corner of the room.

"Your sister survived the surgery, Judge Michaels. But the prognosis isn't good. Do you want me to give you all the medical terminology or put it in lay language?"

"Lay language." Her words were taut. Strained. Laced with fear.

"Okay. The CT scan showed that the bullet entered at an angle from the back of the head, veering toward the right. It lodged behind the right eye. As we discussed earlier, it's very possible your sister heard or sensed a presence and started to turn. Had the bullet gone straight in from the point of entry, it would most likely have damaged both hemispheres of the brain. There would have been no chance of survival."

"Does that mean . . . can she recover?"

Jake evaluated Liz's rigid posture, the pulse throbbing in the hollow of her neck, the whitening of her knuckles—and prepared to spring forward if she started to nose-dive.

"It's possible."

But not probable.

The man's cautious tone spoke volumes. Judging by the sudden tightening of her lips, Liz had picked up his unspoken message too.

"However, we have a long road to travel," the doctor continued. "Let me tell you what we've been doing for the past few hours. The initial CT scan indicated your sister had suffered a significant amount of bleeding in the brain. So we took off a small portion of the skull to evacuate the blood. We also removed dead tissue and inserted a tube to drain off excess fluid. At this point, our biggest concern is swelling. That's why we left the skull open. Swelling can increase pressure inside the head, which prevents blood passage to tissue. That, in turn, leads to further brain injury. Or brain stem issues."

"Is the bullet . . . did you get it out?" Liz's voice shook.

"No. Attempting to remove it would cause more damage. It's better to let it stay where it is."

"What about the baby?"

"We're still picking up a strong fetal heartbeat."

"What happens next?"

"We wait. We watch. We monitor." He pulled off his surgical cap, revealing a head of close-cropped salt-and-pepper hair, and pinned her with an intent look. "You need to be aware that a lot of things can go wrong, Judge Michaels, from cardiac arrest to renal failure to respiratory problems. What we need to focus on now is getting your sister through the next few days. If we succeed in that, we can consider next steps."

"May I see her?"

"Not for several hours. She's in recovery now and will stay there awhile. You can visit her briefly once she's moved to intensive care. In the meantime, it might be a good idea to try and get some rest and come back in the morning. We can call you if anything changes."

She was shaking her head before he finished. "I can't leave." Her voice rasped on the last word.

Watching the muscles in her throat work as she swallowed, Jake joined the conversation. "We can get a hotel room for you close by, if you'd like."

"No. I need to be here."

"She won't know whether you're here or not, Liz." He strove for a gentle tone, hoping it would buffer his practical comment.

When she looked up, he was taken aback by the determination and unyielding conviction in her eyes. "I'll know. I can't leave someone I love alone in their time of need."

Then why were you going to leave Doug?

He scrutinized her face, searching in vain for an answer to his unspoken question.

"Let me see if we can find you a room where you can get a little sleep, then." The surgeon rose, interrupting the charged silence.

Liz leaned forward and touched his arm. "Doctor . . . if

things don't go well, my sister . . ." She swallowed. "Her living will includes an instruction that any usable organs be d-donated."

He covered her hand with his. "I'll pass that information on. And hope it's irrelevant."

"Thank you."

With a nod toward the corner where Jake stood, the man exited.

Hunched in her chair, staring at the stains on her cuffs, Liz was shaking worse than ever. Setting her coffee on a cart beside him, Jake slipped through the door and flagged a passing nurse.

"Could you scrounge up a scrub top for the judge? She's got a lot of blood on her blouse."

The woman nodded. "Let me see what I can do."

As Jake prepared to reenter the room, he caught sight of Tom "Spence" Spencer approaching down the hall. They'd exchanged no more than a handshake and greeting during Jake's introductory tour of the St. Louis office before he'd been called away to Denver, but the man had struck him as solid and competent. The exact kind of backup he was glad to have tonight, when fatigue was beginning to dull the edges of his acuity.

"The reinforcements have arrived. Wait—make that singular. I'm it." The man flashed him a grin as he approached and stuck out his hand.

Jake returned his firm grip. "I'll take whatever I can get. Did Matt fill you in?"

"Yes. As much as he knew, anyway. Sounds like the sister's husband is in the hot seat."

"That's the assumption at this point." Jake relayed the information he'd received from Cole.

"So what's the plan?"

"The doctor tried to convince Judge Michaels to leave for a while and get some sleep, but she wants to stay here until her sister comes out of recovery. He's trying to find a spot for her to rest. Once that's nailed down . . ."

The nurse reappeared and handed him a teal-colored shirt. "It's probably too big, but at least there's no blood on it."

"Thanks."

"No problem. We've also located a private room for the judge not far from the neuro-intensive care unit."

He turned to Spence. "Check it out, okay? We'll wait here until you give us an all-clear. Do you need my cell number?"

"Already programmed into speed dial." He tapped the BlackBerry on his belt.

"Efficient. I need to catch up."

"From what I hear, sounds more like you need to catch your breath."

Jake managed a weary quirk of his lips. "True. But not likely to happen anytime soon."

"We might be able to work something out. I'll call you in a few minutes."

As Spence set off, Jake spoke to one of the two officers flanking the door. "Let your sergeant know I'd like you to accompany me and the judge when we move. After that, we can take over."

Without waiting for a reply, he reentered the room.

Liz hadn't changed position. She was still hunched in her chair. Still shaking. Still fixated on the blood on her cuffs.

He crossed the room and held out the top. "I thought you might want to change out of that blouse. This was the best I could do."

Lifting her head, she met his gaze as she reached for it. "Thank you."

Much to his annoyance, the gratitude in her eyes warmed a tiny corner of his heart. How had she managed that, when he hadn't planned to feel anything but professional concern for his friend's wife? Hadn't *wanted* to feel anything more?

"You're welcome." He gestured to the door. "I'll wait in the hall while you change."

Three minutes later, when she cracked the door, he eased

back inside. She was holding the blouse at arm's length, and he took it from her, passing it to one of the officers outside.

"Find a bag for this, okay?"

Turning back, he found Liz hugging herself and rubbing her arms. He could see the goose bumps on her skin from across the small room. The nurse had been right; the scrub top was way too big. In the voluminous—and no doubt drafty—top, Liz reminded him of a little girl playing dress up.

Another irritating twinge of tenderness tugged at his heart.

"They must be rationing heat." She gave an apologetic shrug.

He reached for her coffee. "Maybe this will help."

"I already tried that. It's as cold as I am. I should have brought my jacket with me when I left the house, but I . . . I wasn't thinking straight."

Jacket.

He had a jacket.

Shrugging out of it, Jake draped it around her shoulders and spoke before she could voice the protest he sensed was coming. "Don't bother objecting, Liz. I'm not cold."

She closed her mouth. Snuggled into the warmth. Let out a sigh. "Okay, I won't. This feels too good."

Her gaze flicked to the exposed pistol in the holster on his belt. She moistened her lips and eased back into her chair. Looking desperately in need of comforting.

He shoved his hands in his pockets and balled them into fists. "Look . . . is there someone I can call who could come and stay with you?"

"No. The police already asked. I've only been in town four months. Not long enough to make a lot of friends. Besides, I wouldn't want to drag anyone else into a mess like this."

His BlackBerry began to vibrate, and he pulled it off his belt. "Taylor."

"It's Spence. The room's secure."

Jake listened as his colleague recited the directions. "Okay. We'll be there in five minutes."

"I also gave the recovery room and neuro-intensive care unit my cell number, in case anyone needs to reach the judge."

"Good."

Slipping the phone back on his belt, he focused on Liz. "We have a room nearby where you can rest."

"In the hospital?"

"Yes."

Taking a deep breath, she stood. The effort seemed to sap her energy, and she grabbed the back of the chair to steady herself as she slung her purse over her shoulder.

Jake opened the door, alerted the two officers that they were preparing to leave, then turned to Liz.

"Okay. We're set. Let's do this quickly. You ready?"

"Yes."

Exiting first, Jake scanned the corridor. Typical ER activity. Nothing to raise a red flag. He took her arm and led her down the hall at a brisk pace, one officer in front, the other in back.

Spence was waiting outside the designated room, and he opened the door as they drew close. Jake ushered her inside.

One quick, sweeping glance told him it was a standard hospital room. Bare bones and impersonal, imbued with a faint antiseptic smell. But it had a bed and a bathroom, and they could keep it secure. It would do.

"If you need anything, we'll be outside the door. Leave the blinds closed. The ICU and recovery room have my colleague's cell number, and they know where we are."

"Okay." She regarded the bed and gripped her arms across her chest. "I hate hospitals."

Join the club.

He tried to blank out the image of Jen's still form lying on a gurney, the eyes of the woman he loved shuttered forever. All because he . . .

"I doubt I'll be able to sleep."

Liz's comment gave him a welcome excuse to switch gears. "You can rest, if nothing else."

"Easier said than done."

He didn't respond to her soft comment.

She didn't seem to expect him to as she dropped her purse onto the nightstand, slipped off his jacket, then handed it back. "I won't need this now. There are blankets on the bed. Thank you for the loan."

He watched as she pulled back the covers, sat, and scooted back onto the raised mattress until her legs were dangling. Looking once again like a vulnerable, lost, innocent little girl.

Jake quashed that thought at once.

Liz Michaels wasn't a little girl. She was a federal judge. A brilliant attorney. A strong woman who went after what she wanted with singular determination. She was not vulnerable. She was not lost. And she most certainly was not innocent.

With an abrupt move, he hooked the collar of his jacket on one finger and slung it over his shoulder. "We'll let you know if we hear anything. Good night."

He didn't wait for her to reply.

"Everything okay in there?" Spence stepped aside as he exited.

"Yeah." Pulling the door closed, he indicated the two cops lingering a few yards away. "Why are they still here?"

"I cleared it for them to hang around if you want to catch some shut-eye. There's an empty waiting room two doors down, on the right. You can probably have it to yourself for four or five hours."

Not a bad idea. He was already digging deep into reserve energy, and he suspected things would only heat up in the light of day. He couldn't afford to be off his game, not with a federal judge in his charge. Liz would be well protected for the next few hours with a deputy U.S. marshal and two cops hovering close.

"Okay. Call me if anything comes up."

"Will do. We'll keep an eye on the door to the waiting room too."

"Thanks."

Two minutes later, Jake dropped onto the couch in the deserted room. After rolling his jacket into a pillow, he tucked it under his head and stretched out. Sixty seconds later, sleep was already claiming him.

But as he drifted off, a faint, pleasing, floral scent invaded his consciousness.

Liz's scent.

It clung to his jacket.

And while he didn't like the woman, he had to admit her scent was very, very appealing.

Lying flat on her back, Liz stared at the dark ceiling. She was exhausted. But, as she'd feared, sleep wouldn't come.

Every time she started to drift off, an image of Stephanie slumped on the white couch, her head centered over a growing crimson stain, pulsed across her mind. And in the silence of the night, she kept hearing the echo of her own screams. They went on and on and . . .

Stop!

Sitting up abruptly, she shoved her hair away from her face, pressed her fingers to her temples, and tried to get her ragged breathing under control. She should have known the firm stand she'd encouraged her sister to take with her husband might backfire. That issuing an ultimatum wouldn't work. That it could lead to violence.

She'd tried the same approach with Doug. And it had failed just as badly.

The pressure of tears tightened her throat. For someone lauded as one of the finest young legal minds in the judiciary, she was a big fat zero when it came to dealing with the people she loved. The insights and good judgment she brought to the bench seemed to desert her in her personal life.

Doug and Stephanie proved that.

The tears she'd held at bay all day spilled out of the corners of her eyes, coursing down her cheeks in silent anguish while her chest heaved and her shoulders shuddered.

Why, Lord? Why are you letting this happen?

No answer came in the silent darkness.

Bowing her head, Liz continued to weep.

In his sleep-drugged state, it took Jake a few moments to identify the source of the vibration against his hip.

His phone was ringing.

Swinging his legs to the waiting room floor, he shoved his fingers through his hair and yanked the BlackBerry off his belt. "Taylor."

"It's Cole. Everything okay there?"

"Yeah." He stifled a yawn and checked his watch: 6:00 in the morning. Four hours of sleep wasn't enough, but he'd take it.

"Was that a yawn? You sleeping on the job?"

"Two of your officers hung around to back up Spence so I could grab a couple hours of shut-eye. What's up?"

"The crime scene technicians will be finished inside the house by 9:00. We'd like the judge to check the place out as soon as possible after that so she can let us know if anything is missing. There's some disturbance around her jewelry box."

"Okay. Any sign of her sister's husband?"

"No. Springfield is watching the house, but he hasn't shown yet. Also, the Feds are nosing around."

"That doesn't surprise me." When a federal judge was involved in a crime, Jake knew the FBI would keep its finger on the pulse of the investigation—and take over if it was determined the judge was the target. For now, that didn't seem to be the case.

"The agent's a good guy, though. Mark Sanders. Heads up the SWAT team. Used to be on the HRT."

Jake arched an eyebrow. Impressive. The FBI's Hostage Rescue Team was the nation's most elite civilian tactical force. If things got dicey, Sanders would be a good guy to have around.

The door to the waiting room opened, and Spence stuck his head in. The grim set of his jaw kicked Jake's pulse up a notch, and he stood. "Gotta go, Cole. Maybe I'll see you at the house."

He strode toward the door as he slid the phone back onto his belt. "What's up?"

"The ICU called. They're taking the judge's sister back to surgery. She's hemorrhaging."

Muttering a word he rarely used, Jake joined Spence in the hall. The man fell into step beside him as they headed toward Liz's room.

"Did you hear anything from her all night—or what was left of the night?"

"No."

When he reached her door, he gave a soft knock.

No response.

He knocked more firmly.

Still no response.

Furrowing his brow, he twisted the handle and pushed the door partway open.

The room was dark, the faint light of dawn nothing more than a pale outline around the blinds on the far window. But the light spilling in from the hallway illuminated Liz as she lay curled into a protective ball facing the door, her hair falling across her cheek.

"Let's try to round up some coffee." Jake spoke softly, keeping his gaze fixed on her. "And see if you can find someone who can give us an update."

As Spence motioned to one of the officers a few feet away, Jake entered the room and eased the door shut behind him. He continued to the bathroom, where he flipped on the light above the sink. That provided some illumination in the room without the need to turn on the harsh bar fixture over the bed.

Moving close to Liz, he was struck by her pallor. And her puffy eyes suggested she'd cried herself into an exhausted sleep.

He wished he had better news to give her. But delaying it wasn't going to change the inevitable.

"Liz."

She didn't stir.

"Liz." He touched her shoulder.

Emitting a troubled sigh, she tried to shift away.

Lightly grasping her shoulder, Jake gave a gentle shake and increased his volume. "Liz."

Her eyelids flickered open. For a brief moment she stared straight ahead. Then, with a sharp gasp, she bolted upright, her disoriented eyes wide with fear, her chest heaving, her posture rigid.

"Liz, it's okay." Jake grasped both her shoulders and put his face close to hers, his fingers absorbing the tremors coursing through her body. "It's Jake. You've been resting in the hospital near your sister." He spoke slowly, giving her a chance to shake off the mind-muddling effects of her exhausted slumber. "Take a few deep breaths."

As she followed his instructions, the haziness in her green irises cleared. Only then did he pass on the news.

"I'm sorry to wake you. But your sister's been taken back to surgery."

Her breath hitched, and she shrugged free of him to swing her legs to the floor. One side of the scrub top slipped off her shoulder as she stood, but she either didn't notice or didn't care.

"What happened?"

"We're trying to get you some details now. All we know is there was some additional bleeding in the brain."

Her response was a small, deep-throated moan that seemed sourced in her soul—and tugged at his gut.

Holding onto the mattress with one hand, she righted her discarded brown pumps with a toe and slid her feet inside. "How long ago . . ."

The knob on the door twisted, and a second later Spence pushed it open to admit a woman in scrubs with a stethoscope around her neck. She headed toward Liz and held out her hand.

"Judge Michaels, I'm Susan Grady from neuro-intensive care. I've been asked to give you an update. Would you like to sit?"

"No." Liz folded her arms across her chest.

The woman gave a quick dip of her head. "Okay. I don't have much yet, anyway. Your sister was being settled into intensive care when she suffered a seizure. Shortly after that, her condition began to deteriorate. We did another CT scan and discovered she'd had a hemorrhagic stroke—in other words, a blood vessel inside the brain ruptured. She was rushed back into surgery about twenty minutes ago, and the doctors are working to get the situation under control. I'll pass on updates as I get them from the operating room."

Shell-shocked was the word that came to Jake's mind as he assessed Liz. She groped for the bed behind her, as if seeking some tangible support, and he edged closer.

"Thank you." Her voice sounded steadier than she looked.

With another nod that encompassed both of them, the nurse exited.

For a few beats of silence after the door closed behind her, Liz stood unmoving. A spasm rippled across her face, and her lower lip began to tremble. She caught it between her teeth, blinked several times, and gestured toward the bathroom as she snagged her purse off the nightstand. "I think I'll freshen up a little."

Jake got the message. She needed a few minutes to pull herself together.

"Okay. I'll be in the hall."

He waited until she pulled the bathroom door shut behind her with a quiet click, then exited.

Spence pushed off from the wall with his shoulder. "I asked one of the aides to round up a toiletries kit, if you want to shave and brush your teeth. Can't help you out on clothes, but at least the rumpled look is in." The other marshal shot him a quick grin as he handed over the small bag. "I also asked her to see what she could find in the way of food."

On cue, Jake's stomach rumbled. Reminding him that his last meal had been a fast-food burger he'd grabbed en route to the airport in Denver more than fifteen hours ago.

"Thanks."

"All in a day's work. There's a men's room down the hall, on the left. Those guys will stay until you get back." He inclined his head toward the two officers who'd remained through the night.

"Give me ten minutes."

"Don't hurry on my account. I'm not going anywhere."

With a wry quirk of his lips, Jake headed down the hall. He'd prefer a long, hot shower, a decent meal, and a soft bed, but he'd make do. If nothing else, freshening up would help him feel more human.

He hoped the same would be true for Liz. Doing routine things often comforted people in stressful situations. A few normal minutes could shore up their stamina, leaving them better equipped to cope with the next trauma.

And Jake had a feeling Liz was going to need all the shoring up she could get in the hours and days to come.

3

Liz gripped the edges of the sink, faced the mirror, and cringed.

It was hard to believe the haggard woman with weary, shadowed eyes and tangled hair staring back was her.

But the stark, shocking reflection—exacerbated by the harsh, merciless overhead light—was all too real.

As real as the nightmare that had become her life.

Lifting an unsteady hand, she brushed her fingers over her cheek. There had been a time in the not-too-distant past when she'd worried that her youthful appearance might be a detriment to her career.

She could now put that concern to rest.

Today, she looked every one of her thirty-eight years.

As for her career . . . she'd trade all her achievements, all her accolades, all her awards for the chance to make things right with Doug and Stephanie. For the chance to have a normal, trauma-free life.

But it was too late.

For all of them.

Fighting back a wave of despair, she turned on the faucet and picked up the bar of soap. As she tore off the paper wrapper, the maroon stains under her polished fingernails caught her eye. Lifting one hand, she examined them . . . and discovered more of the same in her cuticles.

The breath whooshed out of her as if someone had delivered a sharp jab to her stomach.

Stephanie's blood.

Bile rose in her throat, and she gripped the edge of the sink again, willing the nausea to subside. She wouldn't fall apart. Couldn't fall apart. Her sister needed her. Had always needed her. That was what happened when a mother died young and there was a six-year age gap between siblings. And Liz had taken the responsibility seriously, doing her best to be more surrogate mom than big sister.

Yet when it came to the most important decision of her sister's life, her best hadn't been good enough. Ignoring her advice, Stephanie had married Alan—and become his battered wife. It had taken the impending arrival of a baby to give her the courage, with Liz's support, to issue an ultimatum and walk away.

Liz had applauded her decision. Had believed that now, her sister would be safe.

Instead, she was fighting for her life.

And her blood is on your hands.

As Liz stared at her fingers, that harsh indictment echoed in her mind.

Once again, her stomach twisted into a knot.

Adjusting the water as hot as she could stand it, Liz stuck her hands under the stream and scrubbed at her fingers. Determined to scour every trace of blood from her skin.

If only she could do the same with the self-reproach that stained her soul.

How could she not have seen Alan's real character? How could she not have suspected he would resort to lethal violence if crossed? She dealt with criminals every day. Shouldn't that experience have given her more insight?

But her judgment had been lacking with Doug too. After living with him for five years, she should have realized the step she'd taken could send him over the edge.

Liz tried to swallow past the bitter taste on her tongue.

But it was no use. For five long years, her guilt over Doug's death had weighed down her soul. A private burden, known only to her and God. Friends and colleagues hadn't a clue about her culpability.

Except, perhaps, for one man.

Jake Taylor.

Her hands stilled under the running water as she thought about the marshal who'd been assigned to protect her. She didn't know much about him, other than a few stories of their college days relayed to her by Doug. When Jake had flown in for the wedding, she'd been too caught up in the last-minute details and excitement to do more than exchange a few words with her husband's best man. But he'd seemed pleasant enough. His toast at the reception had been witty and warm, and there had been nothing in his demeanor to suggest he harbored any enmity toward her.

In the intervening years, however, his attitude had undergone a dramatic shift. At the funeral, he'd been cool. Distant. Aloof. His stiff posture and stilted language during their brief exchange had spelled disapproval in capital letters.

Since then, she'd often wondered what Doug had shared with Jake during their periodic phone visits to turn his buddy against her.

But now wasn't the time to dwell on that question.

She turned off the water, dried her hands, and reached for her purse. Once this drama was over, she doubted she and Jake would have much contact. In the interim, she trusted him to do his job. As Doug had once commented, Jake seemed like the type who would wear a white hat and ride into Dodge. He might not like her, but he struck her as a suck-it-up kind of guy who took his professional responsibilities seriously. His opinion of her shouldn't matter.

Yet for some disturbing reason, it did.

Forcing herself to refocus, Liz withdrew her comb and lipstick and made a halfhearted attempt to repair her appearance. But it was a losing battle. To restore any semblance of normalcy, she needed a hot shower, clean clothes, and a sound sleep.

The first two she assumed she'd get in the next few hours.

As for the latter . . . she suspected it would remain elusive for the foreseeable future.

As Jake set the tray of scrounged-up food on the adjustable table beside the bed, he heard the bathroom door open behind him.

"Is there any news?"

At the apprehensive question, he glanced toward Liz. She'd combed her hair and applied lipstick. But the color she'd added to her lips only served to emphasize the pallor of her skin.

"No. I brought some food. And drink."

She eyed the eclectic assortment. Small plastic containers of vanilla pudding and lime Jell-O, plus a turkey sandwich. The beverages included a small carton of low-fat milk, a container of orange juice, and two different kinds of soda.

Liz shook her head. "I'm not hungry. But thank you."

"I admit the selection isn't great. But you might want to eat a little until we can round up more substantive fare."

She skirted the bed and took a seat on the far side. Away from the food. "I don't think I can manage anything right now."

"Coffee's on the way, if you'd rather have that."

"No. I had too much caffeine last night." She surveyed the drinks. "Maybe I'll try the milk."

When she started to rise, he waved her back. "Let me see if there are any cups in the bathroom."

He found one, ripped off the covering, and carried it and the milk container around the bed to where she sat. Setting the plastic cup on the windowsill, he opened the carton and poured the milk for her.

As she murmured a thank-you and reached for the cup, he frowned. Her fingers were red. Almost as red as her crimson nail polish. As if they'd been burnt. Or rubbed raw.

After a quick shift into analytical mode, it took him all of two seconds to evaluate the evidence and arrive at a conclusion.

She'd spent the past few minutes scrubbing off her sister's blood.

No wonder the sight of food—and the thought of eating—turned her stomach.

He retraced his route back to the other side of the bed, picked up the tray, and headed for the door. "I'll get this out of the way."

"Aren't you hungry?"

At her question, he angled toward her. "Yes. But I can eat in the hall."

"You don't have to leave on my account. I can tolerate watching someone else eat, even if my stomach won't let me do the same." Her gaze locked with his. "However, if you'd rather not spend any more time than necessary in my presence, don't feel compelled to stay."

Taken aback by her blunt remark, he froze. A flush seeped onto her cheeks as he stared at her—suggesting the comment had surprised her as much as it had him.

Before he could think of a response, she spoke again. "Sorry. I didn't mean to be snippy. Just . . . forget I said that. Chalk it up to stress. Go ahead and eat out there with your colleague. I'm sure he's far better company."

She took a sip of her milk. Lowered the cup.

Jake suddenly found himself fighting an impulse to wipe away the white mustache that clung to her upper lip.

Which was nuts.

He should be hightailing it out of the room instead of thinking about getting up close and personal. She'd given him an out. He ought to take it. Because her assessment was correct. He didn't want to spend any more time in her company than necessary.

Or he hadn't, anyway, when he'd first been handed this assignment.

Yet somehow, in the past few hours, his attitude had undergone a subtle shift. The Liz sitting across the room from him, facing a crisis alone, digging deep for strength as she kept vigil over her sister, didn't jibe with the mental image he'd created of a selfish woman who ranked matters of the heart low on her priority list.

Then again, for all he knew, she might have called her office while he was away. Taken the opportunity to catch up with voice mail or email. He was certain a BlackBerry lurked somewhere in the recesses of her purse.

But somehow he didn't think she'd done that.

And for whatever reason, the thought of leaving her alone in this sterile room didn't sit well.

Besieged by conflicting impulses, Jake went with his gut. "I'll eat in here."

Did the tense line of her shoulders ease a hair? Or was it his imagination? Jake wasn't certain as he set the food back on the adjustable bedside table, propped a hip on the mattress, and opened the plastic container that held the sandwich.

She continued to sip her milk in silence, focusing on the closed blinds as he devoured the sandwich and the pudding. Still hungry, he considered the Jell-O. Passed.

He chose a soda instead, the fizz echoing in the quiet room as he pulled back the tab. After taking a long swallow, he regarded Liz.

As if sensing his perusal, she looked toward him. "How was it?"

"Hospital food." He shrugged. "But when you're hungry, you can't be too picky."

"Not hungry enough for the Jell-O, I see."

He grimaced at the clear green substance in the plastic dish. "I've never been able to stomach food that jiggles."

The ghost of a smile whispered at her lips. "I'm with you. My mom always forced me to eat Jell-O when I was sick, which did nothing to endear it to me. I wouldn't even eat the cherry Jell-O salad with whipped cream and blueberries she always made on Fourth of July, despite the rave reviews it got."

He found himself smiling in response. "My mom's cure-all for any kind of sickness was much more palatable. Homemade chicken soup. Sometimes my brother and sister and I would fake being sick just so she'd make it."

"Pretty devious."

"Hey, it worked. For a while. Now she makes it whenever we come to visit."

"Where's home, Jake?" She took another sip of milk, never breaking eye contact.

"Here. But Mom moved to Chicago a few years ago to live with her sister. They were raised there, and they decided to combine households after they both became widows. Now that I'm based in St. Louis, I should be able to see her more often."

"That will be nice . . . for both of you."

"How about you? Does your mom still make that Jell-O salad?"

As she ran a finger around the rim of her cup, every vestige of her fleeting smile vanished. "She died when I was twelve."

He should have remembered that. At Doug's wedding ten years ago, he'd noted the absence of the mother of the bride and asked his friend about it.

"I knew that. Doug mentioned it once. I'm sorry."

"It's okay. She's been gone a long time. But you know what? I still miss her. Especially on days like this." Her words came out scratchy, and she took another sip of milk. "Dad did his best to fill in the gap for Stephanie and me, though. Hard as he worked in his law practice, he was always there for us." She fingered a loose thread on the oversized scrub top. "He died of a heart attack four years ago. Way too young. He was only fifty-nine."

Meaning she had no one except Stephanie.

Jake couldn't imagine being that alone. He might not have seen his family as much as he'd have liked in the past few years, but he knew they were there if he needed them. Except Dad.

"My father died too young too," he offered. "Sixty-one. He got up one morning five years ago, put on his uniform, and keeled over from a stroke on his way to work. I'll never forget the shock of that phone call." His own voice hoarsened, and he cleared his throat.

"What sort of uniform?"

"Police. He never wanted to be more than a street cop. But he made a difference. People on his beat knew if they had a problem, Joe Taylor would see that justice was served. Everyone loved and respected him. I never met a man with more strength of conviction and integrity."

Liz's expression softened. "I have a feeling our dads might have been cut from the same cloth."

"Could be." Jake tipped his head back and drained his soda can. He had no idea how the conversation had edged into such personal territory. While he wasn't averse to sharing information about his upbringing and his family with friends, Liz didn't fall into that camp. Not even close.

But he had to admit she was easy to talk to. Must be her legal training. Putting people at ease on the stand and encouraging them to talk by asking the right questions would be a critical skill for an attorney. One it was clear she'd mastered.

Jake was saved from having to find a way to shift the conversation back to more neutral territory by a soft knock on the door.

Spence stuck his head inside. "Dr. Lawrence is here."

As Jake's gaze met the other marshal's, some sixth sense told him what was coming. He rose, circled the bed, and stationed himself beside Liz as Spence pushed the door all the way open.

The doctor, still attired in surgical scrubs, entered.

At the man's grim demeanor, Liz drew a sharp breath and her posture went taut as a bowstring. When her fingers clenched, crushing the empty plastic cup in her hand, Jake bent down to take it from her.

The surgeon snagged a chair, placed it at the foot of the bed across from Liz, and sat. Exhaustion had deepened the smudges under his eyes since his visit to the ER, and the lines etched on his brow were mute testimony to sustained, intense concentration.

"There's no easy way to say this, Judge Michaels." His tone was gentle and filled with quiet sympathy. "We did everything we could. But the bleeding and swelling were so severe that your sister's brain stem, which controls the body's most critical functions, stopped operating. We've done an EEG, and there's no electrical activity. In light of our earlier conversation about organ donation, we're keeping her on a ventilator and moving her to the ICU. But brain death has occurred. I'm very, very sorry we couldn't save her."

As the doctor gave Liz the bad news, Jake watched her knuckles whiten on the arms of the chair. Tracked the shudder that rippled through her. Heard the catch in her breathing.

But when she spoke, she once again sounded steadier than he'd expected.

"I know you did your best, Doctor. And I thank you for that. May I . . ." Her voice caught, and she tried again. "I'd like to see her."

"Of course. Just give us a few minutes. One of the ICU nurses will come and get you." He looked up at Jake. "Because of the nature of her injury, we'll need some direction from the coroner before we can proceed with organ retrieval."

"I'll get things in motion."

The doctor nodded, then leaned toward Liz and took her hand, cocooning it between his. "I wish we could have repaired the damage to your sister and given her many more years, Judge Michaels. But some things can't be remedied, even with modern medicine. If it's any consolation, the quality of her life, had she lived, would have been severely compromised. The damage to her brain was extensive."

"Thank you for sharing that. It does help."

With one more squeeze of her hand, the doctor stood and spoke to Jake. "When you have some information, just let the ICU know."

"I'll do that."

In the quiet that descended after the doctor exited, Jake tried to think of some words of comfort. But if they existed, he couldn't come up with them. So he resorted to the standard, trite expression of sympathy. "I'm sorry, Liz."

"Thank you." She blinked and swiped the backs of her hands across her eyes. "I knew all along there wasn't much chance she'd survive. But I . . . I guess I kept hoping for a miracle."

"Can I get you anything?"

"No. Thanks. I'd just like to sit for a few minutes."

"Okay. I'll be in the hall."

With one last glance at her, he exited the room, let the door click shut behind him, and joined his colleague.

"I take it the news was bad?" Spence handed him a cup of black coffee.

"Yeah." Jake took a long swallow of the lukewarm brew and kneaded the back of his neck. "Her sister didn't make it."

"How's the judge holding up?"

"She's still on her feet. But my guess is she's close to folding."

"It's been a rough night."

"Yeah."

"While you were talking to the doctor, I checked in with Matt. He's lined up a condo for her until we sort this thing out. Two of our guys have already done a sweep and are waiting there."

"Good. We should be ready to leave shortly. She wants to

stop by the ICU, so we'll do that on the way out. Also, her sister left a directive to donate her organs. Can you find out what the coroner needs?"

"No problem. I'll arrange for some transport for us too."

"We need to swing by her house on our way to the condo. The police want her to see if anything is missing."

"I'll get a couple of our guys over there."

As the nurse who'd briefed them earlier appeared from around a corner at the far end of the hall, Jake drained his cup. "They must be ready for the judge."

Handing the cup back to Spence, Jake reentered the room. Liz was sitting where he'd left her.

"Susan Grady is headed our way. Do you need a few more minutes before going to the ICU?"

"No."

Standing, she walked around the bed with the exaggerated care of a drunk and picked up her purse. Her slow, precise movements confirmed his assessment of her condition.

She was about to fold.

As she stopped beside him, waiting for him to cue their departure, Jake gave in to his earlier impulse.

"Hang on one sec."

He ducked into the bathroom, dampened a washcloth, reentered the room, and positioned himself in front of her.

She inspected the cloth. Gave him a puzzled frown. "What's that for?"

"Milk mustache."

The furrows in her brow eased. "I never did learn to drink milk properly."

"Easy to fix." He dabbed at her upper lip, trying to ignore those gold-flecked green eyes that harbored so much pain.

"At least you didn't spit on your handkerchief."

"What?" He stopped dabbing, taken aback.

"That's what my mom always did when I had a milk mustache. I hated it." She tried for a smile. Didn't come close to pulling it off.

Admiring her spunk, Jake wiped away the last of the crusty white residue. "I can understand that. Although spit was probably very effective."

"But disgusting."

Flashing her a quick smile, he tossed the washcloth onto the adjustable table beside the remnants of his breakfast and took her arm. "I agree. Let's head out."

The walk to the ICU was short. Once they arrived, Spence took up a position by the door. Jake released Liz's arm, intending to wait outside with his colleague. The nurse pushed through the door and held it open.

Liz didn't budge.

Susan Grady transferred her attention from Liz to Jake and arched an eyebrow.

"Liz." He touched her shoulder. "Would you rather not go in? You don't have to."

"Yes, I do. I have to s-say good-bye." Her voice was determined, but he saw the panic in her eyes. "Would you mind c-coming in with me?"

He shot a quick glance at Spence. "You okay with that?"

"Yeah. I've got it covered."

Taking Liz's arm again, he stepped with her into the ICU.

And into a sea of memories that blindsided him.

It had been a different city, a different hospital, a different set of circumstances . . . but the muted sounds, the equipment, the smell—they took him back four years. To the night he'd lost Jen.

All at once, he was sorry he'd eaten breakfast.

When his step faltered, Liz looked up at him. "Jake?"

He gritted his teeth. Sucked in a deep breath. "Give me a sec."

Understanding—followed by remorse—flashed through her eyes. "I'm sorry. You probably have your own bad hospital memories. I should have realized that. Look, I'm okay. Just wait for me outside. I c-can do this by myself."

The stutter belied her reassurance.

Still, for an instant, Jake was tempted to take her up on her offer. To flee this place that awakened the memories of pain and loss slumbering deep in his heart.

But the truth was, those memories would have been worse if he'd had to face his trauma alone. He'd made it through those dark hours because Cole and Alison had shown up and stuck by him 24/7. That's what siblings did. That's what family was for. But Liz had no one. And no matter his personal feelings toward her, he couldn't let her do this hard thing alone.

Firming his grip on her arm, he urged her forward. "I'm fine."

To his surprise, she held back and searched his face. "Are you sure?"

She was giving him one more chance to change his mind. Putting her own needs secondary to his. Willing to spare him at her own expense—despite her clear recognition of his antipathy toward her.

That was another disconnect with the image he'd drawn of her from his conversations with Doug.

And another reason not to let her down.

"I'm sure."

She drew a shaky breath. "Thank you."

Susan had stopped up ahead by a curtained cubicle, and she gestured toward it when they joined her. "Feel free to stay as long as you like."

As she moved away, Jake kept a firm grip on Liz's arm. "Ready?"

She straightened her shoulders. Lifted her chin. Nodded.

Leaning forward, he took hold of the drape. And as he prepared to pull it aside, he dug deep for a silent prayer to the God he'd neglected of late, asking him to give Liz the courage and strength she would need to get through the next few minutes—and the days and months to come.

4

Liz thought she'd mentally prepared herself to see Stephanie.

She was wrong.

As her sister came into view, her slender form outlined beneath the white sheet, she faltered. Without Jake's steadying grip on her arm, without the bolstering effect of his solid physical presence and aura of strength, she had a feeling she'd have crumpled into a heap on the floor.

For close to a minute, she remained at the foot of the bed, willing the shakiness in her legs to stabilize as she watched the steady rise and fall of Stephanie's chest. And reminded herself that the oxygen flowing through her sister's lungs was being provided by a ventilator. That despite the lifelike movement, Stephanie was gone, leaving only a physical shell behind.

And so was the niece or nephew she'd never know.

She closed her eyes, the double loss and the sudden, empty feeling of utter aloneness twisting her stomach into a tight knot and choking off her breath.

God, please give me strength!

When she at last felt capable of moving forward, she eased free of Jake's grip and walked toward the head of the bed. Tape covered much of Stephanie's lower face, holding the endotracheal tube in place. A white dressing swathed her upper head. Very few of her sister's features were exposed.

But the black eye Alan had inflicted stood out. Visible evidence of the attack that had convinced Stephanie to flee to the refuge of her sister's home. To a place she'd mistakenly assumed would be a safe haven.

A bone-deep coldness settled over Liz, and she shivered.

Seconds later, a jacket infused with warmth was draped over her shoulders. Angling toward Jake, she noted the faint parallel creases etched between his eyebrows. Felt the concern—and compassion—radiating from the depths of his brown eyes. The latter warmed a place deep in her soul much as his jacket was chasing the chill from her skin.

"Thank you."

He acknowledged her expression of gratitude with a nod.

Turning back to her sister, she reached for her hand. It was warm and supple, the fingers long and tapering and graceful. The hand of a ballet dancer. Stephanie had aspired to that career, once upon a time. Until Liz had discouraged her, urging her to choose a more practical profession instead. And so her sister had, earning a business degree that had led her to an executive assistant position. Which had, in turn, led her to Alan.

So much bad advice.

So many mistakes.

Liz's throat tightened, and she stifled a sob. Fought for control.

Holding on to her emotions by the flimsiest thread, she leaned down and pressed a kiss to her sister's forehead.

"Good-bye, Steph." The whispered endearment was more breath than sound. "I'm sorry for all the ways I failed you. I hope you're happy now. And at peace. And I hope you finally get your chance to dance. Always remember how much I love you."

A tear slipped past her lashes, leaving a dark splotch on the pristine sheet. Another followed.

Straightening up, Liz groped inside her purse for a tissue. Swiped at her eyes. Tried to stem the flood of tears.

Failed.

She felt Jake move beside her.

Was it time to go? Already?

But much to her surprise, instead of urging her to leave, he laid a hand on her shoulder.

That silent gesture of support gave her more comfort than any words he could have said.

For an instant, she was tempted to lean back against his powerful chest, to let his solid strength support her physically as his touch had shored her up emotionally. But he was already doing far more than his job required. She didn't want to overstep the bounds of professional propriety.

Taking her sister's hand once more, she gave it a final squeeze, choked back a sob . . . and commended her to God.

As she turned away, she kept her watery eyes downcast and fiddled with her purse. "I'm ready to leave. But I'd like to stop by the chapel on our way out, if that's possible." Though she made a valiant attempt, she couldn't stop the quiver that ran through her voice.

"I'll see what we can arrange."

Jake pulled the curtain aside and she started toward the exit. But three steps outside the cubicle, her vision blurred and she stumbled. He was beside her at once, his hand again firm on her arm through the thin leather of his jacket, supporting her, guiding her as they wove through the ICU.

Once they reached the door, he settled her against the wall beside it, signaling to his colleague on the other side of the glass entry. "Wait here while I talk to Spence about the chapel, okay?"

Not trusting her voice, she simply nodded.

He pushed through the door, and she watched as the two men conversed, aware that Jake was keeping tabs on her. They conferred with a passing aide, and then Jake rejoined her.

"We'll leave by way of the chapel and check it out. If it's not crowded, we can make this work. Let me introduce you to Spence, who will be part of your security detail."

Jake ushered her through the door, and she found her hand engulfed in a strong grip. She liked Jake's colleague at once.

As tall and dark-haired as her husband's best friend, he, too, projected a powerful presence. His eyes were sharp and incisive, and he radiated competence and integrity.

But Jake didn't waste time on social niceties. Before she'd even finished shaking hands, he was propelling her down the hall. Spence fell into step on her other side.

Fortunately, the chapel was empty when they arrived. After escorting her to a pew near the rear, the two men retreated to the back.

Grateful to have a few quiet minutes alone with God before she was plunged back into the craziness that had become her life, Liz closed her eyes, bowed her head, and resolved to make the most of them.

Because she didn't know when she might have this luxury again. And she needed every bit of comfort, fortitude, and strength the Almighty was willing to impart during this brief moment of spiritual communion.

"What's the exit plan?" Standing half in and half out of the chapel, the door propped open with his shoulder, Jake kept one eye on Liz and the other on the hall as he directed the soft question to Spence.

"The Suburban's waiting near a service entrance on the lower level. Dan and Larry are inside. You might have met them on your orientation tour."

"Yeah." As he recalled, Dan O'Leary had the ruddy complexion stereotypical of his Irish heritage, reinforced by strong auburn tints in his brown hair. Larry Olsen, lean and a little gangly, had reminded him of a cowboy in an old western.

"They're good men. Very experienced. Dan's checking out the most expeditious route from the chapel to the service entrance as we speak. Once we're in the Suburban, they'll drop us off at our cars. When we leave, I'll lead, they'll follow, you'll take up the rear."

"That works. We'll swing by the judge's house first, then head to the condo. Where is it?"

"A high-rise downtown. Not far from the courthouse. We've used units there before. There's good security already in place, but it's being beefed up on the judge's unit as we speak, including a camera in the exterior hall. We'll also link into the feed from the security cameras at the entrances to the building. Matt got an adjacent unit for us. The command post is being set up there."

"Sounds like everything is under control."

"On our end, anyway." Spence glanced toward Liz. "I'm not so sure about the judge."

Jake took in Liz's bowed head, the slump of her shoulders. "Not surprising, in light of everything that's happened. But she's a strong woman."

"Good thing." Spence cocked his head. "You two have a history?"

"She's the widow of my best friend. I've only met her twice, though." He pulled his BlackBerry off his belt. "My brother's the lead detective on this case. Hang tight in here while I alert him we're about to leave for the house."

Stepping into the hall, Jake let the chapel door close behind him and stood in front of it as he speed-dialed Cole.

His brother answered on the second ring.

"I've been wondering when I'd hear from you. A couple of your guys showed up at the scene, so I assume you're going to be there soon."

"We got delayed. The judge's sister didn't make it."

Cole muttered a word that wasn't pretty. "We're gonna nail this guy."

"Any sign of him yet?"

"No. But it's only a matter of time. What's your ETA?"

"Half an hour, max. Liz is in the chapel now, and we're out of here as soon as she's ready to leave."

"Okay. I'll meet you at the house. The technicians are just wrapping up inside."

As the line went dead, Spence cracked the door. "I think she's about done here."

Jake looked past him. Liz was settling her purse on her shoulder. "You want to call Dan and see if he's finished mapping our route to the service entrance?"

"Yeah."

He slipped past Spence and reentered the chapel as the other man took his place in the hall.

Liz rose, exited the pew, and walked toward him. Though a profound sadness still echoed in her eyes, they seemed more serene. And she'd regained some of the composure he recalled from their previous encounters.

He hoped it lasted once she left this quiet, peaceful place.

"Thank you for giving me this time. It helped a lot."

"We try to accommodate requests from our charges whenever we can. Are you ready to leave?"

"Yes."

"Okay. Here's the plan. We'll be exiting through a service entrance on the lower level, into a Suburban. Besides being safer, that will allow us to avoid any media people who might be lurking around. We want to do this fast. No stopping."

"All right."

"When we leave here, we'll swing by your house. The police need you to check for missing items. We can't rule out robbery yet. While we're there, you can also pack some things to take to the condo."

Her face went blank. "What condo?"

"Sorry. I guess we haven't gone over that." What was normal protocol for him would be new for her. She'd only been on the federal bench for four months. "In a situation like this, with so many unknowns, it's standard procedure to move a federal judge to a place we can more easily secure."

She took a deep breath. "Right. I knew that. I just never thought it would apply to me. But it's better than staying at the house after . . ." She swallowed. "I understand the need to check out the robbery angle, but I don't have to go in the family room, do I?"

"Is there anything in there worth stealing?"

"No. Besides, most of my stuff is still in boxes. I'm just renting the house while I look for one to buy, so I haven't bothered to unpack."

"Then you can avoid that room." If Cole didn't agree with that decision, tough.

"How long will I be in the condo?"

"Until it's safe for you to leave." He knew she wanted a more definitive answer, but that was the best he could offer.

The door opened, and Spence stuck his head inside. "Any time you're ready."

Jake took Liz's arm. "Now is good. Let's move."

Guiding her out, he set a brisk pace as they traversed a maze of corridors and took a service elevator to the lower level. As it descended, Spence tapped in Dan's number and alerted him they were moments away.

The transfer to the Suburban was smooth and swift. Spence stepped outside the door. The vehicle pulled close to the exit, and he opened the back door. Jake hustled Liz into the car, sliding in next to her. Spence circled the vehicle and took a seat beside her on the other side. He was still closing his door as the vehicle pulled away from the curb.

"Wow. That looked choreographed." Liz's hand tightened on her purse strap, the thread of strain back in her voice.

"We've all been through these kinds of drills a few times. Buckle up." Jake tapped her seat belt. "Liz, meet Dan O'Leary behind the wheel, and Larry Olsen. Guys, this is Judge Elizabeth Michaels."

As Dan lifted his hand in greeting, Liz dredged up the ghost of a smile for Larry. "Marshal Olsen and I met during one of my first cases here. How's your wife doing?"

"Better. Thank you for asking. But it's been a tough pregnancy, and that book of crossword puzzles you sent home with me couldn't have been better timed. It helped get her through one of her roughest weeks."

"I'm glad to hear that."

His curiosity piqued, Jake glanced at Liz. But the Suburban was already pulling to a stop in the ER parking lot, giving him no chance to dwell on her exchange with Larry.

"Spence and I are going to get our cars, Liz. He'll be in front of the Suburban. I'll be behind." He angled toward the door, stopping when she touched his arm.

"Do you want your jacket back now?"

"Later is fine."

After a quick sweep of the parking lot, Jake opened his door and slid out of the vehicle. Spence did the same on his side. Jake waited until he heard the automatic locks click behind him before he headed for his Trailblazer. Spence was already climbing into his Grand Cherokee a few spots down.

As their little motorcade pulled out of the hospital and headed for I-64, Jake checked the clock on the dash: 7:55.

Ten hours ago, he'd been boarding his delayed flight in Denver after nine intense days tracking and arresting a fugitive on the most-wanted list. Ten weeks ago he'd been dodging bullets in Iraq after a mob tried to storm a courtroom during an incendiary trial. Ten months ago, he'd been executing a court order to seize assets belonging to a domestic terrorist group and working a special security detail for a Supreme Court justice in Washington DC.

One thing for sure. This job was never boring.

That was what he liked about it.

But much as he thrived on challenge, much as he relished being pushed to his limits, he wished this assignment had passed him by.

And his reasons today had nothing to do with his negative feelings toward Liz Michaels. Much to his surprise, those had softened during the traumatic hours they'd spent together. In fact, she'd managed to awaken in him a protective instinct that went far beyond what his job dictated.

Jake didn't understand that. Wasn't sure he *wanted* to understand it.

But he did understand risk. Plus, he had a nose for danger. That's why he was good at what he did.

And he was smelling danger now.

For both Liz—and himself.

The first rays of morning sun filtered through the dense woods, reflecting off the small, shiny gold cross in his hand. Looping the delicate chain around his fingers, he lifted it toward the heavens.

How odd that this had been among the handful of jewelry he'd snatched before leaving the house.

But it was fitting.

Because this symbol of pure, perfect, unselfish love—the kind that showed mercy and kindness, that honored vows and commitment—was a stark reminder of her failures.

Worst of all, she'd betrayed the solemn promise she'd made before God.

And wronged him in the process.

Now she'd paid the ultimate price.

As the cross dangled from his fingers, glinting in the clear morning light, he took its presence in his cache as a sign that God approved of his action.

Slowly he inhaled, filling his lungs with the fresh country air.

It was done.

Lowering the cross, he let it drop into the Ziploc bag with the other jewelry and picked up the camp shovel. Brittle, frost-nipped oak leaves had formed a thick carpet on the forest floor, and he brushed them aside with the blade, then began digging. The ground was soft from recent rains, and it took him less than half a minute to create a deep cavity in the fertile earth.

He weighed the bag in his hand for a few seconds, then

wedged it into the bottom of the hole and replaced the earth. Once more using the tip of the shovel, he spread leaves over the disturbed ground.

Stepping back, he surveyed the spot. It looked exactly like the ground around it. There was no indication that anything was buried beneath the surface.

Good.

For all intents and purposes, the jewelry had ceased to exist.

Just as she had.

And as he turned away, two words echoed in his mind.

Good riddance.

"My pearls are missing. So are a couple of costume-jewelry rings, a silver bracelet, and the gold cross necklace I always wear under my robe when I'm presiding."

Finishing her inventory, Liz stepped back from the jewelry box, which was covered with liberal amounts of fingerprint powder, and crossed her arms tightly over her chest.

"You need anything else?" Jake directed the question to Cole, who continued to write in his notebook. They'd been through the rest of the house—except for the family room—and nothing else appeared to be missing.

"No. That should do it. When you have a minute . . ." He tipped his head toward the hall. "Thank you, Judge."

As Cole exited the bedroom, Liz slipped Jake's jacket off her shoulder and handed it back to him.

"Borrowed for the last time, I hope. Thank you."

He took it, resisting the temptation to lift it and inhale her scent. Instead, he handed her the plastic bag containing her blouse. "We can have this cleaned for you."

She peeked inside. Rolled the bag into a ball. Set it on the dresser. "Thanks. But I can't imagine ever wearing it again. What's next?"

"Pack as much as you think you'll need for a week." He

picked up the suitcases they'd retrieved from the guest-room closet during her inventory tour and set them on the bed.

"Would it be okay if I took a shower and changed clothes while I'm here?"

Jake hesitated. He'd prefer to leave ASAP, but there were six deputy marshals, a police detective, and several patrol officers on the premises. It didn't get much safer than that.

"Sure. Keep the shades drawn. I'll be in the kitchen when you're ready to leave."

After closing the door behind him, Jake headed down the hall of the modest bungalow, night-and-day different from the upscale Jefferson City home Doug had shown him through on his one, impromptu visit, when Liz had been out of town. Cole waylaid him en route to the kitchen and directed him toward the dining room, where stacks of boxes were waiting to be unpacked.

The place reminded him of his condo.

"Where's the judge?"

"Packing. Taking a shower. Changing clothes."

Cole surveyed him. Leaned close. Sniffed.

"When's the last time *you* changed clothes? Or showered? It's a little rank in here."

Jake narrowed his eyes and propped his fists on his hips, not in the mood for humor. "Unlike you, I never made it home last night. Back off a few feet if my aroma offends your delicate sensibilities."

Cole arched an eyebrow. "Touchy, aren't we?"

"It's been a very long, unpleasant night."

"Yeah." Cole's levity faded as the muffled sound of a shower joined the muted voices of the marshals conversing in the kitchen. "The judge looks like she's operating on fumes."

"I'd say that's an accurate assessment. So where are you with the investigation, and what do you need to talk to me about?"

"Assuming the husband has an alibi, the robbery motive isn't working for me, even though some jewelry is missing."

"Why not?"

"There were six fifty-dollar bills on the hall table. In plain sight. The assailant had to go past that table on his way into the family room. If he was going to take time to riffle through the judge's jewelry box, why wouldn't he pocket some easy cash?"

Jake rubbed the back of his neck. "He could have taken some jewelry to make it appear robbery was the motive. If the cash wasn't part of his plan, it might not have registered."

"That's my take."

"Did the Crime Scene Unit find anything interesting?"

"Not much. Our assailant got in through a basement window in the back that's concealed by bushes. Taped it so it wouldn't shatter, broke the glass, flipped the lock. The ground back there is hard as a rock, so he didn't leave any footprints."

"What about fingerprints?"

"A few on the window. And some on the jewelry box. The latter are probably the judge's." Cole leaned a shoulder against the wall and stuck his hands in his pockets. "We're running them all through the FBI database."

"Have you talked to the neighbors?"

"Yeah. No one saw or heard anything out of the ordinary. It's like the guy materialized in the room, then vanished."

Jake expelled a frustrated breath. "We know that didn't happen. What kind of security does the house have?"

"A standard home-grade system. But it wasn't activated at the time of the murder. According to the judge, she didn't plan to be here more than six or eight months, and she didn't see the need to enhance the existing system for such a short-term stay."

Silence fell between them as two words echoed in Jake's mind.

Big mistake.

He'd been in the business long enough to know that even if this case was an extension of domestic violence unrelated to Liz, as it seemed to be, there were wackos out there who targeted high-profile judges. The security here should have been beefed up when she moved in—whether she thought it was necessary or not.

But with everything else on her plate, the last thing she needed to do was start beating herself up about that.

"Any word from Springfield?" Jake dug in his pocket, hoping to find a breath mint.

"Nothing. Mr. Long was last seen by a neighbor around noon on Friday as he pulled out of his driveway. The local PD is watching the house, and they've put surveillance on his office. So far he hasn't shown."

"Okay." No luck on the breath mint. He withdrew his hand. "We'll get Liz settled. Keep me in the loop."

"You got it." Cole pushed off from the wall. "By the way, Alison said to tell you she forgives you for standing her up for your welcome-home dinner last week and the lasagna will keep, but did you ever hear of a telephone?"

A grin tugged at Jake's lips. He could picture his little sister uttering those very words, chin jutting out, pert nose stuck in the air. "That sounds like her."

"Yeah. Finally. She's had a tough few months." Cole narrowed his eyes. "How much did she tell you about the accident when she called you in Washington?"

"The basics." Jake mentally replayed the brief conversation he'd had with his sister a couple of days after he'd returned from Iraq, when he'd still been jet-lagged and trying to decompress. "I heard about the broken leg, and she mentioned some internal injuries. I chewed her out for not telling me sooner, but she claimed I was overreacting and said she was doing fine. When I pressed for more information, the best I could get was a promise of more details when I got back to St. Louis. She was much more interested in talking about her new puppy."

"That's what I figured." Cole raked his fingers through his hair. "Look, I agreed—under duress—not to say much until she has a chance to see you. But the truth is, she's not doing fine. She was hurt a lot worse than she implied."

A knot formed in Jake's stomach. "How much worse?"

Several beats of silence ticked by as Cole regarded his brother. "We weren't sure she was going to make it."

A jolt of shock ricocheted through him, followed by a surge of white-hot anger. "And no one told me?"

"Alison's orders. She didn't want you worrying."

"I'm her big brother. That's my job."

"Don't let her hear you say that. Her independent streak is wider than ever. And much as she loves you, she has mixed feelings about you coming home. She's afraid her accident is one of the reasons you suddenly decided to move back to St. Louis."

"It is. It was a wake-up call that I need to spend more time with my family. To be here for you guys."

"A word of warning—keep that tidbit to yourself if you want to preserve the peace. Alison even sent Mom packing back to Chicago, amid much maternal protest."

"Okay. So you tell me how's she doing, since she obviously gave me the sanitized version."

"She's made progress. But she still goes to therapy twice a week. The fractures in her leg are healing. I'm not so certain about the one in her heart."

Jake frowned. "What's that supposed to mean?"

Sticking his hands in his pockets, Cole blew out a breath. "I'm getting in way too deep here. Alison will be furious if she finds out I spilled all this before she had a chance to talk to you."

"You're in too far to back out now. Let's have it."

"I take it she didn't tell you about David."

"What about David?" Last he'd heard, things were heating up between his sister and the up-and-coming Legal Aid attorney she'd been dating. He'd assumed an engagement announcement was imminent.

"He dumped her."

"What! Why?"

"Because as a result of those internal injuries she casually mentioned to you, she can't have children. And he wanted a family."

As he worked through that latest piece of news, Jake's lips settled into a grim line. "What kind of man walks away from a woman because a drunk driver robbed her of the ability to have children?"

"A jerk?"

"I have a stronger word in mind. But better she saw his true character now than before they tied the knot."

"I'm sure she agrees with that assessment. In theory. Anyway, you might want to give her a call when you have five minutes."

"Like that's going to happen anytime soon." Jake shoved his fingers through his hair. "You know, I expected things to be quieter in St. Louis."

True to form, his brother had a smart comeback. "Maybe trouble just follows you around." With a mock salute, he strolled toward the hall. "One of your guys made a coffee run. I think I'll help myself. And when you talk to Alison, do me a favor. Don't mention this conversation."

As Cole headed toward the muffled voices in the kitchen, Jake toyed with the idea of calling his sister now. But he'd rather be focused on her when they talked. And at the moment, he was preoccupied with the safety of a certain judge.

Once Liz was ensconced in the condo and he was satisfied with the security measures, he'd go home for a few hours. Shower. Eat. Sleep. Then, after he was rested and thinking clearly, he'd call his sister. And instead of trying to convince her the accident wasn't the main reason he'd returned to St. Louis, he'd give her serious grief for swearing Cole to secrecy about it until he was back from Iraq.

Because as he'd learned the hard way, with Alison the best defense was always a good offense.

5

Draining the dregs of his coffee, Jake checked his watch. Again.

Liz was taking a lot longer than he'd expected with her shower and packing. Cole had left, and the deputy marshals lounging around her kitchen were getting restless.

So was he.

Setting the cup on the kitchen counter, he addressed the group. "I'll see if I can speed things up. Let's plan to head out in ten minutes."

Thirty seconds later, he knocked on her door. "Liz, it's Jake. Everything okay in there?"

"Yeah. I guess."

He didn't like her vague tone.

"May I come in?"

"Yes."

The woman sitting on the bed was a Liz he'd never before seen. She'd exchanged her usual power wardrobe for jeans and a black knit top, and her hair was still slightly damp, a few loose tendrils around her temples curling softly from the humidity in the bathroom. She was barefoot, one leg tucked under her, and her attention was fixed on the cell phone in her hand.

It would have been an appealing picture. Except for her shell-shocked expression.

He crossed the room in three long strides, noting as he covered the short distance that the tape on two of the sealed packing boxes had been pulled back, as if she'd rooted for some items to take with her. The two suitcases sitting at the end of the bed appeared to be packed.

But she wasn't making any move to leave.

"Liz? What's going on?"

Without looking up, she blinked once. Twice. Again. "I've had my phone on mute. There are twenty-five voice mails since last night. I need to call my boss. Talk to my law clerks. Make funeral arrangements. Cancel some commitments. Get back to my landlord so he can send a plumber to fix the leaky faucet in the bathroom." Panic seeped into her voice. Along with a touch of hysteria. "And I haven't even checked my home machine yet."

She was on overload. Overwhelmed by the enormity of the decisions to be made and the details to be dealt with. Given enough stress, even competent, organized, in-control people like Liz Michaels had their limits.

And she'd reached hers.

Leaning down, he flipped the phone closed. "We'll deal with all that once we get to the condo. And we'll do whatever we can to help you."

She lifted her head, and the searing anguish in her eyes bridged the professional distance he was attempting to maintain. "Can you make this nightmare go away?"

"I wish I could." He swallowed past the sudden tightness in his throat.

With one more look at her phone, she slid it into her purse. Took a deep breath. Exhaled slowly. "Let me put on my shoes and I'll be ready to leave."

She rose, walked to the open closet, and pulled a pair of casual shoes off of a rack.

"Is this everything?" Jake gestured to the bags at the foot of the bed.

"I'll need my briefcase. And my laptop."

"Where are they?"

"On the floor beside my desk in the office."

"I'll get them. And the guys will load your suitcases in the car. Meet us in the kitchen when you're ready."

Jake detoured to the office, found the briefcase and computer, and cracked the blinds on the front window as he passed. Two media vans were now parked in front of the house.

Great.

Back in the kitchen, he delegated bag duty to the two marshals who'd been waiting for them when they arrived—and issued a warning.

"We've got company. Someone tipped off the press that we're here."

Spence crumpled his cup and tossed it into an empty donut bag as the two men exited. "I heard from the coroner's office a few minutes ago. No problem on the organ donation. You want me to call the hospital and pass the word?"

"Yeah. I'll let Liz know once she's settled in at the condo."

"I'll get the engine warmed up." Dan disposed of his own cup and headed out the door.

Three minutes later, as the two marshals returned from stowing the bags, Liz appeared in the doorway. She'd pulled a sweater over her head and carried a jacket over her arm. Meaning she'd have no more need of his.

Stifling an unexpected surge of disappointment, Jake forced himself to switch gears as he addressed her. "We have some media out front, so we're going to make a quick exit. Dan's already in the car."

He took her arm, and the remaining men closed in tight around her.

"It's a good thing I'm not claustrophobic." She surveyed the circle of marshals.

"Bear with us for two minutes. Once you're in the car, you'll have more breathing room."

At Jake's signal, the group exited the front door and headed toward the Suburban.

The instant they appeared, the quiet Saturday morning came to life. The media vans spewed out camera-toting technicians, and reporters waving microphones began calling out to Liz.

Jake tightened his grip on her arm and glanced down. To his surprise, she didn't seem fazed by the shouted questions and circus-like atmosphere.

Then again, she'd been involved in some high-profile cases through the years. Doug had mentioned once that one of them had drawn national attention. She'd even been quoted in *Newsweek*. No doubt she'd had more than her share of exposure to the press.

As she slid into the Suburban and he prepared to close the door, one of the young officers who'd been stationed at the perimeter of the property jogged over.

"Excuse me, sir, but there's a neighbor from across the street who'd like to talk to the judge. Delores Moretti."

"Delores is here?" Liz bobbed her head, trying to find an opening in the wall of men. "I'd like to see her. Jake?" She touched his arm.

He hesitated. The exposed position wasn't good. But it was hard to say no to her after all she'd been through. And as long as they formed a human shield, it should be okay. For sixty seconds.

"This has to be quick."

"I understand."

"Okay." Jake turned to the officer. "Let her come over."

The man walked a few feet away and motioned to a stout, gray-haired woman standing on the sidelines. She ducked under the police tape and trotted up the driveway.

"What's she holding?" Jake eyed the shallow aluminum container in her hands and directed his question to the officer.

"Some kind of food."

Behind him, Jake heard a tiny, soft chuckle from Liz. "That would be Delores."

When the woman drew close, Jake spoke again. "Ma'am, we need to make this fast."

"This won't take but a minute."

Stepping aside, Jake created a gap wide enough for the woman to squeeze through.

During the brief exchange that followed, he did a continuous scan of the neighborhood, as did Spence beside him. But the conversation behind him was more interesting than the view in front of him.

"Cannoli! Oh, Delores, you shouldn't have bothered."

"It wasn't any bother at all. Not that they'll offer much consolation. But words are no good at a time like this. They won't change what happened to your poor sister or take away your grief. So I did what I could. I went to church and lit a candle, and I said a rosary. Then I came home and made your favorite dessert. You know Harold and I are here for you if you need anything, Liz. All you have to do is call."

"I know, Delores. And I appreciate that more than I can say."

Jake felt the woman move behind him, and knew she'd leaned forward to give Liz a hug.

"Don't you worry about anything right now except keeping yourself safe. Just lay low until all this is over."

"I don't think I have a choice in the matter. As you can see, I'm surrounded by U.S. marshals. Will you let Reverend Mike know I won't be able to help at the shelter tomorrow night?"

Jake frowned. Shelter?

"I'll take care of it. And I'll water all your plants too."

Surveying the porch, Jake noted the pots brimming with colorful blossoms that hadn't yet succumbed to the cooling fall nights. There'd also been a bouquet on her kitchen table. Doug had never mentioned that Liz liked flowers.

An elbow in his ribs clued him in that the meeting behind

him was over, and he shifted aside to allow Delores to squeeze through.

"Thank you, young man." She dropped her voice. "And you take good care of her. She's our special angel."

Angel?

Based on Delores's speculative appraisal, he hadn't done a very good job hiding his surprise. "Do you know Liz very well, Marshal?"

"No, ma'am."

She lowered her voice. "We didn't either, until she moved here four months ago. A week after we came over to welcome her to the neighborhood, Harold fell off a ladder and broke his wrist. Had to have surgery and couldn't drive for three weeks. A few days after his accident, I sprained my ankle and couldn't drive, either. Liz stepped right up to help us out, picking up our groceries and prescriptions, busy as she was." Delores shook her head. "She is an amazing young woman. You keep her safe."

"We intend to, ma'am."

As Delores headed back down the driveway, Jake angled toward Liz. Buffered as she was by metal and bodies, he doubted she'd heard much, if any, of his low-pitched conversation with her neighbor. She was focused on the disposable container Delores had delivered, running her finger along the edge.

"We're ready to move out, Liz."

She lifted her head, and he caught the glimmer of tears in her eyes. "Sorry for the delay. But Delores is a treasure. I couldn't not talk to her."

"No problem. I'll see you when we get to the condo."

Closing the door, he turned to Spence. "Same formation?"

"Unless you see a reason to change it."

"No. That works for me." He shook hands with the two marshals who'd come to the house ahead of them to reinforce security. "Thanks, guys."

With a wave they headed toward their own vehicles.

As the little motorcade once again got under way, Jake ignored the media vans and glanced at the house across the street. Delores was standing on her porch. Looking worried.

About her angel.

Back in the early days of Doug's romance with Liz, Jake vaguely recalled him using that term once in reference to her. Jake had passed it off as the delirium of a man in love. And as time went by, Doug had viewed his wife in a far less angelic light. Self-centered, coldhearted, focused on her career to the exclusion of everything . . . and everyone . . . else—those were the qualities Jake had begun to assign to her after his conversations with his friend during the last few years of his life. Before he died in a tragic accident.

Or took his own life.

As far as he knew, no determination had ever been made about the cause of the one-car crash on that cold winter night. But Doug had been despondent after being passed over for a long-awaited promotion. And all these years, Jake had assumed that if Liz had given her husband the kind of emotional support he'd needed, if she'd had her priorities straight, if she'd been there for him instead of spending twelve hours a day at her job, things might not have ended in tragedy.

Now, she was busier than ever as one of the youngest federal judges in the nation. Yet she found time to help out her neighbors. To buy thoughtful gifts for the wife of a marshal assigned to protect her. And what was that business about a shelter?

It didn't compute.

Jake checked his rearview mirror, his professional skills kicking into autopilot as he watched for tails even as his mind continued to wrestle with the conundrum of the judge in his charge.

Had Liz changed . . . or had he been operating on faulty assumptions all these years?

And instead of putting the blame for Doug's demise entirely on her, had he overlooked his own culpability? He'd known his friend was down. Was there something more he could have done to offer support and help avert the tragedy?

The brake lights on the Suburban flashed as the signal in the intersection ahead changed from yellow to red. Jake slowed as well. And redirected his disturbing train of thought. He was too tired for heavy introspection.

But he couldn't stop the little niggle in his conscience that prodded him to admit that maybe—just maybe—he might have been a bit too harsh in his assessment of Liz Michaels.

And perhaps a bit too lenient with himself.

The silence was oppressive.

Closing her phone, Liz leaned back on the low-slung gray couch in the living room, wishing she had more calls to return. More arrangements to make. It was easier dealing with logistics than facing the stark quiet of the impersonal, furnished condo she now called home.

Not that it was a bad place. The open floor plan gave a sense of spaciousness to the compact, two bedroom unit. The living room merged into the dining area, which in turn gave way to a galley-sized kitchen. Modern art hung on the walls, providing the only color in the otherwise neutral palette. The sleek lines were pleasing to the eye, and the furnishings were elegant and sophisticated.

But the decorating didn't fit her tastes.

And it sure didn't feel like home.

Maybe the marshals could help her add a few cozy touches, if she asked. They'd been more than accommodating in stocking the kitchen this afternoon with the items on the list she'd compiled at their request.

However, she hoped she wouldn't be here long enough for the decor to matter much. Once they found Alan, she could go home.

Except the thought of returning to her rental house held

no appeal, either. How could she ever go into the family room again without seeing the image of Stephanie's blood?

Determined to switch gears, she rose and walked over to the picture window. There was probably a great panorama of downtown from this room, if she could see it. The vertical blinds had been closed since she'd arrived, and she'd been told to leave them that way. A quick peek couldn't hurt, though, could it?

She lifted her hand to tilt one of the slats—just as the doorbell rang. With a gasp, she jerked back. Talk about weird timing.

Doing her best to calm her racing pulse, she crossed the room and checked the peephole, as she'd been instructed to do. Jake stood on the other side, juggling a pizza box. He'd left a few hours ago, after a thorough inspection of the condo and the command post—the CP, as he'd called it—had satisfied him the security precautions were adequate.

He hadn't said he'd be back, but somehow she wasn't surprised by his reappearance. He struck her as the kind of guy who took his job seriously and didn't punch time clocks. She could relate.

She was surprised, however, by the pizza.

Unlatching the dead bolt, she twisted the handle and opened the door.

Now that she had a view of him undistorted by the fish-eye lens in the peephole, she found herself taking another kind of inventory. And liking the results. The shadows under his eyes had faded, and based on his clean-shaven jaw and still-damp hair, it was obvious he'd showered and shaved. He'd also changed clothes. Tonight he wore nice-fitting jeans and a cotton shirt rolled to the elbows. The agents in the CP wore suits, meaning he must be paying an off-duty visit.

"I wanted to stop by and check on things before I called it a night. May I come in?"

"Of course." She edged aside, and once he cleared the threshold she closed the door and twisted the dead bolt.

"Any problems?"

"No. It's been very quiet here."

"That's our goal." He hefted the box. "Can I interest you in some pizza?"

Her appetite had been nonexistent all day. But the aromas wafting from the box caused her stomach to growl.

As heat rose in her cheeks, he flashed her a grin. "Shall I take that as a yes?"

"I appreciate the offer. But evidence to the contrary, I'm really not hungry. The other guys brought me some food to stock the kitchen with this afternoon."

"Did you eat any of it?"

She shifted from one foot to the other under his intent scrutiny. It had been a long while since anyone other than Delores had cared what she ate—or if she ate. Although she knew Jake's concern was professional—after all, it wouldn't do much for his career if one of his charges passed out from hunger—it still felt good.

"No. Like I said, I haven't been hungry."

"Well, I'm starving, and I hate to eat alone. Maybe you could nibble at a piece or two while I have dinner. I got a deluxe, so there should be some things on here you like." He paused, and creases appeared on his brow. "Unless you're a vegetarian."

"No. I like meat." She folded her arms. "Aren't you supposed to be off duty?"

Now it was his turn to look uncomfortable. She wondered why.

"I am off duty. But I knew I'd sleep better if I took another run by here to check the security one more time."

That explanation didn't quite ring true, but she didn't press him. "Did you already do that?"

"Yes. You don't have to worry. You're safe here."

"I'm not worried. Alan accomplished his goal. I'm sure he's long gone." Despite her efforts to maintain an even tone, bitterness etched her voice. "Has there been any progress tracking him down?"

"Not yet. But St. Louis County is working the case hard. Springfield has surveillance on his home and office, and there's a nationwide alert out for his car. They'll find him, Liz."

"I'm sure they will. But it won't bring Stephanie back." A lump rose in her throat, and she did her best to ignore it as she gestured toward the dining area. "Have a seat. Is diet soda okay? That's all I asked for."

"That's fine."

She headed for the kitchen, pulling out plates and napkins and retrieving two sodas, keeping busy until she regained control.

When she joined him at the table, he flipped open the box and slid it her direction, letting her take the first piece. She chose the smallest one on her side and deposited it on her plate.

"Did you take a nap this afternoon?" Jake took two large pieces.

"No. I took care of business—personal and professional. I had long conversations with the chief judge and my law clerks. We had to figure out how to juggle the whole docket around. I also spoke with Stephanie's surgeon. They finished retrieving her organs and discontinued life support." She felt pressure build behind her eyes again and fought back the tears. "I had a preliminary conversation with the funeral director too. He's getting the logistics sorted out. Our parents are buried in Kansas City, where we grew up. Doug's in the same cemetery. I'd like her to be with all of them."

"I told you we'd help with some of that."

She lifted one shoulder and began picking the olives off her piece of pizza. "I didn't mind doing it. Idleness is more difficult than busyness."

They ate in silence for a couple of minutes. He wolfed down several wedges of pizza while she nibbled at her small piece. His comment about starving apparently hadn't been much of an exaggeration.

At last he stopped for breath and wiped his lips on a paper napkin. "Is the place okay for you?"

"It's fine for the short time I expect to be here."

"Is there anything missing? Anything you need?"

She tried to coax her lips into the semblance of a smile. "A rocking chair would be nice. With an afghan thrown over the back."

He arched an eyebrow at her as he snagged another piece of pizza. "Funny. I've never thought of you as the rocking-chair type."

Propping her chin in her hand, she gave up the pretense of eating. "What type do you think I am?"

His hand hesitated on the pizza for a fraction of a second. But it was long enough for her to infer he didn't want to answer that question. And his noncommittal reply confirmed that.

"We've only met twice, Liz. I don't know you well enough to have a good feel for your tastes." He deposited the pizza on his plate and edged the box toward her. Four pieces remained.

"Thanks. I'm done. Are you finished?" She gestured toward the box.

"Yeah." He eyed her picked-at wedge and furrowed his brow.

She reached for his plate and stood. "How about some dessert? Delores makes great cannoli, and I put coffee on earlier. It should still be good."

"I'll have some if you'll join me."

"Sure. I can't resist her masterpiece. It's an old family recipe from Sicily."

He rose too. "I'll get the coffee while you dish up the dessert."

It felt crowded in the small kitchen, with Jake's broad shoulders dominating the close quarters. Liz didn't recall him projecting such a powerful, compelling presence in their two encounters in previous years. Then again, emotions had been running high on both those occasions. Not that they weren't now. But this time, she'd spent a lot of hours one-on-one with him. And despite his initial coolness, she'd taken comfort in his steadiness, as well as the authority and competence he radiated.

His attitude toward her had also warmed. Whatever the reason, she was grateful for that too.

"Someone's already put a dent in Delores's offering."

At Jake's comment, Liz inspected the pan of cannoli she'd just unwrapped. Several were missing.

"I offered Dan a sample earlier when he checked in, and not too long after that Larry showed up at the door. He claimed he was checking on me too, but I think he had cannoli on the mind."

"These were supposed to be for you."

She shrugged. "I'll never eat them all before they go bad."

Setting two on his plate and one on hers, she re-covered the pan with foil and slid it in the fridge.

Once back at the table, Jake took a moment to examine the pastry shells that had been dusted with powdered sugar and drizzled with chocolate. Then he dived in.

"Wow. This is amazing."

"Yeah." Liz poked at the creamy filling with her fork. "The combination of flavors is incredible." She took a bite, letting the rich, sweetened cheese dissolve on her tongue.

Jake polished off his two pieces before she got halfway through her first one.

"Would you like some more?"

"No, thanks. I'm full. Finally." He leaned back and took a sip of his coffee, looking relaxed for the first time since he'd walked back into her life last night.

Picking up her own mug, she cradled it in her hands. "I'm sorry to disrupt your weekend. I'm sure you had far better things to do with your Saturday than babysit me."

She couldn't interpret the subtle shift in his features. Nor the flicker of emotion in his eyes.

"I'm used to odd hours. And the only thing on my agenda for the weekend was unpacking. Trust me. It's no hardship to put that off."

Checking his watch, he set his cup down and withdrew a pen and a business card from his pocket. He flipped the card over, wrote some numbers, and pushed it across the table.

"You have the phone number of the command post, but that's the number for my BlackBerry. If you need to talk to me about anything, don't hesitate to use it. Day or night." He took one final sip of coffee and stood. "You need to get some sleep."

She rose more slowly as he gathered up their plates and deposited them in the kitchen. The thought of being alone in the condo for the duration of what she expected would be a long, sleepless night held no appeal.

"Will I see you tomorrow?"

"I'll stop by." He headed toward the door, and she trailed behind. "Remember, there will be two deputy marshals on duty at all times in the CP monitoring the hall and all building entrances. They're also available to take care of anything you need. And don't forget the rules. No venturing out. Don't answer the door unless it's a marshal you recognize. Keep the blinds shut."

He turned at the door, and for an instant she was tempted to ask him to stay. To tell him she couldn't face the long, dark night alone.

But the truth was, she could. And she would. Though the past few years had been difficult, they'd taught her one thing. She was a survivor. She could make it on her own.

Even if she'd prefer to have someone by her side.

6

Jake slept for twelve hours straight. And when he finally woke up on Sunday morning at 9:00, he still felt as if he'd been drugged.

Not a good way to start off a day that he doubted would give him five minutes of downtime. He needed to check in with the CP at the condo. Call Alison. Get an update from Cole on the missing husband. Unpack at least some of his boxes. Stock his refrigerator.

Heaving a sigh, he decided to give himself five more horizontal minutes before attacking his to-do list.

Two minutes later, the vibration of his BlackBerry on the nightstand beside him hosed those plans.

With a groan, he groped for it and checked caller ID.

Alison.

For a couple of heartbeats he considered letting the phone roll to voice mail. But he'd planned to call her anyway. Might as well talk to her now and cross one item off his list.

"Morning, Twig." He grinned, waiting for the disgruntled reaction that his nickname for her from her skinny-as-a-rail preadolescent years would evoke.

She didn't disappoint him.

"I was about to apologize if I woke you, but on second thought, forget it."

Chuckling at her sassy tone, he sat up and swung his legs to the floor. "No apology needed. I was awake."

"Too bad."

"Would you feel better if I said barely awake?"

"Maybe."

"Then I'll give you that. Five minutes ago I was out like a rock."

"Cole told me you had a rough night."

"Did you talk to him today already?"

"Yes. I called to see if he was interested in joining me for church. You want to go?"

A twinge of guilt tweaked his conscience as he examined a ray of sun brightening the room as it streaked across the hardwood floor. He should go. But he and the Lord hadn't communicated much since Jen died. Maybe with Alison around to influence—and prod—him, he'd do better.

Not today, though.

"I have a full plate at the moment. And I need to stop by and check on the judge this morning. I'll think about it next week."

"I got a no from Cole too." She didn't sound happy.

"We both had a long day yesterday. And today could shape up to be just as busy."

"Yeah. The murder's all over the news. Cole says the judge was married to your college buddy."

"That's right."

"Weird coincidence."

"No kidding." He stood and padded barefoot toward the window, cracking the blinds. The sky was blue, and a light breeze was ruffling the leaves on the trees. A perfect day for a jog.

He added that to his to-do list. Along with an hour on the workout equipment in the next room—the first thing he'd unpacked and assembled after moving in. In his business, it didn't pay to get complacent about fitness.

"So if things are quiet this afternoon, you want to come

by for that welcome-home lasagna dinner you stood me up for a couple of weeks ago? You could also meet Bert."

"Who's Bert?"

"My new puppy. I told you about him. He's a charmer."

"Right. I remember. Okay, that sounds good. But could we make it early? I want to stop in at the judge's condo again tonight."

"How about 4:00?"

"That works."

"I'm looking forward to seeing you, Jake. It's been too long." Affection softened her voice.

"I would've been here sooner if you'd let Mom or Cole tell me about the accident."

Her tone went from affectionate to prickly. "That's precisely why I didn't. I don't want my problems disrupting other people's lives."

"We're not people. We're family." Time to play the offensive card. And throw in a little guilt for good measure. "Do you know how terrible I felt, finding out after the fact?"

"I'm sorry about that. But you were in Iraq dodging bullets. The last thing you needed was a distraction. If something had happened to you, I would always have wondered if it was because you were thinking about me when you should've been watching your back. I wouldn't have been able to live with that kind of guilt. But I can live with the kind you're trying to dish out right now."

So much for his strategy. Time to regroup.

"Let's table this discussion until tonight, okay?"

"How about tabling it until you get settled in? Or forever?"

"Nope. You agreed to give me details when I got back in town. I intend to hold you to that promise."

"Hmph. I could renege on my invitation."

Silence while he waited her out.

At last he heard a peeved whoosh of air. "Okay. Fine. I'll let it stand and deal with you after you get here. But if anything comes up and you have to cancel, call. You do have a BlackBerry, you know."

"Sorry about the last get-together. Things got wild."

"I understand. And all is forgiven. Unless it happens again."

He chuckled. "Message received. See you later."

After the phone went dead, Jake checked in with the command post. Everything was quiet. Good. A quick call to Cole confirmed the husband was still AWOL. Not so good.

But at least that news meant he had time for his jog and a workout before he headed downtown to check on the judge in person.

As for stocking his fridge and unpacking—the former chore he'd take care of after he visited Liz. The latter could wait for another day.

At the soft knock on her door, Liz got up from the glass-topped dining room table, where she'd spread out the contents of her briefcase. Massaging her brow, wishing the subtle ache that had begun in the middle of her sleepless night and intensified throughout the morning would go away, she trudged toward the condo's small foyer. Must be another visit from one of the marshals in the command post. They'd been checking on her at regular intervals.

Or perhaps word of Delores's cannoli had spread to today's crew and they were looking for a sample. Her lips softened into the hint of a weary smile as she approached the door. She was glad to accommodate them, but she wasn't in the mood for conversation.

When she peeked through the peephole, however, Jake stood on the other side, once again dressed in jeans and a cotton shirt. Must be his standard off-duty attire.

Suddenly she was in the mood for conversation.

Unlocking the door, she pulled it open and ushered him in. "I didn't expect you to stop by until later in the day."

He waited in the foyer as she slid the dead bolt into place. "Am I too early?"

"No. I just assumed you'd have things to do and places to go on Sunday morning."

"My sister invited me to church, but I declined."

"I hope not because of me."

"Not entirely. I've been less than diligent in my church attendance since Jen died."

She shoved her hands into the pockets of her jeans. "I can relate. I stopped going to services for a while after Doug died too. Faith is a funny thing. It's easy to believe while life is rolling merrily along. But in times of trial, it's tempting to turn away from God. Yet that's when we need him the most."

"You sound like Alison."

"Your sister?"

"Yeah. With her prodding, I'll find my way back sooner or later." He gave the condo a quick sweep. "Any problems? Other than insomnia?"

She arched her eyebrows. "I didn't say I wasn't sleeping."

"You didn't have to."

Heat crept up her neck under his intent scrutiny. "I look that bad, huh?" She tried for a light tone but couldn't quite pull it off.

"Not bad. Just very tired. And very stressed. You've had a tough couple of days." He gestured toward the dining room table. "Working?"

"Trying to. I can usually lose myself in an interesting case. It's not happening today, though."

"Maybe a nap would help."

"Maybe." She gave him an appraising scan. "You look like you caught up a little on sleep."

"Twelve solid hours. And I jogged this morning and got in a good hour-long workout."

No wonder he was in such superb physical condition. "Lucky you. I already miss my daily walk."

"You're a walker?"

"Yes. Thirty minutes every day on the treadmill, no matter how late I get home. I'll go back to it after all this is over. Speaking of which . . . I take it there's no news on Alan?"

"Not yet. I'll let you know as soon as there's a break."

"Thanks." They were still standing in the foyer, and she motioned toward the living room. "You're welcome to come in."

A tinge of some emotion—regret, perhaps?—flashed through his eyes.

"I have a few errands to run. And later in the afternoon I'm having dinner with Alison. I stood her up when I first got back into town, and if I don't show today I suspect I'll end up wearing the lasagna the next time she sees me."

She tried to smile past a sudden surge of panic. She didn't want him to leave. For whatever reason, he was fast becoming her lifeline to normalcy—and sanity—amid all the craziness.

Although she didn't move, didn't say a word, he seemed to discern her thoughts. "I'll be back later tonight to check in on you again, Liz."

"Okay." Relief—and some other emotion she couldn't identify—washed over her. "Look . . . if she's serving lasagna, you have to have an Italian dessert. Take some of the cannoli." She started toward the kitchen.

"If you keep giving them away, you won't have any left." His protest was only halfhearted as he trailed after her.

She slid four onto a plate and covered them with foil. "Good food and kindness are meant to be shared. Enjoy." She held them out.

He took the plate from her in silence, his expression quizzical.

An odd undercurrent in the air unsettled her, and she eased back a few inches. "What's wrong?"

"I'm not sure. But I'll figure it out."

With that enigmatic remark, he turned toward the foyer,

calling over his shoulder as he walked. "Lock up after I leave. And expect me again around 8:00."

He slipped through the door before she could respond. And as she secured the bolt behind him, Liz decided that was just as well.

Because he was talking in riddles. And with fatigue and a headache dulling her thinking, she wasn't up to solving puzzles today.

But come tomorrow, she might just tackle that challenge.

Alison was way too thin.

As Jake greeted his sister with a bear hug at the door while a golden fluff ball cavorted at his feet, he could feel her bones. Every one of them. Or so it seemed. He loosened his embrace, afraid if he squeezed too hard he'd crush her.

He'd known after talking with Cole yesterday that the accident had been a lot worse than he'd thought. Known his sister's recovery had been slow and tedious. So he'd expected to see some evidence of trauma.

What he hadn't expected was her palpable fragility. Though Alison had never carried an extra ounce of fat, she'd always been toned and athletic. Strong. Healthy. Vigorous.

Now she seemed shockingly delicate.

But her spunky spirit appeared to be undimmed. Either that, or she was keeping up a good front for his benefit.

He suspected it was a combination of both.

"Hey!" She shifted in his arms. "I'm glad to see you too, but I'm suffocating in here."

At her muffled comment against his chest, Jake released her. When she tottered a bit as she pulled back, he grasped her shoulders and held on until she got her footing.

"Talk about an exuberant hug." She grinned, attributing her imbalance to his enthusiastic greeting. But he saw the flash of frustration and pain in her eyes and knew better. "Jake, meet Bert." She gestured to the pup at his feet.

He bent down and gave the dog a distracted pat.

"Did you come bearing gifts?" She gestured to the foil-covered plate in his hands as he stood.

Already he could tell that getting her to talk about her injuries, let alone allow him to help in any way, was going to be a tough sell—as Cole had warned. Alison had always been an independent sort, and adversity seemed to have strengthened that trait.

"Cannoli. Courtesy of Liz Michaels. Her neighbor made it for her, and she's sharing the wealth."

"Yum." Alison took it and led the way toward the kitchen, the pup trotting at her heels. "I have spumoni, but this is much better. Let me put it in the fridge."

Jake followed, watching her walk. He could tell she was trying for a normal gait. But she couldn't hide her limp from him. He'd watched her chase butterflies, climb trees, jump rope; he knew every nuance of the easy grace and power of her usual confident stride.

Hearing Cole talk yesterday about how close they'd come to losing her had been bad enough.

Seeing the evidence of it was like a kick in the gut.

"Alison."

At his hoarse summons, she stopped and turned. "What?"

"You're skin and bones. And you're limping."

She flushed. "I know. I had an accident, remember?"

"You said you were fine."

"I will be. Soon."

"It was a lot worse than a broken leg and minor internal injuries."

"Some."

"I can't believe you wouldn't let anyone tell me."

Her shoulders stiffened, and the foil on the plate crinkled beneath her fingers. "We already discussed this. I didn't want you to worry. And be distracted."

"I appreciate your consideration. But that doesn't change

how I feel. I would have found a way to come home. To be here for you. Like you were for me when Jen died."

He caught the sudden shimmer in her eyes before she dropped her chin and made a pretense of recrimping the foil around the plate. "I know you would have. And that means more to me than I can say. But you have enough on your own plate. Besides, I had David."

"That's not what I heard."

Her head snapped up, and she compressed her lips. "Cole's been talking to you."

"He mentioned the two of you had broken up. And why. You didn't tell me that, either."

Ignoring his comment, she turned back toward the kitchen. "I need to put this away."

He followed, the aroma of spicy tomato sauce and garlic bread greeting him as he entered the sunny room. Two places had been set at the café table in the bay window, complete with red checkered napkins, and a small bouquet of fresh-picked flowers from her garden stood in the center. She'd gone to a lot of effort to welcome him home. And he didn't want to spoil the dinner she'd planned. But unless they hashed this thing out, he doubted either of them would be able to do justice to the meal she'd prepared.

She slid the plate of cannoli into the refrigerator and nodded to a bowl on the counter. "You can toss the salad if you want, while I get the bread out of the oven. Here's the dressing." She removed a bottle from a lower shelf and thrust it toward him before closing the door.

Instead of taking it, he waited until she looked over at him. Then he locked gazes with her. "I want details on your injuries, Alison. And your prognosis. We can go over it now or later. But you need to know I'm not leaving tonight until we talk about this."

Setting the dressing on the counter, she locked her arms over her chest and tried to stare him down.

He didn't so much as blink.

She narrowed her eyes. "In case you haven't noticed, I'm trying to put the whole thing behind me and move on."

"I got that message. Loud and clear. And I think it's a smart strategy. Focusing on the future is a good thing, and I'll support you in that 100 percent. Once I get up to speed on the past."

For another few seconds she held her ground. Then she huffed out a sigh. "Fine. You want a download? I'll give you a download. A month after you left for Iraq, I was broadsided at an intersection on my way home from work by a car going at a high rate of speed. The other driver was drunk. He didn't make it.

"My tibia and fibula were broken. The tibial shaft fracture was bad, and a metal rod was inserted and screwed in to hold the tibia in place. In the interest of full disclosure, the procedure is called intrameduallary rodding. I wore a cast from above my knee to below my ankle and used crutches for quite a while. Both of those breaks are almost healed.

"I also suffered an unstable pelvic fracture, which led to severe internal bleeding. The doctors inserted long screws into the bones on each side of my pelvis and connected them to a frame outside my body to stabilize the pelvic area. That allowed them to address the blunt trauma injuries to my abdomen. The worst was uterine avulsion, which required a subtotal hysterectomy. My pelvis was put back together with screws.

"As for the prognosis, it's very good. I've already made tremendous progress, and in time, I should be able to walk normally. Other than never being able to have children, I should make a full recovery." She leaned back against the counter, her knuckles whitening as she gripped the edge. "And now you know the whole story, in all its gory detail. Satisfied?"

Jake was still reeling from the fast-paced data dump. He didn't understand half of the medical terminology she'd used or the subtleties of her injuries, but he filed away the information and planned to check it all out later on the Net.

What he did understand was that she'd recited the facts in a clinical, dispassionate voice—until she'd gotten to the part about not being able to have children. Then her composure had started to splinter and her words had grown shaky.

And that had spoken volumes. She might have come to grips with the physical baggage of the accident, and she might be making her peace with her shattered romance, but she was still working through her inability to conceive.

He'd known, when Cole had dropped that bombshell, how crushed Alison must be. She loved children. Had dedicated her life, through her work with Social Services, to seeking justice for little ones caught in bad situations. Had always talked about having a large family of her own.

As he watched her now, struggling to hold on to her self-control, a lump rose in his own throat. Following his heart, he closed the distance between them and took her in his arms.

"Oh, Twig." He cleared the hoarseness from his voice. "I'm so sorry for everything you've been through."

He felt a shudder ripple through her, mirroring the quiver in her words. "I'll be okay. But I have to admit, an occasional hug is really nice."

"Count on plenty of them from now on."

She leaned back and gave him a watery smile. "In moderation, though, okay? Mom was smothering me; that's why I sent her packing. And Cole never stopped hovering. I need my space."

"I'll try to keep that in mind."

"I'll remind you if you forget."

He gave a soft chuckle. "I don't doubt that."

"Are we all squared away now?"

"Yeah. I guess. But I still wish you'd told me all this sooner."

"Just remember, my motives were good."

"What's that old saying about a certain road being paved with good intentions?" He slung an arm around her shoulders and grinned down at her.

"I'll try to keep that in mind."

As she repeated his words back to him with an impudent tip of her head, he laughed and squeezed her shoulder. "It's good to be home." Releasing her, he picked up the bottle of salad dressing. "Let's eat."

After the emotional prelude to their meal, Jake made a concerted effort to keep the conversation light and pleasant as he devoured her lasagna. Only when they got to dessert did it drift back to serious topics.

"It was nice of the judge to share her bounty with us." Alison dug into the cannoli with gusto, closing her eyes after the first bite as an expression of bliss swept over her face. "Wow. These are as good as the ones from the best restaurants on the Hill."

It had been years since Jake had sampled the famed cuisine of St. Louis's Italian neighborhood, but he didn't dispute Alison's evaluation as he polished off his own offering.

"She said they'll go to waste before she can finish them all. That's probably true. I doubt she's eaten more than a few bites of anything since Friday night."

"Do you think she might like some of my lasagna? You could take a piece with you when you go back tonight."

"It's worth a try."

Alison used her fork to break off a bite of cannoli. "How's she holding up?"

"Better than most people would under the same circumstances. Every time I think she's about to shatter, she manages to pull herself back together. She's pretty amazing."

Squinting at him, Alison speared the last bite of her cannoli and twirled it on her fork. "I seem to recall you making some sort of disparaging remark about her once. After her husband died."

Had he? Jake didn't remember that. But he might have. He and his sister had always been vocal in their opinions with each other. Now he regretted that particular comment.

"It's possible." He fiddled with his coffee cup. "But after

spending time with her these past couple of days, I discovered I may have been operating on some faulty assumptions."

She leaned down to give Bert a pat. "So you think she's nice?"

The conversation had taken an unexpected turn. One he didn't like. He'd seen that gleam in his sister's eye in the past. For all her independence, she was a romantic at heart. Her own love life might be in the doldrums, but it wouldn't stop her from meddling in Cole's. Or his. Not that he had one. Or intended to.

Especially with Liz Michaels.

As he tried to think of some way to redirect the conversation to a less personal topic, his BlackBerry began to vibrate.

Yes!

Praising God for small favors, he pulled it off his belt and scanned the number.

"It's Cole. Give me a sec, okay?" Tapping the talk button, he put the phone to his ear. "What's up?"

"Good news. We've got our man."

7

A bell was ringing somewhere.

From her prone position, Liz struggled to open her eyes. As the shadowy, unfamiliar room came into focus, the bell rang again.

A doorbell.

Trying to jump-start her muddled brain, she pulled herself upright as the pieces began to fall into place. She'd been reading a brief in the condo where she was sequestered. It now lay on the floor beside the couch, where she'd fallen asleep. And based on the dimness of the room, she'd been out cold for a couple of hours.

A knock sounded on the door. A *loud* knock.

Loud enough to suggest the door might be kicked in if she didn't open it. Fast.

"Liz?"

The tautness of Jake's muffled voice propelled her to her feet.

Her shin connected with the edge of the granite-based, glass-topped coffee table, and she yelped as she stumbled toward the door.

"Liz? What's going on?"

A thread of panic wound through Jake's curt question.

"Hang on. I'm on my way."

In the foyer, she paused to peer through the peephole.

Jake stood to the left, almost out of sight, gun in hand. One of the marshals from the CP was on the right, gun also drawn.

Embarrassment warmed her cheeks as she slid the dead bolt back and opened the door.

"Sorry, guys. I fell asleep on the couch and didn't hear the bell."

The marshal beside Jake flashed her a grin and holstered his gun. "No problem."

As he returned to the CP next door, she stepped back to allow Jake to enter. Instead, he bent and picked up a foil-wrapped plate from the hall floor, which he handed her. A bouquet of flowers wrapped in newspaper rested beside it, and he retrieved that as well before joining her inside.

Trying not to be unnerved by the disconcerting juxtaposition of his gun in one hand and flowers in the other, Liz closed and bolted the door. He was sliding the small pistol into a concealed holster on his belt when she turned back.

"Sorry again for the delay in opening the door."

"Don't be. I'm glad you got a little sleep. What was that startled exclamation I heard?"

She wrinkled her nose and reached down to rub her shin. "A close encounter with the coffee table. What's this?" She hefted the plate in her hand. "And that?" She waved her other hand at the newspaper-wrapped bundle.

"A little gift from my sister. I noticed the pots of flowers at your house and the bouquet on your kitchen table, so I sweet-talked Alison into letting me raid her garden."

"They're beautiful." She took the generous, old-fashioned bouquet of roses, mums, zinnias, and feathery ferns from him. The aroma of the roses was like a balm to her soul, and she inhaled deeply.

"She has a way with flowers. And with lasagna." He tapped the foil-covered plate in her hand. "She made plenty and thought you might enjoy some. Have you had dinner?"

"Not yet. And homemade lasagna sounds great. Much

better than a frozen entree. Let me warm it up for a few minutes."

He followed her to the kitchen. After she put one of the two pieces of lasagna in the oven and set the timer, she scrounged up a pitcher that worked fine as a vase for the flowers.

Moving aside the contents of her briefcase, she set the bouquet on the dining room table. "These really help warm the place up. Thank you. And please thank your sister."

"I'll do that." He motioned toward the living room. "Let's talk for a minute. I have some news."

At his serious tone, a surge of adrenaline shot through her. "You found Alan?"

"Yes." He moved to the couch and gestured for her to sit.

Liz complied, perching on the edge as he took a chair at right angles to her.

"Your sister's husband showed up at his house today about 5:00. The Springfield police had it under surveillance and moved in immediately. According to their report, he seemed taken aback by the news of his wife's death and claims he had nothing to do with it."

"I didn't expect him to admit his guilt." Liz clenched her hands in her lap. "Does he have an alibi?"

"Not one he can prove. He claims he went fishing for the weekend. Camped out on some property owned by a friend of his. But no one saw him there."

"What a surprise." Sarcasm dripped from her words.

Twin furrows appeared on Jake's brow. Resting his forearms on his thighs, he clasped his hands and leaned forward. "Here's the thing, Liz. So far, nothing at the crime scene is linking him to your sister's murder. The perpetrator left no trace evidence that we could find. And we've already run the prints the Springfield PD took of your brother-in-law. They don't match any found at the house."

The meager contents of her stomach began to curdle. She knew what that meant.

"You don't have grounds to hold Alan for more than twenty-four hours, do you?"

"No. But we'll be keeping very close tabs on him. And my brother and I, along with an FBI agent, are going down to Springfield tomorrow to question him. He's still our prime suspect. But we can't bring charges without any evidence. You know that."

Liz tried to stay calm. Tried to be rational. But it took every ounce of her self-control to speak in a reasonable tone. "I don't want him to get away with murder, Jake."

"He won't. This case is being given the highest priority. We'll solve it."

His words were steady. As was his gaze. She locked onto it, needing the strength she saw in his eyes. The only thing keeping her going was the conviction that Alan would be brought to justice. That he'd pay for what he'd done to her sister. If she didn't have that to cling to . . .

She cut off that line of thought. Ruthlessly. She wouldn't go there. Couldn't go there.

"Okay." She took a deep breath. Let it out. "I'll just have to trust you all to do your job."

"Count on it."

He leaned down to pick up a sheet of paper that had slipped off the coffee table. Her notes about another painful subject she needed to discuss with him.

"I talked to the funeral director this afternoon." She took the piece of paper from him and stared down at it. The words she'd jotted blurred, and she blinked to clear her vision. "I'd like to have the funeral on Wednesday. I talked to the pastor at Stephanie's church, and he's agreed to go to Kansas City and do a short service in the chapel at the cemetery. The funeral director is making all of the other local arrangements. Will that work for you?" Now that they had Alan under surveillance, she doubted the plans she'd made would present a security risk to her.

"It should be fine. I'll connect with our Kansas City office and line up coverage at the cemetery. Spence and I will drive with you from here, unless you have a strong preference for flying."

"No. Driving is fine.

"What time is the service?"

"At 1:00. I tried to plan it so we could drive there and back in one day."

"Would you like to stay longer?"

"No. Everyone I loved in Kansas City is gone." Her voice choked on the last word, and she dropped her gaze, struggling for control.

When she finally looked up, however, Jake's expression did nothing to help her rein in her emotions. Empathy—and sympathy—lent an unaccustomed softness to his features, and at the tenderness in his brown eyes she again felt the pressure of tears behind her own.

In the next instant, however, his calm, professional demeanor slipped back into place. "Is there anything else we can help with in terms of arrangements?"

"I'd like to have my sister's suitcases. They're in the guest room at my house. I need to pick out some clothes for the . . . to send to the funeral home."

"I'll have them here first thing in the morning."

The timer in the kitchen began to beep, and Jake stood. "I know you haven't been hungry, Liz, but you need to eat. Try a little, okay?"

At his coaxing tone, she wavered. Usually, the aroma of Italian spices that was wafting through the condo would bump her salivary glands into overdrive. Tonight, it turned her stomach.

But the gesture by Jake's sister had been kind. She'd sample a bite or two after he left.

"It smells delicious." Rising, she pushed her hair back from her face. The uncombed mess must be a sight after her two-hour nap. She hadn't bothered with makeup today, either. So much for the always-put-together image of the venerable Judge Elizabeth Michaels.

She started toward the door, but Jake's voice stopped her.

"Aren't you going to eat?"

Angling back, she saw he hadn't moved from his spot by the couch. "Aren't you going to leave?"

"Not if you offer me coffee. I only had one cup at Alison's. She's a great cook, but she never has learned how to make a decent cup of coffee. If you ever tell her I said that, however, I'll deny it." He flashed her a quick grin.

She studied him. Was he being honest about wanting coffee . . . or just hanging around to make sure she ate?

But who cared about his motive? She was glad to have some company. Once he left, the heavy, oppressive silence would descend again in the condo. She might even have to turn on the television—always her last-resort fallback when in need of distraction.

"I'm not the world's greatest cook, but I do know how to brew coffee. I made a pot before I fell asleep, although it might be too strong." She retraced her route.

"Strong is the best kind."

He followed her back to the kitchen, and as she poured the dark liquid into a mug, he took the lasagna out of the oven and carried it into the dining room.

Sliding into her place, she eyed the generous portion—and tried to contain the revolution brewing in her stomach.

As if sensing her dilemma, Jake began talking, asking about her work and the Morettis. In the end, she found herself sufficiently distracted to put a fair-sized dent in the savory pasta while she responded to his relaxed, conversational queries. It almost felt like a normal meal between two friends.

"I couldn't help overhearing Mrs. Moretti mention a shelter." Jake took a sip of his coffee and cradled the mug in his hands. "Sounds like you're involved in some sort of charitable work."

"Yes. People from a lot of area churches volunteer to help out a night or two each month at a shelter for abused women and their children. Serving meals, cleaning up, changing diapers, lending a friendly ear. Whatever needs to be done. It's a temporary, safe place for them to stay until they figure out what they want to do about their situations. I could never get Steph to take that step, but at least I tried to support other women who did, even if only for one night a month."

She poked at the last corner of her lasagna, laid her fork on her plate, and did her best not to let the turn in the conversation to darker subjects depress her.

"I'm surprised you have time for things like that."

The studied casualness of Jake's comment told her he was more interested in her response than his tone indicated.

She gave him a direct look. "In my experience, people *make* time for the things that are important to them."

A few seconds passed while he took another sip of coffee. He seemed to be debating how to frame his next remark. "I got the impression from Doug that your work schedule was intense."

She'd often wondered what the two men had talked about during their periodic phone conversations, and whether Doug had shared much about his marriage. Jake's comment gave her a clue.

Now it was her turn to choose her words with care. "My work is demanding, and I put in long hours. But I've always given time to causes I believe in. And to the people I love."

For a long moment, he appraised her with guarded eyes. Intuitively, she sensed he was wrestling with some sort of disconnect. That her response didn't jibe with information he'd been given by Doug.

Wrong information, obviously.

A deep sadness welled up inside her. She'd known her husband had been losing perspective near the end. And she'd tried her best to help him get his life back on track. Instead, as the weeks and months went by, he'd drifted farther away from her. Far enough to scare her. Far enough to convince her to take desperate measures.

Far enough to make a tragic mistake.

Based on the vibes she'd picked up at the funeral, Liz figured that Jake had suspected that. Had assumed that the blame for Doug's demise rested on her shoulders.

And the hard truth was, he was right about that. Even if he was wrong about other things.

But that was a burden she couldn't think about tonight. Not on top of everything else that had happened in the past forty-eight hours.

No longer able to deal with the silence between them, Liz pushed back her chair and stood. "Please be sure to thank Alison for the lasagna. You're right. It was fabulous."

If he thought her abrupt end to the evening was odd, he gave no indication of it. Instead, he rose too, his gaze flickering to her plate, where only a small piece of pasta remained.

"You did it justice." He drained his mug and carried it into the kitchen. "We'll be leaving for Springfield early tomorrow morning. I'll be in touch when we get back."

As he walked toward the door, Liz followed.

"I don't know what Doug told you about us, Jake, but after things calm down, I'd like to return to this conversation."

She hadn't planned to bring up the subject again. And Jake appeared to be as surprised as she was by her comment.

His step faltered, and he shot her a glance over his shoulder. His eyes were shadowed in the subdued light of the foyer, but she couldn't doubt the sincerity in his tone. "I'd like that too."

He continued to the door and twisted the dead bolt. "I hope you sleep better tonight."

"Thanks. I do too."

After hesitating for a brief second, he let himself out. She peered through the peephole as she relocked the door, noting that he waited until it clicked before he walked a few yards down the hall to check in next door.

Through the fish-eye lens, her view of him was distorted.

Just as his view of her seemed to be distorted.

But before his assignment with her was finished, she intended to set the record straight.

"I'm not getting a good feeling from this."

At the comment by FBI Special Agent Mark Sanders, Jake frowned at the video screen. Cole had been questioning Alan Long for ten minutes in the nearby interview room at the Springfield PD headquarters, and Jake was fast coming to the same conclusion as Mark.

Stephanie's husband sat beside his attorney, Andrew Thomas, his hands tightly clasped on the round table in front of him. Mid-thirtyish with neatly trimmed light brown hair and dressed in a dark gray suit and tie, he didn't look like a wife beater, let alone a killer.

Then again, a lot of violent criminals appeared to be normal, ordinary people when first questioned by the police.

It was the man's demeanor, not his appearance, that unsettled Jake. His grief over his wife's death seemed genuine. It could be an act. But Jake's gut told him it wasn't.

"I'm not, either." He turned to the tall, dark-haired man beside him, who was still focused on the screen.

Mark looked his way. He had the seasoned eyes of a man who'd seen more than his share of violence and trauma. A man with finely honed instincts. A man whose judgment Jake already respected and trusted.

"If he's not the culprit, we have a whole different scenario to deal with."

Meaning Liz could have been the real target.

Jake had already come to the same conclusion.

"Yeah. And it's a whole lot messier." Not to mention unsettling.

"Oh, God, I can't believe this is happening! It's a nightmare!"

At the outburst from the video monitor, both men refocused on the screen.

Alan's elbows rested on the table, and he'd buried his face in his palms. His attorney put a hand on his shoulder and spoke too softly for the mike to pick up.

After a few moments, Alan brushed his knuckles across his eyes and addressed Cole. "I'm telling you, I had nothing to do with this! I loved Steph, even if I didn't always show it. And she knew I loved her. But when she told me on Wednesday she was leaving, I went a little nuts."

"You hit her." Cole pinned him with a hard look.

"Yeah. I did. And I'm not proud of that."

"So you acknowledge you have an anger management problem." Cole maintained a neutral tone.

"You don't have to respond to that," Andrew Thomas interjected.

"I don't mind answering. It's no secret. Yeah, I have an anger problem. Steph bore the brunt of it. And she was a saint to put up with me! But she always believed I could overcome my issues. Believed I was capable of being better than I was. No one in my whole life ever believed in me like she did." His voice broke, and Jake watched as his Adam's apple bobbed and his irises began to shimmer. He swiped at his eyes again.

When he continued, his words were ragged. "She'd been after me for a long time to get counseling. Had hinted it might be the only way to save our marriage. But I never thought she'd really leave me—until I came home Thursday night and found her note. It about killed me.

"At first I was mad. I wanted to smash things. But I knew that was the exact kind of reaction that had caused her to leave. So I didn't. I went to work Friday but took off at noon to drive to the lake. I camped there until Sunday afternoon. I've always been calmer, thought more clearly, out in the woods. And I realized I didn't want to lose her. Or my child. That I wanted to be a better husband and father than my old man was. And I decided I was going to go to counseling, like Steph wanted. Only I never got the chance to tell her that."

Once more, the man broke down.

Cole stood, murmured a few words to the two men in the room, and exited. Thirty seconds later, he joined Jake and Mark.

"What's your take?" He closed the door behind him.

Mark deferred to Jake.

"We're not getting good vibes from this."

"Me neither." Cole turned to Mark. "This investigation might be moving into your ballpark."

"Looks that way."

"You want to take over the interview?"

"I doubt I'm going to get any more than you did, but it might not be a bad idea to let Mr. Long know the FBI has an interest in this too. If he is covering up anything, that might shake him up a little."

"It's worth a try."

Cole stepped away from the door, and Mark exited.

"He doesn't strike me as a murderer." Cole perused the man on the screen. "He has a good job as an engineer, very few debts, no love interest on the side that we've been able to determine. And he appears to be genuinely upset about his wife."

"But I saw Stephanie's black eye." Jake watched the screen as Mark entered the interview room. "Anger can turn normal people into abusers. Or killers. I agree, though. Something doesn't feel right here."

Mark introduced himself, and as he took the seat Cole had vacated, Jake gave the conversation taking place down the hall his full attention.

"Why is the FBI involved in this?" the attorney asked.

"The murder took place in the home of a federal judge. That could move the investigation into our jurisdiction." He addressed his next question to Alan. "Mr. Long, how did you feel about your sister-in-law?"

Alan looked at his lawyer.

"How is that relevant to this investigation?" the man asked.

"It could be very relevant, if she was also a target."

"You think I'd kill not only my wife but Liz too?" Alan stared at him.

"I don't know. You tell me."

He muttered a coarse word. "Look, she wasn't my favorite person, okay? She was always after Steph to leave me. But I didn't hate her. I knew she loved Steph and that she thought she was doing the right thing. In hindsight, maybe she was." He choked on the last word.

"Based on our conversation with Detective Taylor, it doesn't appear to me you have one bit of hard evidence linking my client to this murder." Andrew Thomas folded his hands on the table. "All you have is supposition, which, as we both know, isn't sufficient for a warrant, let alone a conviction. So unless you have more than that, I assume my client is free to go."

Mark took his time answering. "That's correct, Mr. Thomas. However, your client needs to be aware that he will continue to be a person of interest in this investigation. We may have further questions as it progresses."

"I'll help in any way I can. I want Steph's murderer found as much as you do." Alan turned to his attorney. "What about arrangements for my wife's funeral?"

"I understand they're being handled by her sister," Mark offered.

"That sounds like my cue." Jake glanced at Cole. "You staying here?"

"Yeah."

Thirty seconds later, Jake pushed through the door to the interview room. All three occupants shifted their attention to him.

"We were just discussing the funeral plans," Mark told him. "Gentlemen, this is Deputy U.S. Marshal Jake Taylor."

Jake nodded at them. "Judge Michaels has made arrangements for her sister to be interred near her parents in Kansas City. A service is scheduled in the cemetery chapel on Wednesday."

"No!" The word exploded from Alan, and his complexion grew ruddy as he vaulted to his feet. "She's my wife. I want her buried in Springfield. And I want the service at our church."

"Alan." The attorney put his hand on his client's arm.

He shook it off. "This isn't right, Andrew. I'm her husband. I should have the final say on this." He glared at Jake and Mark, bristling with rage.

"Alan." The attorney rose and waited until the man looked at him. "We can discuss this later. In private."

Andrew Thomas's words were measured. Calm. But his eyes were intent. Jake wondered if his client would get his silent "cool it" message.

He did. With what appeared to be a supreme effort, Alan reined in his temper. "Are we finished here?" He kept his gaze on his attorney.

"I believe we are." The attorney looked at Mark, then Jake. "Is there anything else today, gentlemen?"

"No." Mark stood. "But I would strongly recommend your client remain available—and in town—for the immediate future."

Inclining his head in acknowledgment, Andrew Thomas ushered Liz's brother-in-law from the room.

The door had no more closed behind them when Cole stepped inside. "I'd say the man has a definite anger problem."

"No kidding." Jake rubbed the back of his neck. "But that doesn't make him a murderer. So where are we on this?"

Mark gestured to the table and retook his seat. Jake and Cole followed his lead. "Here's my take. It's possible he's still our man. But he did an amazing acting job if he is. Which, as we all know, is very possible. Meaning we can't slack off on our investigation of him. Cole, St. Louis County should probably take the lead on that. We'll assist as needed, since the victim was the sister of a federal judge. Make sense?"

"Yes."

"I'm beginning to think Stephanie Long might not have been the intended victim. That she just happened to be in the wrong place at the wrong time. That puts Liz Michaels in the crosshairs. Jake?"

Much as that possibility disturbed him, Jake found Mark's logic sound. "I agree."

"We asked her early on if she had any enemies, knowing this was a possible scenario. But she said no." Cole tapped his index finger on the table as two parallel grooves creased his brow.

"Known enemies and enemies are two different things," Jake noted.

"And unknown enemies are a lot more dangerous." Mark frowned. "My wife was stalked by one a year ago. He almost succeeded in taking her out, despite our best efforts to protect her."

A chill rippled through Jake. "We need to get with the judge as soon as we return and revisit the enemy discussion."

"Agreed." Mark stood. "You two ready to head back?"

"Yeah." Cole rose. "Let me thank the Springfield guys. I'll meet you at the car."

Fifteen minutes later, as Cole merged onto eastbound I-44 and Mark responded to emails on his BlackBerry from the backseat, Jake watched the passing scenery. The fields were baked from the relentless sun and humidity of a Missouri summer, the parched cornstalks dried and shriveled. A single spark would set the whole field aflame.

That's how he felt about the situation with Liz. Their most promising lead had shriveled and dried up, leaving them with a volatile situation that could explode at any moment.

And he didn't look forward to sharing that news with the woman whose security had been placed in his hands.

8

Jake met Spence in the hall outside the CP as the marshals were changing shifts.

"How's everything here?"

"Quiet as a morgue."

Jake winced at the analogy.

Pursing his lips, the other marshal assessed him. "I'm getting the feeling it didn't go well in Springfield today."

"If by well you mean we got a confession, the perpetrator is in custody, and this protection gig is over, no, it didn't go well. In fact, all three of us have serious doubts Alan Long is our man. And the lack of evidence linking him to the scene isn't helping."

The other man squinted at him. "So you think the judge was the target?"

"That's looking more and more like a serious possibility. Mark Sanders from the FBI is on his way here to talk to Liz. You know him?"

"We've met. He's been assigned to the St. Louis field office for about a year. Came from the HRT."

"So I heard."

"He seems to be a good guy. You need anything before I call it a night?"

"A suspect in custody?"

"I wish." With a rueful shake of his head, he gestured

toward the CP. "I'll alert the guys to be on the lookout for Mark." With a mock salute, he turned back toward the command post.

A quick check of his watch propelled Jake farther down the hall. He had fifteen minutes until Mark showed up. They'd agreed it would be better for Jake to share the outcome of their trip to Springfield—as well as their suspicion—with Liz. And lay the groundwork for the appearance of the FBI.

Wishing he had better news to relay, Jake rang the bell.

Unlike his visit last night, when Liz's slow response had set his adrenaline pumping, she pulled the door open mere seconds after he pressed the button to summon her.

As if she'd been waiting for him.

Ignoring the pleasant little trill that skittered along his nerve endings at that thought, he stepped inside.

"Your timing is good." Liz bolted the door. "I just finished off your sister's lasagna. Please thank her again for me."

"I'll do that. Everything okay?" He studied her. The dark circles under her eyes had diminished, but he couldn't be sure if that was due to restful sleep or skillful application of makeup.

"It's been quiet, if that's your definition of okay." She motioned him toward the living room. "I spent the morning going through Stephanie's bags and picking out some clothing. I also conferred with the funeral director by phone. Everything's set for Wednesday, and I told him you or someone in the Marshals Service might want to discuss security issues." She picked up a slip of paper from the coffee table as she sat on the couch. "This is his cell number. He said to call anytime."

Jake pocketed the number as he opened the button on his suit jacket and took the chair beside the couch. At least the funeral plans wouldn't be disrupted. During the drive home, Andrew Thomas had called Cole on his cell to say his client had had a change of heart and wouldn't interfere with the arrangements Liz had made. Jake assumed the attorney had suggested to Alan that he rock the boat as little as possible.

The bad news was that Stephanie's husband planned to attend the service.

Jake didn't even want to imagine what Liz's reaction would be when he passed on that incendiary tidbit. But they had other ground to cover first.

"I've already spoken to our KC office and they're checking out the location." He'd spent a good part of the ride home, phone pressed to ear, coordinating security plans with his colleagues on the far side of the state. "They'll also give us backup on site during the service."

"Is that really necessary, with Alan accounted for?"

Now came the hard part.

Clasping his hands, Jake leaned forward. "After meeting with him, we have some serious doubts about his guilt, Liz."

She gave him a blank look. "What do you mean?"

"Aside from the lack of evidence linking him to the crime scene, his remorse about Stephanie was very convincing."

Anger flared in her green irises, turning the flecks of gold in their depths into sparks. "You believe him?"

"Let's just say I'm not convinced he's guilty. And neither are Cole or Mark Sanders, the FBI agent who went with us. He's en route here as we speak, by the way. We need to start taking a serious look at other scenarios."

"Like what? You ruled out robbery, didn't you?"

"It's low on our motive list."

He waited, giving her a chance to process all he'd said and come to the obvious conclusion. He knew, from the sudden widening of her eyes, the instant she did.

"You think *I* was the target?"

"You said yourself your sister had no enemies."

"I don't, either."

"Most judges do."

"Jake, I've never even gotten a hate letter, like some of my counterparts have!" She rose, her agitation palpable as she folded her arms tight across her chest and began to pace.

"This doesn't make sense. If I was the target, why did the person kill my sister?"

"It may have been a matter of her being in the wrong place at the wrong time."

He tried to say the devastating words as gently as he could, tried to steel himself against the reaction Liz was certain to have once the implication registered.

But the way her face crumpled twisted his gut.

"Dear God!" The anguished words, half rebuke, half plea, seemed torn from her throat. "If that bullet was meant for me, *I* should be dead! Not Stephanie."

All at once, her cheeks blanched. Clapping a hand to her mouth, she half ran, half stumbled down the hall toward the master bedroom.

Jake rose, unsure whether to follow or give her a few moments alone. Seconds later, the muted sound of violent retching echoed in the quiet room as she lost the lasagna she'd just eaten.

Torn between compassion and respect for Liz's privacy, he opted for the former and started down the hall.

Halfway to her room, the doorbell stopped him.

Mark.

Detouring to the foyer, he used the peephole to confirm it was the agent, then flipped the dead bolt. Silence descended again in the condo as the man crossed the threshold, and Jake kept his voice low as he brought him up to speed on what had transpired in the past few minutes.

A flash of compassion echoed in Mark's eyes. "Hopefully she'll accept in time it wasn't her fault. But guilt—even the misplaced variety—can be overwhelming."

"Yeah." Jake knew that firsthand. And some nuance in Mark's tone told him the other man did too.

He gestured toward the living room. "Have a seat while I check on her."

As he traversed the hall, Jake passed one bedroom with open suitcases on a queen-size bed. Otherwise, the room appeared to be unlived in.

Pausing at the entrance to the master bedroom near the end of the short hall, Jake gave the space a quick scan. The bed was made, and three pairs of shoes were lined up in a neat row beside the chest of drawers. The closet door was half ajar, and a few of the hangers wore garments. Most were empty, as if Liz didn't expect to be here long. A pair of reading glasses lay atop a book on the nightstand.

It was the framed photos on the dresser that captured his attention, however.

There was a small cluster of them, in varying sizes. Based on the attire of the couple in the first one, Jake estimated its age at thirty years. Must be Liz's parents. There was also a picture of Liz and Doug, flower-bedecked drinks in their hands as they stood in front of a backdrop that featured palm trees, a white sand beach, and blue ocean. A honeymoon shot from Hawaii, perhaps? If so, that made it ten years old.

But it was the third shot—an eight-by-ten image of more recent vintage—that sent a wave of adrenaline surging through him.

A smiling Liz was sitting on a boat dock, a large expanse of tanned skin set off by a white tank top, the thin gold chain around her neck glinting in the sun. She had her arm around the shoulders of another woman whose right cheek bore a very faint purple tinge.

Stephanie.

Even without the subtle evidence of abuse, Jake wouldn't have had any problem identifying Liz's sister.

Because the two of them shared the same green eyes. Same generous lips. Same high cheekbones. Same long, wavy blonde hair.

The resemblance was remarkable from the front.

From the back, he suspected it would be impossible to tell them apart.

And a back view was all the killer had had.

The theory that Liz had been the target went from possible

to probable in a heartbeat. Leaving him with a knot in the pit of his stomach. And three key questions.

Who was the perpetrator?

What was the motive?

And would he or she try again?

Liz wrung out the cool washcloth, pressed it to her forehead, and willed the shaking in her legs to subside as she eased down onto the closed toilet seat.

She should be dead. Not Stephanie.

Lord, how am I supposed to live with that guilt?

Drawing a shuddering breath, she leaned against the wall and stared at the tiles in front of her.

"Liz? Are you okay?"

At Jake's concerned question, she closed her eyes and stifled a groan. How long had he been on the other side of the door? Long enough to hear her emptying his sister's lasagna into the toilet?

If ever a person had seen Judge Elizabeth Michaels at her worst, Jake was it. He'd gotten an eyeful in the past seventy-two hours. No doubt he was ruing the day he'd been assigned to head her security detail.

And she couldn't blame him. She wouldn't wish the past three trauma-fraught days on anyone. Either as victim or protector.

"Yes. I'll be out in a minute."

"Take your time."

If she took her time, she'd be in here all night. Hiding in embarrassment. She'd never been prone to public displays of emotion. Had become a master of presenting a placid, calm façade to the world. Strangers weren't privy to her private grief and insecurities and regrets.

Her only consolation was that Jake didn't seem like a stranger. And that was odd. Two meetings in five years and a few stories Doug had told shouldn't have bred the kind of familiarity and sense of closeness she felt with him.

But shared trauma could engender that feeling, she supposed, gripping the edge of the vanity to steady herself as she stood. And they'd had plenty of that during the past three days.

Liz reached for her toothbrush, trying without much success to rid her mouth of the bitter, lingering taste of vomit, wondering if all the subjects Jake guarded felt this way. Relying on someone for both emotional support and physical protection could accelerate a feeling of intimacy that would take far longer to develop under normal circumstances. And it could very well be one sided.

When she opened the door, however, she intuitively knew the warmth and caring in his eyes wasn't his standard operating procedure.

Nor were her feelings one-sided.

Some of her embarrassment dissipated. Replaced by a deeper emotion she wasn't yet ready to deal with.

"I take it you had a ringside seat for the show." She hoped he'd attribute the tremor in her voice solely to the aftereffects of being violently ill . . . even though there were other causes too. Ones that had nothing to do with her stomach and everything to do with her heart.

"No. I was in the bleachers. But I could hear enough from the living room to figure out what was going on. Do you feel up to talking to the FBI agent? He's here."

What she wanted to do was curl up in a ball on the bed, pull the covers over her head, and shut out the world. Pretend that everything was fine. That's what she'd done when her mom died. But it hadn't changed the outcome then. And it wouldn't change it now. As she'd learned through the years, putting off the tough stuff didn't make it any easier to deal with in the end.

"I might as well get it over with."

She flipped off the bathroom light, and as she headed

toward the hall, Jake took her arm in a solid, comforting grip—as if to remind her she wasn't alone.

That helped.

More than he would ever know.

He paused as they approached the door, leaning over to pick up the picture of her and Stephanie. The one she'd asked a passerby to snap last summer when she'd talked her sister into a girls' weekend at Lake of the Ozarks.

"Do you mind if I borrow this for a few minutes?"

"No. Why?"

He turned off the light in the room and guided her down the hall. "I'd like to show it to Mark Sanders. The FBI agent."

Before she could ask him anything else, the doorbell rang. Jake gave her arm a slight squeeze as they reached the end of the hall.

"Wait here."

He crossed the small foyer, peered through the peephole, and opened the door. She heard him murmur a quiet "thank you" before he closed and locked it. When he rejoined her, he was carrying a glass of white soda. After passing it over, he took her arm again.

"This might help settle your stomach."

His gesture of kindness threatened to break the tenuous hold she had on her emotions, and it took every ounce of her self-control to keep her tears contained as they continued toward the living room.

At their approach, a tall, brown-haired man in a dark suit rose from the couch. Once Jake did the introductions and Mark took her hand in a firm grip, they all sat. Jake handed the photo to the FBI agent.

"A picture of Judge Michaels and her sister."

The man studied it, arched an eyebrow, and exchanged a look with Jake. "The resemblance is remarkable. It wouldn't be difficult to confuse the two of you from a distance. Or from behind."

Now Liz understood why Jake had homed in on the photo.

More support for the notion that she'd been the intended victim. She took a sip of her soda, hoping it would quell the renewed churning in her stomach.

"I've already discussed with Liz our theory that the killer might have been targeting her," Jake told Mark.

"That's becoming a very real possibility." He set the photo on the coffee table. "As you may be aware, Judge Michaels, that puts the FBI in charge of the investigation. I'd like to ask you a few questions, if you're up for that."

"I'll help you in any way I can. But as I've already told Jake and the police, I don't have any enemies I know of. In all my years as an attorney and judge, I've never even gotten a threatening letter from a disgruntled client or either party in a lawsuit." She took another sip of soda.

"Still, there's a loser in every case. And not everyone is a good loser." Mark flipped open the folder that rested in his lap. "Our preliminary research indicates you've been involved in some high-profile lawsuits. A few have received national attention and media play."

She shrugged. "Most of those are from my days as a practicing attorney. Ancient history by now, I would think."

"Grudges can have a long lifespan." He consulted the file again. "You've also tried some controversial cases."

"That goes with the territory."

Mark closed the file. "What we'd like you to do, Judge Michaels, is review the cases you've been involved in over the past five years, working backward. Think about anything that happened during those trials that perhaps didn't appear to be sinister at the time, but which, in view of recent events, might merit investigation. Do any cases immediately come to mind?"

Searching her memory, Liz drew a blank. "No. Off the top of my head I can't even remember all the cases I've dealt with in that time frame. If any had struck me as being dangerous, I'm sure I'd recall them. But I'll go through my files and flag any that might be worth investigating. To be honest, though, it seems like looking for a needle in a haystack."

"You never know. It might trigger some ideas." Mark extracted a card from his pocket and offered it to her. "I'll be in regular touch with the police and the Marshals Service. If you want to talk with me directly, however, feel free to call."

As she took the card, he rose. "My sympathies on the loss of your sister, Judge Michaels." He extended his hand, and she found hers engulfed in his strong grip.

"Thank you."

"I'll show you out." Jake stood, and the two men walked to the hall.

She could hear the low rumble of their voices as they conferred in the foyer, though their words were indiscernible. Fingering the card, she read the words: Special Agent Mark Sanders. Federal Bureau of Investigation.

The notion that she was the target of some lethal plot was surreal.

Yet the evidence was all too real. The security of her home had been violated. Stephanie was dead. And she was now under the armed protection of U.S. marshals while the FBI sought the person who wanted her dead.

She was still gripping the card, sipping the soda, when Jake reappeared and took the chair Mark had occupied.

"This helped a lot." She lifted the glass. "Thank you."

He acknowledged her expression of appreciation with a nod. "I'm assuming you may need some records from your home office so you can review past cases."

"Yes."

"We can take you back there, or you can describe what you need and we'll retrieve them."

"I'd rather you get them. All of the boxes are marked, and I can tell you where to find what I need. In terms of more current cases, I can have one of my law clerks bring me some files from my office in the courthouse. A lot of stuff is on my computer too."

He withdrew a small notebook from his pocket. "Just tell me what to look for at your house."

As she did so, she finished off the soda.

"Would you like some more?" He gestured toward the empty glass, pocketing the notebook.

"No. This was perfect. Thank you again."

"Feeling better?"

"Some." More because of his kindness than the soda, though she left that unsaid.

"We'll get these boxes to you first thing in the morning. Is there anything else I can do for you tonight before I leave?"

A hug would be nice.

Instead of voicing that unexpected thought, she wrapped her arms around her middle and held on tight, forcing her stiff lips into what she hoped passed for a smile. "No. I'm fine. Thanks again for everything."

The slight narrowing of his eyes suggested he wasn't buying her reassurance. But he let it go.

"There's one other piece of information I need to pass on."

His careful tone implied more bad news, and she braced herself. "Okay."

"Your sister's husband plans to attend the funeral service."

"What!?" The word exploded from her lips.

"We have no grounds to keep him away, Liz."

"No!" Shaking her head, she lurched to her feet and stumbled to the windows. "I can't deal with that." The closed blinds hid her view of the skyline, but light seeped in around the edges. Struggling to find a point of entry.

She heard him rise and move behind her.

"I know you don't want him there. But he has rights too. He wanted to have the funeral in Springfield and bury your sister there. His attorney convinced him to let your arrangements stand."

Was she supposed to be grateful for the consideration of

a wife beater? And perhaps a murderer? The bitter taste returned to her mouth.

Closing her eyes, she tried to be generous. To muster some kindness and compassion. To live the values her faith taught.

She came up empty.

But Jake was right. She had no legal grounds to stop Alan from showing up. The best she could do was try to ignore him.

"I don't want to talk to him." Her words were brittle.

"We can keep that from happening."

She gave a stiff nod. "Okay. Thank you." She didn't turn around.

A couple of beats of silence passed before he spoke again.

"If you need anything later, remember there are two deputies next door. Don't hesitate to call on them." His inflection underwent a subtle shift, a nuance of warmth adding a more personal touch. "And remember that you also have my BlackBerry number, if you'd rather communicate with me."

Some of the tension melted from her shoulders. It wasn't fair to hold Jake responsible for Alan's decision. He'd already gone above and beyond with this assignment. Even made himself available in his off hours. She should be grateful, not miffed.

Taking a deep breath, she swiveled back toward him. "Sorry. This latest turn of events isn't your fault."

"I'd keep him away if I could."

"I know." And she did. "I also appreciate having your number. But you've put in enough long hours on this assignment already. I don't plan to bother you on your time off."

His brown irises deepened as he regarded her. "It's not a bother, Liz. I mean that."

She could tell he did. The question was, why? Was it because he took the responsibilities of his job so seriously—or something more?

Without giving her a chance to dwell on his comment, he

started toward the foyer. "I'll be back in the morning. Try to get some rest. And you might want to experiment with a piece of toast. It should stay down."

"I think I'd rather have some of your mom's chicken soup."

Flashing her a rueful grin, he twisted the dead bolt. "Yeah. You can't beat it for comfort food. I could use some myself about now. See you tomorrow."

With that, he slipped through the door, closing it with a soft click behind him.

She followed, securing the lock as she pondered his remark. Why did he need comfort food?

The answer was obvious. He was worried about keeping her safe.

And that did nothing for her peace of mind. Or her stomach.

Meaning no toast tonight.

9

Martin Reynolds pulled into the driveway of the two-bedroom brick bungalow he'd occupied for the past year and gave it a quick, disinterested scan in the deepening dusk. It was an okay house, and he'd kept it up since moving in. He mowed the grass every Tuesday—though it was too late to do so tonight. But it had pretty much stopped growing for the year, anyway. He trimmed the bushes when they got shaggy. He'd even painted the garage door a few weeks back.

But he didn't lavish care on it, as he'd done with the house he and Helen had shared for twenty-five years. The one they'd bought six years into their marriage, after scrimping and saving and living off macaroni and cheese until they'd accumulated enough for a down payment.

That had been a home.

This was just a house.

Thank you, Uncle Sam.

Fighting back the rancid bitterness that had become his daily companion, Martin pulled into the one-car garage and set the brake. There had been a time when he'd loved the United States. But the country that had earned his deep affection and devotion was disappearing a little more every day as Big Brother chipped away at the freedoms the founding fathers had fought so hard to defend. If citizens didn't wake up soon and do something about taking America back, there'd be no America left to take.

At least he'd done his small part. Fought back against the terrocrats, as Jarrod called them. A feeling of satisfaction swept over him as he walked down the driveway toward his mailbox.

"Hi, Mr. Reynolds."

He missed a step at the unexpected greeting and peered into the fading twilight. His next-door neighbor—Molly something or other—waved at him from her front porch as she juggled a baby on her hip.

Lifting a hand in greeting, he kept walking. Since moving in, he'd made no attempt to befriend his neighbors. An elderly widow lived across the street, and a yuppie-type couple lived on his other side. The widow only came out in front to retrieve her paper, and the yuppies were gone from first light until dark. They were easy to avoid.

The young mother was a different story. She'd trotted over with a plate of cookies to welcome him when he'd moved in, and despite his efforts to discourage her, she continued to give him a cheery greeting whenever their paths crossed.

"I've been keeping an eye out for you," she called. "I didn't want you to think someone had stolen your papers. I noticed they were piling up, so I collected them and put them on your front porch. I thought maybe you took a little trip."

He ignored the half-question in her inflection and picked up his pace. "Thanks."

"I would have gotten your mail too, but I didn't want to pry."

Disregarding that comment, he withdrew three days' worth of letters, ads, and bills. Mostly bills, he noted in disgust.

"Well, you have a nice night."

The sound of a door closing told him she'd given up trying to start a conversation.

Good.

Back at the car, he opened the rear door and lifted the cat

carrier from the seat. As he used his hip to close the door, Josie regarded him with her almond-shaped green eyes. He'd found her last winter rummaging through his garbage can, and while he'd never been much interested in pets, he'd felt a kinship with the lost, abandoned kitten that had seemed in need of a friend.

"We're home, girl." He reached through the metal cage to stroke her golden hair and was rewarded with a soft, contented purr.

Once he'd toted the travel cage into the house, he set her free and riffled through the mail again. A letter buried among some ads caught his eye, and he pulled it out, squinting at the familiar handwriting and exotic return address.

After three years, he still didn't have a clue what had gotten into his usually sensible sister. She'd taught school for thirty years. Bought her own little house in Cincinnati decades ago, when she'd realized she'd probably never marry. Went to church every week. Lived a nice, quiet, stable life.

Her only idiosyncrasy had been her penchant for annual vacations to far-flung destinations. He'd never even heard of half the places she'd visited.

But her decision to spend her retirement in the Peace Corps—in some African country called Sierra Leone, of all places—had blown his mind. He stared again at the return address, clueless about the pronunciation of the primitive village she now called home.

Yet Patricia seemed happy with her life.

Which was more than he could say about himself.

After retracing his steps to the porch, he collected the newspapers his neighbor had tucked into a corner. He had good reasons for his discontent, though. He was sick of being victimized. Sick of the government turning his life upside down. Sick of feeling helpless.

That was why he'd finally taken some action.

Patricia would never understand what he'd done. Or condone it, Martin knew, as he opened his front door and stepped back inside.

But Jarrod would.

Now there was a true patriot. As far as Martin was concerned, the leader of the Patriot Constitutionalists was as brave as the founding fathers. He was doing his best to let Americans know their liberties were being usurped, that the Constitution was being subverted by the very government whose framework it defined.

Jarrod was a big advocate of using fraudulent legal documents to intimidate and harass public officials. Paper terrorism, he called it. But Martin was convinced he'd support more drastic steps, if they were warranted. It was a tough fight—Gideon against the Midianites, Jarrod had said—but a worthy one.

After months of listening to the leader's rhetoric, Martin had at last joined the battle.

He passed through the living room, dim now as the day waned, and continued to the kitchen. Dumping the papers and mail on the counter, he poured a glass of water and guzzled the whole thing. He hadn't had a drink since he'd left his cabin two hours ago, and the summer-like heat of the past few days hadn't relented one iota, even though fall had begun three weeks ago.

He'd have stayed longer in the country, except he didn't want to miss Jarrod's meeting tomorrow night. Still, the short visit to his hideaway had been good for his soul. There, he felt insulated from the craziness of the world. Someday he might move there full time.

Soon, maybe.

Pouring himself another glass of water, he opened a can of food for Josie and sat at the kitchen table to read Patricia's letter. As usual, the breezy narrative was filled with anecdotes about her daily life and the children she taught. He read the line about eating fried ants twice, thinking he might have misunderstood it on the first pass. But no. There it was, in black and white. This from the woman who hadn't even been willing to try fried shrimp on the one family vacation they'd taken to the East Coast when they were kids.

People sure could change.

Not until he reached the end of the letter, however, did he find her most important piece of news.

"I'll be heading home for some R & R in a couple of weeks, Marty. Just in time to catch the last of the fall color, I hope. I'll swing by Cincinnati first to check on my house, but I'd like to spend most of my three weeks off in St. Louis. I haven't seen you in two years; we need to catch up. Can't lose touch with my kid brother, you know. And you're not the best letter writer. Look for me Sunday, October 27. If this doesn't work for you, call the emergency phone number I gave you. Otherwise, I'll be in touch to give you my flight information so I can bum a ride from the airport!"

A visit from Patricia. In less than two weeks. Martin tapped the edge of the letter against the tabletop, not certain how he felt about that news. He wasn't real social these days. But she was family. And he'd finished the job he'd set out to do, after weeks of planning. He supposed it would be okay if she came.

Pulling the newspapers out of their plastic sleeves, he picked up Saturday's edition first. A quick scan of the headlines told him he hadn't missed much during his brief sojourn in the country.

But when he unrolled the Sunday edition and read the large, bold headline, then the smaller head underneath, his heart slammed against his rib cage.

FEDERAL JUDGE'S SISTER MURDERED

STEPHANIE LONG, SISTER OF U.S. DISTRICT COURT JUDGE ELIZABETH MICHAELS, FATALLY SHOT IN JUDGE'S HOME FRIDAY EVENING

No!

The paper began to shake in his hands, blurring the type.

He set it on the table and tried to breathe as the realization slammed into him like a punch in the solar plexus, driving the air from his lungs.

He'd killed the wrong woman.

"Yea, though I walk through the valley of the shadow of death, I will fear no evil: for thou art with me; thy rod and thy staff they comfort me."

While the minister read the Twenty-third Psalm, Jake inspected the small chapel at the cemetery in Kansas City. From his vantage point near the front, off to the side, he could see the other three marshals from St. Louis and all of the forty or fifty mourners who'd made the trip to the service. Most were friends of Stephanie's from Springfield. A couple of Liz's former colleagues from Jefferson City had come. The remainder were Alan's family. They were clustered around him, on the left side of the chapel.

Liz sat alone in the first pew on the right. Within touching distance of the casket. She'd arrived last, by design, and had taken her seat without so much as a glance in her brother-in-law's direction.

As the soaring notes of a recorded version of "Amazing Grace" filled the chapel, signaling the end of the service, Jake lifted his arm and spoke quietly into the mike at his cuff. "We're winding down inside. Once the service is over, we'll stay in place until the chapel empties, as we discussed. Everything okay outside?"

The four KC marshals assigned to exterior duty checked in one by one, verifying through the earpieces that linked them that all was quiet.

Signaling to Spence on the other side of the chapel, Jake moved in beside Liz. She knew the plan, and she'd remained seated as the mourners had begun to file out. Before the service, she'd pointed out a handful of people who might want to talk with her afterward, and Jake saw them coming forward now. He stayed close as they exchanged a few words with her, keeping his attention fixed on the emptying chapel rather than the muted conversation taking place several feet away.

No one stayed long to chat. One by one, Alan's family members had also filed out. Now, except for the four marshals, Alan and Liz were the sole occupants of the chapel. When her brother-in-law looked toward her, across the width of Stephanie's casket, Jake's pulse ratcheted up a notch and he motioned to Spence.

The other marshal positioned himself in front of Liz and faced Alan across the casket. Jake bent down to her. "Ready to leave?"

With a nod, she swiped at her cheeks with a tissue, tucked it in her purse, and started to rise.

"Liz."

At Alan's quiet but intent plea, she lost her balance and sank back down, her eyes sending a panicked entreaty to Jake.

He took her arm, urging her to her feet as he spoke in a low voice edged with steel. "You don't have to talk to him."

She followed his lead, exiting toward the far side of the pew.

"Liz, I didn't do it."

She stumbled, and Jake steadied her as he shot Alan a warning look.

"The judge doesn't want to speak with you, Mr. Long." Spence moved his suit jacket aside to prop a fist on his hip.

The gesture also happened to display the Glock at his belt. An intimidation tactic Jake, too, had used on occasion. Good for Spence.

But Alan ignored the marshal. And the implied warning. "Liz, please!" The raw anguish in the man's voice seemed amplified as it echoed in the quiet chapel.

She'd reached the end of the row, and Jake expected her to hightail it to the exit as fast as she could.

Instead, she hesitated. Curled her fingers around the back

of the wooden pew. And slowly swiveled toward the man who'd married her sister.

Alan's hands were resting on the casket, and Jake heard the sudden catch in Liz's breath. "Don't touch my sister."

At her fierce, choked command, Alan withdrew his hands. Jammed them in his pockets. "I made a lot of mistakes with Stephanie, Liz." His words roughened, and he cleared his throat. "But I was going to get counseling, like she asked. I decided that last weekend while I was camping. I planned to call her when I got home and tell her. I want you to know I'm still going to go. It's what she would have wanted. And it's what I want too. No matter what you think, I loved her."

She stared at him, and Jake could see the pulse hammering in the hollow of her throat, above the neck of her jade-green silk blouse. "You beat her, Alan."

A spasm of pain twisted his features at her contemptuous denunciation. "I'm sorry for that. More sorry than I can say." His lashes were spiky with moisture, and he brushed the back of his hand across them.

Beside him, Jake felt Liz stiffen. "Tell that to God." She turned away from Alan and looked up at him. She was trembling, and there was desperation in her eyes. "I need to get out of here."

Signaling to Dan and Larry in the back, he took her arm and lifted his wrist. "We're on our way out. Is the Suburban in place?"

"Right outside the front door. The lead and follow vehicles are also in position."

With the threat to Liz heightened now that Alan was no longer as likely a suspect, they'd beefed up the travel plans from St. Louis to include a small motorcade.

"Everything set at the next stop?" He checked on Alan over his shoulder. The man hadn't tried to follow. Good.

"Two of our guys are in place. We'll move to the site too as soon as you're in your vehicles."

Jake wasn't thrilled with the idea of Liz wandering around

the open expanse of the cemetery, but she'd asked to visit Doug's grave, then swing by her family plot after her sister's interment, which the funeral director had arranged to take place immediately following the service. Jake understood her need for closure and was as comfortable as he could be with the security plan they'd put in place.

"Good. Thanks."

As they approached the exit, Dan and Larry disappeared outside. Jake paused on the threshold until one of the KC marshals waved him forward. The subsequent transfer to the vehicle was swift, and within thirty seconds Liz was inside, Spence had taken the wheel, and Jake was sitting in the front passenger seat. Dan and Larry were already in their cars.

Once they were under way, he angled toward Liz. "Sorry about the encounter with Alan."

She gazed at him, her eyes too big, her face too pale. "You couldn't stop him from speaking. But I shouldn't have looked at him. That was a mistake."

Meaning she'd gotten the same impression he, Mark, and Cole had during their visit to Springfield two days ago: the man's remorse was real.

"How can a man grieve over a woman he abused?"

At her bewildered question, he shook his head. "It makes no sense to me either, Liz. I don't get guys like that."

She didn't respond as the Suburban accelerated. Instead, she turned her head toward the blacked-out window. But just as he was about to face front again, she spoke. Her voice was so soft it was almost as if she was talking to herself, and he had to strain to catch the words she aimed at the passing grave markers.

"I'm glad you don't."

Settling back in his seat, Jake mulled over her comment. It was probably nothing more than an expression of relief that others found Alan's behavior as incomprehensible as she did. That the concept of doing physical harm to someone you profess to love was outside the realm of understanding for normal people, who associate love with tenderness and protection rather than brutality and assault.

Yet as they traversed the narrow roads of the cemetery, headed for the grave of the man she'd married, he found himself wishing her comment was more personal. That she was glad he, in particular, couldn't fathom the actions of a man like Alan Long.

Because that would suggest she wanted to think well of him.

That she liked him.

Flummoxed, he stared straight ahead, oblivious for a brief moment to his surroundings—something that never happened when he was on duty. But the 180-degree turn in his attitude toward the woman in the backseat blew him away.

Five days ago, when he'd walked through the doors of the ER at St. John's, he couldn't have cared less what Liz Michaels thought about him.

Now he cared.

A lot.

Because during the past few days, he'd begun to realize that his friend had painted a distorted picture of his wife. He didn't know why Doug had done that, and Liz had offered no clue. But Jake suspected there was a whole lot more to the story of his college buddy's demise than he'd thought.

And he intended to get to the bottom of it—sooner or later.

As the small motorcade pulled to a stop near Doug's grave, Liz gripped the purse in her lap. She hadn't been back here since the day they'd laid her husband of five years to rest. Visiting graves had never offered her much comfort. The people she loved weren't here. Their physical remains might be buried in this parched ground, but their souls were with God.

Still, as long as she was here, it seemed fitting to stop by Doug's final resting place.

"Sit tight for a minute until we get the all clear," Jake told her over his shoulder.

He began talking into the mike at his cuff, scanning the flat terrain through the blacked-out windows as he spoke. Half a minute later, with a nod to Spence, he pushed open his door and stepped out. Dan and Larry joined him. They conversed for a moment, then Jake opened her door and reached behind her seat to withdraw an umbrella. He opened it and extended his hand to help her out.

His fingers held hers in a firm grip as she slid from the car. Clouds had moved in while they were in the chapel, and a light rain had begun to fall.

"It's over there." She gestured toward a gray granite headstone to the right.

"I know."

Of course he would. He'd stood in this same spot five years ago as they'd laid Doug to rest. Just as she had.

Taking her arm, he held the umbrella above her as Dan took the lead and Larry fell in behind. She spotted some of the other agents positioned farther away.

As they approached the grave marker, Dan and Larry dropped back a discreet distance. Jake started to hand her the umbrella. "We'll give you a few private minutes."

Instead of disengaging her arm and taking the umbrella, however, she looked up at him. Hesitated. Took the leap. "You can stay if you'd like."

He arched an eyebrow, as if surprised by the invitation. "Are you sure?"

"Yes. Unless duty requires you to be elsewhere."

He shook his head. "We have plenty of coverage."

The soft rain intensified, and he shifted closer, positioning the umbrella to give her the most protection.

They stood in silence for a minute, her gaze fixed on the grass at her feet, brittle and dry from the long, hot summer. She tried to recall the early days of her marriage, when her love for her husband had been young and fresh and filled with promise. But the bad memories had eclipsed them, leaving the happy times in shadows, their outlines dim and fuzzy, like barely recalled dreams.

Lifting her chin, she read Doug's name carved onto the granite base of the headstone that marked the graves of several members of the Stafford family. "I suppose I should have bought a separate plot for Doug."

A couple of seconds of silence ticked by before Jake responded. "I wondered at the time about that."

She shrugged. "There was an empty spot in the family plot and his mother offered it to me for him. It was the simplest solution in the midst of all the chaos. One less decision to make. One less detail to deal with. Only later did I realize that meant there was no room for me. That Doug and I would be apart in death . . . just as we'd been in life."

Liz didn't need to look up to know Jake was frowning at her, wondering about the whispered comment she'd tacked onto the end. "Our marriage was falling apart, Jake."

Once again, several beats of silence passed, as if he was deciding how to respond. Or if he should respond. "I suspected that."

She tipped her head back and searched his face as they huddled beneath the umbrella. There were questions in the depths of his deep brown irises, and a kindness that hadn't been there on their last encounter in this spot. She saw an openness, as well, suggesting he'd already acknowledged the information he'd gotten from his friend might have been flawed.

"He said you'd threatened to leave him."

So he knew about that. "Did he tell you why?"

He shifted, as if uncomfortable with the topic. Or perhaps the setting. And they were on tricky ground. Literally, considering the close proximity of Doug's mortal remains. How could they communicate about such a sensitive subject without betraying the confidences and loyalties of a friendship and a marriage?

"I had the feeling your decision was related to your career." Jake's words were cautious. Chosen with the same care exercised by soldiers stepping onto a minefield.

A pang echoed in her heart, and she sighed. "I suppose he'd convinced himself it was. But he was wrong. About that—and a lot of things. When did you last talk to him?"

"A few days before he died. That's when he told me you might leave him. He was . . . very upset." He transferred his weight from one foot to the other and shoved his free hand into his pocket. "It's crossed my mind in the past few days that I probably should have . . ." He stopped abruptly, and his expression grew distant as he lifted his hand to touch his earpiece. Furrows appeared on his brow.

"We need to move. I'm sorry to rush you, Liz."

Without giving her a chance to respond, he gestured to Dan and Larry, took her arm, and set a fast pace back to the car. The three-inch heels of her black pumps weren't designed for rapid travel over a sloping lawn, and without his arm supporting her she had a feeling she'd have taken a nosedive.

They were back in the car and under way before she caught her breath.

"Sorry about that." Jake angled toward her from the front seat. "Several cars were headed our direction. No doubt other people visiting graves, but I didn't want to take a chance."

"It's okay. I was finished there."

His gaze locked on hers. "I thought we were just getting started."

At Jake's enigmatic remark, Spence shot him a quick glance. Then he sent a look her direction in the rearview mirror. She felt warmth seep onto her cheeks and braced, expecting him to make a comment. But to her relief, he remained silent.

"We'll swing by your sister's grave now." Jake picked up the conversation again, his tone once more all business. "They're still working there, but the rain is slowing them down a little. With the activity in the cemetery, we'd prefer you remain in the car."

"Okay. The grave is curbside. I don't need to get out."

Two minutes later, as the small motorcade pulled to a stop, Liz scooted toward the driver-side window of the backseat and leaned close to the glass. Someone must have alerted the workers to expect her, because they took a few steps back and rested on their shovels.

The grave was already half filled. The flowers that had covered the casket during the service, a brilliant display of the sweet-smelling Stargazer lilies Steph had loved, were off to the side, waiting to be draped over the mound of fresh earth that would mark her final resting place.

For several minutes, forehead pressed against the cool glass, Liz regarded the spot that held the physical remains of her family.

Now she had no one left to bury.

No one left to love.

She felt the pressure of tears in her throat, behind her eyes, and prayed for the strength to hold on. To shore up her disintegrating composure. To find a way to live with the loneliness . . . and the grief . . . and the guilt.

Lifting her fingers to her lips, she kissed the tips. Pressed them to the window. And whispered a final farewell.

"Good-bye, Steph. I love you."

It was another two minutes before she trusted her voice enough to speak. Scooting back into her place, she kept her head bowed as she tugged her seat belt across her chest and buckled it. "I'm ready to leave."

She heard Jake issue instructions into his mike, but as the Suburban began to move and the men went back to work, she twisted her head for a last look at the plot, once more fighting back tears.

And then she felt a strong, reassuring hand cover her cold fingers as they rested on her knee.

Startled, she turned forward.

Jake didn't speak. With words. But his eloquent, unguarded eyes communicated much—sympathy, caring, and enough warmth to chase away the chill that had settled over her heart as she said good-bye to Stephanie.

Liz had never seen Jake in work mode until the past week. She suspected, however, that he was generally all business. He struck her as dedicated, diligent, and buttoned up. A solid professional with the highest integrity, who never let personal feelings interfere with his job.

She'd felt that way even last Friday, when he'd shown up in the ER. Despite his reserve and her impression that he wasn't thrilled by his assignment, she'd had every confidence he would do his best to protect her.

Now, she sensed his dedication to keeping her safe had a personal element. His demeanor, and the hand resting on hers, seemed evidence of that.

But perhaps Jake would offer the same kind of emotional support to anyone in his charge.

There would be time later to figure all this out, she decided as he gave her hand a squeeze and turned back to the front. When her emotions weren't so tattered and he wasn't occupied with a killer still on the loose—and possibly interested in finishing the job he'd started. They both had enough on their plates for the moment.

But after things calmed down, Liz had every intention of returning to their interrupted conversation at Doug's grave.

And setting the record straight about her marriage to his best friend.

10

"My friends and fellow patriots, we live in troubled times. Dangerous times. Day by day, the unalienable rights set forth in the documents so painstakingly prepared by our founding fathers are being eroded through apathy and ignorance. While many people complain, few take action. I applaud all of you for attending this meeting. It means you share my concern about the fate of our great country. It means you want to learn the truth. But education without action is meaningless. How many of you here tonight can stand up and say, 'I did something'!"

A murmur ran through the crowd as Jarrod Williams leaned forward on the flag-draped podium in the back room of Express Copies and surveyed the seventy or eighty people occupying the rows of folding chairs in front of him.

In his seat near the rear, Martin shifted as he sought a more comfortable position. He'd tried to do something—but he'd screwed it up. And he felt bad about that. Real bad. After reading the story about the judge's sister last night, he'd tossed until the early hours of the morning.

But mistakes happened. When you had the courage to take a stand, there was always the chance of collateral damage, as Jarrod had once called it. It was unfortunate—yet justifiable if it advanced the cause.

"My fellow patriots, we must save our Constitution and

Bill of Rights before it's too late." Martin refocused as Jarrod continued. "Even as we speak, the judiciary is conspiring to oppress us. Despite the Second Amendment, the federal courts want to disarm all Americans. They want to deny us our constitutional right to keep and bear arms. If you think I exaggerate, consider how difficult it has become to own a firearm. Have you tried to buy a gun lately? The regulations and licensing requirements make it an exercise in frustration."

There were murmurs of assent from the crowd, and Martin nodded in agreement. He was lucky. He'd had a number of weapons for years, all now stashed in a locked cabinet in his basement. Purchased before the courts and the government began plotting to undermine the Second Amendment. It was too bad he'd had to drop his favorite .45 into the river as he left town on Friday night. But he'd used it for a good cause. And he had other handguns.

Martin watched as Jarrod came out from behind the podium and moved closer to the crowd. Tall and spare, always dressed in a suit and tie, his face shone with intelligence beneath his shock of white hair. He was a mesmerizing speaker, and Martin had been hooked ever since Tom Harris, the owner of Express Copies, had invited him to attend his first meeting. Here, he'd found like-minded people. Citizens who loved their *country*—not the corrupt government.

"My friends, the press and the terrocrats have called organizations like ours disgruntled fringe groups and subversive factions. Let me tell you something—we're in good company. That's what they called our founding fathers too. Now, like then, the cause is righteous. And we are at a crossroads. America's demise is accelerating, and I fear that in our lifetime, the flickering light of liberty may be extinguished forever.

"Remember this, fellow patriots. Truth and justice are on our side. When your natural birthrights are violated, it is your right to ask for redress from the government. And if our corrupt courts fail you, if our tyrannical government fails you, you are under no obligation to offer them your allegiance or obedience."

He joined his hands in front of him, fingertips touching. Almost like he was praying, Martin reflected.

"Let me leave you with one more thought. Whatever actions you take to reclaim our country, don't keep them hidden. As Matthew reminds us in the Holy Bible, expose them to the world so everyone can see the light. 'Neither do men light a candle and put it under a bushel, but on a candlestick; and it giveth light unto all that are in the house.' Spread the light, my friends. With pride. And if you are persecuted for your commitment to freedom, so be it. For it is up to us to keep the light of liberty burning strong. That is a cause worthy of martyrdom."

The room erupted in applause, and Martin joined the others as they rose to their feet and gave Jarrod a rousing ovation.

But his mind was whirling as he pondered Jarrod's closing comment.

He'd tried to do a good thing, and he planned to finish the job. But perhaps his method was wrong. He'd thought taking out a judge was sufficient. One less judge in America was a good thing, after all. Especially *that* judge. But no one would have known why she died. And that was important. To advance their cause, the world needed to know the reason for such a death. That it wasn't a personal vendetta but part of a bigger purpose.

Suddenly, he saw his failure in a new light—as a God-given opportunity. A second chance to get it right. To shine the light on his actions through the media, so the world would know there were brave patriots dedicated to restoring America to its former glory.

"He was great tonight, wasn't he?"

As the applause died down and the murmur of conversation replaced Jarrod's stirring rhetoric, Martin turned toward Tom Harris. If it hadn't been for Tom, he'd never have found out about this organization. Lucky for him, Tom had struck up a conversation with him fifteen months ago when he'd stopped in to copy some tax records after receiving a letter from the IRS claiming he'd underpaid his taxes. Tom had listened as he'd railed about the obscene fine he'd been slapped with for making an honest mistake, then invited him to his first Patriot Constitutionalists meeting. He hadn't missed one since.

"Yeah. He's always good."

"You staying for the seminar? Should be interesting . . . paper terrorism at the local level." He grinned. "We're going to bury those aldermen on this eminent domain issue."

It was a good cause, and he wouldn't have minded pitching in. Too bad he hadn't known about this group when his own house had been declared blighted a year and a half ago in the interest of "progress." Like the world had needed another strip mall. His lips curled in disgust.

But he couldn't stay tonight.

He had plans to make.

"I'd like to, but my sister's coming to visit, and I have some business to take care of before she arrives."

"No problem." Tom slapped him on the back. "You having any luck finding a job?"

That was another sore subject.

And another kick in the pants by Uncle Sam.

After six months, it was still hard for him to believe his twenty-four-year career was toast. But that's what happened when a company had to downsize after the government reneged on its defense contracts. So at fifty-three, he'd found himself on the street. Too young to retire, too old to find a job. And no one to commiserate with, now that Helen was gone.

Except she shouldn't be gone. Wouldn't be gone, if that doctor hadn't botched things in the emergency room three years ago. Not that the court had seen it that way.

Fighting back the surge of anger those rancorous memories

always provoked, he did his best to keep his tone conversational. "No. Economy's bad."

"Yeah. I hear you. Well, good luck. Are you coming to the next meeting?"

"I plan to." He'd make up some excuse for his absence to Patricia. Tell her he'd gone bowling, maybe. He'd been a bowler once. A long time ago. She'd buy that.

"You gonna say hi to Jarrod before you leave?"

That had been his intention. He'd looked forward to letting the leader know he wasn't one of the cowards who complained from the sidelines without ever joining in the fight. Not that he'd intended to provide details. He'd just wanted the man to know his words had inspired someone to take action.

But he had to finish the job first. The right way.

After that . . . he'd speak with Jarrod.

"Not tonight."

"Okay, buddy. See you next time. Keep the faith."

As Tom dived back into the crowd, Martin headed toward the door at the rear of the copy shop. A tall, thirtysomething dark-haired guy dressed in jeans and a T-shirt was ahead of him, and he held the door open for Martin as he approached. Martin had noticed him at some recent meetings. A construction worker, he figured. Or maybe he had one of the few landscaping jobs not held by illegal Mexicans. You didn't get those kinds of biceps sitting behind a desk.

"Thanks."

"No problem." The man let the door close behind them and fell into step beside him as they rounded the building and headed toward their cars in the front parking lot. "Looks like we're in for a storm."

Martin glanced up at the night sky. The moon was hidden, and no stars twinkled through the clouds. A rumble of thunder sounded in the distance, low and ominous.

"Yeah. Best get home before it hits. See you around."

"I'll be back. You a regular?"

He lifted one shoulder. "I've been coming for about a year."

"I'm newer. Name's Mark." He stuck out his hand.

The gesture took Martin off guard. Most people at these meetings didn't introduce themselves. It seemed to be kind of an unwritten rule. But he didn't see any harm in it. It was only a first name.

He returned the man's firm grip. "Martin."

"Nice to meet you, Martin. Drive safe going home." Lifting his hand, he strolled toward an older model Camry on the parking lot.

Martin headed the other way, toward his newer Accord, picking up his pace as another rumble of thunder sounded. Closer now.

No question about it.

There was unsettled weather ahead.

"Thanks for bringing this by, Neil. You can set it there." As she led the way toward the dining room in the condo, Liz gestured toward the table.

Hefting the box in his arms, the younger of her two law clerks followed. After depositing it in the spot she'd indicated, he brushed off his hands. "Hard to believe you've accumulated this many files after just four months on the job. There are five more boxes in my car."

The faint hint of a smile tugged at her lips. At twenty-six, with the ink not yet dry on his law degree, Neil Clark still had much to learn.

"The practice of law is synonymous with mountains of paper, Neil. And books. That doesn't go away once you leave law school. It only gets worse."

He grimaced. "Good thing you hadn't been on the job *eight* months. We would've had to hire a moving truck."

"I can ask the marshals to bring up the rest of the boxes from the parking garage, if you want."

"No, that's okay. I'm also learning that the practice of law plays havoc with the waistline. Running around campus kept me in shape." He patted his trim midsection. "I've put on a few pounds already since I've been at this job. Too much desk time."

A grin twitched at her lips. She liked Neil. From the shock of unruly blond hair that persisted in falling across his forehead, to the studious horn-rimmed glasses he favored, to his perennial gee-whiz expression, he reminded her of an earnest schoolboy, always eager to please. Looking at him, no one would suspect he had an incredible analytical mind and sharp, intuitive insights. She was glad she'd hired him two weeks into her new job.

"If you've gained any weight while clerking for me, I haven't noticed."

"Victoria has." He gave her a rueful smile.

Her other clerk had already been on the job for a year when Liz had been named to replace the retiring judge, and she valued the woman's experience. It had helped smooth the transition. She'd also watched in amusement as Neil had fallen for her hook, line, and sinker—though as far as she could see, Victoria gave him no encouragement. The woman was a total professional and completely focused on her work. Reminding her of herself at that age.

Before she'd fallen in love with an up-and-coming financial wizard who'd stolen her heart and altered her priorities.

Before their fairy-tale marriage had fallen apart and she'd turned back to work for solace—and escape.

Her smile faded.

"I'll be back up in a jiffy." Neil started toward the front door.

As he shuttled the remaining cartons up from his car, Liz blocked out the melancholy memories and opened the first box. With a sigh, she poked through the contents half-heartedly. Reviewing past case files to look for a needle in a haystack—as she'd described it to Mark Sanders—was a daunting . . . and unappealing . . . prospect.

But the FBI agent, as well as Jake, seemed to think it was a worthwhile exercise. And she supposed that was true. If she had any enemies, it was logical to assume they were buried somewhere in her thirteen-year law career. And the probability was high that she'd find them in a more recent case rather than older ones.

Neil came and went several times, with one of the marshals on duty in the command post acting as doorman to her unit. The young clerk was huffing as he lugged the last box through the condo and set it down with a thud. She noticed he'd ditched his suit jacket in the car during his last trip.

"That's my exercise for the day." He took his handkerchief out of the pocket of his slacks and wiped his forehead.

"I appreciate you delivering these."

"No problem. Got me out of the office for an hour." He flashed her a grin as he tucked the handkerchief away, then grew serious. "I've been wanting to tell you how sorry I am about your sister, Judge Michaels. I can't begin to imagine what you've been through. I hope they find the perpetrator quickly."

"So do I." She closed the lid of the box she'd been riffling through. Since arriving home from the funeral early yesterday evening, she'd tried to focus on doing her part to make that happen. She'd stayed up late into the night, sorting through the case files the marshals had delivered from her home office on Tuesday afternoon. But she'd start her detailed review with the most recent ones, as Mark had asked. The ones that had defined her first few months as a U.S. District Court judge in St. Louis.

Then she'd delve into the cases she'd tried during her three years as a circuit court judge in Jefferson City. Only if those yielded no leads would she go farther back, to her years as a trial attorney.

She hoped it didn't come to that. Jake had hinted she might

need to remain sequestered until she finished the task they'd given her, and she didn't relish the confinement. Her preference was to go back to court next week. Lose herself in her work, as she'd always done when life got tough. It was easier to focus on other people's problems than her own.

"Any idea when you'll be coming back, Judge?"

She gave Neil an amused look. "You must be reading my mind."

"Not quite. I haven't been in your office long enough for that yet. But I'm working on it." He grinned. "It would be a good skill to have as a law clerk, don't you think?"

She returned his smile. "I don't expect miracles. Just keep doing what you've been doing. I'm happy with your work."

"Thanks." A flush stained his cheeks.

"Good work should be recognized." To save him further embarrassment, she moved on. "To answer your question, I talked to Judge Shapiro Tuesday. I know my absence has been hard on everyone." She combed her fingers through her hair and expelled a frustrated breath as she thought back to the conversation she'd had with the chief judge.

"These are extraordinary circumstances."

While she appreciated Neil's loyalty, she deflected the slight edge of indignation in his voice with a smile. "He couldn't have been kinder. But facts are facts. The calendar is backlogged and I have a full docket."

She regarded the boxes of material Neil had delivered, plus the ones the marshals had retrieved from her house. Then there was all the case data stored on her computer . . . it was overwhelming. But she intended to hunker down and plow through it as fast as she could.

"I'm hoping for Monday. At least part-time. I'm going to talk to the marshals and the FBI about it today. In the meantime, hold down the fort, okay?"

"We'll do our best. Is there anything else you need?"

"A normal day would be nice."

"Yeah." He gave a sympathetic nod. "Normal is nice."

As she walked him to the door, Liz pondered his comment. She could recall a time when she'd thought normal, predictable days were boring.

Not anymore. Boring would never again seem banal. She would welcome boring.

Unfortunately, she had a feeling that wasn't a word she was going to be able to apply to her life anytime soon.

Pressing the elevator button in the lobby of Liz's condo, Jake tapped his foot impatiently. He'd meant to get here sooner, but his morning hadn't gone as planned. Thanks to his siblings.

He was still annoyed with Alison. And she was none too happy with him after he'd insisted on driving her to work and arranged for Cole to pick her up. If he hadn't swung by her house last night on his way home after the trip to Kansas City, he'd never have discovered her car was out of commission and that she was planning to take the bus to work. An exercise that would require blocks of walking. Correction. Limping.

Expelling an exasperated breath, he jabbed the elevator button again. She didn't have to do that, not with two brothers willing and able to help. Except that's not the way little Miss Independent saw it. If he hadn't shown up at the crack of dawn, he had no doubt she'd have carried out her threat to take an earlier bus.

The elevator door opened and he stepped inside, pressing the button for the fifth floor. That first detour had cost him an hour. Then, just as he was dropping Alison off, he'd gotten a call from Cole—requiring a second detour to his brother's office, where Mark had joined them. The county crime lab had processed some strands of gold-colored hair the technicians had found in the carpet of Liz's condo, a few feet behind where Stephanie had been shot. And had turned up an interesting piece of information.

The hair was feline.

What made that fact significant was that Liz didn't have a cat. Neither did Alan. Mark had placed a call to him from Cole's office, and Alan had told him that Stephanie had avoided cats like the plague because she was allergic to their dander. A second call, to the owner of Liz's house, confirmed that pets weren't part of the lease agreement. Meaning it was unlikely the prior tenants had been the source of the cat hair, either—unless they'd violated their lease. Mark was tracking them down now to verify they hadn't.

The elevator door slid open, and after a quick stop at the CP and a brief conversation with Spence, Jake continued toward Liz's door and pressed his finger to the button.

It was possible that Liz or Stephanie could have picked up cat hair on their shoes. But as he'd talked it over with Cole and Mark this morning in his brother's office, the three of them had agreed there was a good probability the killer had a cat. Hair could be insidious, clinging easily to clothes and shoes.

It wasn't much of a lead, but so far it was all they had. Unless—or until—Liz spotted a red flag in one of her prior cases.

He pressed her doorbell again.

The FBI was already digging up information on the parties involved in some of Liz's higher-profile cases. Those were older—ancient history, she'd called them—and he was inclined to agree with her skepticism about their relevance. But the FBI wouldn't leave any stone unturned in this investigation. Not with a federal judge involved.

Leaning on the bell again, he frowned. Maybe Liz was sleeping, like the last time she'd been tardy answering. He hated to wake her, but an unanswered door—even in a condo he felt confident was secure—didn't leave him with a good feeling. A small surge of adrenaline kicked his alert status up a notch, but he tried to keep it in check. No sense overreacting.

As he raised his hand to knock, the door was suddenly pulled open—and he froze.

Only one word came to his mind when he saw Liz.

Wow.

Even in the days when his feeling toward her had been chillier than a frigid February night in St. Louis, he'd had to admit she was a beautiful woman. He'd noticed it the first time they'd met, at her wedding.

But today she was drop-dead gorgeous.

Her hair was pulled back into a ponytail, though a few loose tendrils were clinging to her glistening forehead. Her hot pink tank top dipped low enough to reveal a tantalizing glimpse of cleavage, and her spandex shorts left a long length of shapely leg exposed.

This was not the body of the typical thirty-eight-year-old women in his acquaintance. She looked more like a Hollywood celebrity in an ad for a fitness center than a federal judge.

"Jake?"

At her uncertain tone, he checked to make sure his mouth was shut and he wasn't drooling. Okay. He was safe there. But he'd missed whatever she'd said first.

"Sorry. I was worried when you didn't answer." He stepped past her, buying himself a few seconds to regain some semblance of control.

"I'm the one who should apologize." She shut the door and flipped the dead bolt. "When I got up this morning I discovered the treadmill you had delivered while we were in Kansas City yesterday, and that's where I've been since my law clerk left. I had the music cranked up on my headphones and didn't hear the bell until I stopped to get a drink of water. Were you standing there long?"

"No."

"Good."

She smiled at him, and he focused on her face. That was better. And telling. Despite her trim figure and the youthful curves of her body, the lines of strain at the corners of her eyes and the dark circles underneath hinted she was older than she looked. And suggested she still wasn't sleeping.

"I want to thank you for your thoughtfulness. Being cooped up is hard enough, but I hated missing my walks. They keep me in shape."

He gave her another quick scan.

Big mistake.

His pulse leapt again, and he jerked his gaze back up.

Say something innocuous.

"You've got a great body."

A flush tinted her cheeks, and he tried not to groan as heat crept up his own neck.

Brilliant, Taylor. That was real innocuous.

"What I meant was, I can tell you're fitness conscious." It was a lame attempt to remove his foot from his mouth, and he knew it.

"Thanks." She tugged at the hem of her shorts, telling him she knew it too. "Give me a couple of minutes and I'll be right with you. Help yourself to some juice or coffee if you like." She gestured toward the kitchen and fled.

He waited until he heard the door of her room click closed, then wandered into the kitchen, rubbing the back of his neck. What was wrong with him? Never—not one single time—in all his years with the Marshals Service had he let personal feelings intrude on the job. It was dumb. And it was dangerous.

Opening the fridge, he pulled out a carton of orange juice and poured a glass, mulling over his weird dilemma. He needed some logic here. Needed to put his emotions aside for a moment. Needed to look at the facts with a dispassionate eye.

Okay. He could do that. He did it every day on the job. No reason he couldn't do it with more personal matters.

Fact one. Liz Michaels was an appealing, attractive woman.

Fact two. He'd met her years ago, so that history would

naturally engender more closeness than he felt with most of his charges.

Fact three. He'd been thrown off balance by evidence suggesting his entrenched opinion of her was inaccurate.

Fact four. His hormones were going haywire.

Fact five. It was way too hot in this condo.

Running a finger around the collar of his dress shirt, Jake drained the glass of cold orange juice in a few long gulps.

He was still too hot.

Though he usually kept his suit jacket on during duty hours, he dispensed with that rule and slid it off his shoulders.

Better.

Draping it on a chair, he surveyed the pile of boxes in the dining room and the sea of papers spread over the table, the neat stacks covering every square inch except for the small spot occupied by the flowers Alison had sent. Case files, he noted, giving the documents a quick survey. Meaning Liz had already started reviewing them.

"It's intimidating, isn't it?"

At her question, he turned toward the hall. She'd changed into jeans, and her baggy sweatshirt barely hinted at the curves beneath. It was attire designed to hide her assets. Suggesting his appreciative perusal hadn't been appreciated.

Next time she appeared in eye-popping attire—if there was a next time—he'd be sure to keep his eyeballs in their sockets.

"Yeah. You don't have to review it all in one day, though."

"I couldn't if I wanted to." She moved beside the table and fingered a folder. "But I'd like to get through it as quickly as possible. I'm going stir-crazy here. I stayed up late last night to organize everything so I could get a jump on it."

That explained the shadows beneath her lower lashes.

"Maybe you could take a nap today."

She looked up at him. "I'd rather get through some of the files from the last four months that my clerk brought over this morning. Jake . . . I'd like to go back to work next week.

Full-time, if I get through the recent stuff over the weekend. Part-time if not."

"Aren't you rushing things?" He shoved his hands in his pockets, furrowing his brow. "You've been through a lot in the past week, Liz. No one would complain if you took some time off."

"I have a full docket, Jake. And I'm already behind, after only four months."

He studied her. "Is that the real reason?"

Catching her lower lip between her teeth, she folded her arms across her chest. "It's one of the reasons."

"Want to share the others?"

A few seconds ticked by as she considered his question. Finally, taking a deep breath, she motioned toward the living room. "Have a seat. You want some coffee?"

"No, thanks. I had a glass of juice while you changed."

"Give me a sec."

She headed back toward the kitchen, and he heard her fiddling with the coffeepot while he took a seat on the chair beside the couch.

As he settled in, he tried to prepare himself, sensing that whatever she was about to share was going to upend any lingering misconceptions he might still harbor about the woman his best friend had married.

And once that happened, it was going to be harder than ever to maintain his professional distance. Because given the way he was already beginning to feel about her, he suspected he would soon have an even more compelling personal reason to keep her safe.

11

"You look a little frazzled."

Frazzled?

Jake blinked at Liz, trying to regroup as she sat on the couch and cradled her coffee mug in both hands. That wasn't a term anyone had ever applied to him.

But it did fit today. Thanks to the appealing woman across from him. A fact he did not intend to share with her.

"I had a busy morning. Starting with my pigheaded sister."

Her lips twitched as she took a sip of coffee. "What happened? If you don't mind my asking."

He propped his ankle on his knee and shook his head. "She's too stubborn for her own good."

The twitch gave way to the hint of a smile. "Do you care to expand on that?"

He blew out an exasperated breath. "I found out last night she had to drop her car off at the shop yesterday. She was planning on taking the bus to work today instead of asking Cole or me for a ride."

"And that's a problem because . . . ?"

"She was in a very bad accident a few months ago. Broke her left leg in two places and had serious internal injuries. She still goes to physical therapy twice a week. According to her, the limp will go away in time. But she doesn't need to be traipsing to a bus right now. So I strong-armed her into letting me drive her to work this morning. Cole is going to pick her up this afternoon."

"Sounds like she's very independent."

He gave her a disgruntled look. "There's a fine line between independent and foolishly stubborn. And she crossed it."

"Did you share that opinion with her?"

At her amused look, he flicked an imaginary speck of lint off his slacks. "More or less."

"I bet that went over real well."

Narrowing his eyes, he peered at her. "I should have figured you women would stick together."

She lifted one shoulder. "I happen to admire independence. And strength. My guess is your sister has both."

"She does. And for the record, I admire those qualities too." He held her gaze until the surge of color in her cheeks told him his message had been received. "She needs them too. On top of everything else, her serious boyfriend dumped her not long after the accident."

Liz's eyes softened in sympathy. "That stinks."

"Tell me about it."

"Couldn't he handle all the medical stuff?"

"That was part of the problem." He let it go at that. Alison's love life wasn't anyone else's business. Except his and Cole's.

"Did you two make up before you dropped her off?"

"Yeah. Pretty much. She was a little more amenable this morning. Probably because she knows I'm still aggravated that she wouldn't let my brother or my mom tell me about her accident until I got back from Iraq."

"You were in Iraq?" Liz's eyes widened and she froze, her mug halfway to her mouth.

He hadn't intended to let that slip. But it was too late to backpedal now. "Yeah. For most of the past six months. The Marshals Service has been sending its Special Operations Group over there for a while."

She gave him a blank look. "What's the Special Operations Group?"

"A tactical unit deployed for high-risk law enforcement operations and national emergencies. In between, we function as regular marshals in offices around the country."

She took a few seconds to absorb this news. "How does Iraq fit in?"

"SOG teams have been going there for almost ten years to try to improve judicial and witness security. All in the interest of helping stabilize the government and provide a more democratic judicial system."

"Wow. I'm impressed."

He lifted one shoulder. "Don't be. Our troops are doing the real work. Anyway, Alison claims she didn't want me told about the full extent of her injuries until I came home because she was afraid the distraction would put me in danger."

"I see her point." Liz took another sip of coffee, her expression thoughtful.

"I see it too. But I don't have to like it."

Liz stared into the black depths of her mug. "It's odd how doing things you think will protect someone you love can backfire."

He waited, sensing the conversation was shifting toward the subject he was keen to hear about: her relationship with his college buddy.

Lifting her head, she searched his eyes. He tried his best to project empathy and support.

"That's why I threatened to leave Doug, you know. It was a desperate measure, one I hoped would be a wake-up call. I thought if he believed I'd really leave, he might take steps to get his life back on track. Instead, he . . . drove into a tree." She choked and dipped her head.

He was tempted to lean over and give her hand an encouraging squeeze. But he held back. Despite his growing feelings for her, he needed to maintain a professional detachment. Just as Alison had worried about distractions in Iraq making him vulnerable, if he was distracted here Liz could be vulnerable. That wasn't acceptable.

When the silence lengthened, Jake picked up the slack, treading carefully. "I didn't think there was any official ruling about what happened that night."

"There wasn't. But to me, the facts are clear. For once, his blood alcohol level wasn't over the limit. Meaning his reflexes should have been decent. The road was dry. There were no skid marks to suggest he'd applied the brakes or tried to avoid the tree. And I knew his mental state." She swallowed. "It wasn't an accident, Jake."

He knew all the facts from that fatal night too. He'd made it a point to get a copy of the police report. And the evidence suggested her conclusion had some merit. But the absolute conviction in her voice threw him.

"Why would he do that, Liz?"

At his quiet question, she leaned forward to set her mug on the coffee table. The liquid sloshed, and she wrapped both hands around it, easing it onto the glass top.

She was shaking. Badly.

Once again he had to fight off the temptation to enfold her fingers in his.

"Because his life was a mess for the three and half years before he died." She brushed back some loose tendrils that had escaped from her ponytail. "Did Doug drink in college, Jake?"

The question took him off guard. It had been years since he'd thought about their campus career, which had included plenty of wild frat parties. He and Doug had made the rounds every Saturday night, drinking the free booze and flirting with the coeds.

"We both did."

"To excess?"

Oh yeah. On more occasions than he cared to remember, they'd staggered home in the wee hours, holding each other up, then passed out in their respective bunks.

"Sometimes. All the frat guys were into partying in a big way. I'm not condoning it, but it was part of the campus scene."

Liz leaned forward, her posture earnest. "What about after college?"

"I didn't see much of Doug once we graduated."

"But you kept in touch. Did he ever mention drinking to you?"

"No. It was a college thing. I won't deny I've had a few too many beers on occasion in the intervening years, but my job doesn't allow me to make a habit of that kind of behavior. Nor do I want to. I get plenty of adrenaline rushes from my work. I don't need booze to liven up my life. I assumed Doug didn't, either."

As she sank back on the couch, Liz's expression grew pensive. "Unfortunately, he did. Although I didn't know that until we'd been married for more than a year."

Now it was his turn to lean forward, hands clasped between his knees. "Are you saying he had a serious drinking problem, Liz?"

"Yes. And it was compounded by depression. Which got worse after he found out our attempts to start a family were failing because of a medical problem of his, not mine."

Shock rippled through Jake. Doug had always implied the absence of children in their marriage was Liz's choice. That she'd been more interested in her career than in a family.

"You wanted children?"

She gripped her hands in her lap, her knuckles whitening. "He told you I didn't?"

Torn between honesty and loyalty, he skirted the question. "Not in those exact words."

Sadness darkened her eyes, and she took a long, slow sip of her cooling coffee. "I always suspected he might be misrepresenting our situation. And it used to bother me. But I can't dredge up any anger at this point. He had a lot of issues he just couldn't deal with." She wrapped her fingers around the mug, as if warming them. "Did you ever see any indication of depression in him during your college days, Jake?"

He thought back again, digging deep into his memory. Doug had fallen into a funk once after breaking up with his sophomore girlfriend. He'd almost had to drag him out of bed for weeks after that. And there had been other times when his friend had been despondent for a few days. But nothing he'd classify as abnormal. Or clinical depression.

Then again, he wasn't a psychologist.

"I saw him down a few times. I didn't think it was anything to worry about."

"Maybe it wasn't, back in those days." She drew a weary breath and ran her finger around the rim of her mug, then fixed her attention on the drawn shades in the room that held back the sunlight.

"Everything started to go bad the second year we were married, after his dad died. They were very close, and he took the loss hard. He turned to liquor to help him get through it, but that made the depression worse. From there, it was a downward spiral. In the beginning, he only drank on weekends. By the end of his life, he was never far from a bottle.

"He could put up a good public front, though, and he held his liquor well. But it was affecting his performance at work, as I discovered at the wake. His boss told me Doug had lost out on the assistant controller job a few weeks before because of mistakes he made on some key financial documents. And that the day he died, he'd been put on probation."

When she looked at him, the sheen in her eyes twisted his stomach. "I begged him to get help. Offered to make appointments with his internist, with a psychiatrist. To go with him, if he wanted me to. But he refused to believe he had a problem. I prayed harder than I'd ever prayed in my life. Asked God to give him guidance and the strength to tackle the demons that were destroying him. I even considered leaving my law practice." She dropped her chin, and he could see it quivering. "But in the end, my work preserved my sanity. When things got too bad, I could lose myself in a case and get a brief respite from the nightmare. But maybe I should have . . ."

Her words trailed off and she stood abruptly, her head still bowed. "I think I'll get a refill."

Without giving him a chance to respond, she bolted from the couch and made a beeline for the kitchen.

For a moment he thought about going after her. Decided against it. It was clear she needed a few minutes to regroup.

So did he.

From early on in this assignment, Jake had begun to suspect the woman who'd married his best friend, the woman Doug had demonized as a coldhearted workaholic who put career above everything, wasn't the villain he'd painted her to be. Now that suspicion had been confirmed. The problems in his friend's marriage had, for the most part, been of his own making.

Meaning for three and a half years of her five-year marriage, Liz had found herself living a nightmare.

How could you have done that to her, Doug? How could you have subjected the woman you loved to such torment?

The silent indictment came from deep within his heart. Yet even as its echo faded, he knew that while his friend deserved censure, he'd also needed help.

And he'd had an inkling of that during their last phone call. Doug had sounded down that night. Jake recalled trying to cheer him up by reminiscing about a few of their college adventures. Instead, the stories had had the opposite effect. They hadn't talked long, but Jake remembered making a mental note to check back with him in a day or two, to see how things were going. Instead, he'd let a week go by. And his next phone exchange with Jefferson City had been when Liz called to tell him Doug was dead.

"Can I get you anything to drink?"

He looked up. Liz was hovering near the kitchen entry, her

eyes puffy, the shadows underneath her lower lashes more pronounced than when he'd arrived.

"No, thanks."

She retook her seat. Fiddled with the handle of her cup. "Sorry for the data dump. I'm sure that's more than you wanted to know."

"As a matter of fact, it's exactly what I wanted to know."

She shot him a quizzical look but remained silent.

"I have a confession to make." He gripped the ankle he'd crossed over his knee. "I haven't always viewed you in the most favorable light. But I was wrong. I'm sorry I misjudged you. And Doug." He raked his fingers through his hair and shook his head. "I'm also sorry I didn't follow up sooner on my last phone call with him. I sensed things weren't right, and I meant to get back to him. Maybe if I had—"

"Don't go there, Jake." She leaned close and placed her hand on his, her slender fingers pale and delicate against his sun-browned skin, her eyes intent. "At that point, it wouldn't have made any difference. I lived with him. I loved him. I tried everything I could to help him. I even had my pastor come one evening as reinforcement. Nothing helped. You couldn't have stopped what happened. And I'm finally starting to accept that I couldn't, either, even if I can't quite shake the guilt. Or stop the occasional 'what-iffing.' "

"Yeah." He knew all about guilt. And what-iffing. "So how do you cope with it?"

"Not well. I still cry at night sometimes. I work too much, trying to lose myself in my job. I pray. That helps the most. There's a comfort in knowing God is always there, no matter how dark it gets."

"I envy you that."

She took a sip of her coffee and set the mug on the table in front of her. "I take it Alison hasn't convinced you yet to start attending services again?"

"No." He rose, not liking the turn in the conversation. His

relationship with God—what was left of it—wasn't something he discussed with anyone.

Moving to the blinds, he cracked them to look out into the sunlight. This conversation was supposed to be about her and Doug. Not him—and Jen. He needed to get it back on track.

"You're not comfortable talking about faith, are you?"

The knot in his stomach tightened. Maybe if he was honest she'd drop it. "No. It's a very personal subject."

He held his breath. When the silence in the room lengthened, he released it, grateful she'd gotten the hint and . . .

"You mentioned once you'd stopped going to church after Jennifer died."

Shoving his hands in his pockets, he kept his back to her. And remained mute.

"Reestablishing your relationship with God might make a difference in your life, Jake," she said softly, refusing to let the subject die. "It did in mine. Especially if you have any anger or guilt over what happened."

He had plenty of both. And for an instant, he was tempted to explore the subject with the woman across the room, who had somehow infiltrated his heart. Except he didn't talk about stuff like this. It was too risky. Far riskier, in many ways, than dodging bullets in Iraq. That's why he'd buried his feelings deep in a shadowed corner of his heart. Not even Alison or Cole or his mother were privy to them.

They still ate at him, though, in the dark hours of the morning, when he sometimes awakened and found himself reaching for Jen, whose love had filled his life with joy for two short, swift years.

Maybe it was time to expose them to the light.

Digging deep for courage, he turned toward Liz. She remained seated on the couch. Sipping her coffee. Watching him. Waiting.

"I shut God out after he took Jen." He cleared the huskiness out of his throat. "I was more angry than I'd ever been in my life. But the truth is, I also felt guilty."

"Why?" The tone of her quiet question was curious rather than judgmental.

"I pushed her too hard on the last run of the day." Suddenly restless, he jerked away from the window and began to pace. "I knew she wasn't athletic. But I loved skiing, so the second year we were married, I convinced her to go to Breckenridge and let me show her the ropes. I don't know what I expected . . . that she'd be Olympic quality after a day of lessons, I guess. Only she wasn't. She was scared. And cautious. And her progress was far too slow to suit me."

He watched a beam of sunlight as it struggled to infiltrate the barrier at the window, seeking to dispel the shadows in the room. "If you want the truth, I was a jerk about it. I felt like she was holding me back. I kept pushing her and grousing and losing my patience. She was in tears more than once. Finally she told me to go take some black runs while she stuck with the green ones. We agreed to meet for lunch at the base of one of the beginner slopes."

Fisting his hands, he stared at a blank wall in the condo, the cream surface acting like a screen as the final few minutes of the mountainside drama played out in his memory.

"I got to the restaurant early and decided to take the lift up and see if I could catch up with her somewhere on the slope. As I was riding up, I spotted her at the crest of a small hill, and when I waved she saw me. She motioned ahead, like I should watch her. And I did. I watched her take off faster than she should have, trying to impress me with her progress—and make me proud. I watched her lose control. And I watched her plow headfirst into a tree at the side of the run."

He closed his eyes. Sucked in a deep breath. Blinked back the moisture obscuring his vision.

"I couldn't even go to her." His words came out in a broken whisper. "I had to ride the lift all the way to the top while the life seeped out of her as she lay on the cold snow." He swallowed, struggling to regain control. "She was pronounced dead of massive head injuries six hours later without ever regaining consciousness."

Silence fell in the room, broken only by the sound of his harsh breathing. He'd had a lot of moments over the past four years when he'd felt lost. Abandoned. Empty. But all at once, the acute loneliness overwhelmed him, crushing in its intensity. He felt his world spinning out of control again, just as it had when the ER doctor had told him Jen was gone.

And then, a gentle, steadying hand came to rest on his arm. As its comforting warmth seeped through his dress shirt, the world settled back onto its axis.

"I'm so sorry, Jake."

At Liz's emotion-choked words, he swallowed past the lump in his throat and slowly turned.

Her gaze met his, her green irises soft with compassion as she let her hand slip away. He was grateful she didn't try to condone what he'd done, or justify it. She'd simply listened, and accepted, and understood. That was freeing in ways he hadn't expected.

Would it be the same if he laid it before God?

The unexpected notion took him off guard.

"Thank you for sharing your story, Jake. And for reminding me how easy it is to get so caught up in our own traumas that we forget others have suffered too."

"You've had more than your fair share of tribulations."

The corners of her lips lifted almost imperceptibly. "Tribulation. Now there's a biblical word."

"My thoughts weren't very Christian when I said it." His lips settled into a grim line.

"Don't blame God for all the bad things that happen, Jake."

"Who else is there to blame?" Except himself, in Jen's case.

"You make it sound as if God sits in his heavens casting out random lightning bolts to throw people's lives into turmoil."

He folded his arms across his chest. "It feels that way a lot of the time."

"Bad things happen because human nature is flawed and we have free will."

"What about natural disasters? Why doesn't he stop those from happening?"

"I don't know the answer to that. But I trust he does. A key component of faith is accepting without understanding."

He knew that. He'd been raised in a Christian household. And he'd bought into it. Until *he'd* been asked to accept something he hadn't understood.

"My faith has allowed me to accept that suffering is part of the human experience, Jake. Even Jesus suffered, far more than we ever will. I believe God allows suffering not to punish us but to bring about greater good. If I help someone who is hurting, they may see God's love in my support—and I may learn to see Jesus in them." Liz's earnest eyes sought his. "Why don't you take your sister up on her offer? Go with her to services. Maybe you'll find more answers there than you expect."

"I might think about it." It would get Alison off his back, if nothing else. About that, anyway. "I did have some other news to share with you, before we got sidetracked."

This time she seemed to accept that the subject of his faith was closed.

"You want to sit again?" She motioned to the couch.

"No. This will only take a minute. And I'm already late relieving one of the guys in the CP." He told her about the hairs that had been identified by the lab—and their conclusion that the killer owned a cat.

She shrugged. "I don't see how that helps much. Millions of people own cats."

"True. But every piece of evidence we find is part of a puzzle. Gather enough of them, a picture starts to emerge."

"Do you have any other pieces?"

"Not yet. But the FBI is giving this its top priority. And your case review may offer us some other leads."

"What about me going back to work?"

He understood her desire to get back into her routine. To restore some normalcy to her life. But he also knew they needed her to focus on her own case. "Our strong preference is that you give the review your full attention, Liz. At least until you get through the past five years of cases. Why don't you see where you are by Sunday?"

"I know I can get through five years' worth by the end of the weekend."

He narrowed his eyes. "Are you building in any sleep time?"

A soft flush colored her cheeks. "Some. Would you consider half days after that while I finish the rest? I have a full docket, Jake."

He wasn't certain how Mark would feel about that compromise, but he could see how much it meant to her. And staying cooped up here day after day couldn't be healthy. "Okay. We'll plan on that. Subject to change, depending on developments."

A grateful smile was his reward. "Thanks."

"Do you need anything before I go?"

She cast a glance at the dining area, chock full of boxes and stacks of files all tapped into neat, precise piles, and wrinkled her nose. "A reprieve?"

"Sorry." He flashed her a grin. "I can't make a ruling on that. It's not in my jurisdiction."

"Cute."

The saucy comeback and quick grin offered Jake a tantalizing taste of Liz's more playful side. And left him hungry for more.

"Are you hungry?"

Jolted by the timing of her question, he stared at her. "What?"

Tipping her head, she gave him a puzzled look. "I asked if you were hungry. I've got a few cannoli left that are about to expire."

She was talking about cannoli.

Get a grip, Taylor.

"Sure. The guys will appreciate them."

"Hold on a sec."

While she disappeared into the kitchen, he retrieved his discarded jacket and draped it over his arm. It was still way too hot in here.

"Enjoy." She came up behind him and held out a plastic-wrapped plate.

Taking the offering, he followed her to the door. She checked the peephole, flipped the lock, and pulled it open.

"Call if you need anything." He paused on the threshold.

"I will." She rubbed her arms, and he saw a tiny ripple shudder through her.

"Cold?"

"A little. I need to adjust the thermostat."

He could think of another, more appealing way to warm her up.

Get out of here, Taylor.

Backing into the hall, he lifted the plate of cannoli. "Thanks again."

A flicker of some emotion he couldn't identify altered her features ever so slightly. "No problem."

Before he could decipher her expression, she shut the door. The lock clicked into place.

Turning, he found Spence watching him from the CP, one shoulder propped against the doorframe, a smirk on his face. He had no trouble deciphering *that* expression.

"I was just about to come looking for you. Dan's chomping at the bit to go home. He's technically been off duty for"—Spence angled his wrist—"two hours."

"Sorry. I got hung up." When Spence didn't move out of his path, Jake sent him a wary look. "I thought you said Dan wanted to leave?"

"He does. But *I* want to know what gives with you and the judge."

Doing his best to keep the heat inching up his neck from edging above his collar, Jake tried for nonchalance. "What are you talking about?"

"Give me some credit. I'm a trained observer of human nature. And I've been observing some pretty interesting dynamics between you two."

The heat crept higher. "I told you last week. She was married to my best friend."

"Yeah. But you said you'd only met her twice. That's not computing with the intensity my radar's picking up."

"Maybe your radar's defective."

"Nope. Don't think so. Maybe yours is, though, if you're not tuning into the vibes."

"Here, feed your sweet tooth." Annoyed, he shoved the plate of cannoli at the other marshal.

Pushing off from the doorframe, Spence took it, grinning. "Don't mind if I do. Seeing as how you've already fed yours." With a wink, he disappeared inside the CP.

For a full minute, Jake stayed where he was. He'd only been working with Spence for a week, but already the two had clicked, anticipating each other's thoughts and developing the kind of easy banter that made the long hours of a protection detail endurable. He liked Spence. The man was smart, skilled, professional, and insightful.

Jake respected all those qualities. Appreciated them.

But truth be told, he could do with a little less of Spence's insight when it came to his relationship with Liz.

Because he'd rather figure out what was going on between the two of them before his wisecracking counterpart did.

And there *was* something going on.

Score one for Spence.

12

Setting aside the case file she'd spent the past few minutes reviewing, Liz rubbed her bleary eyes and glanced at her watch: 5:30.

A shaft of pain seared through her.

Last Friday at this hour, she'd been wrapping things up at the courthouse, looking forward to a spaghetti dinner and long gab session with her sister. Clueless about the nightmare that lay ahead.

Everything that had transpired in the past week felt surreal. As if any second she'd awaken to find it had been just a bad dream.

Only it was all too real.

A film of moisture blurred her vision and she rose abruptly, determined not to succumb to tears again. She was tired of crying. She felt as if she'd done nothing but shed tears during the quiet, lonely hours she'd spent sequestered in this condo.

Arching her back, she rotated her neck, trying to get the kinks out as she walked toward the kitchen. She'd been culling through her files since late yesterday morning, stopping only to stretch out on the bed for a few fitful hours of sleep last night and to grab a piece of fruit or a bowl of dry cereal when her stomach protested her neglect. Tonight she needed something heartier. Perhaps one of the dinners that had been stocked in the freezer when she'd arrived.

She pulled out the first one her hand touched and read the label. Roasted chicken breast, rice pilaf, broccoli. That would do. After sliding it into the microwave, she leaned back against the counter, trying not to be disheartened as she surveyed the dining room table through the pass-through between the granite countertop and the hanging kitchen cabinets.

It was tough to keep her spirits up, though. She was getting nowhere with her search. Mark's comment that there was a loser in every case and that not everyone was a good loser was true. Meaning any loser in any case she'd tried could have decided he or she wanted revenge. How could she know who might have a penchant for violence? Appearances were often deceptive. The most normal-looking person could have a substance abuse problem. Or anger issues. Or be depressed. A pillar of the community could be a wife beater. Or a killer.

With that in mind, she'd amassed a towering stack of files to give to the FBI. Far too many. In the end, she'd culled it back dramatically, deciding to pass on only those cases in which someone had left a strong negative impression.

Using that criterion, after reviewing almost two years worth of cases, she'd earmarked just three for further investigation. A bank robbery case she'd heard during her first month on the federal bench, plus a domestic violence case and a drug case from her days on the state circuit court. She'd handed those over to Mark earlier this afternoon, when he and Jake had come by.

At the thought of the tall, dark-haired marshal, her pulse lost its steady cadence and her hand stilled as she pulled out the cutlery drawer. Since their tête-à-tête yesterday morning, she'd felt off balance. Especially after that charged moment at the door, when she'd half expected him to put down the plate of cannoli and pull her into his arms.

Had wanted him to pull her into his arms.

In fact—though it shocked her to admit it—she wouldn't even have objected if he'd kissed her.

The high-pitched beep of the microwave shattered the stillness like a red alert, and she jumped at the raucous intrusion.

Shutting the drawer with her hip, she removed her dinner and slid onto a stool at the counter. The red-alert analogy was apt, and she ought to heed it. Thinking about Jake in romantic terms wasn't wise. After the emotional roller coaster of the past week, she shouldn't trust anything she was feeling right now. She was too vulnerable. Too prone to overreact to attention—and perhaps misinterpret it.

Like the glint of appreciation in his eyes when she'd appeared at the door in her workout attire. It probably hadn't meant a thing. She had a decent body. And men noticed that kind of stuff. A look of admiration was par for the course, indicating nothing more than a spurt of testosterone.

The wise thing to do in this situation was let things settle for a while.

Yet as she speared a bite of chicken with her fork, the steam rising from the nuked meal in front of her reminded her of how she'd felt yesterday at Jake's departure. The shiver that had run through her when his brown eyes had locked on hers, then delved deep into her soul, hadn't had a thing to do with the temperature in the room, despite the excuse she'd given him. It had been a shiver of excitement.

And the man himself had been the cause.

The aroma wafting up from her meal set off a rumble in her stomach, and she popped the piece of chicken in her mouth—promptly burning her tongue. Opening her mouth again, she fanned it and groped for her water. Took a mouthful. Swished.

And as the pain subsided, she decided to take the incident as a warning: use caution when sampling anything hot—or you could get burned.

Fifteen minutes later, when her doorbell rang, Liz was still dawdling over her dinner. No way did she intend to put another blister on her tongue. Caution had become her operative word.

Setting down her fork, she slipped off the stool and headed toward the door. Jake stood on the other side of the peephole, broad shoulders front and center, white shirt crisp beneath his dark suit. And though her new operative word was still echoing in her mind, she couldn't stop the little rush of pleasure that warmed her as she twisted the knob.

"Hi." She forced her lips into a shaky smile. "Would you like to come in, or are you heading out for the day?"

"Heading out. I promised to meet Cole for dinner. I just wanted to say good night and see how you were doing with the case review."

She made a face. "It's slow going. And I'm not seeing many red flags, even though it's very possible there's a sleeper I'm missing in one of these cases." Leaning against the doorframe, she slid her hands into the pockets of her jeans. "To be honest, it feels like an exercise in futility."

"Hang in there. The odds are our killer is imbedded somewhere in one of your cases. Unless you've got some enemies you haven't told us about."

"No. I can't think of anyone I've ever met who disliked me enough to want me dead."

"Have you been at it all day?" He hooked a thumb toward the dining room.

"Yes. Except for when you and Mark stopped by earlier."

"Did you eat dinner?"

"Finishing up now. Tonight's special was nuked rubber chicken with mystery sauce." She smiled.

Instead of reciprocating, he frowned. "Not much of a dinner. We can send out for food, if you'd rather."

"That's okay. I haven't been that hungry, anyway." The

ring of her cell phone sounded from the living room, and she pulled the door wide. “Do you mind if I grab that?”

“No. Go ahead.” He stepped inside and closed the door behind him.

Liz dashed for the phone, delighted to discover Delores on the other end.

“I’m not interrupting anything, am I, my dear?”

“Not at all.” Liz motioned Jake into the living room. “How are you?”

“We’re fine. But the real question is, how are you? Harold and I haven’t been able to get you off our mind.”

“I’m doing okay. The marshals are taking good care of me.” She aimed a smile at Jake and mouthed “Delores Moretti.”

“I’m sure they are. But it’s not like having friends around. So Harold and I were wondering if you might like some visitors. We could stop by tomorrow while we’re out and about doing errands. Assuming you can tell us where you are, that is.”

“That would be lovely. Let me ask. One of the marshals is standing here as we speak.” She pressed the mute button and gave Jake a recap of the conversation. “Would that be okay?”

“I don’t see why not. We’ll need to do a security clearance on them, but I don’t expect there will be any problem. Can you let her know first thing in the morning?”

“That should be fine.” Liz pressed the mute button again to disengage the feature. “Delores? I think that will work. They need to run some security checks, though. Can I call you first thing tomorrow morning?”

“Of course. Security, hmm? Do you think the parking ticket I got two years ago will count against me?”

At the woman’s serious tone, Liz smiled and angled toward Jake. “I’m sure a parking violation won’t be an issue, Delores.” Jake’s lips hitched into a one-sided grin. “I’ll get back to you, okay?”

“Sounds good. You take care.”

As Liz rang off, Jake started toward the door. "I'll stop by the CP before I leave and get the security clearance started."

She trailed behind. "Are you off this weekend?"

"Yes. But I'll be by a time or two. And you can always call me on my BlackBerry. We'll regroup on your court schedule Sunday."

"Okay. Thanks."

"No problem. I'll see you sometime tomorrow. Good night."

"Good night."

She closed the door. Locked it. Watched through the peephole until he disappeared.

Back to work.

But as she dumped the remains of her dinner in the garbage disposal and returned to the dining room, she was suddenly grateful for the task that would keep her grief, her loneliness—and thoughts of Jake—at bay.

As the sun peeked over the horizon on Saturday, Martin lifted his coffee from the cup holder next to the driver's seat and took a sip, inspecting the apartment building in the Central West End where Neil Clark lived. It was amazing how much you could find out by simply hanging around. Waiting. Watching. That was how he'd gathered the information he'd needed to devise his first plan to rid the world of Judge Elizabeth Michaels.

Even though it hadn't succeeded, the plan had been good. The outcome wasn't due to faulty thinking or planning. He was always thorough and meticulous. That was why he'd excelled at his job. Why his bosses had put him on the space shuttle assembly work. And the Apache helicopter project. And the Harrier contract. They knew they could count on Martin Reynolds to get the job done right.

Just as he intended to get this job done right.

The front door of the apartment opened and Neil emerged,

his rollerblades already on. The kid looked like he was about fifteen, with that shock of hair falling into his face and his gangly adolescent build. And he was as predictable as the bells that tolled each hour at the church on the corner of Martin's street. Every Saturday morning at 7:00, Neil went rollerblading. Then he headed to the courthouse for a few hours, always dressed in jeans and a T-shirt, lugging a bulky satchel.

Watching the kid take off down the street toward Forest Park, Martin eased his car away from the curb and followed him. When he was first formulating his plan, he'd thought there might be a way to use Neil to gain access to the judge. After seeing the two of them come out of the courthouse together, he'd trailed them on foot when they'd walked down the street to a crowded sandwich shop. The lunch rush had made it easy to get close enough to eavesdrop without being noticed. From their conversation, he'd figured out the kid worked for her as a clerk.

But he hadn't ended up needing Neil. It had been easy to follow the judge home, and easier still to do a little reconnaissance in her secluded backyard. One visit had told him the basement window would provide easy access to the house under the cover of darkness. And one look through the laundry room window had given him a good view of the keypad for her home security system. It was a standard variety. The kind you turned on at night and when you left the house. He'd dealt with enough sophisticated security systems at his old job, with all the classified stuff going on there, to recognize a basic model.

He'd also spent a couple of weeks sitting outside her house, studying her habits. What time she left in the morning, what time she returned, when she tended to run errands, who she talked to. She seemed especially chummy with her neighbors across the street—Delores and Harold Moretti.

No, there had been nothing wrong with his plan. He'd gotten in and out clean, and the police had no clue who the perpetrator was.

His only mistake had been killing the wrong woman.

Next time, there would be no mistake.

He turned into the park, following Neil at a safe distance. It wasn't going to be as easy on the second try, though. The judge wasn't in her house anymore. She was sequestered in a high-rise condo not far from the courthouse, surrounded by marshals. At least he was pretty sure that's where she was, after following Neil there a couple of days ago from the courthouse and watching him haul half a dozen boxes in from his car. Martin had figured she'd eventually want some stuff from her office, and the wet-behind-the-ears clerk had seemed the most likely person to be tapped as a delivery boy. So he'd been sticking like glue.

And it had paid off.

He was hoping the kid would make another trip there, just to confirm the judge's location.

An hour and a half later, as he sat behind the wheel, killing time across from the courthouse parking garage by reading the Saturday paper, he hit pay dirt. The kid's car pulled out less than fifteen minutes after he'd arrived, and instead of moving west, toward his apartment, it headed south. Toward the judge's condo.

Just as he'd done on his last visit, he parked in front. Hauled a box out of his trunk. Headed for the door.

Ten minutes later, he exited, returned to his car, and pulled away from the building.

Martin tapped the wheel, debating his next move. He didn't see any reason to follow the clerk again. The kid had served his purpose. His two trips to the condo were pretty convincing proof the judge was inside.

But why not stick around here for a while? He'd learned a lot by doing that the first time around, at the judge's house. It was possible he'd pick up some more useful information. And you could never have enough information in the planning stage.

Especially when the stakes were this high.

Liz pulled the next file toward her and took a swig of cooling coffee. She'd worked late last night after Jake had left, tossed for a few hours in bed, and gotten up at the crack of dawn to dive back in, determined to get through five years' worth of cases this weekend—plus the box of files Neil had just delivered, after she'd realized one was missing and called him. Not the way she'd choose to spend a Saturday, but she wanted to finish this job as soon as possible.

Her stomach grumbled in protest at the steady infusion of coffee, and she set her mug aside. She'd stop after this file and grab a bagel. Or maybe dig out one of the breakfast sandwiches stashed in the freezer. She was having difficulty focusing this morning—a rare problem for her. No doubt due to a diet that would make a nutritionist cringe. Not to mention her bone-deep fatigue.

Propping her head in her hand, Liz read the label on the file. Martin Reynolds v. Dr. John Voss, St. Gregory Hospital. Off the top of her head, the case rang no bells, but a quick scan of her ruling brought it all back.

The plaintiff had sued an emergency room doctor and the hospital where he worked after his wife's acute appendicitis was misdiagnosed as colitis. She'd died three days later.

Liz did a closer read, refreshing her memory.

Martin Reynolds and his wife, Helen, had been visiting her sister near Eldon when Helen had become ill after eating some popcorn. Her symptoms had worsened, and he'd driven her to a hospital in Jefferson City. After taking her history, which included a long-term colitis condition—and doing some tests that indicated she was, indeed, suffering from an attack of colitis—the ER physician had released her with instructions to rest, ingest only a clear liquid diet for twenty-four hours, and take an over-the-counter pain medication. She had also been directed to seek follow-up care if she didn't show rapid improvement.

Eight hours later, after all of her symptoms had worsened considerably, Reynolds and his wife had returned to the ER. A CT scan was done. The diagnosis was changed to both colitis and acute appendicitis. Before she could be rushed into surgery, her appendix ruptured. Peritonitis set in, followed by sepsis. That, in turn, had led to shock, multiple organ failure, and death. Several months later, Reynolds had filed a malpractice suit.

As Liz perused the material, the details of the case came back to her. Including the plaintiff's raw grief. It had been apparent in his eyes—along with anger and frustration. She'd understood his feelings. Sympathized, even. Yet the so-called expert hired by Reynolds's attorney had admitted on cross-examination that he lacked the qualifications to testify on the standard of care for emergency room doctors. Since the plaintiff had failed to meet the burden of proof, the trial had been over before the defendant had even submitted his evidence. She'd had no choice but to direct a verdict in favor of the doctor. The appellate court had upheld her ruling.

She'd tried to do her best by Reynolds, though, within the confines of the law. When the doctor's attorney had filed a pretrial motion to disqualify the plaintiff's expert for lacking requisite qualifications, she'd thought the motion had merit. But she'd denied it, pending the so-called expert's testimony at trial. However, she'd advised Reynolds's attorney that his expert might lack the qualifications to testify and to consider dismissing and refiling, which would have given him an opportunity to name a properly qualified expert. He'd refused.

Closing the file, Liz tapped her finger against the edge of the folder. She'd dealt with several other malpractice cases during her state court days. Most had been well presented. This one hadn't. There were a lot of marginal lawyers out there, and Martin Reynolds had unfortunately hired one of them—dooming his case.

Liz had felt bad about the outcome. But thanks to her dad, she'd learned early on not to dwell on every case. The emotional toll was too high. He had been the most compassionate man she'd ever met, and his passion for justice had compelled him to work hard on behalf of every one of his clients, paying or pro bono. Yet he'd known how to walk away, leave it behind when he shut his office door. She'd tried hard to emulate his example.

Hefting the file in her hand, she debated which FBI pile to put it in—yes, no, maybe. The latter pile was for the second-round cases—the ones she'd pass on to the FBI if the first group of cases didn't yield any leads.

It wasn't a yes, she decided. There was nothing specific about this case that caused any red flags to pop up. Still, there had been something vaguely disturbing about Martin Reynolds. Nothing she could pinpoint. No threats. No outbursts in her presence. No angry gestures. But his scathing, silent scrutiny had been unnerving.

Her cell phone rang, and she put the file halfway between the no and the maybe pile. She'd let it sit for a while and come back to it later.

Rising, she stretched, then walked to the coffee table and picked up the phone.

"Sorry for the early call." Jake's appealing baritone voice sent a tingle along her nerve endings. "Did I wake you?"

"No." She checked her watch. "I've been up for several hours. Reading case files."

"You're determined to finish by tomorrow night, aren't you?"

"That's my plan."

"Would you consider taking an hour or two off tonight?"

She dropped onto the edge of the couch, intrigued. "I might. What did you have in mind?"

"A Taylor-made pizza party."

She smiled. "Am I picking up a play on words?"

A soft chuckle came over the line. "Good catch. Alison and Cole and I had planned to get together tonight at her house, but pizza's portable. And I think you'd like Alison."

She tried not to take the thoughtful gesture too personally. Jake's job required him to keep her safe. And comfortable. That could be at least part of the motivation for his suggestion.

Nevertheless, the idea was appealing. Very appealing.

"I hate to intrude on a family get-together. Are you sure they won't mind?"

"They're all for it. I asked before I called. Any special requests on the pizza?"

"I like everything. Except olives."

"Already noted. I remember from the last time. Is 7:00 okay?"

"Great. Any word on clearance for the Morettis?"

"That's also why I called. They're good to go."

"I didn't think there would be any problem. Delores's biggest transgression is making fattening desserts. Other than that parking citation, of course."

His soft chuckle came over the line. "Enjoy your visit. And I'll see you tonight."

As they said their good-byes, Liz tapped the end button, headed for the kitchen, and slid a ham and egg biscuit into the microwave. She'd never been the kind of person who needed a lot of social interaction. But this week had been far too quiet. And lonely. She was ready for some conversation that didn't revolve around solving a murder and finding a killer who might, at this very minute, be plotting a second attempt.

Seeing the Morettis would be a good diversion. And she expected the Taylors would provide plenty of distraction tonight too. Cole had seemed like a nice guy, and from everything Jake had told her about Alison, she had a feeling the two of them would click.

Then there was Jake himself. Always a big distraction.

The microwave pinged—in unison with her heart.

No question about it. She was definitely looking forward to tonight.

His patience had been rewarded.

Easing a little lower behind the wheel, Martin watched as the Morettis walked up the sidewalk toward the condo where Neil had delivered the box three hours earlier. The wife, wearing a raincoat, was carrying a large metal tin that looked as if it might contain cookies. The husband wore a short jacket and a baseball cap. They, too, pushed through the glass doors into the lobby.

That was all the proof he needed.

The judge was here.

And she had regular visitors.

A surge of adrenaline bumped up his pulse as an idea began to percolate in his mind. An idea that had a lot of potential.

Putting the car in gear, Martin pulled back into traffic, anxious to get home and think through the details.

It was time to finalize Plan B.

"I can't eat another bite." Alison groaned and pushed her plate away.

"About time. I was beginning to think we'd have to order another pizza." Jake helped himself to one of the three remaining slices in the box on the table, which Liz had cleared of files for the occasion.

"A word of warning, brother. If you go out with Alison for dinner, order Dutch. Otherwise, your stomach may be full but there'll be a hole in your wallet." Cole grinned at his sister and claimed another slice of pizza too.

"Brothers!" Alison gave Liz a pained look and picked up her soda. "Good thing you're here, or they'd *really* beat me up."

Liz chuckled and leaned toward the box, her hand hovering over the last piece. "Anyone want this?"

"It's all yours," Jake answered on behalf of his siblings. He'd hoped a relaxed evening of food and conversation would ease some of the strain in her features—and persuade her to eat a real meal—and he was pleased on both counts. She hadn't added much to the conversation at first, but she'd smiled a lot, even laughed a little.

As the evening had progressed, however, she'd joined more in the banter. Now, with the meal winding down, she was chatting with Alison as if they'd known each other for years, her eyes alive for the first time since he'd stepped into the ER eight days ago and found her reeling from shock, her sister's blood staining her fingers.

Mission accomplished.

"Why not? Jake's going."

At Alison's mention of his name, he pulled himself back to the discussion. "Going where?"

"To church. Cole's still resisting, by the way."

"I'm not resisting. I'm busy." Cole turned his attention to his older brother. "How on earth did Alison manage to strong-arm you into going back?"

"You're going to church with Alison?" Liz gave him a surprised—but pleased—look.

Jake shrugged, hoping the flush warming his neck stayed there. "It was time."

"Since when?" Cole cocked his head and appraised him, then shifted his attention to Liz. "Are you a churchgoer, Liz?"

His brother's tone might be innocent, but the speculative gleam in his eyes wasn't. Jake shot him a silent warning.

"Yes. When I'm not sequestered."

"Ah." A smug smile settled over Cole's lips. "I'm beginning to see the light." He finished off his last bite of pizza. "You two have been spending a lot of time together, haven't you?"

Jake was about to growl a response when Alison took care of the problem by kicking Cole under the table.

"Ow!" Cole leaned down and rubbed his shin, frowning at Alison. "What was that for?"

"Figure it out."

"Thanks." Jake lifted his soda can toward his sister.

"My pleasure." Alison shook her head at Liz. "Like I said, brothers. But whatever you did to make Jake reconsider church attendance, my hat's off to you." She lifted her own soda in her hostess's direction.

Liz's gaze connected with his, and Jake read the apology in her eyes. He couldn't very well follow his impulse and take her hand to assure her he didn't mind the ribbing from his siblings. He settled for a wink instead.

To his surprise, a soft, becoming flush spread over her cheeks before she dipped her head to play with the edge of her napkin. It was a shy, eminently charming side of her he'd never seen. And it captivated him.

When the silence lengthened, Jake pulled his gaze away from Liz and glanced at his siblings. Alison was grinning at him. Cole had a knowing smirk on his face.

A change of subject was in order.

"Who's ready for dessert?"

Alison's eyes widened. "You've got to be kidding! After all that pizza?"

"I'm game." Cole folded his arms across his chest. "What are we having?"

"How about Ted Drewes?"

"Bring it on," Cole declared.

"Okay, okay. I'll find room somewhere," Alison capitulated.

Liz furrowed her brow. "What's Ted Drewes?"

"Just the world's best frozen custard. He sells most of it out of a little stand in the city. It's a St. Louis landmark," Alison offered.

"That sounds great. I can also contribute homemade Italian wedding cookies, delivered earlier today by my neighbor."

"The killer cannoli lady?" Alison asked.

"Yes."

She groaned again. "Then I know they'll be great. Watch out, hips!"

"You can afford to gain some weight." Sliding back his chair, Jake rose before she could respond. "I stashed the Ted Drewes in the freezer in the CP next door. Give me two minutes."

He was back in less, depositing a bag on the table and withdrawing four large cardboard cups. "Take your pick. I got strawberry and chocolate chip. Liz?"

"Strawberry."

"Good choice." He handed it over as his siblings divvied up the rest.

"Wow." Liz's eyes flew open at her first bite. "This is amazing. You can ply me with Ted Drewes anytime."

"I'll remember that." Jake gave her another wink, which elicited a second endearing blush.

As they enjoyed the custard and cookies, Alison shared a charming story about a little boy she'd placed in a foster home that day. Jake had never been able to fathom how his softhearted sister managed to remain so upbeat when her job with the Children's Division of the Department of Social Services brought her into contact with abused and neglected youngsters every day. But he admired her for her commitment to giving those kids a better life.

Liz added a few humorous comments about the Morettis' visit and their reaction to being swept by a security wand. When it had beeped loudly over Delores's tin of cookies, she'd been happy to provide samples to the marshals on duty as proof her offering was innocuous.

"Well, as much fun as this has been, I have to be up early for church." Alison scraped the sides of her cup for the last dregs of her custard, licked the spoon, and pointed it at Jake. "So do you."

"I wish I could join you." Liz dug deep for the last bite of her treat too.

"We can arrange for you to attend services if you want us to," Jake offered.

She dropped her spoon into her empty cup and regarded him. "I have to believe that would be a major security headache for you."

"We've handled more complicated assignments."

"I don't doubt that. But I also don't see any reason to make your job more difficult than it already is. I'm sure God will understand if I communicate with him from a different location for a few Sundays."

"I appreciate the consideration. But if you change your mind, let me know." He rose to collect the empty cups, noting with satisfaction that Liz had finished the whole thing. As far as he knew, this was the first good meal she'd had in more than a week.

As he disappeared into the kitchen, Alison and Cole also stood. By the time he rejoined them, Alison had collected her purse and Liz was walking them to the door.

After a flurry of good-byes, Jake found himself alone with Liz in the foyer. "I should be going too."

She nodded and gripped the edge of the door. "Thanks for tonight. I had a good time . . . despite the guilt."

At her tacked-on caveat, he frowned. "What guilt?"

Shrugging, she examined the area rug at her feet and dropped her voice. "After everything that's happened in the past week, it seems wrong somehow to laugh or feel happy."

Jake's throat tightened with empathy. "I felt the same way after Jen died."

She lifted her head, searching his face. "Do you still?"

"Sometimes." He swallowed and shoved his hands in his pockets. "But I try to remember how much she loved life. How she believed every day was a gift to be cherished and enjoyed. And how she never lost hope, even when things weren't going well. Living forever in the shadow of grief wouldn't honor her memory."

"She sounds like Steph. And I admire your take on how to approach life without her."

"If you want my opinion, I think it's okay for you to take whatever moments of happiness you can find right now, Liz." His words came out tender. Husky. Revealing more than he'd intended to.

Several beats of silence ticked by. When at last she spoke, her soft comment surprised him. "You're a good man, Jake Taylor."

The candid statement, plus the sudden longing in her eyes, stirred him in a way nothing had for a very long while. And not for the first time, he was tempted to pull her close and wrap her in a comforting hug. But he was within sight of the surveillance cameras that were trained on her doorway and being monitored in the CP as they spoke. Plus, he was determined to keep their relationship strictly professional until this assignment ended.

That didn't mean he couldn't pass on a clue about his feelings, though.

"Liz . . . when this is over . . . I don't want to lose touch with you. How would you feel about continuing to see me in a nonprofessional capacity?"

Her soft blush and the graceful lift of her lips gave him her answer before she spoke. "I'd like that, Jake."

He smiled, relishing the flicker of warmth that thawed a long-cold place in his heart. "Count on it, then." Keeping his hands in his pockets through sheer force of will, he took a step back. "I'll talk to you tomorrow. Sleep well."

"I think I might tonight."

As she shut the door with a quiet click and a final smile, he hoped their exchange did help her sleep better. But until they caught the killer who wanted her dead, Jake knew that for him, peaceful slumber would remain elusive.

13

When a knock sounded on her door at 6:30 Sunday night, Liz was just topping off the FBI *no* pile with the final file from her review of five years' worth of cases.

Assuming her caller was Jake come to discuss plans for tomorrow, she decided the timing of her wrap-up was perfect.

A peek through the peephole confirmed her visitor was, indeed, the tall, dark-haired marshal, and she flipped the dead bolt to usher him in.

He smiled as he moved past her. "Did you think I forgot about you?"

A whiff of his rugged aftershave wafted her way, kicking her pulse up a notch. "No. You said you'd be by. And you strike me as a man of your word."

"Always." He shot her a steady look, then strolled toward the dining room and perused the tidy stacks on the table. "Did you meet your goal?"

"Just. Literally. You have impeccable timing."

His mouth twitched into a wry grin. "Not according to Alison. Whenever I call I seem to catch her in the middle of drying her hair or chasing her new puppy or on her way out the door. So did you come up with any more files for Mark?"

"Six." She motioned toward the shortest stack.

"He'll want to walk through them with you, like he did with the first batch. First thing in the morning is my guess, but I'll confirm that later tonight. Want to talk about your schedule for this week?"

"Sure. I was about to reward myself with some of Delores's cookies. Would you like a few?"

He grimaced and patted what she suspected were killer abs. "If I keep eating her goodies, I'll have to double the length of my morning workout. But okay . . . if you're twisting my arm."

She grinned. "How about some coffee too?"

"Sounds good. I'll get that while you focus on the cookies."

Following her to the kitchen, he withdrew two mugs and filled them from the coffeemaker as she popped the lid off the cookie tin. Balancing them in his hands, he gave the table a dubious survey through the pass-through between the counter and the hanging cabinets. "I don't think your dining room can accommodate both cookies and case files."

She peeked through the pass-through herself. Almost the entire glass surface of the table was covered with regimented rows of files.

"Let's eat in here, if that's okay."

"Fine by me." He set the mugs on the granite counter and straddled a stool. "This is what I do at my apartment—the few times I've eaten there since moving back, anyway."

"It hasn't exactly been a peaceful homecoming, has it?" She claimed the stool beside him.

He shrugged. "That's the nature of my job. Never a dull moment." Taking a sip of coffee, he examined the dining room table through the pass-through. "Looks like you've got a job ahead of you just putting things back in order."

"Believe it or not, the piles make sense to me. It won't take long."

He motioned toward a small, neat stack of files set apart on one corner. "What are those?"

"Round two. If the FBI doesn't unearth any leads from

the first batch I gave them, these are the next cases I plan to turn over. Do you know if they found anything interesting in round one?"

"Nothing so far."

She bit into the rich, crumbly cookie filled with ground almonds, enjoying the spurt of sweetness as the powdered sugar coating melted on her tongue. "I'm not surprised. To be honest, I've been pulling files based on gut feel. There's no rational reason to single any of them out."

"Don't discount your gut. It's saved my hide on more than one occasion."

Although she'd have liked him to expand on that intriguing comment, he wrapped his hands around his mug and changed the subject before she could formulate a question.

"Okay, let's talk about this week. What's your ideal schedule?"

She rested an elbow on the counter, propped her chin in her palm, and gave a wistful sigh. "Fly to Bermuda, throw on a bathing suit, and spend every waking hour soaking up rays on a pink-sand beach surrounded by tropical flowers and blue ocean."

The flicker of a smile teased the corners of his mouth. "You like Bermuda?"

"Never been there. But I like what I've heard about it. Maybe someday." She took a sip of coffee, folded her hands on the counter, and got back to business. "In the meantime, I plan to spend tomorrow morning putting away the files I've reviewed and talking to Mark about the new ones I pulled. In the afternoon, I'd like to go to the courthouse and meet with Walter Shapiro, the chief judge. We've been staying in touch by phone, but I need to sit down with him and work out a reasonable schedule that will allow me to keep on top of things at my job while I continue my case review for the FBI. How does that sound?"

"Manageable. I knew you wanted to get back to work, so I've set security protocols in motion for your return."

"Such as?"

"You'll be stuck with me and Spence in the courthouse, for one thing. We'll be outside your chambers, and we'll accompany you to your courtroom. We'll also be present during any proceedings you preside over there. When traveling back and forth between here and there, Spence and I will be in the car with you, and we'll have follow and lead vehicles, like we did for the trip to KC. We'll also keep two marshals at the command post 24/7."

Frowning, she broke a cookie in half and poked at it with a manicured, crimson nail. "The level of security is amazing. And more than a little unsettling."

"You don't need to worry about your safety, Liz. We're very good at what we do."

She shook her head. "That's not what I mean. I absolutely trust you to protect me. I just mean the whole notion that someone might be out there planning another attack freaks me out."

"If he or she is doing that, we intend to find them long before they have a chance to carry it out."

"Cat hair doesn't give you much to work with."

"We also have the files you earmarked for further investigation."

"I'm not hopeful they're going to be a lot of help." She set the cookie aside and gathered the crumbs into a neat pile with her finger.

"Hey."

At Jake's soft summons, she looked up. His steady gaze was confident and reassuring as it captured hers.

"I know this is hard for you. But it will be over soon. Mark Sanders is one of the FBI's finest, and he's giving this investigation top priority. Plus, you've got the U.S. Marshals Service protecting you. Not to mention Delores Moretti supplying you with fantastic desserts. Hang in there, okay?" His expression softened, and he reached over to brush his fingertips against her cheek. "Powdered sugar."

Liz stopped breathing.

His fingers lingered on her skin far longer than necessary to deal with some errant powdered sugar, and she watched his Adam's apple bob. Saw a muscle in his jaw clench. Heard him suck in a sharp breath.

Knew he wanted to kiss her.

Knew, also, that he was struggling to maintain a professional demeanor despite the electricity zipping between them. She could see the conflict in the depths of his brown irises as duty and desire duked it out.

She remained motionless, neither encouraging nor discouraging. Leaving the decision to him, despite the fact her operative *caution* word was strobing across her mind.

In the end, his professionalism won the battle. In one fluid motion, he removed his hand, wiped it on a napkin, wadded the paper square into his fist, and dropped it on the counter. "I need to go."

Even as he made the hoarse comment, he was beating a retreat to the front door. She followed more slowly, pausing a few feet away when he stopped with one hand on the knob, his back to her. "I'll be on duty in the CP tomorrow. We can talk about the specifics of your trip to the courthouse then."

"Okay."

At her soft reply, he angled toward her. Noting the distance she'd left between them, he gave her a strained smile. "Don't worry. I'm too much of a pro to give in to my hormones. But I have to admit, this assignment is proving to be quite a test of my willpower."

She wrapped her arms around her middle. "If it's any consolation, I'm having the same problem."

The strain in his smile eased. "That's good to know. And it gives me an incentive to wrap this case up as soon as possible." He flipped the dead bolt. "Lock up, okay?"

Stepping into the hall, he pulled the door shut behind him. As usual, he waited to hear the lock flip into place before continuing down the hall. She watched through the peephole, craning her neck until he disappeared from sight.

Left alone, she wandered back to the kitchen to clean up the remnants of their snack. After wiping the counter clean, she rinsed their mugs and stacked them in the dishwasher.

But her mind wasn't on her task. It was thinking ahead, to the day she could resume her normal life.

Except somehow, now that Jake was in the picture, she had a feeling her definition of normal was about to change. For the better.

Clinging to that thought, she pressed her finger to the small pile of powdered sugar crumbs she'd gathered earlier, then popped it in her mouth to savor one last burst of sweetness. Because she had an uneasy feeling that before her life took an upswing, there were still some unpleasant days ahead.

From four houses away, hunkered down behind the wheel of his car, Martin watched Harold Moretti pull out of his driveway. The couple seemed to do everything together, except when Harold dropped Delores off after church every Sunday and went to the nearby park for a brisk hour-long walk. Nothing seemed to interfere with his solitary Sunday hour, even heavy rain. But today the man was running weekday errands alone.

That wasn't a problem. It might even work to his advantage.

Turning the key in the ignition, he released the brake and put the car in gear. Once Harold reached the stop sign at the end of the street, he followed. Now that his plan was beginning to jell, he didn't want to make any mistakes. Tip anyone off. The piece of information he needed today was important, and it required him to get up close and personal with Harold. But if he played it right, in the right location, he didn't think anyone would consider his behavior suspicious.

Harold's first stop was at a hair salon that featured discounts for seniors on Wednesday, according to a sign in the window. Martin admired the guy's frugality. But it wasn't a good spot to get the information he needed. Parking several spaces away in the crowded mall lot, he waited him out.

Forty-five minutes later, Harold emerged with his buzz cut whipped into shape at a bargain price, his gray hair standing at attention. Ex-military, no doubt. Lifting his digital camera, Martin zoomed in on Harold's face and snapped a photo. A quick assessment of the image told him it was good enough for his purposes. Setting the camera on the seat beside him, he put the car back in gear to continue tailing him.

Harold's next stop—Home Depot—was promising, and Martin's pulse accelerated.

Again, he parked down the row from Harold. Tugging his baseball cap low over his forehead, he followed the man into the store, moving closer, closer, closer until he was within speaking distance.

But he wasn't here today to talk to Harold.

He just needed to check his height.

The ideal opportunity presented itself when Harold headed for the plumbing fixtures. As the judge's neighbor conversed with a clerk, Martin eased in close, pretending to examine the workmanship on a cabinet. Across the aisle, in a display of vanity mirrors, he caught a reflection of the trio.

And got the answer he needed.

Edging away, he zigzagged through the aisles, toward the exit.

If everything else fell into place this easily, he should be ready to implement his plan soon.

And the world would find itself with one less terrocrat.

As the door to Liz's chambers opened on Friday evening and she appeared on the threshold, Jake broke off his conversation with Spence. Even though she claimed she'd only put in half days during her first week back on the job, they'd been long, packed, tiring half days. More like full days for most people. The smudges of fatigue beneath her eyes attested to that.

"Ready to go home?"

"Yes." She gave a weary nod.

"Give us ten minutes to get our people in place."

"No problem. I owe Delores a call, anyway."

As she pulled the door shut again, Spence raised an eyebrow. "The lady looks beat."

"Yeah." He pulled his BlackBerry off his belt and tapped in a few numbers. As he passed the word to the marshals on motorcade detail, he checked his watch: 7:30. Her departure time never varied more than a few minutes.

Liz, as he'd discovered this week, was a creature of habit. She liked having a schedule and she didn't like surprises. As a result, there was a definite pattern to her days. In the morning, she reviewed old case files at the condo. At noon, she came to the courthouse, where she spent her afternoon reading briefs, hearing oral arguments, and conferring with the chief judge and her clerks. Next week she planned to begin presiding over trials again.

He didn't know if she'd always had a penchant for leading an organized, planned life. But after all the turmoil she'd endured with Doug, after the trauma of Stephanie's murder, he could understand why she'd want an orderly, predictable existence.

From his standpoint as head of her protection detail, however, predictability was dangerous. That's why he varied their route to and from the courthouse each day. After finalizing tonight's travel plans with the driver in the lead vehicle, he slipped the phone back on his belt and glanced at Spence.

"Ready?"

"More than. It's been a long, boring week."

"I'll take boring over the alternative."

"Yeah?" Spence's tone was skeptical. "Then why did you join the SOG?"

As he fumbled for a response, Spence answered his own question.

"My guess is you like action and the adrenaline rush of danger except when a certain lovely judge is involved."

Scowling, Jake tried to think of a way to refute that conclusion. Nothing came to mind, leaving him with only one option.

He ignored Spence and rapped on the door.

A soft chuckle sounded behind him. In the short time they'd been working together, his colleague had managed to figure out almost as much about what made him tick as his sister and brother had. He hadn't been surprised when his siblings had picked up his interest in his charge. But it was annoying that Spence had too.

Liz opened the door, coat over her arm, briefcase in hand. Jake took the bulging satchel from her and passed it over to Spence. As she stepped into the hall, they flanked her and set a quick pace in the direction of the elevator.

"Which exit are we using tonight?" She looked up at him.

"Back service entrance."

"I'm too new here to know where that is." She started to put her coat on as they walked, but Jake stopped her with a touch on her arm. "It's seventy-eight degrees."

"Wow. Talk about Indian summer!"

"Enjoy it while it lasts," Spence chimed in. "Next week we could have snow. Ya gotta love St. Louis weather."

The elevator door opened seconds after Jake punched the button, and he ushered her in. He and Spence followed, standing in front of her as he entered the bypass code that would allow them to travel nonstop to the lower level.

"Delores wants to come by again on Sunday. Is that okay? I got the feeling she's planning to replenish my cannoli supply."

He smiled at her over his shoulder. "No objections from me."

"Me, either. As long as you save me some," Spence seconded. "Jake and I are off this weekend, and *I* won't see you until Monday. I don't want to miss out on my share." He ignored the dark look Jake directed his way.

"Don't worry. There will be plenty to go around," Liz promised. If she'd picked up Spence's intimation, she gave no indication of it.

"What's on your agenda tonight?" Jake tossed the question to her over his shoulder as he watched the elevator's progress and moved toward the door.

"Dinner and bed. I'm beat."

"Sounds like a plan to me." Spence shifted his jacket aside and rested his hand on his Glock as the elevator came to a stop and the door slid open. He stepped out first, then motioned for Jake and Liz to follow. Jake made sure the transfer to the waiting vehicle was swift and efficient. Less than half a minute later, they were moving out.

"You know what's sad? This whole routine is beginning to feel normal to me." Liz buckled her seat belt.

The dark interior hid her features. But Jake had no problem picking up the thread of melancholy woven through her voice.

It wasn't the kind of comment that required a response, so he didn't offer one. Besides, he was still mulling over Spence's observation about him joining the SOG because he liked action. It was dead-on. After Jen died, he'd needed action. Needed a job that demanded intense, singular focus. It had been the only way to keep the pain at bay. And that strategy had worked. The SOG required every bit of his energy and concentration.

In the nearly four years he'd been part of the elite group, he'd dealt with plenty of life and death situations. Had been entrusted with countless lives. And he'd done his best to protect everyone in his care. But truth be told, he'd thrived on outwitting the bad guys. Had liked the high-stakes challenge.

He didn't like it this time.

Thanks to Liz—as Spence had suggested.

And much as she yearned for routine and predictability, no one would be happier than him when things returned to normal.

The weather wasn't cooperating.

Frustrated by the meteorologist's report, Martin punched the off button on the television remote and settled back in his recliner, stroking Josie, who lay curled in his lap. It was the end of October, for pity's sake. It should be forty degrees tomorrow, not eighty. Cold enough to require coats and hats. Yet when he'd followed the Morettis to the judge's condo this morning and watched as they'd delivered another pan of food, Harold had been wearing shorts!

He'd hoped to implement his plan before Patricia arrived. Now he'd either have to wait until she left in three weeks, or figure out a way to pull it off while she was here.

Then again, her presence might not be a bad thing. He didn't intend to leave any clues for the authorities, but alibis were always good to have. And he could count on Patricia for that. He might think she was nuts for going to Sierra Leone, but he'd never questioned her loyalty. She'd always stood up for him, taken his part. If he needed a champion, Patricia wouldn't fail him.

Giving Josie one final pat, he set her on the floor and stood. Might as well take a final inventory of his equipment and double-check the letters. The more prepared he was, the less margin there'd be for error. And he didn't want any more errors.

Because the next time he went after Judge Elizabeth Michaels, he didn't intend to fail.

Good heavens!

Was that Patricia?

Martin squinted at the woman barreling toward him down the concourse from the gate area at Lambert International Airport. She'd trimmed down, and her skin had taken on what appeared to be a permanent, deep tan. The fan of lines around her eyes was also new, as was the mannish cut of her silver hair. If he hadn't been watching for her, she could have walked past him a few feet away and he wouldn't have spotted her.

She seemed to be having trouble picking him out too, based on the way she was scanning the crowd.

No surprise there. He looked in the mirror every day. Knew his face had grown lined and haggard over the past couple of years. He'd lost a fair amount of weight too. And the gray hair and buzz cut would throw her. Last time she'd come to St. Louis, his hair had been on the shaggy side, and more pepper than salt. He'd grayed up some since that visit, but not enough for his plan. Dye had solved that problem, though.

All at once he saw recognition dawn in her eyes as her gaze connected with his. For an instant she appeared shocked. But then she broke into a smile and lifted her hand in greeting.

He waved back, forcing up the corners of his mouth. It wasn't that he didn't want to see his sister. But he still didn't like the timing. While it had some advantages, there were challenges too. Like finding ways to slip away without arousing her suspicions.

As she passed the security checkpoint and left the concourse, he hoped she'd been sincere about not wanting to disrupt his life. When she'd phoned to give him her flight information, she'd made him promise not to change any plans on her behalf. Good thing. Waiting until she left to finish the job he'd botched two weeks ago wasn't an option.

Unfinished business bothered him.

He'd been that way for as long as he could remember. Back in his school days, whenever he'd had a paper to write, he'd tackled it right away, unable to rest easy until it was done. That compulsion hadn't lessened with age. For his own peace of mind, he needed to take care of Judge Michaels sooner rather than later.

"Marty!" Patricia stopped in front of him, set down her carry-on bag, and threw her arms around him. "Give your big sister a hug!"

"Hello, Patricia."

He patted her back awkwardly, self-conscious as always with public displays of affection. He hadn't even felt comfortable holding Helen's hand in the ER that last night, despite the silent plea she'd sent his way. His father had always belittled that kind of behavior as sentimental fluff. Called it sissified. And Martin had never wanted to be a sissy. What he'd wanted was his father's approval. His respect. Some sort of tangible proof of his love.

No matter how hard he'd tried, though, nothing he'd done had been good enough to earn him any of those things. But he'd found them in other places. From Patricia. And Helen. He'd gotten a healthy dose of respect on the job too.

He hadn't gotten it from his government, that was for sure.

Swallowing past his bitterness, he tugged free of Patricia's embrace and bent to pick up her bag. There was no way to condone snatching away the house a man had scrimped and saved to buy and called home for twenty-six years. Or depriving him of the work that defined him. Or fining him an exorbitant amount for making an honest mistake.

That wasn't just disrespect. It was robbery.

It made a man feel like a victim.

And he didn't like being a victim.

He trudged toward baggage claim, his fingers clenching on the handles of the bag. That was water under the bridge, though. He couldn't change the past. But he could do his part to fix the broken judicial system and freedom-sucking government that stole from a man and let an ER doctor get away with murder. That was what Jarrod always—

"Marty!"

At Patricia's summons, he looked over his shoulder. She was standing where he'd left her, watching him with a puzzled expression.

Retracing his steps, he rejoined her. "What's wrong?"

"I was in the middle of asking you a question and you just walked off." She peered at him. "Is everything okay?"

"Sure. I'm a little preoccupied, that's all." Heat suffused his face, and he struggled to come up with a reasonable explanation for tuning her out. "I was trying to remember if I filled Josie's water bowl this morning."

She gave him a blank look. "Who's Josie?"

"My cat."

Her mouth dropped open. "You have a cat?"

"Yeah. A stray I picked up last winter."

"I thought you disliked animals. When I suggested you get a pet after Helen died you claimed they were more trouble than they were worth."

She was staring at him as if he'd sprouted two heads, and he shifted from one foot to the other. This was going to be trickier than he'd expected. Patricia had known him for fifty-three years. She was well versed in his habits and personality quirks. He'd have to be careful not to arouse any suspicions or she might start watching him. That wouldn't be good.

"A man can change his mind, can't he? And she's been a real fine companion. Let's go get your luggage." Without giving her a chance to respond, he set off again for baggage claim.

She fell into step beside him, and he found that if he fed her questions about her trip, he didn't have to worry about contributing much to the conversation. Patricia had always been a talker. Even as a child, she'd been blessed with the gift of gab, as their mother used to say before the flu cut her life short when Martin had been ten. No question about it, his sister had been born with the social gene.

Funny that he was the one who'd married while she'd remained single.

Life sure could be hard to figure out.

By the time the carousel belched out her bags twenty minutes later, he'd heard the entire saga of her journey and she'd launched into a running narrative about life in the tiny village she called home.

Once more, Martin tuned her out. For the past three years, he'd lived a quiet, solitary life. He doubted he'd had a social conversation with anyone that lasted longer than five minutes. And he liked it that way. Always had. Fortunately, he'd found a woman to marry who had understood that. Helen hadn't needed a man who used a lot of words. And his job hadn't required him to communicate much, either.

Since Helen had died and he'd been laid off, however, his minimal social skills had atrophied. He didn't mind. But he had a feeling Patricia would.

He sighed.

It was going to be a long three weeks.

14

She should have rented a car.

Scooping Josie up, Patricia huffed out a breath and watched through the mini blinds on the front window of Martin's house as the taillights of his car disappeared down the street. She hadn't expected her brother to spend every minute with her during her visit, but the man was always on the go. Touchy, too, when she inquired about his activities.

Like tonight. Over dinner, he'd told her he'd joined a bowling league and was committed for the evening. She'd been delighted. He'd always kept too much to himself, and she'd been afraid that with Helen gone, he'd withdraw even more. She was glad he was getting out. Truth be told, after three days cooped up in the house, she'd been ready for some social interaction too. But when she'd asked about joining him, just to watch, he'd practically choked on his coffee.

It was a guys' night out, he'd told her. Women weren't welcome.

So much for that idea.

Now she had a whole evening to kill. Already she was missing her village and the charming children who'd given her a new lease on life after early retirement had left her bereft and feeling useless.

She scratched the kitty under the chin, eliciting a purr.

"Looks like it's you and me, kid. What do you think about watching some television?"

Josie burrowed closer and buried her head.

"Yeah. My sentiments exactly."

The sudden ring of the doorbell startled her, and Patricia cracked the mini blinds again with her fingers, peering sideways at the front door. A young woman, juggling a baby, stood on the porch.

At the prospect of company, Patricia's spirits took an upswing and she hurried toward the door, setting Josie down as she opened it.

"Hi." The thirtyish blonde-haired mother smiled. "Sorry to disturb you, but the mailman left this in my box by mistake today." She held out an envelope. "I thought it might be a bill, and I didn't want it to sit out overnight, so I decided to deliver it instead of putting it in Mr. Reynolds's mailbox. I'm Molly Stephens, by the way. From next door."

Patricia took the letter. "Nice to meet you, Molly. I'm Patricia Reynolds, Marty's sister. Thanks for bringing this over."

"It wasn't any trouble. I was getting ready to run to the grocery store anyway. Are you visiting from out of town?"

"Yes. A long way out of town. I'm with the Peace Corps in Africa."

The woman's eyes widened. "Wow! That must be fascinating. I'd love to hear about it while you're here. These days, I'm pretty much confined to the house, thanks to my little stinker here. Otherwise known as Jack." She bounced the baby on her hip, her lips curving into a tender smile as she patted his back. "I took six months off after he was born, and my husband travels a lot. I'm craving some adult conversation."

Hallelujah! Patricia praised in silence. This young woman could be the answer to a prayer.

"I'm in the same boat. Marty seems to have a lot going on, and since I didn't rent a car, I'm stranded. He's gone again tonight. Stop by anytime."

"I'll do that. Maybe tomorrow, if that's okay. In the meantime, can I bring you anything from the store?"

Patricia hesitated. She'd never been the pushy type, but she'd gotten more assertive during her years in the Peace Corps. Why spend a long, dreary evening alone if there was the chance of a reprieve?

"I do need a few things. Marty's pantry is in desperate straits. The man exists on cereal and microwave dinners. Would you mind very much if I came along?"

"Not at all. To be honest, you'd be doing me a favor. My husband worries about me running to the store after dark, and he'll be glad to know I had some company."

"Wonderful. Let me get my purse and lock up, and I'll meet you in your driveway in two minutes."

By the time she joined Molly, Jack was strapped in his car seat and gurgling happily in the backseat.

"He seems like a very contented baby." Smiling at the infant, Patricia slid into the passenger seat and buckled her belt.

"He is. After hearing some of the horror stories my friends tell about how fussy their newborns are, I know I've been blessed." Molly backed out of the driveway and headed down the street. "I want to hear all about your work in Africa tomorrow, but how about a little preview tonight?"

Patricia was happy to comply. She never tired of sharing her experiences, especially with an interested listener. Marty had asked a few perfunctory questions, but it was hard to work up much enthusiasm for storytelling with an indifferent audience. Molly more than made up for her brother's apathy, however, plying her with questions, and she found herself sharing far more than she'd planned.

She was in the middle of a story about one of her students when the young mother pulled into the parking lot.

"My! I've talked your ear off all the way here."

"I've enjoyed every minute of it."

"Well, I ought to save a little for . . ."

Her voice trailed off as she spotted a dark blue, late model Accord that looked a lot like Marty's parked in front of a print shop. She squinted, trying to make out the license plate. Usually she didn't pay attention to such details, but his plate had caught her eye at the airport because it contained his initials. She'd kidded him about the coincidence, pointing out that he'd gotten a vanity plate for free.

The overhead security lights in the parking lot didn't offer enough illumination for her sixty-two-year-old eyes to read the whole plate, but as they passed she did pick out three letters.

MTR.

It was Marty's car.

Puzzled, she scanned the strip mall. There wasn't a bowling alley in sight.

"Patricia? Is everything okay?"

Realizing she'd stopped midsentence, she tried to regroup. "Yes. Sorry. I got distracted for a moment. Is there a bowling alley in this mall?"

"No. Are you a bowler?"

"Not much of one." She gave her brother's car another distracted glance over her shoulder. "But I've rolled a few gutter balls in my day."

Molly chuckled and swung into a parking spot. "Sounds like a description of my brief and unremarkable bowling career." She set the brake and opened her door. "Give me a sec to extricate Jack from his seat."

"No hurry. In fact, why don't I meet you in the produce section in five minutes? I want to make a quick stop at that copy center." She indicated the adjacent shop, which occupied the last spot in the strip mall.

"Okay. Sounds good."

Leaving Molly to deal with Jack, Patricia headed for the small business, noting the unfamiliar name as she pushed through the door. Express Copies. Must be an independent store. It didn't have the rubber-stamp look of a chain.

The high-school-age girl behind the counter was busy with a customer, and Patricia took the opportunity to wander through the aisles of stationery and office supplies. A few people were milling about, but not nearly as many as the cars parked in front would suggest.

And Marty was nowhere in sight.

Had he stopped in at the mall for some other reason? Run into the grocery store on his way to bowling, perhaps?

"May I help you find something, ma'am?"

At the question, Patricia turned toward the teenage clerk, summoning up a smile. "No, thank you. I'm just browsing."

"Well, if you need help, let me know." She trotted down the aisle to offer assistance to the next customer.

After working her way to the front of the store, Patricia headed for the exit. As she pushed through the door, a car pulled into an empty spot a few spaces down, and despite her distraction, she couldn't help noticing the tall, dark-haired man who got out. She thought he was planning to go into the copy shop, but much to her surprise he bypassed the front door and headed around the side of the building.

Although she felt a bit cloak-and-daggerish, Patricia walked to the corner and peeked around. The powerful overhead lights that illuminated the asphalt lot didn't reach far enough to dispel the shadows along the wall, but she could see the outlines of the man as he disappeared around the back of the building.

How odd.

Most people who lurked in shadows were up to no good. But that guy hadn't struck her as the devious type. He'd been clean cut, and his jeans and T-shirt hadn't been dirty or shabby. Nor had he skulked around the back as if he had anything to hide.

Was Marty back there too?

If so, what was he doing?

And why had he lied to her about his destination for the evening?

Lost in thought, Patricia switched directions and went to join Molly. She was probably fretting over nothing. It was possible her first inclination had been correct, after all. Marty might have stopped at the mall to pick up some grocery items.

But she didn't see him anywhere in the store as she and Molly wandered through the aisles.

And when they returned to the parking lot loaded down with plastic sacks, her brother's car was still in front of the copy shop.

Leaving her with an uneasy feeling she couldn't shake.

Liz was good.

Really good.

As Jake observed the proceedings in her courtroom on Friday afternoon, his admiration and respect for her rose another notch. Each of the cases she'd presided over this week had been complicated, and with each she'd demonstrated razor-sharp insights and a cut-to-the-chase manner that showed no mercy or patience for frivolities or sloppiness.

In yesterday's accident case involving trucks from two states, she'd cut off the pompous, patronizing attorney who'd begun instructing her on the details with a curt reprimand. "I already did my homework," she'd said. "I know the facts. Let's discuss legal issues."

Jake had had to stifle a grin at the man's discomfiture. And he gave a silent cheer for Liz. As she'd aptly demonstrated to the condescending chauvinist, drop-dead gorgeous and a precise, clear-thinking mind weren't mutually exclusive.

She'd ended up remanding the case to the state circuit court.

Today's legal liability case involved a faulty bicycle made by an out-of-state company that had gone out of business. She'd discussed it with her law clerks in the morning, and after lunch she and the attorneys had selected a six-member jury and six alternates. Then the trial had begun.

Liz didn't waste a minute of her day.

Now, as five o'clock approached, she adjourned the bicycle case until Monday.

As she rose, he and Spence moved forward. By the time she reached the door behind the bench that led to her chambers, they were behind her. After two weeks, she was familiar with the routine, and she waited for Spence to go first and give the go-ahead.

Once she was in the hall leading to her chambers and the door closed behind them, she expelled a long breath. Although she looked tired, her eyes had grown more alive with each passing day. And while he'd questioned the wisdom of her decision to go back to work so soon, Jake realized it had been the right choice for her. It was clear she loved what she did, and returning to her comfort zone had been therapeutic.

"Ready to go home?" She hadn't yet left work before 7:00, but he decided to ask anyway. "It is Friday night."

She led them toward her chambers, a rueful smile playing at her lips. "It's not like I have any exciting plans for the weekend, other than giving myself a long-overdue manicure." She waved her chipping crimson nails at him. "But it is a relief to be done with the case review for the FBI. I was thrilled when I closed the final file last night."

"You should celebrate." He followed her across the reception area of her suite and into her office while Spence lingered at her door.

She unzipped her black robe and started to shrug out of it. "Maybe I'll have a double serving of cannoli. And I think I will go home early."

"Five o'clock isn't early."

"It is for me."

"Judge Michaels, Neil would like to speak with you."

At Spence's comment, Jake turned toward the door. The studious-looking law clerk hovered behind the other marshal.

"That's fine, Spence. Come in, Neil." Liz let the robe settle back on her shoulders.

Spence angled sideways, and the clerk edged past, pushing his glasses up his nose as he gave the marshal's Glock a nervous look.

"Sorry to bother you this late on Friday, Judge, but the lawyer for the defendant in that drug conspiracy case we discussed this morning showed up with his client and the prosecutor. He wants to offer a guilty plea. They're in the courtroom."

With a resigned nod, Liz rezipped her robe. "Okay. Sorry about that, guys." Her apologetic glance encompassed both of the marshals. "I'm sure you have better ways to spend your Friday night."

"No problem." Jake motioned to Spence, and they accompanied her back to the courtroom.

Forty-five minutes later, Liz was once again in her chambers, unzipping her robe. "I think we should beat a hasty retreat before something else comes up."

"I second that." Spence moved to the door.

"Hot date?" Jake arched an eyebrow.

Spence grinned. "Yeah. Eat your heart out, buddy."

"And I was going to invite you both to stay for cannoli." Liz shot Spence a teasing look.

"Now that's almost enough to make me change my plans. But"—he feigned a heavy sigh—"I can't disappoint a lady. Jake, however, might be persuaded. I have a feeling he's at loose ends."

He was going to have to have a long talk with his impertinent colleague soon, Jake decided. Very soon.

"As a matter of fact, I promised my sister I'd take her new puppy to the kennel. She's working late. And all of us are leaving early tomorrow for Chicago. It's my mom's seventieth birthday and we're planning to surprise her."

Besides, he didn't need the temptation of a Friday night alone with Liz in her condo. Why subject his self-discipline to that kind of test?

"What a nice gesture."

At Liz's warm comment, he looked over at her. The tenderness of her smile jolted his libido, and it was a struggle to maintain a neutral tone.

"I think she'll get a kick out of it. It's been a lot of years since all three of her kids were there to celebrate her big day." He shifted toward Spence. "You want to alert the motorcade guys?"

"Already done. They're moving into position as we speak."

"Okay. We're out of here. Liz?" He gestured toward the door.

She slipped her coat off its hanger. "I think I'm going to need this. I hear the temperature has been dropping all day."

"Let me help you with that." Jake took the briefcase out of her hand and passed it over to Spence. As he held the coat for her, a faint, pleasing floral scent wafted his way. The one he'd come to associate with Liz.

He fought the temptation to lean close and inhale a lungful.

"Thanks, Jake."

He released the coat. "My pleasure."

"Are you sure I can't convince you to stay long enough to sample some cannoli?"

She turned his way, and when she smiled up at him he had to remind himself to breathe. How she'd managed to get under his skin in such a short time was beyond his comprehension. But he couldn't dispute the evidence. His heart was beating double time.

"Not tonight, Liz." His voice rasped, and he cleared his throat. "But thanks for the invitation."

"Okay. Your loss."

She meant the cannoli. He knew that. But as far as he was concerned, missing an evening in her company was a far bigger loss.

The problem was, if he'd accepted her invitation he'd have been tempted to sample far more than the cannoli.

And given the roguish grin Spence directed to him over Liz's head as they fell into step on either side of her, he suspected the other marshal had figured that out.

This was the weekend.

Martin wiped his palms down his slacks and picked up the snub-nose .38 revolver he kept in his dresser. He'd never had occasion to use it, but he'd always believed in being prepared. The world was getting more dangerous every day. A man couldn't be too careful.

Or afraid to right wrongs.

As Jarrod always said, if peaceful means of redressing grievances failed, citizens had an absolute right to use force to remove an abusive government and rid the world of a rotting judicial system. Or maybe he'd read that in some of the literature he'd been collecting. In any case, the mandate was clear. And this weekend, he would—

"Marty?"

At the knock on his bedroom door, followed by Patricia's annoyed call, he fumbled the gun. It fell onto the carpet at his feet, and he snatched it up. He'd been afraid the timing of her visit would make things difficult, and those fears had been realized. She asked too many questions and looked at him strangely every time he left the house.

He'd put his plan on hold if he could, but he wasn't going to get a decent night's sleep until it was done. Besides, for all he knew those marshals might move the judge to some new location and he'd have to start all over figuring out where she was. But the clincher was the weather. It was finally cooperating.

No, he wasn't going to wait. This was his window.

"Marty?" She knocked again.

He shoved the gun under some T-shirts in his dresser and

closed the drawer. After crossing the room, he twisted the knob on the door.

"I heard you the first time, Patricia."

She planted her hands on her hips and gave him one of those narrow-eyed looks he remembered from his childhood. The kind she'd pinned him with when he was behaving in a way that didn't meet with her approval.

"Are you going to spend the entire evening in your room?"

"No. I just had a few things to take care of." Josie rubbed against his leg, and he stooped to pick her up, cradling her in his arms. As a companion, she was turning out to be far preferable to his sister. She made no demands and didn't expect him to communicate.

"You didn't even try the apple pie I made for dessert."

"I was too full from your great meatloaf. But I'll have some now."

That seemed to appease her. Some of the tension left her face, and she motioned him to follow her back to the kitchen.

"The coffee's still hot. Have a seat." She gestured to the table.

He put Josie on the floor and took his place. After setting the plates of pie and two mugs on the table, she joined him.

"You know, Marty, I've been here five days and I've seen more of your neighbor Molly than I have of you. I had no idea you led such a busy life. With you being off work and all, I thought we'd have more time to spend together."

He broke off a bite of pie with the edge of his fork. "You've been talking to Molly?"

"Yes." Concern sharpened her features. "I told you all about it yesterday at dinner. How she came by Wednesday night and I went to the grocery store with her. And how she dropped by for a visit yesterday. Don't you remember?"

He vaguely recalled her mentioning his neighbor. But he didn't pay a whole lot of attention to Patricia's rambling monologues. His mind was occupied with his plan for the judge. Still, he couldn't risk having her think he was getting senile. After all, their father had died with early onset Alzheimer's.

"Of course I remember. I'm just surprised you two hit it off. She's only a kid. I wouldn't think you'd have much in common."

"She's a very nice young woman. And she's fascinated by my stories from Africa."

Ah. A willing ear. That explained it. Martin took another bite of pie.

"Anyway, she took me out again with her today while you were . . . what was it you were doing again?"

He tried to remember the excuse he'd given her for his four-hour absence while he'd gone to buy the bales of straw and driven to the country to stash them. A visit to the outplacement firm. That was it.

"I was working on my resume and doing some practice job interviews at that place the company sent all the laid-off employees."

"Oh yes. Now I remember." She took a sip of coffee, still watching him. Like this was a test or something. "Anyway, with you so busy and all, I thought I might rent a car for the duration. That way, I can tool around and entertain myself while you're gone."

Perfect! He should have suggested that sooner. If she was occupied, she'd be less likely to pay as much attention to him.

"That's a great idea. I'll run you over to the car rental place tomorrow morning first thing. By the way, did I mention I was going deer hunting this weekend?"

She stared at him. "No."

"Yeah. Joe Abernathy and I go every fall. He's got a cabin upstate. We're leaving Sunday morning and I'll be back Tuesday evening."

"I thought you gave up hunting years ago."

He pressed the tines of his fork against the crumbs from his piecrust. "I did. Helen didn't much care for it, and I stopped hunting after we got married. Now that she's gone, I've picked it up again with Joe. His wife's never had a problem with hunting." The season didn't start for two weeks, but he doubted Patricia knew that.

"I never did see the fascination in tracking down innocent animals for sport. And I don't like guns."

"Neither does the government."

"What do you mean?" She gave him a puzzled look as she scooped up her last bite of pie.

Martin stifled a disgusted sigh. That was the problem with most Americans. The government was undermining their freedom right and left, and they didn't even realize it.

"Do you know how hard it is to get a gun now?"

"I know there are regulations about it. To protect people."

He snorted in disgust. "That's a crock of . . ." He bit off the last word. Leaned forward. "Patricia, wake up. The government wants to destroy our Second Amendment rights. To disarm all Americans. Our liberty is in jeopardy from the very arms of government that are supposed to protect it, especially our courts and our judges."

"Goodness, Marty." Her eyes widened. "I haven't seen you this riled up since your eminent domain fight. When did you start worrying about the government?"

Back off. Let it go.

As the warning sounded in his mind, he bit his tongue. Patricia wasn't a recruit for Jarrod's group. She didn't even spend much time in the United States anymore. And he didn't need to further arouse her suspicions by acting out of character.

"I've been reading a lot lately is all." He adopted a nonchalant tone. "Seems like the country's in a lot of trouble these days. I guess you're a little out of touch over there in Africa."

"I keep up with things. I haven't read much about people

being up in arms over gun control, though. Pardon the pun."

"Depends on who you talk to, I guess. Do you want me to drive you to the rental place after breakfast tomorrow?"

"That would be fine."

"Good pie, Patricia." He pushed his plate aside. "Best I've had since Helen died."

"I'm glad you liked it, Marty. I know apple was always your favorite. I remember once when you were about eight, Mom had a pie cooling on the counter and you ate off the entire crust." She chuckled and shook her head. "Mom was fit to be tied."

"That doesn't ring any bells."

"I guess not. That's a long time ago, and you were little. Do you remember Mom at all?"

"Not anything specific. I have much clearer memories of Dad."

Twin furrows appeared on Patricia's brow. "I'm not sure that's a good thing. He was always too stern and controlling. And he was awfully hard on you. I'll always remember the time you won first place in that art fair and he wouldn't let you go accept the prize because you didn't get an A on your calculus exam."

He remembered it too. It had been one of his bitterest disappointments. But he hadn't thought about it in years. And he wasn't going to start now.

"That's ancient history, Patricia."

"Maybe. But I was always sorry you gave up your drawing after he told you it wasn't a manly pursuit. You had a lot of talent."

He lifted one shoulder. "I guess he was being practical. Can't make much of a living drawing pictures."

"Some people do."

"It's a tough life, though. Things turned out okay. I liked my work."

"You still miss it?"

"Yeah. It was a good job. I felt like I was doing something important, something that mattered." A surge of anger welled up inside him. "Too bad the government didn't."

She reached over and patted his hand. "Priorities change, Marty. Times change. You have to go with the flow."

"If we keep going with the flow, this country's going to go under."

"My! I think my low-key brother is becoming a radical in his old age."

She smiled, but he saw the speculation in her eyes.

Somehow he dredged up a smile of his own. "I wouldn't worry if I were you. You know what they say about teaching an old dog new tricks." Rising, he picked up his plate and carried it to the sink. "What do you say we watch an old movie tonight? I've got a DVD of *North by Northwest*."

"Cary Grant! Now that would be a treat." She gave him a pleased smile. "Maybe we can make popcorn later too."

"Sure. That would be nice."

She joined him at the sink and put her arm around his shoulders. "You've seemed really different since I've been back, Marty. But tonight I'm seeing the little brother I remember."

"He's still inside, Patricia. I've just had a few rough years."

"I hear you. Let's hope it's smooth sailing from here on out."

It would be, Martin resolved, as he went to retrieve the DVD.

Particularly when it came to finishing off Judge Elizabeth Michaels.

15

"Happy birthday to you!"

As the three Taylor siblings finished their rousing if off-key rendition of the familiar ditty and the waiter delivered a cake glowing with candles, Eleanor Taylor beamed at them. "This is the nicest Saturday night I've had in years. And I couldn't ask for a better birthday present—all my children with me to celebrate."

Jake grinned at his mother, pleased to see her so happy. "You didn't think you'd get rid of us just by moving to Chicago, did you? We're not that easy to shake."

She smiled and shook her head. "As if."

"Make a wish, Mom," Alison encouraged.

"And make it good," Cole added. "You only get one shot at this every year."

She looked around the table. "My wish has already come true. But I think I'll make one for all of you." Taking a deep breath, she blew out the candles.

"Wow! Now I know where Alison gets all her hot air." Cole winked at his mother and grinned at his sister.

Alison countered by jabbing an elbow in his ribs.

"Hey!" He feigned injury. "Watch it or I'll have to book you for assault and battery."

"Try it." Alison made a face at him. "So what did you wish for, Mom?"

"I think I know."

They all turned toward Eleanor's sister. Six years older than her sibling, she was tall and thin as a rail, with snow-white hair she'd worn piled on her head in a loose chignon for as long as Jake could remember. His mother, on the other hand, was shorter, more stout, and still had quite a bit of brown in her stylishly coiffed graying hair. No one would ever guess they were related.

"Catherine! If you tell, it won't come true," Eleanor admonished her sister.

"I bet these three smart children of yours can figure it out, anyway." Aunt Catherine scanned the table, then glanced toward a young couple holding hands in a nearby booth.

Noting Alison's sudden pained expression, Jake was about to step in when Cole beat him to it.

"Well, if you're wishing what I think you're wishing, your oldest son might come through for you."

At his mother's interested—and hopeful—look, Jake's neck warmed. His brother was as bad as Spence.

"Do you have some news to share, Jake?"

"No, Mom. I don't. And Cole has a big mouth." He shot Cole a dark look.

"Oh, go ahead and tell her about Liz." Alison joined in the fun, making an obvious effort to shake off her melancholy. "If you don't, we will."

"Liz who?" His mother directed the question to him.

He was stuck. Four pairs of eyes were riveted on him. And he'd rather his mother hear *his* version of his relationship with Liz than the embellished one his siblings would no doubt concoct.

"Liz Michaels, Mom. She's a federal judge. I'm heading her protection detail. She used to be married to Doug Stafford. She kept her maiden name."

"I remember Doug well from your college days. Nice young man. It was such a tragedy when he died in that car accident a few years ago."

"Yes, it was. Anyway, Liz and I have enjoyed getting reacquainted. She's a very nice woman."

He shot a silent warning to his siblings. Alison was grinning as she cut the birthday cake. Cole was sitting back, arms crossed over his chest, enjoying the show.

"Is she in danger, Jake?"

At his mother's question, he refocused on her. Unlike his brother's and sister's smirks, which suggested they were getting a kick out of putting him in the hot seat, a slight frown marred her brow, and she was leaning forward, her posture intent.

He'd never told his mother much about the dangers of his job. When they talked, he tended to share the humorous or glitzier elements, trying to shield her from worry.

Kind of like Alison had done with him when he'd been in Iraq.

That sudden realization forced Jake to view his sister's actions in a more sympathetic light.

Before he could respond, his aunt touched his mother's shoulder. "Eleanor . . . Elizabeth Michaels is the judge we've been reading about in the *Tribune*. The one whose sister was murdered."

His mother's complexion paled. "Oh, dear." She reached for his hand and squeezed it. "Are you worried someone is after her too?"

"It's possible. But we have a full contingent of deputies assigned to her detail. And the FBI is working hard to find the person who killed her sister."

"I'm certain she's in good hands, then. But I think I'll say a few prayers for her safety, anyway."

Alison distributed the slices of cake, and the party shifted back into a lighter mood. But as he ate his piece, Jake was grateful for his mom's promise of prayer.

Because even though things were quiet at the moment, his gut told him the danger wasn't over.

And as he'd confided to Liz not long ago, he always listened to his gut.

"You sure you don't want to go to services with me, Marty?"

Martin stopped shaking his cereal into a bowl and surveyed Patricia, who was all gussied up for church. When Helen was alive, he'd gone every week. Now, he got there once a month. Maybe. And today he had other things to do.

"I'm sure, Patricia. I need to get my stuff together for my hunting trip. I'll be gone when you get home, but if anything comes up and you need me, call my cell phone. I'll leave the number on the kitchen counter."

"I expect I'll be fine. Molly's husband is heading out of town again this week, so we're going to lunch tomorrow. And I thought I'd play tourist on Tuesday. Visit the Arch and the Art Museum."

"Sounds like fun."

"I agree. You'll be back on Tuesday night, right?"

"Yes."

"Okay. I'm off." She bustled over and gave him a hug. "Good hunting."

"Thanks."

He remained at the counter, cereal in hand, until he heard her car door slam in the driveway. Setting the box down, he hurried across the kitchen and through the living room to the front window. As she pulled out and headed down the street, his pulse kicked up a notch.

This was it.

No longer hungry, he dumped the cereal in his bowl back into the box and headed for his bedroom. After pulling the flat garment box out from under his bed, he took a quick inventory. Latex gloves. Regular gloves. Heavy-duty cording. Strips of rags. A large round tin, filled with cookies he'd bought at the bakery yesterday. The mustache and spirit gum he'd purchased earlier in the week at a theatrical supply shop, plus a gray woman's wig. Sunglasses. Several pairs of nylon restraints a cop buddy had given him years ago as a gag gift. The two letters. Large sheets of clear heavy plastic. Preaddressed, stamped envelopes. Extra ammunition.

The only thing he still needed to retrieve was the gun in his dresser. His rifle was already at the cabin—hidden under the floorboard, in case someone with sticky fingers broke in.

Opening the drawer, he withdrew the revolver and slipped it in his pocket. Then he took the plastic and a roll of duct tape and headed for the garage, where he set about covering the front seat of the car with the plastic, taping it firmly in place.

It was important not to leave any trace evidence. He knew all about that stuff from the television cop shows. It was amazing how they could nail a person with the littlest thing. A fingernail, even. That's why he'd been extra careful when he'd gone to the judge's house, wearing latex gloves and a stocking cap that covered his hair. Right before he went, he'd also washed the black clothes he'd worn, just in case any of Josie's hair had been clinging to them.

He'd found a piece of gum wedged under the heel of his shoe after he'd arrived home, though. And he'd wondered briefly if there might have been cat hair stuck to it. But even if there had been, thousands of cats in the city had gold hair. There would be no reason for anyone to link him to a stray cat hair found in the judge's house.

But to be safe, he'd put Josie in the basement this morning. No reason to take chances.

Once he finished his taping job on the seat, he covered the carpet in the front with plastic too. After the job was finished, he'd dispose of it.

Satisfied, he backed out of the car, opened the door between the garage and the house—and froze.

The doorbell was ringing.

His pulse began to hammer as he stepped inside. No one ever came calling on Sunday morning.

No one ever came calling, period.

Moving through the house, he sidled up to the front door and peered through the peephole.

It was that young woman from next door. Looking for Patricia, he presumed.

As he watched, she pressed the bell again.

He could ignore her. But she was a bit of a busybody, always watching the comings and goings in the neighborhood. She probably knew he was at home. If he didn't answer, she might think he was ill or injured. And she was the type to call 911, all in the interest of being a good Samaritan.

A flutter of panic rippled through his stomach. Better to deal with her and send her on her way.

"Good morning, Mr. Reynolds." She gave him a perky smile as he opened the door. "I tried to catch your sister as she left, but it was too late. She offered to let me borrow a Bundt pan for a cake I'm making to take to a potluck dinner, and I wondered if I might trouble you for it. Those are the pans with the hole in the middle, you know? She said she saw one in a box in the basement at the foot of the stairs."

A Bundt pan.

He did his best not to roll his eyes.

"I'll check for you." He started to turn away, then hesitated. The polite thing to do would be to ask her in. The temperature had dropped into the upper thirties, and a wind was whipping her hair around her face. "You want to wait inside?"

"If you don't mind. It sure has gotten cold all of a sudden, hasn't it?"

She eased past him. The front door opened directly into the living room of the small bungalow, and she hovered just inside.

"I'll be back in a minute." He didn't offer her a seat.

Without waiting for a response, he hightailed it to the basement door. Josie hated being relegated there and usually parked herself on the top step, meowing loudly until he let her out. She'd been quiet today, though.

Easing the door open, he could see the coast was clear. She wasn't waiting on the step, ready to rush past him and escape her shadowy confinement.

It took him less than thirty seconds to find the pan. After moving in, he'd removed only the essential items from the boxes of kitchen stuff. But he'd had to rummage through every box to find what he'd needed, and he hadn't done the best job repacking them. Patricia must have noticed the Bundt pan on one of her trips down here to do some laundry.

As he grabbed the pan, he saw Josie by the wall a few feet away, wedged behind some boxes. She wasn't paying any attention to him, which was unusual, and curiosity got the better of him. Squeezing between the cartons, he kept his distance but leaned over.

She was playing with a dead mouse.

Mystery solved.

He backed away, ascended the stairs, and closed the door.

Molly hadn't strayed far from where he'd left her. "Here you go."

"Thanks, Mr. Reynolds. I'll save you and Patricia a piece. She sure is a nice lady."

"Yeah." He opened the door.

"See you around."

The instant she stepped through the door, he closed it behind her.

Back in his bedroom, he pulled on the boots with the thick soles, left over from the square-dancing class Helen had dragged him to five years ago. He hadn't liked the lessons, but he'd enjoyed being more than an inch and a half taller. Today the added height had a practical advantage as well.

After putting two nylon restraints and a few strips of rags in his pocket, he carried his box of supplies to the car. Stowed it on the passenger seat. Locked the door to the house. Slid behind the wheel.

It was D-Day.

Martin smiled.

Harold was right on time.

Though the blustery wind was creating whorls of leaves along the gravel path in the deserted park, the judge's neighbor was marching along at a good clip. He always made four circuits of the twisting path that wound through open fields and small wooded parcels. He was now halfway through the first one.

As the man disappeared around a small copse of trees, Martin removed the spirit gum and mustache from the box beside him. He'd practiced at home, and it took him less than a minute to secure the small, neat mustache to his upper lip. Once it was affixed, he put on a pair of sunglasses and pulled a stocking cap low over his forehead. After snapping on a pair of snug-fitting latex gloves, he covered them with a pair of leather gloves. A quick touch to the pocket of his coat confirmed his gun was in place.

Martin waited until Harold was less than a hundred yards away before exiting his car. He took a quick look around to verify they were still alone in the quiet park and palmed his revolver. Then he started down the path toward the approaching man, who was bundled up in a bulky winter coat with a scarf around his neck and a baseball cap on his head.

He stopped as the man drew close. "Good morning, Harold."

Harold stopped too, his expression quizzical. "I'm sorry . . . do I know you?"

"No. But you're about to do me a big favor." Martin angled his hand so the man could see the gun.

The color drained from Harold's face, and he took a step back. "Look . . . I-I don't have much cash with me, but what I have is in a money clip in the pocket of my pants."

"I don't want your money, Harold."

Panic gripped the man's features, and he did a quick scan of the park.

"There's no one here today, Harold. And I don't plan to hurt you *or* Delores, as long as you cooperate."

Harold's head snapped back toward him, and the fear

in his eyes was almost palpable. "What have you done with Delores?"

"Nothing yet. And I won't, either, if the two of you cooperate. Now let's walk nice and casual over to your car, like you just met up with an old friend and we're having a little chat."

The man complied, though his gait was stiff as Martin fell in beside him.

When they arrived at the car, parked as usual at the far end of the lot, Martin gestured to the trunk. "Open it."

Harold fumbled in his pocket for his keys and fitted one in the lock as beads of sweat broke out on his forehead and began to trail down his temples. The trunk lid swung up.

For a moment, Martin felt bad. Harold was just an innocent bystander in all this. It didn't seem fair to cause the man such distress.

On the other hand, plenty of people had caused *him* distress these past few years. And he'd been innocent too. At least Harold's distress would be brief. Unlike his.

"Get in. Lay on your side, facing away from me, hands behind your back."

At the command, Harold sent him a pleading, terrified look. "Please, mister, don't do this."

"I don't want to hurt you, Harold. I just need you out of the way for a couple of hours. But if you don't get in, I'll have to use this." He hefted the gun.

"Okay, okay." The man lifted his hand in a placating gesture and awkwardly climbed in.

Once he was in position, Martin holstered his gun and bound Harold's wrists behind his back with one of the plastic restraints. Then he twisted the other around the man's ankles and wound a long strip of cloth around the man's mouth, tying it behind his head. Finally, he tugged the man's wedding ring off his finger and slipped it in the pocket of his coat. He'd have taken the man's keys if the ring hadn't come off, but this was more personal. And persuasive.

"Relax, Harold. You'll be out of here in time for dinner.

Just lay nice and quiet until someone comes to let you out. Because if you cause any problems before then, you'll never see Delores again. Got it?"

The man gave a jerky nod.

"Good."

Closing the trunk lid, Martin once more checked out the park. Considering the biting wind and the cold, he doubted anyone would venture into the corner of this little parking lot anytime soon. Even if Harold tried to attract attention, there'd be no one to hear him.

But given the fear on the man's face when Martin had threatened Delores, he didn't figure he had to worry about the man causing any trouble.

As he slid into his own car, he shot a quick glance at the bouquet in the vase on the floor beside him, all wrapped up in that fancy paper florists used. That had been his only stop en route to the park.

And now it was time for the flowers to play their role.

At the ring of the doorbell, Delores set down the knife she was using to cut up the potatoes for the pot roast and wiped her hands on her apron. Odd. She and Harold never had callers on Sunday morning.

She peeked around the semi-sheer curtains in the living room, which gave her an angled view of the front porch. A man was standing by the door, juggling a flower arrangement wrapped in green floral tissue.

Liz. They had to be from her. That was exactly the kind of gesture her lovely neighbor would make as a thank-you for the treats she'd been dropping off at the condo.

Smiling, Delores bustled toward the door and swung it open.

"Good morning, ma'am." The delivery man was half hidden behind the tall bouquet. "These are for Delores Moretti."

"That would be me." She reached for the arrangement. "My, what a nice surprise on a gloomy Sunday. No one's sent me flowers in years. Thank you for . . ." The words died in her throat as she looked back at him.

The man was pointing a gun at her!

"Move back, Mrs. Moretti."

Panic surged through her. Yet one thought was clear: she couldn't let this man into her home. If she did, she'd be at his mercy.

Tightening her grip on the vase, she inched it up, took a deep breath, and prepared to heave it at him and slam the door in his face.

"I wouldn't do that if I were you, Mrs. Moretti. Not if you want to see your husband alive again."

Stunned, she watched as he withdrew Harold's wedding ring from the pocket of his coat and displayed it in his palm.

"Dear God!" She choked out the whispered words, her gaze riveted to the familiar wide band of burnished gold with the tiny nick on one side.

"Move back, Mrs. Moretti."

Too shocked to think, she stumbled back a few steps. He slipped inside and closed the door behind him, the gun never wavering.

"Set the flowers down, Mrs. Moretti."

She complied numbly.

"Your husband is fine. For now. Whether he stays that way depends on you. Why don't you have a seat while I tell you what I want you to do."

As the gun-toting intruder laid out his plan, an icy chill settled over Delores. This wasn't about her and Harold. They were simply pawns in his nefarious plan to get to Liz. And the thought of betraying her neighbor by aiding and abetting this man twisted her stomach into a knot.

Yet what option did she have? All she could do was go along with his plan and pray that before he was able to carry it to its conclusion, she'd think of some way to thwart him.

Because if she didn't, Harold might live.

But Liz would surely die.

16

"What! When did this happen?" In the marshals' command post next door to Liz's condo, Larry Olsen vaulted to his feet, shock rippling through him.

BlackBerry pressed to his ear, he listened as his sister-in-law recounted the hemorrhage that had sent his pregnant wife to the ER. At the same time, the Morettis appeared on the hall video monitor. The security cameras had picked them up coming in the front entrance, bundled up against the cold, so he'd known they were on their way up to visit Liz. But the timing couldn't have been worse.

To complicate matters, Dan was deep in conversation with their boss in the kitchen, discussing an upcoming trial that would present the marshals with some major security challenges.

Grabbing the hand-held metal detection wand off the foyer table, he spoke into the phone. "Trish, I need to put you on hold for thirty seconds. Don't hang up."

As he stepped into the hall, the couple stopped. Harold bent his head and fiddled with the lid on the latest tin of goodies they'd brought for the judge, sunglasses hiding his eyes. Delores had told the judge he'd had cataract surgery on Friday, and Liz had alerted the marshals to expect the sunglasses. The man also had a baseball cap pulled low over his forehead. But his distinctive gray mustache was clearly visible.

"Hello, Mr. and Mrs. Moretti. The judge is waiting for you." He swept the wand over them quickly, his mind focused on his wife. They'd lost their first baby late in a pregnancy. Neither of them were prepared for a second loss. As soon as he cleared the Morettis, he needed to find someone to replace him in the CP, then get to the hospital. Fast.

The wand began to beep as he ran it over the tin of cookies. Nothing new there. The food containers Delores brought set it off every time.

"Mr. Moretti, may I take a quick look in there?"

"Sure."

He pried open the lid, and Larry glanced at the sugar cookies. "Thanks. Go right on in, folks."

With a wave in the direction of Liz's condo, he returned to the CP.

Dan was strolling into the dining room, where the monitors were arrayed, as he came through the door. "What's up?"

"The Morettis are here." Larry motioned to the monitor, where the couple could be seen standing at Liz's door. "Give me a minute." He finished the conversation with his sister-in-law, then filled Dan in. "Bottom line, I need to find a sub ASAP."

Dismay flattened Dan's features. "I'm sorry, Larry. I'll help you make some calls." As he spoke, he was already pulling out his BlackBerry.

"Thanks." Larry scrolled down his speed-dial list of deputy marshals. Maybe he could tap a newer guy who was anxious to make points. They didn't need one of their top people for this gig.

Because if the pattern held, it was going to be a long, boring Sunday.

At the ring of her doorbell, Liz smiled. Now that she'd finished the case file review, she'd been at loose ends for much of the weekend. Jake was gone to Chicago for his mother's birthday, so there'd been no impromptu visits from him or pizza parties with his siblings. Although she'd filled much of her Saturday and Sunday reading briefs for upcoming cases and catching up on law review articles, eventually her mind had refused to focus. The unexpected offer of a visit from the Morettis had been a godsend.

Peeking through the peephole, she saw Delores frowning beneath her floppy-brimmed, oversized rain hat. That didn't bode well. In general, the woman bubbled with unbridled optimism. But she'd also sounded a little tense on the phone. Had there been a glitch in Harold's cataract surgery? He was standing behind Delores, head bent, and she could see his sunglasses. Funny that Delores hadn't told her anything about the surgery until today. She was usually chatty about such goings-on in their lives.

After flipping the dead bolt, she opened the door and ushered them in.

"I've been looking forward to this ever since you called, Delores." She waited until the couple cleared the door, then shut it and flipped the dead bolt. As she started to turn, she heard the top being popped off the tin of cookies. "It's been really quiet here all . . ."

Her words died in a sharp gasp. Harold tossed the cookies to the floor, lifted a revolver from underneath, and pointed it at her.

Only . . . it wasn't Harold. The mustache wasn't quite right, and his body build was more angular than her neighbor's.

"I'm sorry, Liz." A tremor ran through Delores's words. "But he's got Harold, and he said unless I cooperated I'd never see him again."

At the tearful apology, Liz focused on her neighbor. The woman was quivering, and her complexion had a gray cast.

"That's right, Judge," the intruder interjected. "And the same goes for you. Harold's fate is in your hands. So is Delores's. You cooperate, they live. You don't, they die."

Between the glasses and the baseball cap and a muffler wrapped high around his neck, not much of the man's face was visible. Liz had no idea who he was.

But one thing was clear.

She was looking at the man who'd killed her sister.

The man who still wanted her dead.

As fear clawed at her throat—and her composure—she struggled to rein in her panic. She had to keep her wits about her. To think clearly.

Her life depended on it.

She forced herself to examine the facts, just as she did in the courtroom, doing her best to take emotion out of the equation.

And the facts were straightforward.

The intruder was intelligent; he'd devised a plan that had gotten him past the marshals in the CP, which was no small feat.

He was committed to finishing the job he'd set out to do in her house three weeks ago; otherwise, he wouldn't have risked coming back.

And since she was his target, not the Morettis, she needed to do everything she could to keep them safe. There was enough secondhand blood on her hands already from Doug and Stephanie; no way did she want to add the Morettis to that list.

"Did you hear me, Judge?"

At his prompt, Liz gave a jerky nod. "Yes."

"Good. Both of you go into the living room and have a seat." He stripped off his leather gloves and waved a latex-encased hand that direction, and the two women preceded him. Liz perched on the edge of the couch, Delores beside her. The man remained standing. "Delores, take off your coat, hat, scarf, gloves, shoes, and skirt. Judge, get rid of the jeans and put on Delores's skirt. Tuck one of those flat cushions in the waistband. And do it fast."

He wanted her to impersonate Delores, as he'd impersonated Harold.

Meaning he wasn't going to kill her here.

Why not? That would be the quickest, cleanest way for him to finish the job. There were plenty of silent ways to eliminate someone. Why take the risk of spiriting her away to another location? It wasn't logical. And given the methodical way the man had thought this through, he wasn't some half-cocked nutcase. He had a reason for doing it this way.

Whatever it was, she was grateful for the delay. It gave her more time to come up with an escape plan.

Delores sent her a frightened look, and she gave the older woman's hand an encouraging squeeze as she stood.

After drawing her up, Liz helped her shed the clothing items the man had specified. Tugging Delores's skirt up over her own hips, Liz unzipped her jeans and shimmied out of them until they puddled at her feet. She bent down and tossed them on a nearby chair. But as she reached for the flat cushion on the couch, the man stopped her.

"Before you do that, both of you—in the bedroom." He gestured toward the hall with his gun.

When Liz sent him a panicked look, he gave a mocking laugh. "Don't flatter yourself, Judge. Move." He gestured again with the gun.

Taking Delores's arm, Liz urged her down the hall. As they approached the guest bedroom, the man spoke.

"In there."

He followed them in and scanned the room, homing in on the closet with sliding doors along the hall wall. "This will do. Delores, get inside and lay down on the floor."

The gray-haired woman lurched toward it, opened the door, and stiffly lowered herself to the floor, jangling the empty hangers above her as she did so.

As Liz watched, the killer withdrew two long plastic bands from his pocket and tossed them on the floor near Delores. "Tie her wrists behind her back and bind her ankles together."

Dropping to her knees, Liz picked up one of the restraints and touched her friend's shoulder. "I'm sorry, Delores."

"No talking." The man's sharp command echoed in the room. "And pick up the pace."

Liz followed his instructions as fast as her shaky hands would allow, then prepared to stand.

"Wait." The man tossed a strip of cloth beside her. "Gag her. Delores, open your mouth. Judge, put the band of cloth around her mouth and tie it in the back. Tight."

Liz fought down the bile that rose in her throat. She hated doing this to her neighbor. But if it saved her life, it was a small price to pay.

After affixing the cloth, Liz rose.

"Over there." The man gestured toward the far side of the room. "Lay on the floor, face down, and put your hands over your head."

Once she complied, he moved beside Delores. Liz heard the older woman gasp, and in her peripheral vision she saw the man pulling the restraints and the gag tighter. Much tighter. She also saw him toss a sheet of paper on the floor beside the older woman.

When he finished, he stood and closed the closet door. "All right, Judge. Get up." As she did so, the man motioned her toward the hall. "Find a couple of bulky sweaters or sweatshirts in your room."

He kept his distance as she exited and continued down the hall to her bedroom. But he stood close enough to watch as she pawed through the drawer. As if he was afraid she had a gun hidden among her clothing.

She wished.

After pulling out a maroon sweatshirt, she took as long as she could selecting a sweater. She had to think of some sort of clue to leave behind.

But what? She didn't even know who the guy was. Maybe if she fished a little . . .

Angling toward him, she studied his face. "Why are you doing this?"

"You're not in the courtroom, Judge." His lips twisted into

a smirk. "I don't have to answer your questions. And you can't shut me up, either. This time, you have to listen to me." He waved the gun at the black, V-necked pullover in her hands. "That will work. Now go back to the living room."

This time she had to listen to him. Meaning they'd had a prior encounter in the courtroom. But as she retraced her steps down the hall, Liz had no idea which case was involved.

"We've met before, haven't we?" She stopped at the couch and faced him.

"That doesn't matter. I'm not here because you let the man who killed my wife go free. I'm here because the whole court system is rotten to the core, and somebody needs to start cleaning it out so it doesn't fail other people."

Martin Reynolds.

The name flashed through her mind as she looked into his intense, hate-filled eyes. The same eyes that had burned into hers when she'd directed the verdict in favor of the doctor in the malpractice case.

"Your attorney failed you, Mr. Reynolds. Not the court system."

His face went blank with surprise for a moment. Then his expression hardened again. "Doesn't matter. This isn't about me. It's about saving America by stopping the courts from being used as a weapon of oppression. By shoring up the power of the Constitution. By restoring respect for life and property and freedom."

As she listened to him rant, a cold, hard knot formed in Liz's stomach. Dealing with a killer was one thing. There was a chance you could reason with someone driven by personal motives. Or bargain with him.

Dealing with a zealot was a different story. People who did things for a "cause" didn't mind being martyrs. There was little that would dissuade them from their mission.

"Put on the clothes. You have one minute."

His cold command yanked her back to the present, and

she pulled the sweater over her shirt, trying desperately to think of some way to leave a clue for the marshals.

"What kind of security is there with visitors as they exit?" He barked out the question as she tugged down the sweater.

Could she scare him? Make him nervous enough to do something suspicious, something that might catch the marshals' attention?

"They check out people who are leaving, like they do coming in."

He leaned close to her face, the gun mere inches from her temple, and she stopped breathing. "You're lying. I asked Delores. She said they just walk out. And since she told me the truth about the security coming in, I think I'll believe her." He pressed the cold barrel against her skin. "You know, you'd penalize someone in your courtroom if they lied. Guess I'll have to do the same for you. Later. Keep moving."

Liz finished dressing. With all the bulk she'd added, she doubted the security cameras would detect much difference in body build between her and Delores. Except for the hair.

As if reading her mind, he reached into the deep pocket of his coat, pulled out a gray wig, and tossed it to her. "Put it on."

Her heart sank. He hadn't missed a trick.

Fingering the wig, her gaze fell on the small pile of second-tier cases she'd compiled to pass on to the FBI if the first tier didn't pan out. They still rested on the edge of the dining room table. In the end, Reynolds's file had made that cut. If there was some way she could give it some prominence . . .

"What are you waiting for?"

At his sharp question, she gestured toward the kitchen and said the first thing that came to mind. "I need a rubber band to hold my hair back. And a safety pin for the skirt. It's too big. I think I have both in the drawer in there."

"Fine. Get them. And don't try anything."

She walked the long way around, and he followed. As she passed the files, she dropped the wig. Leaning down to retrieve it, she reached over to balance herself on the table. And pushed the files to the floor.

"What are you doing?"

For the first time, she detected a touch of fear in the man's voice.

"Sorry. I-I dropped the wig." She gathered the files together as quickly as she could, trying not to draw attention to them. She didn't put Reynolds's on top, but she did pull one sheet out a few inches. And she left the files in an uncharacteristic messy stack. Hoping they would catch someone's eye.

Like Jake's.

It wasn't much. But it was the best she could do.

He came around the table and examined the top file. Thank goodness she hadn't put his there. "Hurry up."

She retrieved the rubber band, put her hair in a ponytail, and pulled the wig onto her head. Then she pinned her skirt.

"Now the hat. And tug it low."

After she complied, he walked over to her. "Now here's what we're going to do, Judge. You and I are going to walk out that door. I'll hold your arm. I want you to keep your head down low. Rummage around in your purse, like you're searching for your keys. You make one wrong move, and this game will end right here. For you *and* Harold. I'm the only one who knows where he is. You understand?"

"Yes."

"Good. Let's go."

As he guided her toward the door, she opened Delores's purse. He tucked the hand holding the gun under their linked arms, the barrel pressed against her side. Near her heart.

And as they stepped into the hall, Liz knew that unless a miracle happened, Martin Reynolds was about to finish the job he'd started three weeks ago.

Brett Holmes settled back in his chair in front of the bank of monitors showing the video feed of the hallway and the entrances and exits of the condo where Liz Michaels was sequestered. Sunday duty wasn't his favorite, but as one of the newest deputy marshals in the St. Louis office, he was used to being tagged for the less favorable shifts.

At least he only lived five minutes away. And this was a high-profile assignment. Protecting a federal judge who had an active threat against her life was a lot better than escorting some low-life prisoner to and from the airport.

The door to the judge's condo opened, and he leaned forward. Before Larry had taken off less than three minutes ago, he'd played back the tape of the Morettis arriving and given him a good description of the couple. The man and woman exiting the condo fit it to a T.

"Anything going on?" Dan poked his head in from the kitchen, where he was making a sandwich.

"The Morettis are leaving."

"Yeah?" Dan strolled in and took a quick look at the screen, juggling a knife in one hand and a jar of mustard in the other. "I wonder what goodie she left this time?"

"What do you mean?"

"You haven't heard about the cannoli?"

"No."

"Never mind, then."

As Dan returned to the kitchen, Brett watched the couple enter the elevator. The doors closed. He leaned back.

"Any other visitors coming today?"

"Nope." Dan reappeared and tossed him a bag of chips. "The judge leads a very quiet home life. Jake will probably stop by when he gets back from Chicago, though."

"I haven't had a chance to meet him yet. I hear he's just back from Iraq. Those SOG guys see all the action."

"You know what? They can have it. I'll take a nice, quiet protective detail any day. Like this one's been." He indicated the monitor displaying the empty hall.

"Yeah."

But two minutes later, as Brett watched the monitor that

displayed the older couple exiting the building, he couldn't help wishing he'd see a little action once in a while.

Except he doubted that was going to happen on this assignment.

At 5:15, when Jake opened the door to the command post, he was surprised to find an unfamiliar deputy on duty.

"You're back from Chicago earlier than I expected." Dan rose from the couch and stretched.

"I left after we took my mom to church." He and his siblings had planned to drive up together, but at the last minute he'd decided to take his own car. He wasn't certain why. Nor was he certain why he'd felt the need to cut and run after church instead of going to brunch with his family. It was true he wanted to spend part of the evening with Liz. But an odd feeling of restlessness had also pushed him to start the drive back even earlier than he'd planned.

The blond guy in front of the video monitors rose and held out his hand. "Brett Holmes."

"Jake Taylor." He returned the man's firm grip. "Where's Larry?"

"At the ER." Dan filled him in.

"How's his wife doing?"

"Okay so far. The bleeding's under control, and she hasn't lost the baby."

"Good." Jake checked the monitors. "Everything quiet here?"

"Very. The Morettis stopped by around 1:00. That's been the only activity." Dan headed for the kitchen. "You want a soda?"

"No, thanks. I'm going to stop in and see the judge."

"How come I knew that?" Grinning, Dan tossed the remark over his shoulder.

Jake ignored the comment. It was obvious the man had been talking to Spence. "I'll swing by here again on my way out."

"We'll be around."

Stepping into the hall, Jake pulled the door shut behind him and covered the distance to the adjacent unit in mere seconds, anxious to see Liz. It was amazing how much he'd missed her after being separated less than forty-eight hours. Even their brief phone conversation yesterday hadn't helped much. Talking long distance was more tantalizing than satisfying.

As he pressed the bell to her condo, Jake wondered if he could convince her to let him send out for Chinese. Sharing dinner with her would be a perfect way to end the day.

When there was no response to his first ring, Jake tried again. She might be napping. Or taking a shower. Or she could be on the treadmill again, with the music cranked up. Wearing those amazing spandex shorts.

A slow smile curved his lips, and he pressed harder on the bell.

After the second ring failed to produce a response, Jake pulled out his BlackBerry and punched in the number of her cell phone.

After three rings, a recorded voice asked him to leave a message.

His smile faded.

He tried calling the phone in her unit. He could hear it ringing on the other side of the door, but no one picked it up.

Telling himself not to overreact, that there was surely a logical reason for her lack of response, he strode back to the CP and pushed through the door.

"Where's the key to Liz's unit?" He glanced around. Each set of marshals on duty kept it in a different location.

Brett swiveled around from his seat in front of the bank of monitors. Dan frowned and crossed the living room to retrieve it from a small ginger jar. "What's up?"

"She's not answering."

"The key won't help if she has the dead bolt on."

"It's worth a try before I kick the door in." He looked at

Brett. "You stay here. Keep your eye on the monitors. Dan, come with me."

The other man fell in behind him as he retraced his steps.

Fitting the key in the lock, he turned it.

The door opened.

His alarm escalated.

"Liz?" He stopped in the middle of the foyer and listened.

Nothing.

"Check the front part of the unit. I'll cover the bedrooms."

Without waiting for Dan to respond to his curt command, he pulled out his gun and moved down the hall.

He started with Liz's bedroom. A quick survey showed nothing amiss. Everything looked in order in the closet too.

As he headed back down the hall, Dan joined him at the threshold of the second bedroom, where the treadmill was located.

The man shook his head, his expression grim. "Nothing."

"Her bedroom's clean too." Jake did a quick sweep of the exercise room, then reached for the closet door. His mind already racing ahead to next steps, he pushed it open to do a cursory check.

And stopped breathing.

A bound-and-gagged, slip-clad Delores Moretti stared up at him from the floor with wide, frightened eyes.

But it was the large block letters screaming at him from the computer-generated note beside her that sent his pulse into overdrive.

Harold Moretti is in the trunk of his car in Morgan Park.

But the judge is mine.

17

As Delores dissolved into tears for the second time, Jake was glad Mark Sanders had assumed the lead in taking her statement. His patience was deteriorating with every minute that ticked by.

At least she was a little more coherent now that her husband had been freed and was being brought to the command post to join her. But so far she'd revealed little that would be of any help in their investigation. She couldn't even remember the make or color of the car she'd been forced to drive here.

"I'm sorry, Agent Sanders." The gray-haired woman dabbed at her eyes with a tissue. "I was so scared—all I could think about was that gun pointing at me. And I was so worried about Harold."

"It's okay, Mrs. Moretti. That's a perfectly normal reaction." Mark picked up the glass of soda he'd poured for her and held it out. "Drink a little of this and we'll talk more in a minute."

Rising, the FBI agent motioned to Jake. He followed him to a corner of the living room. The busy CP wasn't the best place to talk with a victim, but the FBI's Evidence Response Team had taken over Liz's condo and they needed information from Delores. As soon as possible.

"We're going to have to give her a few more minutes."

Mark angled away from the older woman and dropped his voice. "I think we have a trauma spike going here."

"Yeah." Jake had witnessed that phenomenon on numerous occasions. Adrenaline, fear, and disorientation could push important information to the edges of a witness's or victim's consciousness. They often needed time to calm down in order to process it.

But time was in short supply.

"Maybe she'll remember more once she sees for herself that her husband is okay," Mark offered.

"Maybe."

"After he gets here, why don't you have your people talk to him, and we'll work with Mrs. Moretti?"

"Okay."

Mark gave him an appraising look. "You all right?"

No, he wasn't. The woman he'd come to care for more than he'd ever thought possible in just three weeks had been snatched from under their noses. He might not have been on duty, but he was responsible for her security detail. For protecting her.

And he'd failed.

Now her life hung in the balance.

A tsunami of guilt crashed over him, pulling him down, down, down into a dark, forsaken void. Cutting off his oxygen. Contorting his stomach into a painful knot.

Exactly the way it had after Jen died.

But Liz wasn't dead. He had to believe that. If her abductor had wanted her to die quickly, he'd have killed her here.

As for the guilt—there would be time later to beat himself up about that. Right now, he needed to focus on the task at hand: rescuing Liz before the killer finished the job he'd set out to do three weeks ago.

Sucking in a deep breath, he shoved his hands in the pockets of his jeans. Fisted them. "Yeah. I'm okay. We just need to find this guy. Fast."

"I agree."

An EMT from the ambulance they'd summoned when they'd found Delores approached them. "You guys want us to hang around?"

Jake shook his head. "I don't see why." After submitting to a quick exam, Delores had refused further medical attention. Likewise for Harold, according to the police who'd freed him from the trunk. Neither had suffered any major physical injury from their traumatic experience.

After gesturing to his colleagues, the technician disappeared out the door as Deputy Marshal Todd Nelson stepped inside. Catching sight of Jake, the other St. Louis-based Special Operations Group member joined them.

With a nod to Mark, he quickly turned his attention to Jake. "Matt's got a whole contingent from the SOG on the way."

"I'm not surprised." For a pending arrest in high-profile crimes, members of the elite group were always brought in. That's why he'd been called to Denver so soon after arriving in St. Louis.

Only they weren't even close to an arrest at this point.

"Matt briefed me. Anything new in the past half hour?"

"No. Mrs. Moretti has been too upset to give us much. We're hoping that changes once her husband gets here. In the meantime, let's watch the video."

He led the way to the dining table containing the monitors. The younger marshal—Brett, Jake reminded himself—had gone a few shades paler while they'd grilled him about what he'd observed on the screens. His features were still taut and his complexion on the ashen side as they approached.

"I've got the feed from the camera in the lobby and the one from the hall both queued to the couple's entry." He gestured to the center monitor.

Jake gave a curt nod as he, Todd, and Mark clustered behind him. "Okay. Let's take a look."

The first video showed the couple everyone had assumed

was Harold and Delores coming through the front door of the building.

"Zoom in as close as you can."

As Brett complied with Jake's instruction, all three men leaned closer.

"Between the sunglasses and hat and muffler, plus the way he kept his head down, I can't make out a thing." Jake shook his head. "Anyone see anything I'm missing?"

At the negative response, they moved on to the video of Larry using the security wand. Again, no matter how close they zoomed in, the man's bowed head gave them little to work with.

"Okay, let's see the exit videos."

They already knew the killer had spirited Liz away by disguising her as Delores. The older woman had told them that much. So Jake was tuned in to the subtle height difference between the man and woman in this clip versus the couple in the lobby video. The woman's gait was different too.

But he couldn't blame Brett for failing to notice those things. One quick viewing of the couple's entrance wouldn't have given the man enough context to red flag the minor differences.

"You'd have to look really close to see the discrepancies." Mark echoed his thoughts, peering at the screen. "And that floppy hat the judge is wearing doesn't help. Her face is almost completely hidden."

"Queue up the exit video from the front entrance," Jake said.

Brett tapped a few keys, and the sequence began to play.

Again, the man's features were impossible to discern. And at this point, they didn't need any more proof he'd kidnapped Liz. No clear image of her face was necessary.

But as the couple stepped through the front door, she gave them one. It was only a quick, stolen glance toward the video camera. Yet it was enough to reveal her terrified eyes.

The image clutched at his gut.

And Jake knew it would haunt him until she was safe again.

From her seat on a plain wooden chair in the rustic cabin, hands cuffed in front of her, one leg shackled to a support beam, Liz watched Martin Reynolds unwrap a deli sandwich and begin to eat. He hadn't said more than ten words since they'd left the condo, other than to instruct her to put on a pair of latex gloves when they'd reached his car and to give her driving directions as he kept the gun aimed at her. They'd made one brief stop, at a drive-up mailbox.

But first, he'd told her to pull over, handed her a pen, and dictated a message for her to write at the bottom of a typed document. The single sentence had sent a chill racing down her spine. Then he'd told her to sign it.

As she'd done so, she'd tried to read at least a few of the words. But he'd snatched it away too quickly. Tipping a bottle of water against a paper napkin, he'd moistened the flap of the envelope and sealed it.

When he'd instructed her to drop the envelope down the mail chute, she'd gotten the first inkling of why she'd been spared. It had been addressed to the news desk at the St. Louis *Post-Dispatch* and marked "urgent, time-sensitive material."

Meaning he wanted to make a statement by killing her. To tell the world why he was disenchanted with America and its judicial system. She'd noticed another similar-looking envelope on the table in the cabin. Was he trying to stretch this out, milk it for as much press as possible? If so, how much time did that give her?

She supposed she could try engaging him in conversation and hope he would drop a hint about the timing of his plans. But so far, the few questions she'd asked had been ignored.

The only time he'd acknowledged her presence had been when she'd asked to use the bathroom. He'd pulled out his revolver, cut through the plastic of her leg restraint with a wicked-looking hunting knife, and gestured toward the door. The bathroom had turned out to be a tiny outhouse behind the cabin. She'd finished her business as quickly as possible in the fading daylight, and been back in the chair ever since.

Her hair was still tucked inside the uncomfortable gray wig, and he'd ignored her request to remove it. She wished she knew what time it was, but the latex gloves covered her watch. Considering it felt like hours since any hint of light had seeped around the drawn shades of the only window without closed shutters, it had to be at least 9:00.

She watched her abductor take a swig of water and licked her parched lips.

"May I have a drink, please?"

No response.

When he finished eating, he gathered up his trash and deposited it in a plastic garbage bag with a drawstring top. Then he extinguished the stubby candle that had provided the only illumination and lay down on the bed, pulling a pile of blankets over him.

As the darkened room grew quiet, Liz suddenly felt pressure behind her eyes. She'd been too tense and frightened to cry until now, but with Martin preparing to sleep and the immediate danger suspended for the moment, tears welled up, blurring her vision.

But crying was a waste of valuable time. She needed to use this respite to assess her situation, not give in to an emotional meltdown.

There was one major problem, though. She didn't know what Martin had done with Harold. If her neighbor was being held hostage somewhere, his fate could still be in her hands. And if she attempted to escape—and failed—he might die.

But if she didn't try—if she couldn't find a way out—*she* would definitely die.

Yet how could she take the chance of putting Harold at risk?

Feeling trapped, Liz did what she'd always done in times of fear and darkness. She closed her eyes and sent a silent plea heavenward.

Please, Lord, show me what to do!

By 11:00 p.m., after FBI agents, marshals, and the local police had joined forces to canvas the neighborhood around the condo, hoping to find someone who had seen something—anything—that would help them identify or track the kidnapper, they had precious little new information.

Delores had remembered that the abductor's car was a dark blue midsized sedan. She had no idea of the make.

And after an up-close-and-personal search of the carpet in the condo, Clair Ellis, the FBI's lead ERT investigator, had found a golden-colored hair. She was fairly certain it would match the feline hair they'd found in Liz's house—confirming their assumption the perpetrator was the same guy.

The ERT was still at work both in the condo, along the route of entry and exit, and at the Morettis'. The team was also giving Harold's car a thorough going-over.

The situation, however, was much like the one they'd encountered in Liz's house after her sister was murdered. The killer had apparently left nothing but a cat hair as a calling card.

Shoving his hands into his pockets, Jake stared through the window of the CP, feeling as chilled and bleak as the cold autumn darkness outside. Their only hope was that the ERT would unearth some piece of information that would allow them to ID the guy.

But he knew that was a long shot.

"He's not giving us much to work with, is he?" Mark joined him, the frustration in his voice matching Jake's own.

"No."

"I'm heading home to grab a few hours of shut-eye. You might want to do the same so we can hit the ground running tomorrow. Clair will let me know if anything significant turns up in the meantime, and I can call you. It's not like the night crew isn't going to be all over this for the next few hours."

Jake knew that was true. This case would be worked 24/7 until it was solved. But he couldn't leave. Not yet.

"I think I'll hang around awhile. No sense going home when I know I won't sleep, anyway."

A few seconds of silence ticked by.

"You know, when I was on the Hostage Rescue Team, my partner and I had a similar experience with a dignitary protection assignment. Everything that could go wrong did. But if it makes you feel any better, we salvaged the situation against all odds. He's now happily married to the woman we were protecting, by the way."

Jake frowned at him. "What's that got to do with me?"

The agent shrugged. "I'm picking up some vibes that suggest Elizabeth Michaels is more than a job to you. We're all committed to finding her in time, Jake. Hang in there."

As the other man said good night and wove his way toward the door of the CP, Jake knew Mark meant well. And he didn't question the commitment of the FBI or his marshal colleagues.

But he also knew the killer wasn't likely to wait long to finish the job. The clock was ticking very fast. And with every second that passed, time was running out.

If it hadn't already.

The sound of her teeth chattering woke her. That, and the crick in her neck.

Opening her eyes, Liz squinted at the shadowy outlines around her, trying to orient herself. Even after three weeks, the condo felt strange and unfamiliar.

Except this wasn't the condo.

The memories came back in a sudden, jarring rush, and a

surge of adrenaline cleared her mind and set her pulse racing as her gaze sought the bed in the far corner of the room.

The man who had killed her sister in cold blood—and who planned to kill her—continued to sleep under a mound of blankets in these predawn hours of what might be her last day.

Resentment and hate bubbled up inside her as she pulled herself into as tight a ball as possible to conserve body heat in the dank coldness of the unheated cabin. Her faith taught forgiveness, but nowhere in her heart could she find a shred of sympathy or mercy for Martin Reynolds.

If it were up to her, she'd consign him to hell in a heartbeat.

And she wasn't going to meekly go along with his plan to kill her off so he could fulfill whatever misguided mission he was on.

Assuming Harold was safe by now—and she chose to assume that—she could come up with only one escape plan. She had to find a way to render Reynolds unconscious long enough to get some of his plastic restraints on him. And the best opportunity to do that would be during a trip to the outhouse, when her legs were free.

She didn't have a clue how she could accomplish that, especially with her hands restrained. But there had to be a way. On her next trip out there, she'd take a closer look at the area and the interior of the small structure. Maybe she'd spot something that would inspire a plan.

The odds were against her, though. She knew that. Reynolds could overpower her with little effort. Yet she couldn't give up without a fight.

With the possibility of failure so high, however, she needed to leave some proof she'd been here. Plant a few pieces of DNA evidence for the authorities to find. Because she wanted Martin Reynolds brought to justice.

Whether she survived or not.

Fingernails, she decided, would be a good place to start.

Catching the end of the latex glove in her teeth, she peeled it off. Then she lifted her thumb to her mouth and worked the nail with her teeth. She wanted a sharp edge on the first one.

After ripping the top of it off, she went to work on two more. Setting them carefully in her lap, she pressed her fingertips against the chair in several places, worked the glove back on again with her teeth, and waited—praying her abductor would give her a chance to set the fingernails on the floor once there was sufficient illumination in the cabin for her to scope out the area within arm's reach.

An eternity later, as the first light of dawn began to peep around the window shade, Reynolds stirred. He did no more than cast a quick glance her direction before heading out the door.

This was her opportunity. Leaning over, she surveyed the floor. The dead bugs and line of dirt along the wall suggested he didn't sweep often.

Good.

Bending down, she placed one polished nail upside down near the edge of the wall, beside a dust ball. The second she tucked halfway under the beam to which her ankle was shackled. The third she slipped into her shoe.

She was just finishing when he returned.

Without a word, he advanced toward her, revolver in one hand, hunting knife in the other. She tensed, but all he did was cut her ankle free from the plastic cuff, jerk her to her feet, and shove her out the door, in the direction of the privy.

Perfect.

Once inside the tiny structure, she took the fingernail out of her shoe and set it in the corner, beside a small pile of dirt, polish-side down. Then she worked off the glove on the hand with the jagged nail, pulled off a square of toilet paper, and folded it into fourths.

Taking a deep breath, she lifted her bound hands, reached inside the top of her cardigan, and dragged her ragged thumbnail across the tender skin near her sternum, cutting deep enough to draw blood. She pressed the scrap of toilet paper against the cut and held it in place as long as she dared. Though the light was dim, she could tell when she withdrew it that there was a sizable splotch of blood. Squeezing it into a tiny ball, she wrapped it in another square of tissue and tucked it in her shoe. Later, when she had the opportunity, she'd find somewhere near her chair to plant it.

While she used the so-called facilities, she worked her fingers under the wig, separated a few strands of her own hair at the nape, and yanked. Hard. It brought tears to her eyes, but she blinked them away as she coiled the strands and stashed them under some dust.

A sudden pounding on the door made her heart stutter.

"I-I'm hurrying as fast as I can, but it's hard with my hands bound." She quickly left a few more fingerprints, then worked the glove back on.

Taking a rapid inventory of the outhouse, she saw nothing with any potential to be a weapon. The place was bare except for a roll of toilet paper stuck on a wooden peg.

Half a minute later, when she opened the door, Martin grabbed her arm and propelled her back to the cabin, clearly not happy about the delay. As she stumbled along beside him, she scanned her surroundings. A few sturdy boards lay on the ground near their route, beside a bin of firewood. If she yanked free, maybe the element of surprise would give her a chance to grab one and take a swing that would stun him long enough for her to get in a blow to his head.

But at the pace he was walking, she had no time to implement that plan. She'd have to wait until her next trip outdoors.

If there was a next trip.

Please, God, let there be a next trip!

Back in the cabin, he shoved her into the chair and tossed a restraint toward her, keeping a safe distance away as he kept the revolver trained on her.

She knew the drill by now. He expected her to secure her ankle to the support beam.

Once she'd done so, he checked it, tightening it a notch for good measure.

"Please, could I have a drink of water?" Liz doubted he'd respond, but she'd had no fluids in eighteen hours, and her mouth felt as dry as the shriveled cornstalks in the rural Missouri fields.

As she'd suspected, he ignored her request. Pulling on his own latex gloves, he took a sheet of paper out of the envelope on the kitchen table, extracted a pen from his pocket, and walked over to her.

Now that he'd gotten rid of the mustache and the baseball cap, she had no trouble recognizing him as the man who'd given her such a venomous stare after she'd directed the verdict in the malpractice case. The loathing and hate in his eyes hadn't diminished one iota.

"Take this." He shoved the pen at her.

She fumbled it as he retrieved a yellowed magazine from the table. Setting a typed document on top, he put it in her lap. She noted that it bore today's date.

"Write these words at the bottom. Then sign your name."

As he recited the single sentence, a chill raced through Liz that had nothing to do with the penetrating cold in the cabin. Her hand began to shake so hard her script was barely legible.

When she finished he picked up the sheet of paper. For a moment, he studied it, as if deciding whether it was readable. Apparently satisfied that it was, he returned to the table, folded it, and slipped it inside the envelope. Once he'd sealed the flap with a rag he dampened from a water bottle, he pocketed the envelope and exited through the front door. A couple of minutes later, she heard the engine of his car, followed by the crunch of gravel.

Liz had no idea how long he would be away. But she didn't intend to assume she had another day to live. Every hour he held her captive increased his risk of being found. He had to know that.

Maybe she could find a way to free herself and get away before he returned.

Although the isolated cabin was deep in the woods, she'd paid attention during the drive and knew she could find her way to the tiny town they'd passed through a few miles from here. If she succeeded, the police could be waiting to welcome Martin home.

Clinging to that hope, she set to work.

18

Midmorning on Monday, as his BlackBerry began to vibrate, Jake took one hand off the steering wheel and pulled the device off his belt. A quick glance at caller ID set his pulse racing. Mark.

He wasted no time on a greeting. "Did the ERT come up with something?"

"No. But our man sent a letter to the *Post-Dispatch*. We just got the call. A couple of our guys are on their way over to pick it up now and get some elimination prints from whoever's handled it there."

"What does it say?" Jake switched lanes on I-64, heading for an off-ramp so he could reverse direction. His quick trip home from Liz's condo for a shower and change of clothes could wait.

"Apparently it's a long anti-government diatribe. From the initial read, it doesn't offer any clues about where he's taken the judge. But his intent to use her to gain attention for his cause is clear."

"Maybe we'll find some prints. Or DNA, if he licked the envelope."

"Only if he was sloppy."

They both knew he wasn't.

"What's the postmark?" Jake sped up the exit ramp.

"Afton."

A South St. Louis suburb. "That could be the direction of his destination. Why would he drive around with Liz in the car any longer than necessary and risk detection? My guess is he wanted to get wherever he was going ASAP."

"I agree. Where are you?"

Crossing the overpass, he wove around several cars, then turned onto the entrance ramp. "Heading eastbound on I-64. Are you at your office?"

Sometime during the night the higher-ups had made the decision to relocate the operations center to the FBI field office. There was no need to hang around the condo anymore.

"Yes. We may have the letter in hand by the time you arrive."

Jake floored the Trailblazer. "I'll be there in ten minutes."

Eight minutes later, Jake pushed through the front door of the FBI office. After clearing security, he was directed to one of the conference rooms that lined the cubicle-filled bull pen in the center of the first floor.

Mark and a mid-fortyish man with salt-and-pepper hair were seated at the rectangular table, poring over copies of the letter as he entered. Mark handed him one as he introduced Luke Garavaglia, assistant special agent in charge of the St. Louis operation.

Sparing the man no more than a quick handshake, Jake read the typed note, beginning with the bold quotes at the top of the page.

> **"Don't interfere with anything in the Constitution. That must be maintained, for it is the only safeguard of our liberties."**
>
> **Abraham Lincoln**
>
> **"The Constitution is not an instrument for the government to restrain the people, it is an instrument for the people to restrain the government—lest it come to dominate our lives and interests."**
>
> **Patrick Henry**

Today, I abducted federal judge Elizabeth Michaels.

Soon she will die.

Here is why.

America is disintegrating. Our Constitution is being destroyed. Our rights are being violated by our government, just as they were in the days of our founding fathers.

Much of the blame rests in the hands of the decaying judiciary—the very courts that are supposed to serve *us*. We, the people. Instead, they are stripping away our rights. Day after day they break their vow to support the Constitution.

Our corrupt government has become an intimidating big brother filled with terrocrats, and the judiciary is its enabler.

It is time to stop the courts and the lawyers and the judges from crushing the life out of our Constitution and snatching away our freedoms. They are the criminals—not the people they prosecute . . . and persecute.

Look at what they've done to our constitutional right to bear arms. The restrictive rules and regulations that have been put in place are a direct threat to our life and liberty.

The courts of America belong to the people, not to government prosecutors and tyrannical judges. It's time we took them back . . . and took the first step in returning this great country to the principles on which it was founded—self-reliance, respect for life and personal property, and the protection of our unalienable God-given rights.

When peaceful measures fail, as they have, it is our right—our *duty*—to use force to remove and replace abusive government and its agents.

Wake up, Americans. If you are a patriot, heed this call before it is too late.

Take back your country.

One terrocrat at a time.

At the bottom, handwritten and signed by Liz, was a brief, bloodcurdling message.

I am a sacrifice in the cause of liberty.

"Wow." Jake fought back a wave of nausea as he groped

for a chair and sank into it, the slight tremble in his hands the only visible indication of the roiling in his gut.

"That was our reaction." Mark folded his hands in front of him. "We're couriering the original to the lab, along with some handwriting samples we got from the judge's office, and we've already faxed this to our profilers in Quantico. But I suspect we're dealing with a fanatic associated with one of the sovereign citizen groups. Some of this stuff sounds as if it was pulled right off their literature and websites."

"I agree." As a U.S. marshal charged with protecting the judiciary, Jake was well briefed on the loose network of disgruntled individuals who claimed no accountability to the federal government and who often lashed out at courts and judges they felt had wronged them. The fifty-year-old movement was a mixed bag of tax protestors, white supremacists, fringe religious groups, desperate individuals—even prisoners.

Although its popularity had ebbed and flowed through the decades, he knew the past few years had seen a sharp increase in activity and threats against the judiciary. That was one of the reasons the Marshals Service had opened a high-tech Threat Management Center in Virginia, where intimidation tactics against judges were monitored and analyzed, and personnel could tap into classified FBI and CIA databases. He'd had contact with the center on a couple of occasions.

This might be another one.

As Jake scanned the copy of the letter again, his lips settled into a grim line. "This guy's over the top."

"Yeah. He's way past paper terrorism."

That was the typical tactic of such groups, Jake knew. They liked to file frivolous lawsuits and liens against public officials and law enforcement officers to intimidate them and clog up the court system.

Unfortunately, Liz had run into one of the zealots who had no compunction about using violence to dismantle the system. All in the name of patriotism.

"Do you think this has any connection to the Patriot Constitutionalists?" Luke asked.

Jake narrowed his eyes. "Who are they?"

"A very active local sovereign citizen group," Mark replied. "I've been doing some undercover investigation on them, but I haven't discovered anything incriminating. The leader, a former IRS agent turned psychologist named Jarrod Williams, is very charismatic—and very careful. I've been to a dozen meetings of his group, and I've never heard him advocate violence . . . or anything illegal. He's masterful at coming up with ways to subvert the system within the confines of the law."

"You think our guy might be part of that group?" For the first time, Jake allowed himself to hope they might have a lead, however slim.

"I don't know." Mark tapped his finger on the table as twin creases appeared on his brow. "The members are very close-mouthed. Most only share first names, if that. And I've never heard anyone mention violence. That doesn't mean there aren't some fanatics in the group, though."

"We can't blow your cover by sending you to talk to the guy," Luke said. "I'll have Nick pay Mr. Williams a friendly visit. See if he can ferret out any names of potential suspects."

"I'd like to go along," Jake spoke up. At least he'd be doing something; sitting around waiting for leads would drive him nuts.

"Okay by me." Luke rose. "I'll round up Nick. Mark can brief the two of you on Williams, and then you can head over to his office. Let's take him by surprise. Give me five minutes."

As he exited, Mark looked at Jake. "I know the judge said she never received any threats, but she clearly made an enemy somewhere along the line in her career."

"Yeah." Jake massaged his forehead with one hand. "I take it none of the files she turned over to you produced anything?"

"Not yet. We're still checking out a few personalities. A lead may yet surface."

A muscle clenched in Jake's jaw. "We don't have much time."

"I know." Mark's somber expression matched Jake's mood. "Let's hope Quantico comes up with some trace evidence on the letter. Or Mr. Williams shares a piece of information that's helpful."

As they waited for Luke to return, Jake reread the letter, the word *hope* echoing in his mind. He hadn't thought a lot about hope—or faith—since Jen died. Nor communicated much with God. His last plea to the Almighty, torn from his heart as he'd knelt on the snow-packed slope beside her, had been to spare her life.

God hadn't listened.

And after she died, he'd realized his so-called faith had been a sham. It was Jen's faith that had carried them as a couple. It was her urging that had compelled him to attend church each week. But though he'd gone through the motions, he'd never achieved the personal connection his wife had found so comforting.

He supposed dealing with criminals day in and day out was one of the reasons for that—along with the senseless violence he witnessed on a regular basis. On some subliminal level, the juxtaposition of evil and good must have negated his faith.

But until tragedy had shattered his own life, he'd never given that paradox much thought. And when he'd tried to reconcile a loving God with all the bad things that happened in the world—including Jen's death—he'd failed. The admonition of the minister at her funeral, to trust in the Lord's goodness and mercy, had fallen on deaf ears. His trust had been shattered. So he'd walked away.

And one visit to church, thanks to Alison's prodding, hadn't reestablished his connection with the Almighty.

Now, however, faced with another life-and-death situation,

he was tempted to again ask the Lord to show him some of the goodness and mercy the minister had talked of.

But the words wouldn't come. He'd have to leave the formal prayer to his mother.

And hope God might tune into the desperate plea echoing in his heart.

As Patricia stepped through the front door after her extended lunch with Molly, anxious to escape the wind that was making the thirty-five-degree temperature feel more like twenty, she frowned. The house was far too chilly.

With a loud meow of complaint, Josie padded in from the hall and twined herself around Patricia's legs.

"I'm with you, kid." Patricia leaned down and gave her a distracted pat.

Leaving her coat on, she walked to the thermostat in the hall. It was still set on seventy-two, as it had been since she'd arrived. But the temperature gauge read only sixty degrees.

Patricia huffed out a breath. It figured that Marty's furnace would wait until he was out of town to act up.

She hadn't planned to bother him during his short trip, but rather than pick a heating and cooling company at random from the phone book, it might be best to see if he had a preferred service company.

His cell number was where he'd left it, tucked between the canisters of tea and coffee on the counter, and she tapped it into the portable phone, hugging her coat around her.

"The party you are trying to reach is unavailable. Please try again later or leave a message at the tone."

Great. Either he was out of range, his battery was dead, or he'd forgotten to turn on his phone.

She pressed the off button. It didn't matter why he wasn't answering. The furnace needed attention. Now.

As she set the phone back in its cradle on top of the built-in desk, she eyed the drawers. She didn't make a habit of snooping in other people's business—even her brother's—but if he used this desk to pay bills and keep house records, she might find a receipt or check stub that would give her a clue about what service company to call.

Pulling open the pencil drawer, she found Marty's checkbook and several stacks of check stubs held together with binder clips. She'd resort to sorting through those if necessary, but perhaps the two side drawers would yield faster results.

The top one was full of what appeared to be brochures, printouts, and newspaper clippings. She sifted through them, noting the headings. They covered all kinds of subjects, from patriotism and punitive taxes to criticisms against elected officials and gun control information.

How odd. She'd been kidding him the other day when she'd made that comment about him becoming an activist. But maybe she hadn't been off base. For a guy who'd never shown much interest in political stuff, he'd collected an awful lot of government-related material.

Closing that drawer, she checked the bottom one. It was empty.

With a sigh, she went back to the pencil drawer and pulled out a recent stack of check stubs. She didn't intend to waste a lot of time on this exercise. The furnace needed to be serviced today or she'd be facing a long, chilly night. If she didn't find a likely candidate on a check within ten minutes, she'd resort to the yellow pages.

Nine minutes later, after riffling through four packs of stubs, she gave up. There hadn't been a name on any of the checks that bore a remote resemblance to a heating and cooling firm. They were just the usual utility, credit card, and insurance kinds of payments.

The only thing that had caught her eye was an odd notation at the bottom of each check in the most recent stack. Above his signature, her brother had written "without prejudice UCC 1-308."

What in the world was that all about?

Not that it mattered. Her priority was to get the furnace fixed.

All at once the ring of the doorbell echoed through the house, and she set the last stack of checks on top of the desk before heading back through the living room.

Molly smiled as she opened the door, juggling Jack on her hip. "You left your gloves on the front seat."

"Goodness. I must be getting absentminded in my old age. Thank you, dear." She took the knit gloves she'd purchased a few days ago when the weather had taken a cold turn. "I'm afraid I may need them indoors. Marty's furnace seems to be on the blink."

Molly wrinkled her nose. "They always pick the worst times to go out, don't they? We had that same problem last year. The morning of Christmas Eve, of all days. But a friend from church recommended a company to us, and they sent a guy right out. Would you like me to look up the name and call you when I get home?"

"That would be wonderful. Josie's already complaining about the cold, and I'm not far behind."

"Give me five minutes." With a wave, Molly took off, tugging the blanket higher around Jack's head to shield him from the wind.

As Patricia closed the door, Josie gave another loud *meow*.

"Hang in there, kiddo. Help is on the way."

By the time Liz heard Reynolds's car pull up outside the cabin, hope had given way to frustration, which in turn had degenerated to despair. Though she'd tried for hours to free herself, all she had to show for her efforts were raw wrists and a swollen, bruised ankle where the plastic restraint had bitten into her flesh as she'd tugged and pulled.

Failing to free herself meant she'd have to revert to her original plan—try to surprise him by lunging for one of the boards near the woodpile. If she could hit him behind the knees so he fell, she might be able to deliver a whack to his head that would buy her enough time to take his gun and get some plastic restraints on him.

At this stage, that was her only option.

But she prayed Reynolds had left a clue somewhere that would put Jake and his law-enforcement counterparts on his trail. That was her best hope of survival.

The door swung open. Reynolds spared her no more than a quick glance as he stepped inside, a white deli-type bag in his hands, a newspaper tucked under his arm. As he set the bag on the table, the paper slipped and fell to the floor—landing close enough for her to read the headline of the Monday morning edition.

FEDERAL JUDGE ABDUCTED
SISTER SLAIN IN JUDGE'S HOME IN OCTOBER

What captured her attention, however, were the photos. Her official court portrait was prominently displayed—but she focused on the shot of her neighbors. Harold's arm was around Delores's shoulders, and underneath was a bold quote: **"He said if we didn't cooperate, he'd kill us."**

Harold was safe.

She could now attempt her escape without worrying that it would put him in danger. Relief coursed through her.

Tugging off his leather gloves, Reynolds picked up the paper and waved it in her face. "We made the front page, Judge."

She recoiled, lifting her hands in an automatic gesture of defense.

The next thing she knew, her arm was taken in a crushing grip. His eyes narrowed as he examined her abraded wrist. Then he checked the other one. She tried not to shake as he stared at her with cold eyes that contained not a flicker of empathy.

"You aren't going to escape your due this time, Judge."

Turning his back, he sat at the table and proceeded to eat a poor boy sandwich.

Despite her lack of appetite, Liz's stomach growled. And when he took a drink of water, the dryness in her mouth intensified. If he continued to withhold food and water, she'd begin to weaken. That would make it far more difficult to muster the strength to deliver a blow hard enough to disable him.

Time was running out.

On the next trip to the privy, she was going to have to give her escape plan her best shot.

"How much longer do you want to give this guy?"

At Jake's irritated question, Special Agent Nick Bradley crossed an ankle over a knee and leaned back in the leather chair in Jarrod Williams's plush office. "Five minutes?"

That was four minutes too long, as far as Jake was concerned. He narrowed his eyes at the thirtysomething, sandy-haired agent with the all-American-boy look. "Max."

They'd already been cooling their heels for almost fifteen minutes. Jake suspected Jarrod had hightailed it out the side door when his secretary had called to tell him he had visitors. She'd stalled for a couple of minutes, then shown them to the man's office with the promise he'd be back shortly.

Right.

No doubt the guy's delay was a statement. He was doing his best to disrupt their investigation. Practicing what he preached.

But Jake didn't have the patience for his games. Not with Liz's life hanging in the balance.

Just as he was about to suggest they start putting some pressure on the secretary to round up Jarrod, the side door opened and a tall, spare man with a full head of white hair joined them. Dressed in a well-tailored suit, crisp white dress shirt, and silk tie, he exuded confidence—and the charisma

Mark had mentioned. The man's attire was in marked contrast to Jake's wrinkled khakis, open-neck cotton shirt, and scuffed leather jacket. Too bad he hadn't had a chance to go home long enough to shave and put on a suit. Another reason to let Nick, in his dark gray power suit, take the lead with Jarrod, as they'd agreed on the way over.

"Good afternoon, gentlemen. How can I be of help?"

After they shook hands, introduced themselves, and handed over business cards, Nick wasted no time on preliminaries.

"We have a few questions about your Patriot Constitutionalists organization, Mr. Williams. We have reason to believe the person who killed Judge Elizabeth Michaels's sister and abducted the judge herself on Sunday may be a member of your group."

Jarrod raised an eyebrow as he took his seat behind his desk. "I don't advocate violence, gentlemen. If you've investigated me enough to know about my organization, I suspect you know that as well."

"We're not suggesting you aided or abetted this person." Nick fixed him with a steady look. "But there are zealots in any group. People who take extreme measures. Perhaps misinterpret directives. What we'd like to know is whether you think anyone who belongs to your group might be capable of the kind of violence that's been perpetrated against the judge and her sister."

Resting his elbows on his desk, Jarrod steepled his fingers. "It's not a group in the sense you're suggesting. It's simply a loose collection of individuals who happen to believe, as I do, that our government needs reforming. I keep no membership roster. People may come and go as they choose without making any sort of commitment."

"But I'm sure you're familiar with the regulars," Nick pressed, maintaining an even tone. "And I would think you'd know whether any of them have a propensity toward violence."

"I'm sorry, Agent"—he referred to the card on his desk—

"Bradley. When people come to my meetings, I promise them their presence will be known only to me and them. I can't violate their trust."

Jake stepped in, fixing the man with an intent look as he leaned forward. "Mr. Williams, let me put it this way. We have one murder on our hands already. We don't want another one. But that's what we'll have if we don't get some helpful information quickly."

For several moments Jarrod regarded him, his expression cool and unflinching. "Perhaps you could tell me why you think someone in my organization is involved."

They'd anticipated that question. Drawing a copy of the kidnapper's letter out of the portfolio on his lap, Nick handed it over in silence.

A frown appeared on Jarrod's brow as he read it.

"I'm sure you recognize the sovereign citizenship language," Jake said when he finished.

Passing the letter back to Nick, Jarrod once more steepled his fingers. "Many of those thoughts do represent principles of current-day patriots. But as I noted before, I don't advocate violence. There are peaceful means to achieving our ends. I would never condone murder or kidnapping."

"A misguided follower who's checked out other sovereign citizen groups on the Net might believe that's the next step in the professed battle to save America," Nick countered.

Jarrod lifted his hands palms up and shrugged. "What can I say? It's possible. But I can't take responsibility for someone who's chosen to resort to extreme measures."

They were getting nowhere.

"Where were you on Sunday between the hours of 11:00 and 1:00, Mr. Williams?" Nick asked.

The question seemed to surprise the older man. "Am I a suspect?"

Nick countered with a question of his own. "Do you have an objection to telling us your whereabouts?"

The ghost of a smile flickered at his lips. "I was at church.

My pastor and dozens of people will vouch for that. First Congregational. Pastor Adam Burnett."

Shooting Jake a look, Nick closed his portfolio and stood. "If you think of anything that could help prevent a second murder, we'd appreciate a call."

"Of course."

As they exited the man's offices and headed down the hall to the elevator, Nick turned to Jake. "What do you think?"

"Either he truly believes no one in his group is responsible, or he's a very good liar."

"Yeah." Nick pressed the elevator button. "We'll check out the church, but I think that's going to be a dead end."

"I agree. We could get a search warrant for his home and office to see if we can find a Patriot Constitutionalists roster, but even if we did uncover one—and I doubt it exists in any sort of easily recognizable form—we'd have to run intel on every single person. That would take time we don't have."

The door opened, and they moved inside.

"It might still be worth doing. Let's regroup at the operations center. See if the profilers have weighed in yet." Nick selected the lobby button.

As the elevator descended, Jake's spirits plummeted as well. The visit with Jarrod had yielded nothing. The profilers were unlikely to tell them much more than they'd already surmised. The odds of the abductor's fingerprints or DNA being on the letter or envelope were miniscule, based on past experience.

They needed a break. Badly.

And they needed it fast.

Please, Lord!

The desperate, silent entreaty came unbidden, from deep within his soul, surprising him.

But he let it stand. Because while he and God might not be on the best of terms, they needed all the help they could get to find Liz before it was too late.

19

"I hate to be the bearer of bad news, but you need a new furnace."

As Bill Lewis, the repairman from Premier Heating and Cooling, pronounced his verdict, Patricia let out a disgusted sigh. "Can you do anything to make it run for just a couple more days? My brother gets back tomorrow night, and I'd rather leave this decision to him."

"I'm sorry, ma'am. It's a twenty-year-old unit that's been patched and repaired too often already. I could try to shore her up for a few days, but it would be like throwing money into a black hole. The valves are corroded, and the heat exchanger has several cracks. There's also a lot of rust in the manifold tube going into the gas valve from the main line. To be honest, I think there's a serious risk of a carbon monoxide leak."

Patricia had no idea what half of that meant, but none of it sounded good.

"If you have an electric space heater, that could keep the chill off the bedroom at night and the kitchen during the day, until your brother gets back," the man suggested.

"I'll have to look around." She hadn't seen one, but it was possible Marty had one in the basement. If not, she could always buy a cheap unit to tide her over. Or maybe his hunting buddy's wife could reach them and she could convince him to come home early. She should have thought of that sooner. "Do you have a card you could leave?"

"Sure thing." He withdrew one from his pocket as Josie wove around his ankles.

"Sorry about that." Patricia shooed her away from him. "She's been sticking close to me too. I think she's trying to stay warm."

"No problem." He handed over the card. "We can give you prices and install a new unit within twenty-four hours once you make a decision."

"Thanks. How much do I owe you?"

He quoted the amount, and she moved to the desk, where she'd left Marty's checkbook and the check stubs. After Helen died, he'd added her name to all his accounts. Good thing. That meant she could write a check on his account for the service call.

As she signed it, Patricia hesitated. Was she supposed to include that UCC 1-308 code he always used?

Hesitating, she turned to the repairman. "Do you have any idea what this means? It's on all of my brother's checks for the past year or so." She pointed out the notation on one of the stubs.

He squinted at it, his expression puzzled. "I haven't a clue. I've never seen anything like that."

"Me neither." Deciding to skip it, she signed the check and handed it over, then walked him to the door. "I'm sure my brother will be in touch in a day or two."

"No hurry from our end. But get yourself an electric heater for tonight. It won't be cold enough to freeze your pipes, but the house will get mighty chilly."

"I will. Thanks."

After closing the door behind him, Patricia returned to the kitchen and pulled out the phone book. Scanning the listings under Abernathy, she found two Josephs. One of them had to be Marty's hunting pal.

The first call was a bust. The man who answered had never heard of Marty.

A woman picked up at the second number.

"Mrs. Abernathy?"

"Yes."

"This is Patricia Reynolds. I'm trying to reach the Joe Abernathy who's on a hunting trip with my brother, Martin Reynolds. Is this his number?"

The silence on the other end of the line stretched so long that Patricia wondered if they'd been disconnected. "Hello? Are you still there?"

"What did you say your name was?" There was a note of caution in the woman's voice.

"Patricia Reynolds. Martin's sister. I'm staying at his house while I'm in town, and the furnace went out. I tried to call him, but his cell phone isn't working. I was hoping your husband might have a phone with him. If he's the Joe Abernathy who's with my brother."

"Ms. Reynolds, I'm confused. I recognize your brother's name, but my husband died three years ago."

Speechless, Patricia stared out the kitchen window at the shriveled, decaying maple leaves being tossed about by the frosty autumn wind, their fall beauty long faded.

"Ms. Reynolds?"

"Yes." She pulled herself back to the conversation. "Perhaps I misunderstood my brother. I'm sorry to have bothered you."

"No problem. Good luck tracking him down."

As the phone went dead, an ominous chill settled over Patricia. Slowly she lowered the phone into its cradle. Ever since she'd arrived in St. Louis, she'd picked up strange vibes from Marty. He'd been distant, distracted, and uncommunicative. While he'd never been the most social person, they'd always been close. And they'd always managed to share some laughs.

There'd been little laughter on this trip. And only when he'd talked about gun control had he seemed focused.

Then there was all that material in the desk drawer. Some of it had looked kind of radical.

Lowering herself into a kitchen chair, she propped her elbow on the table and rested her chin in her hand, unable to shake her sense of unease.

What in the world was her brother up to?

Although his eyes felt gritty from lack of sleep, Jake fought off his fatigue as he settled into a chair in the command post at the FBI office. Quantico was ready with a report from both the forensic team examining the letter and from the profilers, and a full contingent of FBI agents and marshals had assembled, including the SOG guys who had been filtering in over the past few hours. Jake surveyed the crowded conference room. Luke Garavaglia was at the head of the table. His own boss, Matt Warren, sat beside him. Spence was across the table.

BlackBerry still in hand, Todd slipped back into the seat beside him. "Thanks for saving my spot." As he tucked the phone into its holder on his belt, he inspected Jake. "When's the last time you slept?"

"Saturday night."

"You must be running on fumes."

Jake lifted one shoulder. "I'll crash tonight for a while if there's nothing new."

Not that he expected to sleep. How could he, when the image of Liz's terrified eyes as her abductor had guided her out of the lobby kept strobing across his mind?

The phone squawked to life as Luke pressed the speaker button and dropped the handset back in its cradle. "Christy, are you on the line?"

"Yes."

"Okay. We have a full house on hand to listen to your report. For those of you here who haven't dealt with Christy, she's a profiler in our Behavioral Analysis Unit. Christy, you're on."

"Several of us have reviewed the letter, and we all reached

the same conclusion. As you suspected, we believe you're dealing with a radical member of a sovereign citizen group. These people have often been victims of the system—on multiple occasions in some cases. That fuels their feeling of persecution. Many ascribe to conspiracy theories of one sort or another. The most radical ones get desperate and feel violence is their only option."

"Any thoughts on our man's age?" Luke asked.

"No. This movement crosses generations and all walks of life. But I'd say you're looking for someone who's angry, socially isolated, and obsessed with revenge. You should assume he has access to weapons and may be well-armed. As most of you know, these sovereign citizen types have no trust in government and operate from what they believe is very high moral ground. They're absolutely convinced their position is correct and are often willing to die for it. Timothy McVeigh is a good example of that. We saw the same phenomenon with Waco, Ruby Ridge, and the Montana Freemen. These types of people consider themselves martyrs for a greater cause."

"Do you think the fact the guy is playing the press angle buys us some time?" Jake threw out the question.

"I wouldn't count on it. These people can be very methodical and logical. Unless he wants to be discovered—which doesn't appear to be the case, given the care he's exercised to conceal his identity—I doubt he'll risk holding on to the judge more than a couple of days."

While Christy's answer didn't surprise him, hearing an expert profiler confirm his own opinion did nothing to quell Jake's growing anxiety.

"Any other questions?" Luke glanced around the silent room. "Okay. We appreciate the input, Christy. Thanks."

"I hope it helps. Good luck."

Pushing a different button on the phone, Luke spoke again. "Sam, you with us?"

"I'm here."

"Sam's been overseeing the lab work," Luke told the assembled group. "All right, Sam, what do you have?"

"Not enough, I'm afraid. There's nothing unusual about the paper the letter was written on or the envelope, and the few prints either matched the elimination prints that were sent or didn't show up in NCIC. There's no DNA on the adhesive, so your guy didn't lick it."

No trace evidence. No prints in the National Crime Information Center database. A muscle in Jake's jaw twitched.

"Paul Sheehan, our handwriting expert, did confirm that the message and signature written at the bottom of the letter are the judge's," Sam added.

"What about that gold hair the ERT found in the condo?" Luke tapped a finger on the table.

"Definitely feline. And it matches the one from the previous crime scene three weeks ago."

"Anything else?"

"No. We tried to clean up the surveillance tapes from the judge's condo to see if we could sharpen the guy's face, but with the glasses and hat and muffler, we still can't pick up any distinguishing features."

"Okay. Questions?" When no one spoke, Luke leaned toward the phone to disconnect the call. "Thanks, Sam."

A heavy silence hung in the room as Luke sat back. Leading Jake to conclude that everyone was as stymied as he was by the rapidly cooling case.

"From our end, Jarrod Williams, the leader of the Patriot Constitutionalists, had a valid alibi for Sunday," Luke told the assembled group. "Matt, you want to jump in here?"

Matt rested his elbows on the table and knitted his fingers together. "All we have is a profiler's assessment, a cat hair, and an essentially worthless video." He shook his head. "We need a break. I'm open to ideas."

"Mark, when's the next meeting of the Patriot Constitutionalists?" Jake asked.

"Not until a week from Wednesday."

No good.

"While you and Nick were paying a visit to Jarrod Williams today, I did go through some databases of sovereign citizen groups," Mark offered. "I found Mr. Williams's photo, but I didn't recognize anyone else from the meetings I've attended. If our guy is part of that group, he's not on any official radar screens."

"Okay. We can't just sit around hoping for something to turn up." Luke jabbed his fingers through his hair and blew out a breath. "Let's do another canvas of the area around the judge's condo, broadening the scope by a few blocks. And let's do the same on the judge's street. I know none of the immediate neighbors saw anything on Sunday, but let's expand our perimeter there too. Matt, why don't we divvy up the assignments between your people and mine?"

"That works."

"All right. Everyone hang close while we sort this out."

As the meeting broke up, Matt exchanged a few words with Luke, then detoured to Jake and Todd. After sizing Jake up, he planted his fists on his hips.

"Go home. Take a shower. Get some sleep. We have plenty of people working this. If there's a break, I need you fresh."

Jake wanted to protest, but his boss was right. Any agent or marshal could question possible witnesses as effectively as he could. And the lack of sleep was beginning to dull his reaction time. He needed to be at the top of his game if they got a solid lead on Liz's abductor.

"I'll be back in a few hours."

"Eight o'clock tomorrow morning," Matt countered.

Jake thought about arguing. Decided not to. "Okay. I'll see you then."

As their boss walked away, Jake angled toward Todd. "Are you working tonight?"

"Looks that way."

"Page me if anything turns up. Anything."

"You heard the boss. Go home and sleep."

"If you won't, I'll find someone who will."

Giving him the steady, piercing stare that made him such a good sniper, Todd crossed his arms and shook his head. "Fine. I'll page you. But to be honest, I'm not expecting much to develop tonight."

Jake turned away, not liking Todd's conclusion. Yet as he made his way out of the building into the dark night, shivering as a gust of wind cut through his thin leather jacket, he couldn't dispute it. Considering the dearth of leads, there was a very good chance Liz's abductor would elude them for the immediate future.

They'd catch him eventually, though. In the vast majority of cases, even the most careful criminals made mistakes that came back to haunt them sooner or later.

In this situation, however, later wasn't good enough. Time was a luxury they didn't have. The window to rescue Liz was closing fast. At best, Jake estimated they had thirty-six to forty-eight hours.

As he put his key in the ignition and started for home, he tried not to dwell on the odds of success. But he knew they weren't good.

And he also knew that with so little to go on, it would take a miracle to save Liz.

By the time Reynolds heeded Liz's request for a trip to the outhouse, night had fallen. And implementing her plan in the dark didn't make a lot of sense. It would be difficult enough to pull off when she could clearly see both the board she intended to use as a weapon and her target. As she stumbled through the pitch blackness toward the tiny privy, she could only pray she'd get another chance tomorrow, in the daylight.

Shivering, she hurried to finish. While she could see her breath in the cabin, at least no cold wind seeped through the cracks in the walls, as it did here in the outhouse. *Warm*, she had come to realize, was a relative term. She wished Reynolds would light the woodstove in the cabin, but she supposed he was afraid the smoke would advertise his presence. Thank goodness she was still wearing the bulky sweatshirt and sweater he'd insisted she put on before leaving the condo. Nevertheless, she felt chilled to the bone. And her head was pounding.

Five minutes later, she was back in the chair she'd occupied for most of the past thirty hours. After verifying her ankle was securely attached to the post, Reynolds sat at the table, close to the stubby candle that provided the only illumination. Pulling a deck of cards out of his pocket, he began to play solitaire.

As she watched him calmly lay down card after card, Liz's stomach lurched with disgust, and a fierce rage welled up inside her. This was the man who'd killed Stephanie in cold blood. Taken an innocent life through a case of mistaken identity. And he knew that. Yet she'd seen zero evidence of remorse. Or any feelings at all. What kind of animal was he?

"I don't know why you're doing this, but no matter how noble you think your cause is, nothing exonerates murder."

She hadn't intended to voice her thoughts. But the bitter words came out before she could stop them.

Reynolds's hand froze for an instant in the process of laying down a card, and her breath caught in her throat. *Stupid, stupid, stupid*, she railed silently. If she antagonized him, he might decide to kill her sooner than he'd planned.

After a few moments, he went back to his game and she let out her breath. For once, she was glad he'd ignored her. She needed to make it through this night.

Two hours later, when he extinguished the candle and burrowed under the mound of blankets on the bed, Liz's tense muscles went limp. She was safe for a few more hours.

Letting her head drop back to rest on the rough plank wall behind her, she tried to force her brain to shut down. She needed to rest and conserve her strength. Get some sleep, if possible.

Because when dawn broke, she wanted to be as ready as she could be for what she knew would be her one and only chance to escape.

The laser point of a sunbeam nudged Jake awake, pulling him back from what felt like a drug-induced sleep. Blinking, he shifted to escape the sun and peered at his watch: 6:30. The last time he'd checked prior to falling into a fitful slumber it had been 3:30.

Three hours of sleep wasn't enough.

But it would have to do. Now that he was awake, there was no way he'd be able to drift off again.

Swinging his legs to the floor, he wiped a hand down his face. Todd hadn't called, so he assumed there'd been no break in the case.

As he rose and headed bleary-eyed for the bathroom to take a quick shower, he scrolled through the email messages on his BlackBerry. None of them required an immediate response. Same with voice mail. He did owe Cole and Alison return calls, though. They'd both tried to reach him twice since the news of Liz's abduction had broken yesterday morning, but he'd let their calls roll to voice mail. For now, he needed to focus on the case.

The brief, hot shower woke him up, and as his brain began firing on all cylinders again, he settled on a plan of action. He'd only taken a quick look around Liz's condo after she was abducted. Nothing had seemed amiss, and he'd felt no need to return while the ERT was in the unit.

But the technicians were gone now. And it was possible, on closer inspection, he might notice something he'd missed on Sunday. It was worth a trip, anyway. Nothing else was producing any leads.

Fifteen minutes later, fortified with a triple espresso from the drive-up coffee shop near his apartment, he headed for his office in the courthouse downtown to pick up the key for the condo. Matt had said to report back on duty no earlier than 8:00, so he should have half an hour to poke around.

Swigging the high-octane brew, he merged onto the highway. His little excursion might very well turn out to be a wild goose chase. But maybe—just maybe—it would offer some overlooked clue that would give them the lead they desperately needed.

Liz hadn't expected to sleep much, if at all. Her mind had been too busy running through the plan she intended to implement in the morning.

But her body had had other ideas. Exhausted, sapped of strength and energy, it had apparently shut down sometime in the wee hours of the morning. It took the sudden slam of a door and a vibration in the wall behind her head to rouse her.

Despite a subconscious awareness of imminent danger, her brain was slow to respond as she tried to blink herself awake. She watched as Reynolds crossed from the door to the table. Picked up his hunting knife. Turned toward her.

A rush of adrenaline brought clarity to her sluggish brain. Did he intend to finish her off now?

When she tried to speak, her tongue stuck to the roof of her mouth. Only one word emerged. "Bathroom."

She didn't need to use the facilities, but that was her ticket to the outside—and the woodpile.

Without speaking, he bent down beside her and cut the ankle restraint. Tipping his head toward the door, he waited while she stood. The pounding in her temples returned with a vengeance, and it took her a moment to get her balance. As she stumbled toward the exit, an odd weakness caught her off guard, and she grabbed the door frame to steady herself when the room started to swim.

"Move."

Praying for strength and courage, she stepped through

the door, Reynolds close behind as a gust of wind buffeted her. He left both the knife and revolver on the kitchen table, perhaps assuming her strength was weakening and she presented no threat.

That was an advantage she hadn't expected.

The early morning sun filtered through the trees around the cabin, providing sufficient light for her to clearly see the pile of boards as she passed. One in particular caught her eye. Hand-span width, it was long enough to reach her captor's legs and topple him if she swung it with sufficient force.

Inside the tiny wooden privy, Liz leaned her forehead against the rough boards and took several slow, deep breaths to quiet the pounding of her heart. She was trembling, both from cold and fear. If she blew this, only Jake and his counterparts would be able to save her. And considering how little evidence Reynolds had left in her home when he'd shot Stephanie, she didn't hold out a lot of hope he'd left much for law enforcement to work with this time, either.

Taking one final deep breath, she pushed open the door, exited the smelly structure, and set off toward the cabin fifty yards ahead, her gaze fixed on the board she intended to grab.

As she approached it, a sideways glance told her Reynolds was about three feet behind her. Perfect. Her pulse began to hammer, pounding so hard and loud she was almost afraid he'd hear it.

One step past the board, she turned and dived for it. Wrapping her fingers around the wood, she swiveled and swung at Reynolds's legs with all the force she could muster.

A startled yelp of pain was her reward. He stumbled and fell to his hands and knees, giving her the opening she needed—and fueling her hope she could pull this off. Raising the board high, she aimed for his head.

And then everything fell apart.

Scuttling to one side as the board descended, he grabbed her ankle and yanked. Thrown off balance, she fell hard on her back, unable to cushion herself because of her bound hands.

Though dazed and struggling for breath, terror pushed her to her knees. But by then, Reynolds had regained his footing. She saw the fury in his eyes as he loomed over her. Lifting his arm, he backhanded her across the face with such force that she toppled over, the metallic taste of blood warm on her tongue.

As she lay on the cold ground, the stark reality of her situation crashed over her.

Her plan had failed.

And today she would die.

Staring up at the man who'd killed her sister, she half expected him to retrieve his knife or gun from the cabin and finish her off now.

What she didn't expect was the hard kick he delivered to her rib cage.

She gasped as pain exploded in her side. When he drew his foot back again, she curled into a tight ball, trying to protect herself. But it didn't help. The toe of his boot connected with her tender flesh again. And again. And again. Pain blurred her senses, and she began to fade in and out of consciousness.

Just when she thought he intended to kick her to death, the attack ceased. She was jerked to her feet and half dragged back to the cabin. With every step, a sharp, searing pain shot through her midsection. Moaning, she tried to suck some air into her lungs. Couldn't.

"Please . . . I can't . . . breathe."

He ignored her. Hauling her over the threshold, he shoved her back in her chair, secured her leg to the post again, and stood.

Slumped sideways against the support beam, Liz doubled over, fighting back tears, every breath agony.

As waves of pain washed over her and her awareness dimmed, she tried to focus on the one good thing in her life of late.

Jake.

If she was going to die, she wanted his face to be the last image in her mind.

Letting her eyelids drift shut, she pictured his intense brown eyes, strong chin, and chiseled features. Who would ever have thought her husband's aloof best friend would somehow manage to infiltrate her heart? Yet with his innate confidence and quiet competence, his dedication to justice, his compassion and kindness, he'd done just that.

As she labored to breathe, she thought about all the ways he'd made her feel cared for and protected. His supportive, protective hand at the small of her back in the hospital. His steady grip as he'd guided her over the uneven ground in the cemetery when she'd paid a visit to Doug's grave. His gentle touch as he'd brushed the powdered sugar from her cheek in the condo.

She'd wanted so badly to see what the future held for her and the tall, dark-haired marshal.

Once more she fought back tears. She'd done everything she could to save herself. To protect that future.

Now it was in the hands of Jake, his colleagues—and God.

20

Letting himself into Liz's condo on Tuesday morning, Jake tried not to think about all the times she'd welcomed him with her warm smile.

That would only make the emptiness harder to bear.

As he closed the door behind him, a residue of fine, sticky fingerprint powder clung to his fingers. Brushing it off, he examined the small foyer. Nothing out of place here.

He moved into the living area and made a slow circuit of the spare, modern room. It looked exactly as it had the last time he and Liz had been here together. No clues were waiting to be discovered.

He headed for the dining room. Liz's laptop was in its usual place, centered precisely at one end of the glass-topped table. It was still on, in sleep mode. Mark had told him the computer forensics people had checked it out on the off chance she'd somehow left a message, but they'd found nothing.

A stack of folders rested next to the laptop. He picked them up and flipped through. They appeared to pertain to an upcoming case and contained nothing that looked relevant to his search. He set them back down.

On the other end of the table, the smaller stack of folders that had been there for a couple of weeks caught his eye. Round two for the FBI, Liz had told him—in case the first batch didn't yield any leads. He'd stopped noticing the neat little stack on his visits; it had become part of the furniture.

Except today it wasn't neat. The files were in disarray, as if they'd fallen to the floor and gotten shuffled around. Or been quickly gone through and then thrown back together.

He frowned. That wasn't the way Liz operated. As he'd learned, she liked things neat, precise, organized.

It was possible the ERT had gone through the files and left them in this messy state. But what if they hadn't? What if somehow Liz had planted a clue, calling it to his attention with this out-of-character jumble of papers?

As Jake rounded the table, he noticed one piece of paper sticking out farther than all the others. A fluke? Or a desperate effort to highlight some important piece of information?

Without disturbing the rest of the pile, he slid one of his business cards in as a place holder and eased out the sheet. A quick scan told him it related to a malpractice case she'd heard two years ago, during her state court days. He noted the names of the plaintiff and defendant—Martin Reynolds and Dr. John Voss.

Pulling his BlackBerry off his belt, he fished Mark's cell number out of his pocket and punched it in. The FBI agent answered on the second ring.

"Mark, it's Jake. I need to ask Clair Ellis, the ERT technician who worked Liz's condo, a question."

"What's up?"

"Maybe nothing. But I stopped by on the off chance I'd pick up some clue I missed on Sunday. I just noticed a stack of thrown-together files on the edge of the table. That's not Liz's style. I'm thinking the ERT people either moved them when they were working here, or she might have tried to leave us a clue. These were the second round of case files she intended to pass on to you if the first group didn't yield any leads."

"I'm pulling into the parking lot at my office. Let me find Clair and I'll call you back."

The line went dead.

As Jake waited for Mark to get back to him, he gently tugged the Reynolds file out of the stack and skimmed through it. The man had filed the malpractice suit on behalf of his wife, who had died at a hospital in rural Missouri when they were visiting the area. Liz had directed a verdict in favor of the doctor because Reynolds's attorney had failed to meet the burden of proof.

Jake stared at the file. Why had Liz included it in her second-round pile? Had Reynolds been angry with her verdict? Had she considered him capable of violence? Was he their man?

Probably not, Jake cautioned himself, trying to rein in a sudden surge of hope. If Clair said the ERT had messed with the files, he was back to square one.

If, however, they'd been in disarray when the ERT arrived, there was a slim possibility they were about to get their first solid lead.

"Sorry I'm late." Bill slid into the booth across from Cole in the noisy diner. "It was one of those mornings, you know?"

Cole took a sip of coffee from his heavy crockery mug and grinned at his best buddy from high school. Even though their lives had taken different directions, they'd remained close. He looked forward to their twice-a-month breakfast get-togethers.

"No problem. Did somebody's furnace give up the ghost overnight?"

"I wish." Bill signaled to the waitress and pointed to Cole's mug, then himself. "Dad called to make sure everything was copacetic before he and Mom headed to the airport for their cruise." He shook his head and heaved a long-suffering sigh. "I'm thirty-five years old. I've been married for almost a decade. I have three kids. I've been working with him for twenty years, learning the ropes from the ground up. You'd think he'd trust me by now."

The waitress set his coffee down. "I'll be back for your orders in a minute."

"Thanks, Judy." He shot Cole a wry look as he added two packets of sugar to the dark brew. "Oh, the joys of being part of a family business."

Cole chuckled. "You love working with your dad."

With a sheepish grin, Bill stirred in the sugar. "Yeah. I do. He's a good guy. Say, speaking of family, how does it feel to have your brother back in town?"

"I don't know. I've hardly seen him. He's working a high-profile case."

"Yeah?"

The waitress reappeared. "The usual, guys?"

"Sounds good to me." Bill handed her back his unopened menu.

"Me too." Cole followed suit.

She shook her head. "I don't know why I bother to give you menus. I always place your standard orders the minute you walk in the door." She smirked at them and headed for the kitchen.

"Cute, Judy," Bill called after her, then turned his attention to Cole. "So can you talk about your brother's case?"

Cole wrapped his hands around his mug. "Nope."

"Too bad." He stirred his coffee. "Your stories are usually better than those law enforcement shows on television. The way you guys piece together clues is amazing."

"There's a fair amount of luck involved. And we don't always figure things out. Some mysteries go unsolved."

"Say . . . speaking of mysteries, here's one you might be able to clear up for me, given all the weird stuff you run into in your line of work. I was at a lady's house yesterday, and when she was writing out a check for the service call she showed me an odd notation on some of her brother's check stubs. She asked me if I knew what it meant, and I didn't have a clue.

It was above the signature line, and it said something about prejudice. Then there were the letters UCC followed by some numbers . . . 308, I think. Any idea what that means?"

Cole's antennas went up. He'd been following the Michaels kidnapping case through the media and the law-enforcement grapevine, since Jake wasn't returning his calls. He knew the FBI profilers suspected that a member of a sovereign citizen group was the perpetrator. While there were lots of those around, it was an odd coincidence that his friend had encountered one yesterday.

"Yeah. UCC stands for Uniform Commercial Code. It's a system of law that deals with taxing and commerce. I can't give you a technical explanation about what it means, but there are groups of people out there who believe certain kinds of documents constitute a contract with the government that undermines their freedom. So they use the 308 thing when endorsing checks or applying for driver's licenses or car registrations. It's related to the 14th Amendment."

Bill gave him a skeptical look. "They sound like nutcases."

"They consider themselves patriots."

"Right."

The waitress delivered their breakfast, and Cole picked up his fork. "The scary thing is, some of what they say makes sense. But a lot of the stuff they do is plain silly, like signing legal papers with red crayon because they think that keeps the documents from being subject to United States law. At the other extreme, though, they've been known to use guns and bombs when it suits their purpose. What was this guy's name, anyway?"

"Hey, I don't want to get anyone in trouble. Or lose a customer." Bill poured a generous portion of syrup over his pancakes. "His sister was a real nice, normal lady. I don't think this guy was one of your more radical groupies."

Cole used the edge of his fork to break off a bite of his ham and cheese omelet. "Did you meet him?"

“No. He’s out of town on a hunting trip. His sister said he’d be home tonight sometime.” He set the syrup back on the table, grimacing as he eyed his sticky fingers. “That thing leaks.”

He reached forward to pull a few napkins out of the holder—and knocked his fork off his plate. It clattered to the floor.

“Sheesh.” He rolled his eyes. “Like I said, not my day.” Bending down, he snagged the fork.

At his muttered grumble, Cole leaned sideways to look down. “What’s wrong?”

Straightening up, Bill examined his hand in disgust. Several gold hairs clung to his sticky fingers. “I’ve been pulling these off my pants legs since yesterday. I knew there was a reason I disliked cats. This one was a real pest. The guy’s sister tried to shoo her away, but she kept coming back.”

Cole stared at the cat hair. Thought about the UCC code on the checks. Reached for his cell phone.

“Bill, I need the name of that guy with the funny checks. And I need it now.”

As his BlackBerry began to vibrate, Jake glanced at caller ID. Mark.

“Jake? I’m in Clair’s office. I’m going to put you on speaker.” He heard a click. “Okay, we’re good. Clair . . .”

“Good morning, Jake. I pulled the photos we took Sunday of the dining room table before we moved anything. There were two piles of files. Which one are you asking about?”

“The pile on the far side of the table, across from the computer. I need to know if it was messy or neatly stacked.”

“Messy. Is that important?”

His pulse kicked up a notch. “Maybe. That pile had been sitting there for two weeks, perfectly aligned. Liz likes things neat.”

“The kidnapper could have knocked it off the table.”

"That's possible. But I can't see any reason why he would have been in that part of the room. And a sheet from one of the files looks as if it could have been pulled out on purpose."

"What file is it?" Mark asked.

"It's for a malpractice case she heard a couple of years ago. Martin Reynolds versus Dr. John Voss." When silence greeted his response, Jake frowned. "Are you guys still there?"

"Yeah. Who won that case?" Mark asked.

"She directed a verdict in favor of the doctor."

"Okay . . . this may be pure coincidence, but one of the guys I met recently at a Patriot Constitutionalists meeting is named Martin."

A surge of adrenaline set Jake's nerve endings tingling. "I think it's time to pay Jarrod Williams another visit."

"I'm heading out the door for Luke's office to fill him in as we speak," Mark responded. "I can meet you in the lobby of Mr. Williams's office in fifteen minutes."

"Sounds good. I'll give Matt an update too."

As Jake rang off and strode toward the door, preparing to dial his boss, his BlackBerry began to vibrate again. Checking caller ID, he saw it was Cole. This was the second time in the past twenty-four hours his brother had tried to call him. But he let it roll to voice mail. Talking to his boss was more critical.

Once in the hall, he pulled the door of the condo shut behind him and headed for the elevator.

Once more, his BlackBerry quivered to life.

A glance at the screen told him this was a page, not a call. From Cole.

He frowned. Cole never paged unless it was an emergency. Maybe something had happened to his mom or Alison.

Putting the call to Matt on hold for sixty seconds, he keyed in his brother's number, then punched the down button beside the elevator.

Cole answered immediately. "Sorry to bother you. I know things must be crazy. But I might have a lead on the judge for you."

That got his attention. "Okay. I'm listening."

"I'm having breakfast with Bill Lewis, my high school buddy. He was doing some work at a house yesterday for a guy who's out of town. After the sister wrote him a check, she showed him some of her brother's check stubs. Above the signature line, he'd written 'without prejudice UCC 1-308.' That fits with the whole sovereign citizen thing the FBI profilers came up with. And get this . . . Bill was picking gold hairs off his pants legs. From a cat that kept brushing against him at that house."

Jake stopped breathing. "What's this guy's name?"

"Martin Reynolds."

His breath whooshed out of his lungs.

Bingo.

The evidence might all be circumstantial, but Jake knew they'd found their man.

"Do you have an address?" He dug through his pocket for a notebook as he jabbed the elevator button again.

"Yes."

He jotted it down as Cole recited it. "We're on it. If this pans out, I owe you. Big time."

"I'll keep that in mind. By the way, Alison said to let you know she's praying for the judge."

"Tell her I said thanks." The words came out raspy, and he cleared his throat. "I'll be in touch when this is over."

As the elevator door opened, he punched in Mark's number.

After he relayed the news, they agreed to meet at Reynolds's house. While Jake placed a second call to Matt to bring his boss up to speed, Mark got a search warrant in the works. Not that they needed it. They had grounds to search on the basis of exigent circumstances. But it never hurt to cross all the t's and dot the i's.

Five minutes later, as he slid behind the wheel of his Trailblazer and fumbled for his key, he realized his hands were shaking. That had happened only once before in his career.

In Iraq. When he and two other SOG members had been ambushed en route to the courthouse by a band of militant jihadists intent on disrupting a high-profile trial. They'd been badly outnumbered, and he'd expected to die.

But he and his colleagues had fought hard. And they'd survived.

Today, he intended to fight just as hard for Liz.

Because as the tremors in his fingers proved, saving her life was as important to him as saving his own.

The judge's moaning was getting on his nerves.

Martin glanced over at her from his seat at the wooden table. She was still slumped against the support beam, and the right side of her face had taken on a purple hue. The edges of her eye were also turning black. For a brief instant, a tiny flicker of remorse licked at his conscience. Hitting a woman went against everything he'd ever been taught. He'd been raised to respect the opposite sex.

But this wasn't about gender. This was about ridding the world of tyrannical, corrupt judges. Defending the Constitution. Saving America. It was about preserving freedom and liberty and God-given rights.

The anger he'd directed at her when she'd whacked him with that piece of wood had been justified.

Pressing his lips into a thin line, he turned his back on her.

Besides, she didn't have long to suffer.

In less than four hours, she would be dead.

Mark was waiting in his car when Jake pulled up in front of Martin Reynolds's house. The agent met him on the sidewalk near the concrete path that led to the front door, falling into step beside him as he picked up his pace to escape the steady rain that showed no signs of abating.

"Luke sent Nick and one of our other agents to have another chat with our friend Jarrod. And two of our people are on their way to the copy shop where the meetings are held to talk to the owner. We're also running intel on Reynolds."

"Okay. Let's see what the sister has to offer." Jake pulled out his badge and pressed the bell.

A sixtyish woman with cropped silver hair and a deep tan answered. She was wearing a coat, as if they'd caught her about to leave.

"Ms. Reynolds?"

"Yes."

Jake flashed his badge. "I'm Deputy U.S. Marshal Jake Taylor. This is Special Agent Mark Sanders from the FBI." He waited while Mark displayed his creds. "Is your brother at home?"

The woman's eyes widened, and a flicker of panic sparked in their depths. "No. He won't be back until this evening. Is there a problem?"

"May we come in? We'd like to ask you a few questions."

Her hand tightened on the edge of the door, and Jake had a feeling she was going to refuse.

"Ma'am, it's a matter of life and death," he pressed.

At his grave tone, she drew in a sharp breath, and the color drained from her face. Pulling back the door, she moved aside and gestured for them to enter.

"The furnace is out. The kitchen is the warmest room. We can talk there." A tremor ran through her words as she closed the door and started toward the back of the house.

Jake eyed her stiff back. She was way too nervous . . . suggesting she knew—or suspected—something. He glanced at Mark as they followed her. The other man quirked an eyebrow, confirming he'd picked up the same vibes. He also pointed to a photo on a side table in the living room as they passed, then nodded. It showed a man with salt-and-pepper hair standing beside a middle-aged woman on a beach.

Jake interpreted that gesture to mean that the man Mark

had met at the Patriot Constitutionalists meeting and the owner of this house were one and the same.

Conclusion: they needed answers from Patricia Reynolds. Fast.

As the two government men followed her into the kitchen, Patricia slid into one of the wooden chairs around the table, perched on the edge, knotted her hands, and tried to suppress the shiver that rippled through her. She couldn't blame her sudden chill on the room temperature, either. The small electric space heater she'd picked up at Walmart was doing a stellar job of keeping the kitchen warm. This ominous coldness came from deep in her heart. And it was accompanied by a paralyzing dread.

"Ms. Reynolds, do you live with your brother?" the FBI agent asked.

"No. I'm in the Peace Corps. In Sierra Leone. I'm just here on vacation."

"Where is your brother, ma'am?"

"I don't know." She tightened her clasp, whitening her knuckles. "I thought he was on a hunting trip, but when the furnace went out yesterday I called the wife of the man he said he'd gone with and found out his buddy died three years ago."

"When was the last time you saw your brother?"

"Sunday morning. Before I left for church. He was gone when I got back."

Josie padded into the room, surveyed the scene, and jumped into her lap. The warmth of the little body was welcome, and she cuddled her close. Stroking the cat helped comfort and calm her.

But the appearance of her brother's cat had the opposite effect on the two men sitting at her table. Their tension was almost palpable, and they exchanged a look she couldn't interpret.

When neither spoke, she leaned forward, fear clutching her heart. "Is Marty in trouble?"

The marshal folded his hands on the table. "Ms. Reynolds, are you aware that your brother is active in an organization called the Patriot Constitutionalists?"

"No. What kind of group is that?"

"Have you ever heard the term sovereign citizen?"

She searched her memory, then shook her head. "No. What does it mean?"

"Essentially, people who ascribe to the sovereign citizen theory believe the United States government is illegitimate and is encroaching on the freedoms and rights guaranteed by the Constitution. Some work to subvert the government through peaceful means. Others resort to violence. We have reason to believe your brother is in the latter category."

Shock drove the breath from her lungs. "You think Marty would do something violent?"

The intent gaze the marshal fixed on her was deadly serious. "We believe he may be the person who kidnapped federal judge Elizabeth Michaels."

Her mind grappled with that bombshell. Marty, a kidnapper. And if the articles she'd been reading in the paper about that case were true, the authorities believed the kidnapper was the same person who'd killed the judge's sister.

They thought Marty was a murderer.

The room tilted.

"Ms. Reynolds . . . would you like a glass of water?"

The question from the FBI agent seemed to come from far away. Forcing back the dizziness, she shook her head. "No. I'm just trying to . . . I can't believe my brother would be involved in anything like that. He's always been a churchgoing, law-abiding citizen. Are you sure you have the right man?"

"We think so," the agent replied. "And we need to find him as soon as possible. As far as we know, the judge is still alive. But if he told you he plans to be back tonight, I suspect time is running out. Do you have any idea where he might be?"

"No. I'm sorry."

The grim expression on the faces of the two men grew more somber.

"Ms. Reynolds, we have a search warrant in process for this house. But we need to start searching now."

Patricia's first instinct was to protest. She'd always done everything she could to protect her baby brother. As a child, she'd lavished him with love, trying to mitigate the damage their father had inflicted with his constant hounding and criticism. She'd always known Marty was a sensitive soul, and she'd tried to shield him from hurt, both inside and outside their home. She hadn't wanted him to carry any psychological scars into adulthood. And she thought she'd succeeded. He'd gone on to live a productive life, and he'd been blessed with a wonderful, supportive wife and a happy marriage.

Sometime in the past few years, though, Marty had changed. A lot. In many ways, he seemed like a different person. Where once she would have called the suspicions of these men ridiculous, now she wasn't certain. And with the judge's life hanging in the balance, how could she refuse to cooperate?

Yet how could she betray her brother?

As she struggled with her dilemma, a sentence from one of the readings at church the previous Sunday echoed in her mind. The pastor had focused on an unfamiliar passage from Deuteronomy in his sermon, and it had stuck with her.

You shall not distort justice.

The meaning was clear. Saving a life had to take precedence over love and loyalty. She had to cooperate with these men who were dedicated to serving justice.

Even if Marty would pay the price.

Lacing her hands tightly together, Patricia took a deep breath. "You can start searching whenever you like. And I'll help you in any way I can."

21

"The *Post* got another letter."

At Mark's comment, Jake stopped sifting through the incendiary material in the drawer of Reynolds's built-in desk. Todd and Spence had joined them, along with two more FBI agents, and all of them were working at warp speed. After half an hour of tearing apart the house, they'd uncovered a veritable arsenal in the man's basement—but were no closer to figuring out where he'd gone than they had been when they'd started.

Mark's grim expression did nothing to quell Jake's burgeoning anxiety. He gripped the back of the desk chair, trying to brace himself. "What does it say?"

"It has yesterday's date at the top, and for the most part it's a continuation of the same diatribe. Except for the last line, which the judge again hand wrote and signed. It says, 'Tomorrow I will die.' "

A sudden boom of thunder rattled the windows, echoing the panic that shook Jake to the core and sucked the breath from his lungs.

"We also have some intel on Reynolds. In the past couple of years, in addition to losing the malpractice lawsuit, the house he'd lived in for more than twenty years was declared blighted through eminent domain, he was hit with a sizable fine from the IRS for underreporting his income, and he lost his job."

"Wow." Jake's grip tightened. "That's a recipe for rage and a persecution complex. And a perfect fit for the profile Christy laid out."

"I agree. I don't think there's much doubt he's our man. Now we have to . . ." Mark stopped speaking, pulled his BlackBerry off his belt, and pressed it to his ear. "Sanders." He listened for half a minute, then reached for a pad of paper and pencil on the desk and jotted down a few words. "Got it. We'll stand by."

Pressing the off button, he slipped the device back onto his belt. "That was Luke. The owner of the copy shop caved once our guys exerted a little pressure. Told them Reynolds bought a cabin a year or so ago somewhere near Potosi, close to Mark Twain National Forest. Our office is running property deeds. We should have an address momentarily. In the meantime, you might want to get with your boss. We'll give you backup, but you guys are the arrest specialists."

"Do you have any agents in the area?" Jake pulled his own BlackBerry out and speed-dialed Matt.

"One guy in Rolla. He's up in northern Gasconade County working a case, according to Luke. We have a few agents in Cape Girardeau. But none of them are any closer than we are."

"Potosi's at least an hour by car, isn't it?"

"Yeah. Maybe a little longer."

They both knew that might not be good enough.

"Okay. Let's pull in the local police or highway patrol to meet us in Potosi with some vehicles. I'll get us helicopters from County or the city. We need to move as—"

"What have you got?" Matt's voice crackled over the line, cutting off his exchange with Mark.

Jake shifted away from the agent and gave his boss his full attention. "I have an ops plan to run by you."

Forty-five minutes later, with the helicopter rotors beating out a pounding rhythm that vibrated through his already taut nerve endings, Jake checked out the group assembled in the aircraft. Mark now wore jeans, a Kevlar vest, and an FBI jacket. The five SOG members were attired in their standard uniform and assault equipment—Royal Robbins khaki pants, long-sleeved black T-shirts, Kevlar vests, tactical holsters, and boots. He'd exchanged his suit for the assault gear in the helicopter. They all had earpieces tucked away in case things got dicey and a tactical resolution was needed.

Todd sat next to him, a Remington 700 sniper rifle outfitted with a 40-power spotting scope beside him. All the other SOG members were armed with MP5 submachine guns and .45 caliber Springfields.

There was no lack of firepower for this takedown.

And there was another helicopter of SOG members on their tail. FBI agents were following by land.

Through the rain, the single-runway Washington County Airport near Potosi came into view. As the helicopter sped toward it, Jake saw several vehicles gathered near the main building, including a couple of SUVs. Good. They'd be set to head out the instant they landed. And Reynolds's cabin was less than eight miles away.

If all went well, this would be over in less than an hour.

The rain had stopped.

It was time.

Rising from the wooden table where he'd spent the past hour cleaning his favorite hunting rifle, a .22 Winchester Rimfire, Martin carefully set it down and made a final, slow circuit of the cabin, picking up trash, straightening the bedclothes, looking for any evidence he'd had company on this trip. He didn't plan to come back here today once his mission was finished, and he wanted nothing left behind that might incriminate him.

When he was satisfied the rustic structure held no evidence of its second occupant, he hauled the trash bag out to the car, deposited it in the trunk, and opened the passenger side door. After closing and locking the one set of shutters he'd opened, he went back inside and tugged on a pair of latex gloves.

The judge hadn't moved a whole lot in the past few hours. Nor spoken. In fact, she'd gotten real quiet. Even her moaning had stopped awhile back.

As he approached the support beam where she was tethered, her eyes flickered open. They were kind of dull, and the way she was blinking, he figured she was having trouble focusing.

Leaning down, he cut the restraint on her leg, tucked his hunting knife into a sheath on his belt, and pulled her to her feet.

She groaned and doubled over, pressing her bound hands against her rib cage.

"Please . . . that hurts."

She gasped out the words, like she couldn't catch her breath.

No matter. She wouldn't be breathing much longer, anyway.

Blocking out her moans, he dragged her to his car and shoved her into the passenger seat. She huddled over, and he saw a sheen on her cheeks as he shut the door.

How about that? He'd made a judge cry. Just like so many of her ilk made average people cry when they used their power to undermine justice and chip away at freedom.

But they weren't so high and mighty once you got them out of their courtroom.

He returned to the cabin, locked the dead bolt and the padlock on the front door, then joined her in the car. As he put the key in the ignition and turned on the engine, he spared her one brief glance.

She was shaking. Badly. And her eyes were kind of sunken in. As if she'd had all she could take.

Too bad.

Because the dramatic grand finale was still ahead.

One that would make front-page headlines all over the country—and serve as a call to arms for all the patriots out there to join the fight to restore the unalienable rights the founding fathers had fought so hard to protect.

Reynolds's cabin was deserted.

After approaching it by stealth and seeing no sign of movement or any evidence of a vehicle, the marshals had pried off a shutter. One look through the dirty glass was all it had taken to confirm there was no one inside.

As the reality sank in, Jake's spirits plummeted. He'd been convinced Reynolds had brought Liz here. They all had. It had been their only hope of finding her in time. They had no backup sites to investigate.

Now, Liz would die.

"I found some tracks on the side of the cabin." Todd joined the small group gathered in front of the ramshackle structure. "There are fresh tire impressions in the mud. Since they haven't been washed away by the torrential rain we had up until the last half hour, I'm thinking the driver left very recently."

A flicker of hope ignited in Jake's heart. Maybe they weren't too late after all.

Unless . . .

He didn't want to consider the possibility, but they had to check out every scenario. "We need some people to search the woods for disturbed ground."

He couldn't bring himself to say the word *grave*.

"Clair and her people are on the way," Mark offered.

Turning to their chauffeurs—two highway patrol officers hovering in the background—Jake motioned them over.

"We think our man is in the area. I need you guys to make sure area law enforcement is aware of the BOLO alert the FBI issued with his license number and car description."

As they jogged back toward their vehicles, Jake headed for the door of the cabin. "Since Liz managed to leave a clue on the dining room table in the condo, my guess is she might have tried to do the same here. We need to get in. Now."

No one argued. Todd retrieved a sturdy piece of wood from the nearby pile, and several hard downward blows on the latching side of the padlock were all it took to release the bale.

"You want me to try a few bump keys on the dead bolt before we knock in the door and maybe destroy evidence?" He produced a key ring from his pocket and jiggled it.

"You carry bump keys?" Jake raised an eyebrow. Keys with specially designed teeth that worked on a variety of locks weren't part of a marshal's standard equipment.

Todd shrugged. "You never know when you might need one."

"Okay, give it a shot. You've got thirty seconds."

It only took him twenty.

As the door swung open and Todd stepped back, Jake crossed the threshold. "I need some light in here."

While another SOG member went to retrieve one of the powerful flashlights from the highway patrol officers, Jake peered around the dim interior. The furnishings were sparse and basic. A bed covered with blankets. An upholstered chair that was losing its stuffing. A small table with a lantern on top. A wood-burning stove. A couple of cabinets with a chipped Formica counter underneath. A battered table with one chair. A matching chair stood near the wall, catty-corner from the table, near a support beam.

Jake's gaze lingered there. Why weren't both chairs at the table? If Reynolds wanted to relax away from the table, wouldn't he be more likely to use the overstuffed chair rather than a hard one?

"Here's the flashlight."

Jake grabbed it, clicked on the beam, and homed in on the chair. He wasn't an evidence technician, but he had a good eye. Although he didn't intend to contaminate the scene by touching anything, he wanted some proof Liz had been here.

He swept the light over the chair and the base of the support joist. At first he saw nothing. But on a second pass of the joist, he thought he detected a slight variation in the color of the wood near ground level.

Dropping down to balance on the balls of his feet, he took a closer look.

"Did you find something?" Mark joined him.

Jake indicated the lighter-colored ring on the beam. "That's been rubbed."

"As if someone was tied here and was trying to get away," Mark theorized.

"That's my take." He flashed the light along the edge of the wall, where it met the floor. A small, irregular shape half wedged under the joist caught his eye. Pulling his knife off his belt, he flipped it open, got down on his hands and knees, and handed the flashlight to Mark.

"Shine it there." He pointed to the object.

As the light illuminated it and Jake leaned in, he realized what it was.

A fingernail.

Using the knife blade, he worked it out. Flipped it over. Stopped breathing.

"She was here."

"How do you know?" Mark bent down to take a closer look.

"That's the color of the nail polish she always wears."

Rising, Jake exited the cabin, motioned the two highway patrol officers over to join the group, and gave them a quick update.

"We need every available law enforcement person in a fifty-mile radius on this," he concluded. "But I don't want anyone moving in unless it's a life and death situation. The marshals need to handle this rescue and arrest. You guys"—he gestured to the representatives from the highway patrol—"contact the police in the area and alert them to the situation. Todd, call Matt. Get the ETA of the rest of our people. Mark, can you do the same for your agents?"

The other man was already pulling out his BlackBerry. "I'm on it."

Jake angled toward Todd. They were on the same SOG assault team and had worked together on a number of dicey assignments, including high-risk arrests and search warrants. Todd was one of the best snipers in the group. And after a week of advanced training, his skills would be razor sharp.

"We may need you on this one."

"I hope it doesn't come to that."

In general, Jake felt the same way. He preferred arrests that went smoothly, where no one was hurt.

But as he looked back at the cabin where Liz had been imprisoned, he really didn't care what happened to Reynolds.

All he cared about was saving Liz.

Whatever it took.

"Hey, Colin . . . do you hear that?"

Stubbing out his cigarette on the wet ground, Colin readjusted the slippery, waterproof jacket insulating his rear from the damp wood of the downed tree and shot Brian an annoyed look. "You need to chill, man. Even if we get caught, what are they gonna do? Throw us in jail for skipping out of school after a couple of classes and smoking in the woods?"

"No. But we could get into big trouble for that." Brian nodded to what was left of the six-pack sitting between them on the dead tree. They'd finished most of it in the car while they sat out the rain, pulled off the road behind some pine trees a quarter mile down the little-used rural route. But it was better to smoke in the open. That way there'd be no telltale smell in the upholstery. So they'd left the car and hiked down a ways until they'd found a good place to sit.

"Trust me. No one's gonna find us. I told you, I've done this before. Cutting out early is no big deal. We're only missing lunch, study hall, and two—"

"Shh." Brian leaned forward, his posture tense. "I hear it again. It sounds like tires on gravel!"

Humoring his paranoid friend, Colin pretended to listen as he pulled another cigarette out of the pack. All he heard was the chirp of the birds, the rustle of the dead leaves still clinging to the trees, the . . .

He froze. Now he heard it too. And it was getting closer.

"Okay. We're outta here. Grab the beer."

As Brian scooped up the plastic holder with two cans still attached, Colin pocketed the cigarettes. The crunch of gravel grew louder, and before they could flee, a dark blue car came into sight.

The only good news was that it wasn't a police cruiser.

Muttering a word he knew his father would smack him for—even if he was sixteen—Colin grabbed Brian's arm and yanked him down behind a cluster of scrubby cedar trees.

"We're gonna have to wait until he passes. I don't want him to spot us."

Beside him, he heard Brian's rapid breathing. Felt him shaking. Disgusted, Colin shook his head. Brian was too skittish for this kind of clandestine stuff. He'd have to pick his drinking buddies more carefully in the future.

"Chill, Brian." He leaned close and whispered the instruction in his companion's ear. "As soon as he gets past us, we'll take off for the car."

It was a good plan. Colin had every confidence it would work and they'd escape undetected.

Until the car pulled to the side of the overgrown gravel lane, behind a stand of evergreens that hid it from the road, and rolled to a stop.

Less than twenty feet from where they were hiding.

Colin would have said that word again, except a man got out of the car, and he was afraid the sound would carry.

Burrowing deeper behind the cedars, he peered through a tiny opening. The driver was an old guy, with gray hair. He was looking around, as if checking to make sure no one was watching him. The same way he and Brian had done when they'd picked this spot.

But why should an older guy be worried?

Unless he was doing something illegal. Like dumping trash, maybe. That was against some kind of ordinance. His dad had talked about the problem at dinner a few nights ago. Lots of people ditched stuff that wasn't easy to get rid of, like broken washing machines, along the road.

Except this guy's car wasn't big enough to hold anything like that.

Brian was shaking worse now, and Colin sent him a dark look. If he jiggled the tree they were crouching behind, it could call attention to their hiding spot.

He elbowed him and mouthed the word *relax*.

Not that it did any good. Brian looked ready to puke.

He was definitely off Colin's fun and games list.

Peeking through the branches again, he watched the old guy circle around to the passenger side and open the door. He reached in, and a moment later a gray-haired lady appeared beside him. Her back was to him, but she was kind of bent over. Like maybe she had arthritis. Or didn't feel too good.

The guy tugged her forward, toward the front of the car, and she stumbled.

The moan that followed sent a chill down his spine.

And when she turned so he could see her face, his heart did a weird stop-start kind of thing. She had a really bad bruise on her cheek, and her eye was kind of black. Plus, she didn't seem to want to be here. The guy was dragging her along. Forcing her.

Something bad was going on.

"Colin." Brian's urgent whisper reminded him he had company. "Did you see that lady's face?"

"Yeah."

"Do you think that guy did that to her?"

"I don't know."

"Why would he be taking her back into the woods?"

"I don't know."

"Do you think we should call the cops?"

The couple disappeared down the gravel road, and Colin frowned. "They'll be able to trace the call to my cell. How am I going to explain why I'm here instead of at school? I'll be toast. My old man will ground me, like, forever."

"Yeah, but that lady looks like she needs help. What if we find out later he did something bad to her, and we knew we could have stopped it? Man, that would be a boatload of guilt to carry around for the rest of our lives."

Brian had a point.

"Look, you want me to call?"

As Brian pulled out his cell phone, Colin was tempted to let him take the heat. But that wasn't fair. He'd been the one who'd come up with this idea and dragged Brian along with him. If anyone got in trouble, it should be him.

A woman's muffled cry of pain echoed through the woods, galvanizing him into action.

Opening his cell phone, he tapped in 911.

She was moaning way too loud.

Martin picked up his pace. He should have gagged her before he pulled her out of the car. Not that anyone was around to hear her, other than maybe a few deer. But he'd silence her once they got to the lean-to. He didn't want to run the risk of having anyone hear her scream. And without a gag, she'd be doing a lot of that.

The crude structure came into view up ahead, set back from the gravel road in the center of a clearing about a hundred feet in diameter. It sure wasn't a place he'd want to sleep, exposed to the elements and all. But the owner belonged to some kind of mountain man group and liked to come out here in buckskins and shoot his black powder rifle and sleep in the open.

Go figure.

Still, he was glad he'd met Jeff in the café in Potosi, where he'd stopped for breakfast on one of his first weekend trips to his cabin a year ago. The place had been packed, and the guy had claimed a stool next to him at the counter. He'd been real friendly, and they'd struck up a conversation. When Martin had told him he owned property nearby but complained he didn't have enough acreage to allow for good hunting, Jeff had invited him to hunt on his three hundred acres anytime. And he'd done so on a number of occasions. Jeff had also offered him the use of his "cabin," then explained it was just a lean-to he used for protection from the wind or rain.

Who knew it would end up serving a higher purpose?

Arriving at his destination, Martin pulled the judge into the open-ended wooden structure and dumped her against the single sloping wall. After balancing himself on one knee, he fished in his pocket and withdrew a strip of cloth.

The judge's head was lolled to one side, her eyes half closed, and when she opened her mouth to moan again it was easy to slip the cloth between her teeth, pull it taut, and tie it behind her head.

Her eyes flew open, wide with fear, as he gagged her. As if she knew the end was near.

It made him feel good.

Righteous.

Like a patriot.

Thanks to him, in just a few minutes there would be one less freedom-sucking judge to undermine America.

He pulled out two plastic restraints from the pocket of his jacket. With one, he secured her ankles together. She struggled a little, but an elbow to her ribs took care of that. She collapsed with a moan.

With the other restraint, he attached her wrists to a metal hook sunk deep into the wood of the lean-to above her head, where Jeff maybe hung a lantern or draped a canteen. As he stretched her arms up, she made a noise deep in her throat, and he glanced at her again. Her features were contorted with pain, her expression pleading. Like she thought he might take pity on her.

Fat chance.

No one had ever taken pity on him. Not the government. Not his employer. Not his father. Why should he feel one iota of sympathy for a corrupt judge who reveled in controlling people's lives?

Backing out of the lean-to, he retrieved the plastic-wrapped bales of straw he'd hidden under cedar branches in the woods. Then he jogged back to his car to get his rifle—just in case—and to remove the plastic from the car seat and floor. Bundling it in his arms, he returned to the lean-to and stuffed it around the judge. In just a few minutes, any trace evidence or stray fingerprints would simply melt away.

Along with the judge.

22

At the impromptu command post that had been set up at Reynolds's cabin, Jake tried to ignore the fact that the woods around them were being searched. He chose to believe Liz was still alive.

It was the only way he could stay focused. And in control.

Motioning to Todd to join him, he strode toward the tire tracks the other marshal had discovered. If there were tire prints, there might also be footprints.

Two sets, he hoped.

The rocky ground didn't offer much. But as he scrutinized the tire tracks, then widened his scan to what he assumed was the area around the car, he picked up an indentation that, from a distance, looked like it could be a shoe print.

As he moved toward it, Todd fell in behind him. "See something?"

He pointed toward the disturbed area. "That might be a print."

Todd squinted at it as they approached. "Maybe."

Stopping a foot away from the muddy patch, Jake dropped down to study the impression. It was definitely a shoe print. More like a boot print, based on size.

But it was the scuffed mud next to it that drew his attention. It appeared to be a much smaller partial shoe print.

Yes!

Todd knelt beside him. "It looks as if he was dragging something—or someone."

"Yeah. Or partly dragging, anyway." He did his best to contain his burgeoning hope, trying to engage the left side of his brain. "I see part of a shoe print. That means Liz was still on her feet when she left here. And if they've only been gone for . . ."

His BlackBerry began to vibrate, and he pulled it off his belt, glancing at the display area. The caller ID was unfamiliar.

"Taylor."

"Marshal Taylor, this is Hal Davis, chief of police in Potosi. The Highway Patrol patched me through to you. We just had a call from two juveniles who say they saw suspicious activity about four miles from your position. It involved a gray-haired man and an elderly woman who appeared to be injured. The man pulled his car behind some evergreens to shield it from the road, then took off with the woman down the gravel path that leads into the property. The kids didn't get the license plate, but the color matches the BOLO alert. I have an officer in your area who should be arriving momentarily. He can lead you to the entrance."

Jake's pulse skyrocketed. Motioning to Todd and the other marshals milling around the area, he rose and took off at a sprint for the vehicles parked a couple hundred yards from the cabin.

"Okay. We're heading for the main road as we speak. Alert your officer we'll meet him or her there. Are there any buildings on the property?"

"Not that we know of."

"How far back does the road go?"

"I don't have that information. It's a three-hundred-acre parcel, but most owners don't go to the expense of building roads too far back. Just enough to get them away from the main road."

"All right. Tell your officer no siren. We'll stop an eighth of a mile away from the entrance and go in on foot. I don't want to advertise our presence."

"I copy that."

"I also need an EMT crew standing by. Make sure at least one of them is a paramedic. They should wait half a mile away until we give the signal to move in."

"Understood."

Ending the call, Jake stopped beside the Highway Patrol SUVs that had transported them here. The other marshals gathered around as he filled them in.

"We'll fan out and go in through the woods." He fitted his voice-activated earpiece into place as he issued the clipped instructions, and the other marshals followed suit. "We'll work on the assumption that our guy isn't going in too deep. If Liz is injured, he won't want to transport her very far. Let's do it."

By the time they piled into the two Suburbans and arrived at the main road, the police cruiser was waiting for them. Jake motioned through the window for the officer to move out. The man floored it, and they fell in behind him, spitting gravel.

Pulling out his BlackBerry, he punched in Matt's number. When his boss answered, he brought him quickly up to speed.

"We also need a medevac helicopter ASAP," he finished.

"I'll take care of it. Just rescue the judge."

"That's my plan."

As he ended the call and they sped down the two-lane road, Jake sent seven silent words heavenward.

Please, Lord—let us be in time!

She couldn't breathe.

Every time Liz tried to suck air into her lungs, pain exploded in her midsection.

She felt the hovering, shadowy presence of death.

Pressure built behind her eyes, but no tears came. Through a haze of pain and dizziness, she watched her tormentor moving about as she tried to inhale tiny breaths that wouldn't cause further agony. It didn't work. No matter how slight the rise and fall of her chest, searing shafts of pain shot through her.

She couldn't even cry out. Not only had the gag silenced her, it had also sucked out whatever moisture had remained in her mouth. Her tongue felt huge and parched.

All at once a muscle cramp seized her shoulder, and she gasped at this new torture. She tried to maneuver herself into a different position, tried to rise to her knees, to flex her shoulders—anything to alleviate the spasm. But weakness had robbed her limbs of their ability to respond to the commands of her brain.

Her body stiffened as the cramp twisted the muscle in her shoulder, and a despair deeper than any she had ever known rolled over her, crushing in its intensity, sucking the hope out of her.

All her life, she'd been a fighter. A woman who'd never believed in giving up. Who'd always battled to survive. To endure. That's why she'd tried so hard to escape. Why she'd left clues every chance she'd gotten.

But she'd finally reached her limit.

She was ready to concede defeat.

Until the pungent smell of kerosene seeped into her fading consciousness and jerked her attention back to her abductor.

Blinking, she tried to focus. Straw was piled high around the lean-to now. So high she could barely see over the top.

And Reynolds was dousing it with kerosene, his movements methodical, impassive.

A splash of the noxious liquid hit her face, trickling down her chin, soaking into the rag around her mouth. She gagged at the taste, but there was nothing in her stomach to retch up.

As the final horror registered, revulsion and fear clawed at her.

No!

She tried to scream the word.

The gag muffled her cry of terror. But it couldn't stop the surge of adrenaline that shot through her, giving her a final burst of panicked energy. She'd been ready to die. But not like this. Not engulfed in flames.

Desperately she yanked at the restraint holding her wrists. Again. And again. And again.

But it didn't give.

Then Reynolds lit a match. Threw it in her direction. Repeated the action. Over and over again. Like he was playing some macabre carnival game.

As flames began to curl up from the straw and smoke started to waft her direction, he finally spoke.

"Good-bye, Judge. And good riddance."

Jake was out of his vehicle and sprinting toward the woods even before the SUV came to a full stop. Gesturing toward the other marshals to spread out, he plunged into the thicket of branches, grateful that much of the stubby undergrowth had been nipped by frost and died back.

He was making steady progress when a puff of smoke rising above the trees up ahead caught his attention—and sent his pulse rocketing off the scale.

"We have smoke. Move in!" As he issued the curt instruction into the mike on his cuff, he broke into a flat-out run.

Thirty seconds later, he emerged into a small clearing. He could see billows of smoke, and through it some sort of lean-to structure. Here and there, fingers of flame licked upward.

Then, as a gust of wind whipped the smoke aside for a brief instant, he saw Liz.

In the middle of the inferno.

He whispered a word he rarely used.

"What's wrong?" Todd's voice.

"I see Liz. She's in the lean-to. I'm going in." He raced toward the blaze, adrenaline pulsing through his body. "We need to—"

The crack of a rifle ricocheted through the woods.

It wasn't one of theirs.

Jake dived for the ground as another bullet ripped past him, so close he could feel the vapor bulge.

His gaze riveted on the lean-to still thirty feet away, he pressed himself flat to the ground. Now he could smell kerosene as well. Reynolds had used an accelerant.

They had very little time.

"Jake—are you hit?" Mark's terse question crackled through his earpiece.

"No. But I can't budge till we get this guy." He tried to keep the panic and desperation out of his voice. "Todd . . . can you spot him?"

"Not yet. But I'm working on it."

He looked again at the lean-to, the smoke and flames increasing by the second. Terror tightened his throat. He couldn't lose Liz. Not when they were this close.

Not when he could no longer imagine a future without her.

"Work faster! We've only got seconds!"

How in the world had they found him?

Martin hunkered down among some large boulders near the edge of the woods. Good thing he'd taken one more look over his shoulder as he trekked back toward his car or he would have missed the guy running toward the lean-to.

If he hadn't checked back, the judge might have survived.

And he couldn't allow that.

He wasn't going to fail a second time.

Peeking over the rocks, he saw that the man was still on

the ground. A marshal or FBI agent, maybe, based on his attire. And he wasn't moving. Martin wasn't sure he'd hit him, though. Surprise had thrown off his usual precise aim. But it didn't matter. If the man wasn't hit, he was pinned down. There was no way he could get to the judge to save her. That was all that mattered.

Except . . . he wouldn't have come alone. The place was probably swarming with law-enforcement types.

The reality slammed into him, stealing the breath from his lungs.

He wasn't going to get out of this alive.

His stomach coiled into a knot of fear. He hadn't planned to die carrying out this mission.

But a lot of patriots had put their lives on the line back when the country was just beginning. Thousands had died fighting for independence and freedom. It was a noble way to go. An honorable way.

A strange peace settled over him as he tightened his grip on his rifle and scanned the area around him. All he had to do was hold them off a little longer.

Then he would take his stand.

Just as the patriots had at Bunker Hill.

23

"I have him in my sights. He's behind the boulders on the west side of the gravel road."

As Todd's terse words crackled through his earpiece, Jake responded without hesitation. "Take him out."

A second later, the retort of a rifle splintered the still air.

Jake didn't wait for Todd's all clear. Before the echo of the shot faded, he was on his feet. Running.

As he approached the lean-to, a staggering wall of heat hit him. Coughing, he peered through the swirling smoke, desperately seeking a way through the ring of fire.

A sudden gust of wind whipped the acrid cloud aside for a brief instant. Long enough for Jake to spot one section where the flames hadn't yet engulfed the straw.

Shielding his face with his arm, he took a deep breath, held it, kicked aside the smoldering straw, and plunged through.

The smoke stung his eyes, and he blinked to keep his vision clear. Liz didn't appear to be burned, but her bound hands were secured to a hook on the lean-to and her head was slumped on her chest.

She was unconscious.

Or worse.

Smoke inhalation could kill quicker than fire.

Pushing that terrifying possibility aside, he pulled out his knife and went to work on the nylon restraint. Heat scorched his upper arm, but he ignored it and kept sawing.

When the restraint gave way at last, he gathered Liz into his arms. Doing his best to protect her from the fire, he exited the same way he'd come in, flames licking at his legs as he passed through.

Once in the clear, he knelt and gently lowered her to the ground. Sitting back on his heels, he sucked in deep breaths and wiped his streaming eyes on his sleeves.

"The EMTs are seconds away." Todd dropped to one knee beside Liz and pressed his fingers against her neck. "I'm picking up a pulse." Cutting off the gag, he leaned down and put his cheek close to her mouth. "And she's still breathing."

For the first time in his professional career, Jake's composure shattered. Tears streamed down his cheeks while Todd made short work of the restraints binding Liz's wrists and ankles, but he could no longer blame them on the smoke. At some peripheral level, he was aware of the buzz of activity around him. But all that registered in his consciousness was Liz. Her face was battered, and the restraints had left deep abrasions on her wrists and ankles. But she was alive.

Leaning over, he eased the gray wig off her head. Her blonde hair spilled out, and he fingered the silky strands. Stroked her cheek.

Thank you, God!

"Sir, we need to get in there."

The EMTs nudged him aside none too gently, and as he stood he heard the sound of the medevac helicopter's rotors in the distance.

"You need to get your arm checked out."

Todd's comment barely registered, and he aimed a distracted frown over his shoulder. "What?"

"Your arm. You've got a bad burn back there."

"It'll keep." Dismissing his own injury, he refocused on Liz.

"There's no reason they can't work on you while they work on her."

Before he could protest, Todd waved over a third EMT.

"Take a look at that." He gestured toward the back of Jake's arm.

Irritated, he turned to his SOG teammate. "Let it go, okay?"

The EMT was already poking at him. "Looks like a second-degree burn. If you'll sit on that rock over there, I'll be able to do a better job of treating it."

"I'm not moving."

"Fine." Todd pressed him down with a firm hand on his good shoulder. "Sit here."

Normally Jake would have jerked away and told the other marshal to back off. But for some reason, the stiffening in his legs gave out. Capitulating, he sank to his knees and sat back on his heels again, staying within touching distance of Liz.

As the EMT cut away his sleeve and went to work, he blocked out the pain in his arm and focused on the clipped conversation between the technicians treating Liz. They'd already put an oxygen mask over her nose, taken her blood pressure, and were trying without much success to start an IV. But he was picking up some words he didn't like.

Shock.

Dehydration.

CO poisoning.

All at once one of the technicians began cutting off her sweater.

"What's wrong?" He jerked forward, and the EMT working on him muttered a startled "hey." He ignored him.

"We can't get good vitals through all these clothes."

As the man sliced through her sweatshirt, then her sweater, the bottom edge of her shirt rode up.

Revealing a mass of black and blue.

Jake sucked in a sharp breath.

The EMT paused for a moment to do a quick inspection. "We've got some possible broken ribs. Maybe internal damage." Dispensing with the sweater, he fitted the stethoscope into his ears and listened to her heart.

The paramedic finally got the IV going. Only to deliver more bad news.

"We need to intubate."

The second technician looked up. "Airway edema?"

"Yeah." Even as he replied, the other man was pulling out a plastic-wrapped package and ripping it open. Withdrawing a tube, he fed it into Liz's nose and down her throat, then attached the oxygen.

"What's wrong?" Jake was vaguely aware that the EMT dealing with his arm had gone back to work.

"The airway seems to be swelling. We don't want it to close up."

He rested a hand on Liz's leg. "Will she . . ." His voice rasped, and he cleared his throat. "Is she going to be okay?"

"I hope so."

The man's noncommittal response did nothing to alleviate the fear churning in his gut.

The paramedics from the medevac helicopter arrived, and as the two emergency medical teams exchanged notes and prepared to transfer Liz, Jake stood. Todd materialized next to him.

"I'm going on the helicopter." Jake kept his gaze fixed on Liz.

"I am too. This protection detail isn't over yet."

"Yeah." Jake pressed his lips into a grim line. "Like we've done such a great job."

The team from the helicopter lifted Liz, and Jake started to follow.

"Hey! I'm not done yet!" Another protest from the EMT working on his arm.

"Yes, you are."

"At least let me put this on." He held up a gauze pad.

Jake kept an eye on the group approaching the helicopter. "Ten seconds."

The EMT slapped it on and taped it in place. "Have them finish up at the hospital."

"Right. Thanks."

As he jogged to catch up with Liz, Todd fell in beside him. A moment later they passed the group of rocks where Reynolds had taken his last stand. He lay where he'd fallen, sprawled on the ground, his body twisted at an awkward angle.

Jake gave him no more than a passing glance.

Usually he felt at least a twinge of remorse when they had to take someone out. He respected the sanctity of life. Even a misguided life.

But as he passed Reynolds, he felt nothing but enmity. And relief.

Every breath, every movement, hurt.

But the pain had lessened a bit.

Why?

Liz opened her eyes. Frowned. There was some kind of mask over her nose, obstructing her vision. She tried to lift her arm to pull it away, but a sharp pain stopped her. Repositioning her head, she squinted toward her elbow. But her eyes weren't focusing very well. Nor was her brain hitting on all cylinders.

"It's okay, Liz. Lay still. You're going to be fine."

A voice that sounded a lot like Jake's came from her other side. Except it was much deeper than usual. And not quite steady.

A warm hand engulfed hers in a gentle grip, and she turned her head.

It was, indeed, Jake. Though it didn't look much like him. Crevices lined his haggard face, dark circles hung beneath his lower lashes, and there was a streak of soot on his cheek.

She tried to speak, but only a croak came out.

"Just relax, Liz. Don't try to talk. You'll be hoarse for a while from the smoke. You're safe now. In the hospital."

Smoke. Hospital.

All at once, the memories came rushing back. The abduction. The cabin. The fire. Her surrender to her fate.

Yet somehow she'd survived.

And she had a strong suspicion her rescue had been orchestrated by the man standing beside her. The man whose arm was sporting a large white bandage where his long-sleeved black T-shirt had been cut away.

Tugging her hand free of his, she pointed to the dressing and raised her eyebrows.

He dismissed her silent question with a shrug. "It's a small burn. I'm fine." Leaning close, he stroked her cheek, his touch oh-so-gentle, his velvet brown eyes tender and filled with caring, warmth—and an emotion far deeper than mere affection.

Maybe she'd died and gone to heaven after all.

A nurse appeared at his elbow and leaned over to look at her. "You're awake. That's good. On a scale of one to ten, ten being the worst, how's the pain?"

Liz flashed five fingers, then three.

"Okay. We can give you some more meds."

As the nurse worked with the IV, Liz reached for Jake's hand again. Her voice was gone, but she wanted him to know that the emotion she'd seen in his eyes matched the one in her heart.

The world began to swim as the pain medicine kicked in, but before she gave in to it, before she let sleep claim her, she thought she heard him whisper four beautiful words.

"Tomorrow is ours, Liz."

Three hours later, when Mark stuck his head into the door of Liz's room, Jake rose and met him on the threshold.

"How is she?" The FBI agent glanced toward the bed.

"She's had a battery of tests, from chest X-ray to blood count to something called a bronchoscopy. There doesn't seem to be any serious damage. If we'd been even sixty seconds later, though . . ." His voice choked.

"But we weren't. Thank God."

"I've been doing that all afternoon."

"Good plan. I stopped by to check on the judge, but I also wanted to let you know that our ERT technicians found some interesting things around the cabin. Another fingernail. A small ball of tissue by the chair that contains blood I'd wager belongs to Judge Michaels. And in the outhouse—a third fingernail and several strands of blonde hair coiled into a ball and tucked into a corner."

Liz had done her best to leave them clues. To plant evidence so her kidnapper could be brought to justice, whether she survived or not. Jake shook his head, awed but not surprised. "That sounds like Liz."

Mark cast an admiring glance her way. "She's quite a woman."

"No argument there."

Spence joined them, and after getting his own update on Liz's condition, he squinted at Jake. "You need to go home and sleep."

"What is it with you and Todd? I think you both have a latent mother hen complex."

"Okay. Fine. Keel over from fatigue. Then we can get you admitted too."

Mark chuckled and extended his hand to Jake. "I'll leave you two to sort this out."

Taking the man's fingers in a firm clasp, Jake gave him a steady look. "Thank you for everything."

"All part of the job." He nodded toward Liz. "And on the personal front—good luck."

One corner of Jake's mouth lifted. It was the closest thing to a smile he'd been able to manage since her abduction. "Thanks."

As Mark headed down the hall, Spence propped one shoulder against the wall and folded his arms across his chest. "We have kind of an interesting situation. Reynolds's sister is here. Has been for the past two hours. She wants to talk to Liz."

Jake's lips settled into a grim line. "No way."

"I figured you'd say that. But here's the thing. We checked her out, and she's totally on the up-and-up. A model citizen. Churchgoer. Dedicated teacher. Peace Corps volunteer.

She's very distressed about what her brother did and wants to apologize."

Liz stirred, and Jake angled toward the room. "She's been through enough. She doesn't need some stranger crying on her shoulder."

"You could ask, anyway. It ought to be her decision, don't you think?"

Yeah, he did. But he also wanted to protect her from any more emotional trauma.

"I'll think about it."

"Okay. I'll be right here."

Closing the door, Jake returned to Liz's side. A few seconds later her eyelids fluttered open.

"I feel like a truck hit me." She rasped out the words in a husky voice he didn't recognize.

"Close enough." He took her hand. It felt right in his. Like that was where it belonged. "But all the tests indicate you'll be fine. Once your two cracked ribs and all those bruises heal, that is. You may be stuck with that sultry voice for a while, though."

"Sultry, huh?" She managed a small smile. "That's an adjective that's never been applied to me before. So why are you still here? You look exhausted."

One side of his mouth quirked up. "Trying to get rid of me, huh?"

"You need to go home and sleep."

Tenderness tightened his throat. "Later."

She sighed and shook her head. "You're one stubborn man, you know that?"

"I've been called worse." A grin tugged at his lips.

Hers twitched in response. "I'll bet. Okay, if you're going to stay, why don't you fill me in on what happened?"

"How about later? When you're feeling better."

"How about now?"

"And you're calling me stubborn?"

She made a face at him. "Get used to it."

He gave her a slow, warm smile. "I think I'd like that."

Her eyes widened, but rather than give her time to dwell on his comment, he launched into a quick, top-line recap.

When he finished, twin furrows creased her brow. "There was no way to get to me without taking Reynolds down?"

"No." He squeezed her hand, and his jaw hardened. "It was you or him, Liz. And that was no contest. He doesn't deserve one ounce of sympathy."

"It sounds like he had a lot of bad breaks in his life."

"That doesn't condone murder." His tone was flat. Cold. "He killed your sister. And he almost succeeded in killing you."

"I know."

Her eyes filled with tears, and he softened his voice. "I'm sorry. I shouldn't have been so blunt. But I have no sympathy for the guy."

"It's okay." She blinked and swallowed. "I feel the same way. And I'm struggling with that. We're supposed to love our enemies. But I can't even contemplate forgiveness at this point, let alone love."

"That's understandable." More than. Personally, he doubted he'd ever get past the hate.

She played with the edge of the sheet. "Did he have a family?"

"One sister." He gave her a few facts about the woman.

"Does she know what happened?"

"Yes." He hesitated. Spence was right. This was Liz's decision. "Actually, she's here at the hospital. Hoping to see you. To apologize, I think. Spence says she's pretty broken up about the whole thing."

Liz caught her lower lip between her teeth, her expression uncertain.

"You don't have to talk to her."

"I know. But maybe I should. Maybe I can find the route to forgiveness through her."

"Don't count on it." He gave her a skeptical look.

"It's worth a try, though. Let her come in, Jake."

Not at all certain she was making the right decision, Jake moved to the door. Spence was still outside. Still on protective duty.

"She says she'll talk to the sister."

"Take over for a minute while I get her, okay?"

"Yeah."

Jake stayed by the door, one eye on the hall, one on Liz. Her generosity blew him away. Despite being battered and traumatized, she was trying to follow the dictates of her faith. And setting an example he wasn't sure he could live up to.

Two minutes later, Spence appeared with Patricia Reynolds. The woman was dressed as she had been earlier, but her complexion had lost all its color, and grief had strained her features, pulling her mouth into a taut line.

When they drew near, Jake turned toward Liz. "She's here. But it's not too late to change your mind."

Although her fingers bunched the sheet, she shook her head.

Stepping aside, he ushered Patricia in and motioned Spence to the other side of the bed. He wasn't letting the woman out of arm's reach.

Patricia's face crumpled as she looked down at Liz. "Oh my!" The appalled words were breathed more than spoken. "They told me you were badly hurt, but I had no idea . . ." Her fingers flexed on her purse, and her knuckles turned white. "I'm so sorry for everything, Judge Michaels. I just wanted you to know that. And to tell you Marty wasn't always like this. He used to be a fine, responsible, caring man."

She started to open her purse, and Jake's hand shot out to stop her.

"We already checked it, Jake."

At Spence's quiet comment, he withdrew his hand.

Patricia pulled out a snapshot and held it up for Liz to see. "This is him and his wife ten years ago. Working at a soup kitchen on Thanksgiving. They used to do a lot of that kind of thing, he and Helen." She blinked as she studied the photo, then tucked it back in her purse. "But something inside him must have broken. I'm so sorry I didn't recognize that in time to save you from . . . this."

A tear rolled down her cheek, and she covered her mouth with her hand, stifling a sob.

Jake saw a matching tear well in Liz's eye.

"It's not your fault, Ms. Reynolds. People change." Liz's hoarse reassurance scratched its way past her throat. "It happens. Sometimes there's nothing we can do to save them—no matter how strong our love is."

She was thinking of Doug, Jake knew. He could see the remnants of regret pooled in her jade-colored irises. Along with sympathy for this woman's grief, born of personal experience.

"Thank you." Patricia fished a tissue out of her purse.

"I'm sorry for your loss."

"I think I lost Marty a long time ago." She wiped her nose, took a breath, and straightened her shoulders. "My prayers will be with you for a quick recovery."

"And mine will be with you."

With a dip of her head, Patricia walked out the door. Spence followed, closing it behind him.

In the quiet that followed, Jake twined his fingers with Liz's. "You're amazing, you know that?"

She gave him a sad smile. "Far from it. I've made way too many mistakes in my life."

"Haven't we all? But I stand by what I said."

She squeezed his hand. And held tight. "I guess your job is finished here, isn't it?"

He nodded, trying to read her eyes. "We'll hang around until you're released. But yeah, after that, the protection detail will end."

Her fingers played with the edge of the sheet. "You said once that when this was over you'd like to see . . . to stay in touch."

Jake heard the trepidation in her endearingly wistful tone.

Felt it in the anxious grip of her hand. "I still feel the same way. How about you?"

Her gaze locked on his. "Yes. Very much."

Warmth—and hope—filled his heart.

Smiling, he bent down until he was a mere whisper away, her breath soft on his cheek. "I was hoping you'd say that. Because I have plans for us."

"Do you want to share them?" The flecks of gold in her green eyes sparkled as her own lips curved into a sweet, appealing—irresistible—smile.

"Why don't I demonstrate instead?"

Closing the distance between them, he claimed her lips in a tender, careful kiss.

After a few moments, he started to draw back. But much to his surprise, she pulled him near again, extending the kiss. He didn't protest.

When he broke contact at last, he stayed close, their faces inches apart. "I want you to know I don't usually kiss the people I'm assigned to protect."

"I'm glad you made an exception for me." She sighed, and her smile faded as she touched his stubble-roughened cheek. "It's been a tough few weeks, hasn't it?"

"Yes. But they're behind us now. Let's focus on tomorrow. And getting to know each other better."

"I like that idea." She rested her hand on his shoulder and gave him a gentle tug. "In fact, I think you should present me with some more evidence as to what tomorrow might hold. And how we might go about getting to know each other better."

He chuckled, loving the teasing light in her eyes. And the longing in their depths. "Are you angling for another kiss?"

"Absolutely. Any objections?"

"No objections, Your Honor."

And claiming her lips once more, he set a precedent for their future.

Epilogue

Five Months Later

As the doorbell of her tiny rented bungalow rang for the third time, Liz huffed out a breath and gave up trying to secure the flimsy strap on her second sandal. Pulling it off her foot, she dangled it from her finger and limped over to the door, off-balance in her single two-inch heel.

It took only a quick peek through the peephole to banish her frustration and bring a smile to her lips.

Jake stood on the other side—looking heart-stoppingly handsome in tan slacks, an open-necked white dress shirt, and a subtly patterned sport jacket. Perfect attire for church and the birthday brunch for Alison that would follow.

Twisting the dead bolt, she slid back the lock, then pulled open the door. "Hi."

His slow, intimate smile turned her knees to jelly. As did the appreciative perusal he gave her clingy floral sundress.

"Nice."

"Thanks."

He gestured to the sandal in her hand. "Were you taking that off or putting it on?"

"On."

"Too bad." He winked at her.

Heat stole onto her cheeks. As she'd discovered over the past few months, Jake knew how to flirt. Big time.

And she loved it.

"Come on in. I'm having trouble with the clasp on this strap."

She hobbled toward the couch, and he set down the small shopping bag he was carrying to reach for the sandal.

"Let me take a look."

She handed it over, and he examined the catch. "I think it's just a little stiff. Are these new?"

"Yes."

He sat and motioned for her to do the same. "I like them. Let me have your foot."

She lifted it, and he slid the shoe on, pausing to touch a polished toenail. "Pretty."

"I thought my first sandal event of the season deserved a pedicure."

"No arguments from me. Painted toenails arc very sexy." As he slipped the sandal on, cradling her foot in his hand a few seconds longer than necessary, he grinned at her. "Do you feel like Cinderella?"

She chuckled. "That would make you Prince Charming."

"If the shoe fits . . ." He secured the strap.

"Cute."

Setting her foot on the floor, he rested an arm along the back of the couch while she rose to collect her purse.

"Don't we need to leave?" She snagged a lacy shawl off the wing chair that was too big for the tiny room. One of these days she had to get serious about looking for a bigger, more permanent place.

"In a minute."

At his pensive tone, her heart skipped a beat and she clenched her hands around her purse. "Is something wrong?"

"No. But we got a letter addressed to you a couple of days ago."

" 'We' as in the U.S. marshals?" A shiver of anxiety rippled through her, and she sat back down beside him.

"Yes." He frowned and linked his fingers with hers. "It's nothing bad, Liz. I'm sorry. I didn't mean to scare you."

She clung to him and took some deep breaths. She was getting over the trauma from last fall. Slowly. The physical evidence was fading, and she was doing better psychologically too. There were sometimes even consecutive nights when she didn't wake up trembling or screaming or crying. But the slightest whiff of danger was enough to bring on the shakes.

Her counselor said that would pass in time.

She hoped he was right.

"It's okay." She managed a shaky smile. "You just got very serious all of a sudden. What kind of letter is it?"

He withdrew the envelope from the inside pocket of his sport coat. It was larger than a business-letter size and a bit bulky.

"It's from Patricia Reynolds. We opened it for security reasons. I wasn't sure you needed to revisit all the bad memories, but after debating the pros and cons, I think it may actually help you move on."

He held it out to her, and for the space of several heartbeats Liz regarded the hand-addressed envelope with the strange stamp and the Sierra Leone return address. If it was anyone but Jake suggesting she read it, she'd have refused. She didn't need any reminders of the trauma. But over the past few months, she'd learned to trust his judgment.

Taking the envelope, she pulled out the single sheet of paper that was folded around several photographs. She set the photos in her lap, opened the letter, and read the short, handwritten note.

Dear Judge Michaels,

I have prayed for your full recovery over these past few months. I trust this finds you healing both physically and emotionally.

I wanted you to know that as my brother's sole heir, I sold all his possessions except for a few sentimental items and used the money to construct a school building here in the village where I live and work and teach. Now my bright, eager students are protected from the elements as they learn, and they have access to resources that have opened a whole new world to them. I've enclosed a few photos.

While nothing can ever make up for the loss of your sister or the terror you were forced to endure, I hope you can take some comfort in knowing that out of all that adversity, the children in one tiny African village have been blessed with a brighter tomorrow.

My prayers will be with you always, Judge Michaels. May the Lord comfort and sustain you all the days of your life.

Blinking back tears, Liz sifted through the photographs. Children with ebony faces smiled back at her from a cheery, modern classroom. There was also a group photo taken in front of the new school building.

Fingers brushed against her cheek, tender, consoling, and then she was pulled into two strong arms and nestled against a broad, solid chest.

"Are you okay?"

Jake's gentle query came out muffled against her hair, and she nodded.

"Yes. I'm glad you showed it to me. I do think it will help me move on. And push me a little farther down the path toward forgiveness."

She stayed in the shelter of his arms as long as she could, but at last—reluctantly—she tugged away and stood. "We're going to be late for church. I don't want to keep your mom and Alison and Cole waiting."

"We have plenty of time." He refolded the letter around the pictures, slid it back into the envelope, and set the packet aside.

"I thought you said the service at Alison's church was at 10:30?"

"I lied."

She shot him a startled look. "You want to explain that?"

"Sure." He patted the seat beside him. "Come sit by me again. I have something else that may help you move on."

An odd nuance in his inflection put her on alert. It sounded like a touch of . . . nervousness? But that was completely out of character. She'd never met anyone more steady and in control than Jake.

Curious, she joined him on the couch. Once she'd settled beside him, he reached into the small shopping bag at his feet, withdrew a ten-inch square box wrapped in silver paper and topped by a fresh hibiscus, and held it out to her.

She tipped her head, puzzled. "It's not my birthday."

"Presents aren't only for birthdays."

Giving him a speculative glance, she reached for the box.

"Use both hands." He kept a firm grip on it until she obliged.

She understood why when he released the package. It weighed a ton.

"What's in here? A brick?"

He grinned. "Open it and see."

Carefully removing the hot-pink tropical flower, she ripped off the silver paper to find a sturdy white box. Intrigued, she lifted the lid.

It was filled almost to the top with sand.

Pink sand.

Confused, she looked over at him. "I don't get it."

"How many places in the world have pink sand?"

"Only one that I know of. Bermuda."

"The very place you mentioned to me once that you'd like to visit."

"Okay. And that's significant because . . . ?"

"Dig around a little. You never know what you'll find. That's why beachcombing is so popular."

Burrowing her fingers into the fine sand, Liz fished around—then froze when she encountered an object that felt a lot like a ring.

Heart racing, she slowly pulled out an exquisite marquise-cut diamond set in a gold band.

She stared at it for a long moment before she could tear her gaze away. "Is this . . . Are you . . . ?"

"Yes, it is. And yes, I am."

He plucked the ring from her fingers, set the box aside, and took her hand. No trace of levity remained on his face.

"Over the past few months, I've come to believe our reunion wasn't coincidence, Liz. And that this"—he lifted the ring—"was the road we were meant to travel. Especially since I love you more than I thought I could ever love anyone." His voice hoarsened, and he cleared his throat. "Sorry. I'm not all that great with touchy-feely stuff. But the fact is, I can't imagine my life anymore without you in it. So, Judge Michaels, I rest my case. Will you marry me?"

As Jake gazed at her, the love shining in his eyes warmed a place deep in Liz's soul. She'd known this day was coming. Known she was falling in love, and that Jake felt the same way. So after much prayer in the quiet of countless lonely nights, she'd made her peace with her mistakes, put her guilt over Doug's death in God's hand, and opened herself to the future the Lord had planned for her.

The future Jake was offering her now.

A flicker of uncertainty flashed through his eyes when she didn't respond, and she felt a tremor in his hand. The same hand that had always been steady and sure and unshakable, no matter the crisis or danger he faced.

Her heart melted.

"So what's the verdict?"

Smiling, she held out her left hand and wiggled her ring finger. "The verdict is . . . a happy ending for both parties."

A grin chased the tension from his features, and he slid the ring on her finger.

"You weren't really nervous, were you?" She looped her hands around his neck, loving the feel of the gold band on her finger.

"Am I under oath?"

She chuckled. "Cute. So am I to assume a Bermuda honeymoon is included in this deal?"

"That would be a safe assumption."

She scooted closer and touched the tip of her nose to his. "What date did you have in mind for the big occasion?"

"The sooner the better?"

At his hopeful tone, she laughed and backed off a little. "I have a very full docket, Marshal Taylor. It could take some time to clear my schedule."

"I could give you a reason to speed things up."

At his husky response, her heart skipped a beat. "It would have to be a very persuasive argument."

His eyes darkened. "I'm very good at persuasive arguments."

And as his lips claimed hers, Judge Elizabeth Michaels had to admit that Jake made a very compelling case for a wedding.

The sooner the better.

Acknowledgments

Writing a book like *Fatal Judgment* requires intensive research. Although much of my background information is gleaned from books or the internet, I rely on expert sources to fine-tune and vet my work. A number of them deserve special mention for their assistance with this book.

I offer my heartfelt thanks to the following:

U.S. Marshal Don Slazinik, who not only served as my technical expert throughout the writing of this book, patiently answering my many questions, but who also read the entire manuscript. His suggestions allowed me to portray the U.S. Marshals Service with a degree of accuracy I could not otherwise have achieved.

Circuit Judge Richard Bresnahan, whose tweaks to the judicial sections provided a final touch of authenticity.

Attorney Jack Horas, who walked me through the intricacies of a malpractice suit.

Barry M. Levine, MD, who reviewed the medical sections to make sure I got it right.

FBI veteran Tom Becker, now the chief of police in Frontenac, Missouri, for his always gracious answers to my FBI-related questions.

Captain Ed Nestor from the Chesterfield, Missouri, Police

Department and attorney Laurel Siemers for their invaluable referrals to authoritative sources.

I also want to thank the amazing team at Revell—especially Jennifer Leep, Kristin Kornoelje, Twila Bennett, Michele Misiak, Cheryl Van Andel, Deonne Beron, and Claudia Marsh. You are the best!

A special thank you as well to the master of inspirational romantic suspense, Dee Henderson, who was kind enough to read this book and offer me a fabulous endorsement. I am honored by her praise.

Finally, loving thanks to my parents—my favorite proofreaders and tireless cheering section!—and to my husband, Tom, whose keen interest in my literary career is one of my greatest blessings.

Irene Hannon is a bestselling, award-winning author who took the publishing world by storm at the tender age of ten with a sparkling piece of fiction that received national attention.

Okay . . . maybe that's a slight exaggeration. But she *was* one of the honorees in a complete-the-story contest conducted by a national children's magazine. And she likes to think of that as her "official" fiction-writing debut!

Since then, she has written more than thirty-five romance and romantic suspense novels. A four-time finalist for Romance Writers of America's coveted RITA award (the Oscar of romantic fiction), she took the golden statuette home in 2003. Her books have also been honored with a HOLT medallion, a Daphne du Maurier award, and two Reviewers' Choice awards from *RT BOOKreviews* magazine.

Irene, who holds a BA in psychology and an MA in journalism, juggled two careers for many years until she gave up her executive corporate communications position with a Fortune 500 company to write full-time. She is happy to say she has no regrets. As she points out, leaving behind the rush-hour commute, corporate politics, and a relentless BlackBerry that never slept was no sacrifice.

A trained vocalist, Irene has sung the leading role in numerous community theater productions and is also a soloist at her church.

When not otherwise occupied, she loves to cook, garden, and take long walks. She and her husband also enjoy traveling, Saturday mornings at their favorite coffee shop, and spending time with family. They make their home in Missouri.

To learn more about Irene and her books, visit www.irenehannon.com.